FEN

Also by Freya North

Sally
Chloë
Polly
Cat

To find out more about the novels of Freya North,
visit her website at www.freyanorth.co.uk

FREYA NORTH

Fen

WILLIAM HEINEMANN: LONDON

Published by William Heinemann in 2001

1 3 5 7 9 10 8 6 4 2

First published in the United Kingdom in 2001 by William Heinemann

The Random House Group Limited
20 Vauxhall Bridge Road, London SW1V 2SA

Random House Australia (Pty) Limited
20 Alfred Street, Milsons Point, Sydney, New South Wales 2061, Australia

Random House New Zealand Limited
18 Poland Road, Glenfield
Auckland 10, New Zealand

Random House South Africa (Pty) Limited
Endulini, 5a Jubilee Road, Parktown 2193, South Africa

The Random House Group Limited Reg. No. 954009

www.randomhouse.co.uk

A CIP catalogue record for this book is available from the British Library

Papers used by Random House UK Limited are natural, recyclable products made
from wood grown in sustainable forests. The manufacturing processes conform to the
environmental regulations of the country of origin

Typeset by SX Composing DTP, Rayleigh, Essex
Printed and bound in the United Kingdom by
Clays Ltd, Bungay

ISBN 0 434 00536 3 (Hardback)
ISBN 0 434 00540 1 (Trade Paperback)

For Andy and Felix – my two.

PROLOGUE

Always keep in touch with nature, always try to get close
to your model.

Auguste Rodin

Paris 1889

Julius Fetherstone had absolutely no need to sketch Cosima Antoine. Having met her, just the once, six days previously, and having fallen in love with her immediately, he knew her features off by heart instantly. Julius could have created a portrait bust of Cosima with his eyes closed. Literally. For, whenever he closed his eyes, there she was soliciting his every thought, setting his senses on fire, firing his artistic desire.

So it was a deplorable double con. Professionally, he had no need to see Cosima again. Ever. Whether commissioned or not, he would have been sculpting her. Again and again. Now he was charging his patron, her fiancé Jacques, more than he'd ever dared ask for a portrait bust. The fee would clear the debt to his landlady that a placating fuck every Thursday had done so far. More than just pay the rent and preclude further unsavoury carnal commerce; it would also keep him in clay and casting for a good long while. But far more valuable than the financial gains, Cosima's image, imprinted in his soul, was now destined to provide source material for all future works.

He need never see her again. As he flipped through his

1

sketch-book of the last week, her features stared back at him from every page apart from one with his copy of the new Manet he'd seen on display in the *Salon des Indépendants* and another with a charcoal of a maquette by his master, Rodin. But Cosima dominated all other pages. No further analysis today could make any portrait more complete than these done from memory, from knowing someone for less than twenty minutes. Yet in half an hour, she'd be at his studio and he'd be given carte blanche, plus a sizeable purse, just to stare at her.

Cosima Antoine was herself about to deceive her fiancé and con the sculptor. Julius Fetherstone had dominated her thoughts, asleep and awake, for the last six days. She told herself she was not in love with him because love was a state that should be avoided at all costs. She had decided this from an early age when witnessing how her mother's love for her father was rebuffed by his compulsive infidelities with a succession of maids, friends and young cousins. No, Cosima told herself she was not in love with the brooding British sculptor, but feelings for him she certainly had. For her fiancé, she had no feelings, rather she had *reasons*. He would be a good man to marry. He would make a good husband. He would make a good father to her children. Sometimes, she found all that inherent goodness just a little unsavoury, but Cosima could cope because still the dark places in her heart and mind were free to take her wherever she pleased. And now her fiancé was taking her to the sculptor, walking her to a place where her fantasies of the past week might just take solid form.

Never had Paris looked so beautiful. It was autumn, leaves on trees were burnished bronze and breathtaking, those underfoot crunched and disintegrated most satisfyingly. The October sun, rosy and mellow, infiltrated her body and brought a rare warmth to her soul which saw her nodding politely at the inane witterings of her fiancé, though she chose not to hear a word.

'I think we should ask Monsieur Fetherstone what he feels

about a hat,' Jacques was saying. 'I think it would be most avant-garde for a portrait sculpture to be crowned by a hat. Otherwise, it might be like any old bust. We need to define you. To have a sculpture that says "1889; Cosima Antoine at twenty years old".'

Cosima nodded thoughtfully; glad she had decided to leave the house hatless despite her fiancé's concern and her maid's horror.

There is absolutely no need for Cosima to undress. Julius has not asked her to, nor has she offered. They have simply exchanged cordial salutations and she has calmly walked over to the carved wooden screen in the corner of his studio. She has slipped behind it, unhooking her clothing as she goes.

'I won't be a moment,' she says.

'That's fine,' he replies, loosening his cravat with one hand, unbuttoning his trousers with the other.

Naked but for his loose, damask shirt, he folds the window shutters almost closed, affording his studio privacy as well as investing it with sultry shadows. October sun seeps through, licking all it touches with melancholy gold; a visual swansong of summer edged with the faintest prelude of forthcoming winter. He pads, barefoot, across the rug, closing his eyes to feel the transition between fabric ending and the well-worn, warm run of smooth old floorboards. He recalls how floorboards in Derbyshire, at the height of summer, were never as warm and welcoming as these in Paris in autumn. One more reason never to return. The other, just then, appears from behind the screen and time is suspended for Julius.

Ten twenty-two, the first Wednesday in October, 1889.

He, Julius Fetherstone, is wide awake in dream-time.

The briefest glimpse of Cosima's nudity would have sufficed. Instead, she is walking over to him, fantastically naked. His senses are ablaze; his past, his twenty-three years until this moment, have lasted but a blink. His future will be governed by his ability to savour the present.

They stand, a foot apart, staring at each other. They have not touched but the heat emanating from their bodies seems to meet and merge. They have not kissed, but their lips are as wet as if they have. He stares at her. This body before him, the flesh and muscle, the curves and hair, is the composite of all his fantasies to date and will constitute the standard for all future fantasies. She can be everything. Angel–virgin–whore–wife.

Cosima takes her fingertips to his face and hovers them over his lips. His mouth parts and she can feel his breath on her fingers. He licks his lips and her fingertips are caught, like bees to honey paper. His tongue flicks over them. His hands encircle her waist and pull her against him. She brushes her now damp fingers over his cheek and down, so that she cups the back of his neck, dragging his hair between her fingers. Her other hand she takes to his chest, slipping behind the cotton of his shirt to meet his skin. He makes to kiss her but she turns her face at the last moment.

'How long do we have?' he breathes.

'How long does a portrait take a sculptor these days?' she asks, quite loudly, with a sly smile.

'I need a day,' he says, 'that's what I told your – him.'

'Jacques,' she states.

'Jacques,' he confirms.

'My fiancé,' she elaborates.

'Your fiancé,' he verifies.

'Who,' she says, licking her top teeth, 'is commissioning my portrait in bronze.'

'As a celebration of your impending union,' he states.

'So,' she says coyly, 'I suppose there was no need for me to undress?' She eases Julius's shirt over his shoulders and away.

'No need at all,' he confirms, skimming his hands up from her waist to her breasts. He places a thumb over each of her nipples and rubs small circles. The sound of her gasp causes his eyes to close and he sinks his mouth against hers, their tongues talking passion while their bodies begin to taste each other.

Since arriving in Paris three years ago, Julius Fetherstone has had sex with four prostitutes, two wealthy clients his senior by extremes, one of the studio models, and his landlady – coupling with whom is a necessity in lieu of rent, but necessitates closed eyes throughout. This afternoon, though, with Cosima, sex is different. New. They are both virgins together. Exploring and experiencing pleasures that are a taste, a smell, a sensation. At times tender, at others lewd, they fuck and make love, alternating seamlessly between the two, all afternoon.

At four thirty, he comes inside her one final time and they sleep for half an hour on the rug. When they awake, she walks calmly over to the screen and dresses. Barefoot, but in his shirt again, he folds the shutters back. The sun has gone. It surprises him. The studio had radiated such heat, appeared to be bathed in brilliance, time standing still. Cosima appears from the screen, neatly dressed. She sits demurely on the high stool and obediently turns her face this way and that at Julius's command. He does not lift a pencil. He spends an hour just looking at her.

'That's fine,' he declares, folding down the cover on the blank sheets.

'I shall marry Jacques,' Cosima proclaims, still holding her pose and looking out of the window. 'He is rich and kind and he treasures me.'

'I wish you happiness and health,' Julius says, but he says it quietly. It doesn't seem fair. Timing is lousy. He meets a mesmerizing woman, but she is betrothed to another to whom, ultimately, Julius is beholden.

'Now that I have had you,' Cosima adds, a breath of softness to her voice, 'I can say that I truly want to marry Jacques. For whatever may be, however my life will unfurl, I will always have the memory of today.'

'And now that I have had you,' Julius clears his throat,

'every time I sculpt a nude, your body will be at its core. Every time I model a pair of breasts, or carve the lips of a cunt, I will be feeling you again.'

'Jacques arrives,' Cosima whispers, taking her gaze from the window to the sculptor.

'Goodbye, Cosima,' says Julius.

'Goodbye, Monsieur Fetherstone,' says Cosima.

ONE

Art has the objective of leading us to the knowledge of ourselves.

Gustave Courbet

*T*he lurcher, who appeared to be wearing a 1970s Astrakhan coat dug from the bottom of a jumble-sale pile, strolled nonchalantly up to the McCabes. The dog regarded Pip McCabe cursorily, expressed mild interest in Cat McCabe's plate of food and then thrust its snout emphatically, and wholly uninvited, into Fen McCabe's crotch. When Django McCabe, the girls' uncle, roared with laughter, the dog took one look at him, at his *genuine* 1970s Astrakhan waistcoat, and lay down at his feet with a sigh of humble deference. The dog's tail, like a length of rope that had been in water too long, made a movement more akin to a dying snake than a wag.

'Barry!'

The dog's owner, whose exasperation suggested this was a regular occurrence over which he had no control, gave a whistle. The dog leapt up, seemed as startled by the McCabes as they were by him, and swayed on four spindly legs as if trying to remember from whence his owner's voice had come. The solution – to escape, to feign deafness – seemed to lie in Fen's crotch. This time, he attempted to bury his entire head there, as if hoping that if he couldn't see a thing, no one else could see him.

'Barry! Good God!'

Reluctantly, Barry could not deny that his owner's voice was now very near and very cross. He extracted his face from his hiding place, gave Fen a reproachful look, dipped his spine submissively and slunk to his master's heels, out of the pub and, no doubt, into disgrace in the back of a Land Rover.

'He comes from a broken home,' the owner said on his way out, by way of explanation, or apology. 'Derbyshire via Battersea.'

Django McCabe, who'd brought up his three, Battersea-born nieces single-handedly in Derbyshire, nodded sympathetically. Pip and Cat McCabe thought they ought to close their mouths (especially as Pip still had some steak-and-kidney pie to swallow). Man and dog left, Pip swallowed. Cat gulped.

'I thought dogs were meant to look like their owners,' Cat said incredulously. 'There's justice in the world that he looks nothing like his dog!'

'Be still, my beating heart!' said Pip theatrically.

'Country squire?' Cat mused.

'Farmer needs a wife?' Pip responded.

Fen hadn't a clue what they were talking about. She'd had her back to the man throughout. 'I'd love a dog,' she said, 'but I'd settle for one sculpted by Sophie Ryder or Nicola Hicks in the meantime.'

'Jesus, Fen,' Pip sighed, pressing the back of her hand against her forehead, 'can you not retrain your eye to appreciate the finer points of real life?'

'Pardon?' Fen looked at her sister, and then assessed the level of liquid in Pip's pint of cider, as well as that in her own. 'Django?' Fen turned to her uncle for support. Django, however, puffing away on his old meerschaum pipe, regarded her quizzically.

'Fenella McCabe is a lost cause,' Cat asserted, arranging peanuts into complex configurations on the table. 'She's studied as an Art Historian for far too long—'

'—and had one too many disasters in love—' Pip

8

continued her sister's sentence, picking peanuts from Cat's pattern.

'—to allow her eye to appreciate the merits of any man now *not* hewn from marble,' Cat went on.

'—or cast in bronze,' Pip added for good measure, forming the remaining peanuts into a 'P'.

'Django!' Fen implored her uncle, with theatrical supplication, to come to her rescue and defend her from her goading sisters.

Django merely tapped his pipe on the heel of his shoe and gave Fen a smile. 'I think another pint,' he remarked, 'is the order of the day.'

'You'll have us sloshed,' Pip enthused, looking at her watch. To be sipping very good cider in their uncle's local, in Derbyshire, at half three on a Saturday afternoon in March, seemed a very good idea.

'Nonsense!' Django said, as if offended by the remark. 'I've brought you girls up not to fear alcohol – the fact that you've known the taste of drink since you were tiny means, I do believe, that it has no mystique.' He popped his pipe into the breast pocket of his waistcoat and went to the bar.

Fen McCabe watched her uncle wend his way, his passage hampered by the number of people whom he met and talked to en route.

Funny old Django, his attire so out of kilter amongst the flat caps, waxed jackets and sensible footwear. I mean, it's not just the waistcoat – he's teamed it with a Pucci necker-chief today, and truly ghastly shirt that wouldn't look amiss on some country-and-western crooner. Jeans so battered and war-torn they'd have done Clint Eastwood proud, plus a pair of quite ghastly cowboy boots that shouldn't see the light of day in Texas, let alone Derbyshire. And yet; Django McCabe, who came to Derbyshire via Surrey and Paris and had three small nieces from Battersea foisted upon him, is now as indigenous as the drystone walls. He fits in, in Farleymoor. Like he suited Soho when he was a jazz musician. But he fitted his life around us when we came to live with him. He's

9

barking mad and he's the most important man in my life.

'If our mother hadn't run off with a cowboy from Denver,' Fen said, 'but if our dad had still had the heart attack, do you think we might have been brought up by Django anyway?'

This was a conundrum upon which each girl had mused frequently, though never in earshot of Django.

'I would guess,' Cat said measuredly, though she was merely giving back to Fen a theory her older sister had once given to her, 'that the whole "cowboy-Denver-I'm-off" thing was probably a key ingredient in his heart attack.'

'Sometimes,' Pip reflected, 'I feel a bit guilty for not caring in the slightest about my mother and not really remembering my father.'

'I've never envied anyone with a conventional family,' Fen remarked, 'in fact, I felt slightly sorry for them.'

'I used to wonder what on earth their lives were like for want of a Django,' Pip said.

'Me too,' Cat agreed.

'Do you remember when Susie Bailey hid in the old stable, made herself a kind of hide-out from Django's old canvases?' Fen laughed.

'And her mum had to promise her that she'd make Django's midnight-feast recipe of spaghetti with chocolate sauce, marshmallows and a slosh of brandy!' Pip reminisced.

'Do you remember friends' houses?' Cat said. 'All that boring normal food? Structured stilted supper-time conversation? Designated programmes to watch on TV? Bedtime, lights out, no chatter?'

'Django McCabe,' Fen marvelled. 'Do you think we're a credit to him? Do you think we do him proud? That we are who we are, that we're not boring old accountants?'

'Or housewives,' Cat interjected.

'Or couch potatoes,' Pip added.

'Or socially inept,' Cat said.

'I'm sure he's delighted that my career entails me being a clown called Martha rather than an executive in some horrid advertising agency,' Pip said hopefully.

Django returned, his huge hands encircling four pint glasses. 'Philippa McCabe,' he boomed, 'every night I pray to gods of all known creeds and a fair few I make up, that you will be phoning to tell me of your new position as a junior account manager on the Domestos Bleach account.'

Pip raised her glass to him.

'And you, Catriona McCabe,' Django continued, his eyes rolling to the ceiling, while he produced, from pockets in his waistcoat that the girls never knew existed, packets of peanuts and pork scratchings, 'speed the day when you trade your job as a sports columnist for a career in the personnel department of a lovely company making air filters or cardboard tubing.'

Cat took a hearty sip of cider and grinned.

'Fenella McCabe,' Django regarded her, 'how long must I wait before you exchange a dusty archive in the bowels of the Tate Gallery for the accounts department of a financial services company? And the three of you! The three of you! Why oh why have I been unable, as yet, to marry any of you off?' He clutched his head in his hands, sighed and downed over half his pint.

Fen laughed. 'Hey! I've only just landed this job. I'm going to spend my days with Julius!'

'Oh Jesus,' Cat wailed, finding solace in cider, 'Julius.'

'Bloody Julius,' Pip remonstrated, chinking glasses with Cat.

'Oh Lord, not that Fetherstone chap,' Django exclaimed, rubbing his eyebrows, letting his head drop; a strand of his silver hair which had escaped his pony-tail dipping into his pint, 'please, dear girl, please fall in love with a man who is at least alive.'

'Who's to say,' Cat mused, 'that while you're waiting for the right bloke to come along, you can't have lots of fun with all the wrong ones!'

'*Please*,' Fen remonstrated but with good humour, 'my new job starts tomorrow.' She regarded her two sisters and her uncle. 'One for which I *was* head-hunted,' she emphasized. She ate a peanut thoughtfully, took a sip of cider and looked out of the pub window to the moors. 'So, my life wants for nothing at the moment.'

TWO

Julius Fetherstone (1866–1954) arrived in Paris in 1886 at the age of 20. There, he begged, bargained and all but bribed his way into the studio of Auguste Rodin, for whom he worked as a technician in return for materials and tutelage. However, though the great Master esteemed his foreign pupil, Julius was never truly accepted by the French who firmly believed, at the exclusion of all visual evidence to the contrary, that the English could no more sculpt than they could cook. When Julius returned to England for a one-man-show in 1935, the British art world looked the other way. 'Vulgar in theme and execution' was the The Times review in its entirety. Only 3 works were bought, all of them by Henry Holden. Holden became something of a patron to Julius until the sculptor's death in 1954.

F.A.McCabe
Unpublished MA thesis

*F*en McCabe first came across *Abandon* by Julius Fetherstone four days after losing her virginity at the age of eighteen. She was in Munich, on her A level Art History study trip when she found herself trans-fixed by a mass of bronze depicting two figures embroiled in the very moment of orgasm. To her humiliation and regret, it made her realize that the fumbling poke she had recently endured was utterly at odds with what the experience obviously should have been.

13

From that point on, Fen has been obsessed with the sculptor and his work. On her return from Munich, she unceremoniously dumped the virginity-taker and spent eighteen months apparently celibate. In body at least. However, the more she studied Fetherstone's work, the more she analysed his drawing and physically handled his sculptures, the more worldly she became. She studied the fall of light on mass, the relationship between form and space. She also learnt about the tension that intertwining figures could create. She came to understand how bodies could stretch to accommodate both their own desire and that of another. She discovered how the sensation of orgasm could manifest itself in facial expression, the throw of a neck, the twist of the stomach, the flail of arms, the jut of a breast, the buck of buttocks.

She devoted both her Bachelor and Master degree theses to Fetherstone, resolutely ignoring her tutors' advice that she stand back from the material and certainly refrain from referring to the sculptor by his Christian name.

She fantasized about being the woman in *Abandon*. She forsook film stars as masturbatory stimulus in favour of the image of the male in *Abandon*. She looked forward to the day or night when she too could enjoy a coupling commensurate with that of the bronze figures; when she would be seduced to a state of abandon by the desire for, and of, such a man. Consequently, she spurned the advances of a relatively long queue of students who all fell short of her ideal. Too puny. Or too gym-induced beefy. Too uncouth. Too affected.

In her mid-twenties, two men came close; but the reluctance of the first to commit and then Fen's reluctance to commit to the second, rang the death knell on both. Now, at twenty-eight, Fen is single. She isn't spending much time looking for a partner, nor is she losing sleep over the situation. After all, would a man enhance her life that much? It's rather good as it is, in Chalk Farm, North London, where she rents a terraced house with damp and with two friends, bohemian neighbours and her two sisters nearby. Life's busy with her new job and her bi-monthly lectures at the Courtauld and Tate galleries, which she gives voluntarily. No time for romance and all its panoply. Yes, she recently bought a pine double bed from Camden Lock market, with a king-size duvet for added luxury. However, the wink wink nudge nudging from her housemates met with her rebuttal.

'Hasn't it come to your attention,' she told them, 'that our landlord sees fit to provide us with mattresses apparently filled with sand and gravel which, in places, congeal into concrete?'

Monday morning, the first of April. After sleeping undisturbed through the last night of March, Fen awakes and finds herself sprawled at a luxurious diagonal across her bed. With Radio 4 making her reverie all the more civilized, she cocoons herself in her duvet and stares at the window, whose frame is clearly visible through flimsy curtains. Pinch and a punch for the first of the month. What kind of idiot starts a new job on April Fool's Day, Fen wonders as she gazes across her room?

After *Thought for the Day*, which Fen doesn't think much of today, she leaves her bed and checks her reflection in the mirror.

My hair needs a wash. What do I feel like wearing? What ought I to wear? Do I dress for the weather? Or for the job?

She peers out through the curtains but soon enough she forsakes meteorological reasoning (it's sunny and bright) for sky gazing instead. But that gets her nowhere so she goes to her cupboard and looks inside. Then she looks from the palm of her left hand to the palm of her right, as if reading one theory and then another, pros and cons; an idiosyncrasy that she knows causes friends and family much mirth and sometimes irritation, but which provides Fen with the answers she seeks. She regards her left hand.

It's April, it's positively spring-like. Time for my Agnès B skirt – bought in the sale and worn only once so far.

She looks at her right hand.

I'm an archivist. My office is to be a small room of dusty papers, acid-free boxes, brass paper-clips and shelving with sharp edges. There'll be no one to see me in Agnès B.

She dons jeans.

'I've hardly slept,' Abi moans, sitting at the table-cum-storage-surface in the sitting-room-cum-dining-room, rubbing the small of her back and rolling her head cautiously from side to side, 'bloody *bloody* bed.'

'Ditto,' Gemma says drowsily from the settee, holding a mug of hot tea, her eyes, though partially hidden by her mass of dark curls, drawn to breakfast TV with the volume off. 'God, my head. Why do I invariably start the week as I end it – with a hangover? Why don't I learn?'

'I slept like a babe,' says Fen, who has appeared at the foot of the stairs, 'and awoke to a room spic, span and fragrant with Shake 'n' Vac.'

Abi and Gemma regard their housemate, who looks annoyingly fresh herself both in countenance and clothing.

'Take your halo—' Abi starts.

'—and shove it!' Gemma concludes.

Fen grins and makes much of sashaying past both of them en route to the kitchen. 'Toast?'

'Can't eat a thing,' Gemma groans, 'bloody hungover.'

'Can't eat a thing,' Abi bemoans, 'bloody on a diet.'

Fen returns with heavily buttered toast and takes a seat at the table next to Abi, balancing the plate on a pile of CDs which are themselves atop a heap of Sunday papers.

'It's one of life's great injustices,' Abi decrees, glowering at Fen's plate, 'that you basically have toast with your butter and you're still slim and spot free. Bitch. I hate you.'

'Hate you too,' Fen says with her mouth full. The two of them sit affably and procrastinate over 14 Across in Saturday's *Guardian* crossword.

'And me,' Gemma chips in, having been momentarily

distracted by the weather girl's quite staggering choice of lipstick, 'I hate you.'

'*Hate* you,' Abi stresses non-specifically.

'*Hate* you,' Fen says with no malice and to no one in particular.

'Hate *hate* you,' Gemma recapitulates. And then they all laugh and sigh and say oh God, what are we *like*? Sigh some more and moan about Monday mornings.

'Are we going to Snips this evening?' Fen asks.

'Yup. Every sixth week at six o'clock,' Abi confirms.

'Do you think it a bit odd,' Gemma wonders, though her eyes are caught by TV presenters doing extraordinary things with sarongs, 'our obsession with little rituals?'

'It makes sense to have a communal outing to the hairdressers,' Abi shrugs, analysing her housemates' hair: Gemma's ebony ringlets, Fen's dark blonde long-top-crop. She twists pinches of her own hair, bleached and razor-cut short into pixie-like perfection. 'It's all about synchronization. What's the point of spending time apart on the mundanities, when we can actually make them something of an institution?'

'What, even the dentist?' Gemma asks, turning away from the television, the sight of cooking in a bright studio kitchen making her decidedly queasy. 'And leg waxing?'

'Which reminds me,' Abi says, stroking her calves.

'Not yet!' protests Gemma, for whom the pain of a leg wax is on a par with her fear of the dentist.

'How did we manage to coincide our periods?' Fen wonders, dabbing at toast crumbs and thinking she could do with another slice, were there another slice left to toast.

'That'll be the Moon Goddess,' Abi says, very earnestly. 'We'll dance in her honour next time we're on Primrose Hill.'

'Abi,' says Gemma, 'you need *help*.'

'I'm not going to bother to wash mine this morning then,' says Fen.

'Wash *what*?' the other two shriek.

'My hair – if we're going to Snips.' Fen fingers her locks gingerly. 'Anyway,' she reasons, 'who's going to see me in my little archive? Just a bunch of dead artists and benefactors.'

'Are you excited?' Abi asks, excited for her friend.

'Nervous?' Gemma asks, nervous for her friend.

Fen upends her right palm. 'Nervous? Yes,' she says. Then she upends her left palm. 'Excited? Yes,' she says. Then she clicks her fingers and punches the air: 'But I get to have Julius all to myself!'

'Bloody Julius,' mutters Abi, when Fen has shut the front door behind her.

'Bloody Julius,' murmurs Gemma. 'Fancy fancying a dead sculptor.'

Abi sighs. 'It's not the dead sculptor she's obsessed with but some lump of marble he made in the shape of two people having a shag.'

'Our Fen is way overdue a bonk,' Gemma reasons.

'So am I,' Abi rues.

Gemma counts the months off on her fingers. 'Er, and me.'

'Maybe we should set aside some time and synchronize,' says Abi.

THREE

Man's love is of man's life a thing apart,
'Tis woman's whole exixtcnce.

Byron

O*h God. Oh Gawd. Oh Jesus.* Matthew Holden has just woken up. The start to the day, to the week, could not be much worse. He has a hangover. He has a bad taste in his mouth. He's late for work. And his ex girlfriend is lying in bed next to him. With a contented smile on her sleeping face. He has a very bad taste in his mouth indeed. He tries closing his eyes but realizes that to stare at the ceiling, at the blooms of new paint on top of old, is far preferable to confronting all the current hassles of his life which parade around his mind's eye as soon as his eyelids touch. Wake up. But he's so damn tired. Wake up. Stay awake. Force eyes open. Monday. Monday. April Fool's Day. Only this is no joke. No prank. He's been a fool, full stop. It would be easier to just go back to sleep, slip into nothingness, to will it all to be a bad dream. However, while sleep might be a good antidote to his raging hangover, it won't actually remedy the situation in hand or make it any less real. In fact, he'd have to wake again and do the whole oh God oh Gawd oh Jesus thing once more.

He daren't move. Memory tells him that if he does, she'll reach for him, claim him with encircling arms and clamping legs. Never let him go.

I wanted to get away.

The severity of his sigh is pronounced enough for her to turn to him, wrapping her limbs around him. She sighs herself. Triumphant.

Oh God. Oh Gawd. Oh Jesus no.

And then the phone starts to ring and Matt has an escape route though he knows in an instant that it is Jake's mobile phone. He slithers from his bed and hurries through the flat, very naked.

Jake had, of course, answered his mobile phone. Jake was also late for work. But at least he was dressed. Jake just had a hangover, no ex-girlfriend in his bed. Not today. He had, in fact, bedded Matt's ex-girlfriend. Quite recently. But never again. And not that Matt was to know. Certainly not today. Matt slumped into the armchair, placed a cushion over his dick and stuck two fingers up at Jake's superciliously raised eyebrow. He couldn't remember whether the clock on the mantelpiece was five minutes slow or five minutes fast. Whichever, he was categorically late. Jake had finished on the phone. He let his eyebrows soften though he refused to erase the vestiges of a smirk from his face. He sat down on the sofa. Though dressed, he placed a cushion across his crotch in a gesture of camaraderie.

'Julia's in my bed,' Matt groaned, head in hands.

'April Fool?' Jake asked, in a vaguely hopeful way. Matt shook his head and cast his eyes to the ceiling. Only, unlike that in his bedroom, it had been replastered and repainted fairly recently and there were no hairline cracks or nuances of old against new paint to provide any welcome distraction.

Neutral nothingness.

It was realizing that I felt neutral nothingness that saw me finish a five-year relationship two months ago.

'I could say,' Jake mused, looking out of the window and deciding that it appeared to be spring-like enough to roll up shirtsleeves, 'you've made your bed, now you must sleep in it.'

'And my only reply would be, "I can't, my ex-girlfriend is sprawled all over it",' Matt groaned.

'How on earth did it happen?' asked Jake.

Matt looked at him and couldn't resist giving an elaborate, if quite medical, description of the sex act.

'Really?' Jake marvelled, playing along. 'You put your weenie *where*?'

'In a lady's front bottom,' Matt joshed.

'How the *hell* did it *happen*?' Jake asked again, seriously, stroking his goatee contemplatively.

Matt shook his head, shrugged and made a knocking-back-of-glasses motion before scratching his tufty cropped hair. 'Oh God,' he groaned, 'oh Gawd. I'm late for work. Jesus.'

Clean, dry, if crumpled clothing in the washer-dryer provided Matt with no reason to go back to his bedroom. He dressed in the kitchen, hopping around trying to wriggle crumb-soled feet into odd socks. Shoes. Shoes? Matt had a rather sizeable shoe collection. But they were all under his bed. Jake had an enviable selection himself. Distributed quite evenly around the various rooms in their flat. Matt honed in on a pair of smart loafers behind the hi-fi.

'Can I?'

'What! My Patrick Cox? With *those* trousers?'

'Excuse me – they're Paul Smith, thank you.'

'Well, that's fine then.'

'Cheers, mate.'

Though Jake could barely function without being fuelled by a hefty injection of caffeine, he left the cafetière full and smelling gorgeous so he could leave the flat with Matt. He didn't want to be alone with a sobbing girl, nustling up to his neck, pleading for comfort and affection, advice and inside information. If he answered her direct questions with direct answers, she'd cry and nustle and need comfort and affection all the more. If he didn't, she'd believe there was still a chance to rekindle the relationship with Matt. And he couldn't do that to Matt. Plus, quietly, he found weeping women craving affection and comfort rather difficult to resist. And how she had sobbed that day a month or so ago. And they'd ended up in bed. And all the while, deludedly, he'd told himself he was performing not just a selfless act, but a charitable one which was useful too. He was doing it for Julia. He was doing it for Matt. A good distraction. Get her off his case. Help her get over him. Proof for her that she's attractive to other men. Bla bla. Etcetera. When he had come, however, he had come to the more fitting conclusion.

Big mistake. Bad idea.

The two men stopped for bagels and coffee en route to Angel tube. Nourished by the former and woken up by the latter, they chatted.

'Oh God,' said Matt, 'why, why, why?'

'I'd've done the same, mate,' said Jake.

'But what now?'

'Dunno? Give up drinking?'

'You *what*?'

'Celibacy?'

'You *what*?'

'Find a distraction,' Jake concluded. 'You can't go on the rebound with your ex-girlfriend. It defeats the object of the exercise. You need a good old zipless fuck.' Jake was rather proud of such logic despite his hangover and juggling a bagel, a coffee and a ringing mobile phone.

'Who was that?' Matt asked, when Jake had finished the call.

'Your ex-girlfriend,' Jake said, 'asking me if she could stay at ours. That she'd clean the flat and have dinner awaiting our return from work. Asked whether she thought you'd like her to iron all your shirts. And change your sheets.'

'Oh Jesus,' Matt moaned, losing his appetite and throwing the bagel away, the coffee too – knowing nothing could help a headache whose provenance was now not alcohol driven.

'Hey, Matt,' Jake called, as they headed for their separate platforms.

Matt turned.

'April Fool!' Jake laughed, winking and making to pull an imaginary pistol. 'It was just Jim on the phone. About five-a-side on Thursday.'

'Wanker!' Matt mouthed very clearly.

I did love her. Really love her. I was madly in love with her, for a while, way back when. But it faded. I didn't really love her at all towards the end. I guess I kept hanging on in there because I was in love with the idea of it all. That it seemed easier to stay together than to split up. On a practical and emotional level. We went through months of arguing. And then months of indifference. Which was worse?

Matt! Pimlico station. You're about to miss your tube stop.

Splitting up hurt. Though it was something that, amongst the acrimony and indifference, had seemed like a good idea, it still hurt. I was afraid that the decision was wrong. It took some getting used to, but I never actually missed her. Not Julia herself. Her position in my life, yes. The familiarity of having her, yes. But her? In person? No.

Matt! It's a red pedestrian light and there's a double-decker haring along Vauxhall Bridge Road towards you.

Oh God. Last night. It happened but it can't happen again. Shit. It happened and it can't happen again. Jake is right. I should take a leaf out of his book. Dip in here and there. Just like he does. Dips his dick here and there. No relationship-incumbent panoply. Have a laugh. Be light-hearted. I'm twenty-nine. Thirty soon. Rebound? Sure, whatever.

You've arrived at the Trust Art offices, Matt. And you're following Fen McCabe along the corridor. You have no idea who she is. You're too preoccupied to really notice anyway. You're late. Not very seemly for the editor of the Trust's bi-monthly magazine, *Art Matters*. Don't make a habit of it.

FOUR

*F*en McCabe firmly believes one should trust art because art matters. Henry Holden, who died sixteen years ago aged eighty-three, founded Trust Art in 1938 specifically to enable national art institutions to acquire works of modern art by grant, bequest or gift. Since his death, the Trust has published a bi-monthly magazine, *Art Matters*. Fen is unsure whether this is Happy Coincidence or Fate though she has consulted her left palm and right for an answer. She thinks it has to be more than coincidence and fate that the man who founded the organization for which she now works also championed Julius Fetherstone, befriending the artist in the 1930s, buying his works and bequeathing them to British galleries. Fen feels that Henry Holden is somehow passing the baton on to her. Lucky Julius. Safe hands.

Along with the Arts Council and the National Art Collections Fund, Trust Art ensures that works of art which may otherwise be sold overseas, are given homes in galleries and museums in Great Britain and the Commonwealth. It has stayed true to its original aim of saving modern art for the nation.

Originally, Henry Holden was the only salaried member of staff. The other six workers were volunteers and all but one were the eyelash-fluttering sisters of his Oxford rowing fraternity; the odd one out being the mother of the cox. They were all utterly in love with Henry. All had double-barrelled surnames, flats in SW Somewhere and places 'in the country'. Trust Art now employs fourteen people, of whom three are part-time and three are volunteers. Continuing the tradition, these three are minor aristocracy.

Trust Art has long been housed in a clutch of rooms which are part of the labyrinthine network in Tate Britain's back buildings. Not for them the prestigious Millbank address or approach. You cannot see the Thames from Trust Art's offices; the view from the John Islip Street windows is of the nicely maintained mansion blocks. There's little more than a sandwich bar and a newsagent nearby and the shops at Victoria necessitate a veritable march; consequently little more than brief window-shopping during a lunch-hour is possible. Fen is quite relieved that most her earnings will see their way into her bank account, and not be squandered on some impulsive lunch-time purchase, as Gemma's and Abi's invariably are.

Fen had arrived at her new job a full quarter of an hour before her contractual start time. And that was with a delay in a tunnel just after Camden Town. There was a veritable welcome brigade awaiting her. If she analysed the palm of her left hand, she was really rather embarrassed by the fuss. Her right hand, however, said that she was quietly rather flattered. Amongst the croissants and coffee set out in the boardroom-cum-library, Fen soon realized that it was all at the whim of Rodney Beaumont, the director of Trust Art; not so much to welcome her as to indulge himself. Consequently, watching him tuck into pastries and talk animatedly about anything but shop with his staff, made Fen feel much less conspicuous. And it was nice to meet the fourteen staff who, it soon occurred to Fen, were as diverse as the art the Trust was saving for the nation.

From Fundraising, three girls with pearls, hearts of gold and hyphenated surnames provided a nice contrast with the two dowdy accountants, sweet but dull, with little interest in art but a near-obsessive passion for stretching the Trust's funds in all directions. The sober Acquisitions team, essentially art historians rather than administrators, dressed demurely and talked art earnestly with Fen, in hushed tones and with much eye contact. The two women in Membership could double for headmistress and hockey captain and Fen found herself promising them that she'd deliver Trust Art leaflets to all the streets within walking distance of her own.

Fen particularly liked Bobbie, the receptionist, who was clad in an extraordinary polka-dot ensemble as daring for a woman in her fifties as for an institution as seemingly staid as Trust Art. Bobbie was as categorically Cockney as Rodney Beaumont (who looked like an extra in a Merchant Ivory production of any Evelyn Waugh novel) was wholly Home Counties. He lolloped around the room like a young labrador, or an overgrown schoolboy (though he must be nearing fifty), tucking into the croissants. Fen mused that there were probably conkers and catapults and dusty pieces of chocolate in his pockets. He was affable and ingenuous and kept grinning at Fen, sticking his thumbs up or saying crikey! what goodies you are going to unearth! terrifically exciting, *terrifically*!

And then a tall man, much her own age and appearing to be constructed from pipe-cleaners and drinking straws, such was his thinness, introduced himself. Sidling up to her, he ate his croissant in a silent and contemplative fashion whilst visibly assessing Fen from top to toe. After much teeth sucking and de-crumbing of fingers, he smacked his lips, held out his hand and made her acquaintance.

'Otter. I'm Otter. *Charmed* to meet you,' he said in a voice so camp that Fen initially thought he was putting it on.

'What do you do here?' Fen asked, wanting to stroke his hand for fear of breaking it on shaking it. 'And why are you called Otter?'

'I work in Publications,' he said, running bony fingers through a surprisingly dense flop of sand-blond hair, 'and I am called Otter because Gregory John Randall-Otley is a mouthful.' He paused, licked his lips and leant in close. 'A *fucking* mouthful,' he bemoaned. 'Anyway, what sort of a name is Fen, then?'

Fen whispered, 'It's short for Fenella.'

Suddenly, she felt utterly buoyant; as if she'd just been afforded a glimpse, via coffee and croissants and people coming to say hullo, of future fun to be had at work. Fen had been excited enough about the job itself and now she discovered, almost as an added bonus, colleagues so affable. On the face of it, backgrounds were distinctly contrary and yet (hopefully not just on the face of it) the staff of Trust Art seemed non-judgemental, genuine and unconditionally friendly. Apart from Judith St John, deputy director, whose steely exterior and somewhat cursory handshake Fen had told herself must just be an unfortunate manner, surely.

'And when are you Fenella?' asked the man called Otter. 'Only on very special occasions?'

'I am only ever Fen,' she declared, pausing for effect, 'unless I'm being told off.'

Otter narrowed his eyes and put his hands on his skinny hips. 'And are you told off often?'

Fen feigned offence and clasped her hand to her heart. 'The dread of being called Fenella ensures that I behave perfectly all the time.' She kept her eyes wide whilst Otter narrowed his all the more.

'It will become,' he said, with great conviction, 'my aim in life to make you misbehave. I shall then call you Fenella at the top of my voice and with much satisfaction,' Otter proclaimed triumphantly. 'Now Ed,' he said, looking around the room, 'Ed would have you misbehaving in no time, Fen McCabe. Where is he, the bugger? Late. Must have been misbehaving himself.'

Fen laughed. 'Does that mean we're going to call him Edward or Edwyn, or whatever his full name is, very sternly all day today?'

Otter regarded her quizzically but before he could answer, Rodney whistled piercingly through his fingers, compounding Fen's overgrown-schoolboy theory. 'The meet and greet is over!' the director exclaimed with gusto good enough for a town crier, or a master of ceremonies, or a soapbox at Speaker's Corner. 'There is art to save for the nation – and, more to the point, no bloody croissants left!'

The Archive room was smaller than Fen remembered from her interview, and the boxes seemed to have increased twofold. She sat down in the typist's chair and swivelled hard, discovering that however hard she propelled herself, the chair conscientiously returned her dead in front of the computer. She ran her fingers lightly over the keyboard, as if eliciting soft notes from a piano, then rotated herself once clockwise, once anti-clockwise. She stared out of the window to the courtyard below which separated Trust Art from the Tate. The incongruous floral roller blind was half down and she gave it a tug to zap it up and let in more light. However, it unfurled with a clacketting whoosh, like a roll of wallpaper from on high, and subsequently refused to be rolled up by hand, let alone spring back by a pull at its cord. Let it hang. Switch on the light instead. A travesty on a fine April morning but better than wrestling with the blind or being held in the dark.

Fen regarded the floor-to-ceiling metal shelving standing up valiantly under the tonnage of brown archive boxes. She felt simultaneously unnerved and excited.

Julius is in there, somewhere. I can't believe I'm being paid to do a job I'd gladly pay to do. Where on earth do I start? Only half the boxes are labelled and most of those are 'Misc.' or have question marks. Six miscs. See here: '1954?', and there: 'Symposium?'. I'll start here: 'Members' gala dinner (1963) + Trip to Blenheim + Poster for Post Impressionism show + Misc. correspondence'.

Cross-legged on the floor, having hauled the box off the shelf and been sent staggering under its weight, Fen eased the lid off and grinned at the contents as if she'd just prised open a treasure chest. She was engrossed. When the phone rang, she leapt.

'Hullo?' she said, as if the call had come through to the wrong extension.

'Miss McCabe?'

Fen was silent before she clicked that she was Miss McCabe and the call was most certainly for her.

'This is Barnard Castle Museum.'

'Hullo! Barnard Castle Museum!' she greeted them with excessive delight.

'Just wondering whether you've received our package?'

No, she hadn't but she assured them she'd go down to Reception to check and would call them as soon as it arrived. By the way, what is it? Oh, only photos and documents. Only? *Only*? Fantastic!

'I'm expecting a package from Barnard Castle Museum!' Fen announced triumphantly in Reception, where Rodney was peering with intent into the biscuit barrel.

'Marvellous,' he said, though whether this was about the Bourbon biscuit or Barnard Castle was unclear.

'Not arrived yet, ducks,' said Bobbie. Seeing Fen look a little crestfallen, Bobbie suggested a biscuit. Seeking some solace in a Jammy Dodger, Fen climbed the stairs and walked briskly back along the corridor to the Archive.

And that was when Matt Holden was a few steps behind her. But as he had arrived so late for work, and she was eager to return to the treasure, neither noticed the other.

'Have you met the new archivist?' Otter asks Matt, an hour later.

'Nope,' Matt replies, 'not yet. But I think it's time for a biscuit break so I'll go and make my acquaintance. How old is this one? The last one was older than any of the documents.'

'Nah,' says Otter nonchalantly, rather amused and starting to scheme, 'she's a little bit younger, this one.'

Matt knocked and entered. Fen was sitting amidst dunes of papers and appeared too engrossed to have heard him. He was quite surprised that she was not old enough to be his grandmother.

She looks too young to be an archivist! Who am I to judge on what an archivist should or shouldn't look like? And who am I to complain!

'Hullo, archivist.'

'Fantastic!' Fen said, spying a large brown envelope tucked under the arm of a man she presumed to be a courier. After all, she didn't know what the editor of *Art Matters* looked like. 'Are you from Barnard Castle?'

'Er,' said the courier, looking a little perplexed, 'no, Gloucestershire originally.'

'Oh,' said Fen, nodding at the envelope, 'isn't that for me?'

'No,' he said, 'just thought I'd say hullo.'

'Oh,' said Fen, slightly taken aback by his forthrightness and wondering whether it was harassment and whether she should have Bobbie phone or fax or e-mail a complaint to his delivery company. 'Nothing for Fen McCabe?' she asked, giving him the benefit of the doubt.

'Er, no,' said the courier.

'Bugger,' said Fen, disappointed and now disinterested; turning from him to regard the boxes instead. 'You probably want Fund-raising next door,' she said with her back to him.

'Do I?' the courier asked.

'Or Acquisitions,' she continued breezily, as if she was a long-term member of staff, 'down the corridor, before Publications.' Then she stood on tiptoes to retrieve the box marked 1956. 'Bugger Barnard Castle,' she said under her breath and obviously to herself.

The courier raised his eyebrows. At her language, at her turned back, at her neat bottom; at the fact that she was working in a room with the lights on and the blind down on a particularly fine April day. At the fact that she worked here now. But Fen didn't notice. Not just because she had her back to him. She had lifted the lid off the box and was already enthralled by its contents.

'Blimey,' she murmured. The box had revealed an original catalogue to the Picasso–Matisse exhibition at the Victoria and Albert Museum. Matt left her to it, hearing her mutter, 'But that was 1945, what's it doing in 1956? Matisse was already dead,' as he shut the Archive door.

Fen was blazing through 1956 when the phone in the Archive rang. She scrambled up from 1942, 1958 and 1979 (all found in the 1956 box – despite it being the only box without a question mark on the label, for goodness' sake), and grabbed the receiver.

'Barnard Castle?' she asked hopefully.

'It's Otter. Ed and I are ready for our lunch. Come to our room in five minutes. Next to Acquisitions.'

My God, lunchtime already.

Only Otter isn't in the room. Just the overfamiliar courier.

'Oh,' says Fen, 'still lost?'

'Hullo,' says the courier, 'again.'

She makes to leave. 'Are you looking for someone?' he asks.

'Yes,' she says, 'Otter and Ed.'

'I'm Matt,' he says.

Fen nods somewhat cursorily at him.

As she made to leave a second time, Otter came in.

'Fen!' he greeted her. 'Meet Ed.'

Fen was starting to feel a little exasperated and she glanced from Otter to the Man With Two Names. 'Who?' she shrugged. 'Which? *What?*' Otter looked worryingly non-plussed at Fen's confusion. But the courier came to her rescue.

'I'm Matt,' the courier persists, 'I edit *Art Matters*. Hence "Ed". Although I hasten to add that it is only Otter who calls me Ed.'

31

'You're not a courier?' Fen asks, frowning first and then blushing, much to Otter's delight and Matt's surprise.

'No,' confirms Matt generously, 'just an editor. Sorry to disappoint you. Hullo.' He held out his hand which Fen took. They shook hands just a little gingerly.

'Hullo, Matt, then.'

'Thyu.'

'Sorry?'

'Matthew. I edit *Art Matters* and anything else you want to know you can ask over lunch. I'm starving.'

'Hangover?' Otter said not so much presumptuously as from experience.

'Worse than,' Matt groaned and hoped that Otter wouldn't pry or comment.

Otter, however, was now near-obsessed with his self-crowned role as matchmaker. 'Matthew Holden is a modest sod,' he said as the three of them walked along John Islip Street to the sandwich shop, 'he's twenty-nine, he is a brilliant editor – if a quite dastardly cad. He's relatively solvent and comes with car and mortgage.'

Fen backtracked and ground to a halt as she did so: 'As in Henry?'

'Henry Moore-gage?' Otter quipped.

'*Holden*,' Fen stressed, staring at Matt.

Please please please! Please let it be so! I'll cook and clean and perform base acts for him. I'll marry him and bear him an heir. But please please please!

'Any relation?' she said, with hastily employed non-chalance.

'Father,' Matt confirmed without fanfare, 'late.'

'How fantastic!' Fen said, wincing as she did so. 'I'm sorry. I didn't mean . . . I'm sorry for your loss. But I'm a huge Julius Fetherstone fan, you see, and your father was such a wonderful patron.'

'I applied under a pseudonym,' Matt said almost defensively, 'and anyway, most of his Fetherstones were already bequeathed to national art institutions.'

32

Fen touched Matt's arm. He felt firm. 'I'm sorry. I didn't mean . . .'

Matt reassured her by laying his hand fleetingly between her shoulder-blades.

Otter noticed the physical contact with satisfaction.

'Did you say "most"?' Fen asks, as they take their sandwiches into the little gardens opposite the Trust. 'Did you say *most* the Fetherstones were bequeathed?'

Matt nods because he has a mouthful of pastrami and ciabatta.

'Can I marry you?' Fen asks, all wide-eyed and winsome.

'OK,' he confirms through a muffle of bread and sausage.

Otter is delighted with their exchange.

'It's not an April Fool,' Fen stresses, glancing at Matt's profile and liking it so much she has to cast her eyes away, alighting on his legs instead; feeling suddenly a little light between hers.

Oh God. Not on my first day at work. Not a colleague. Not after so long without. Not after landing my dream job after so long doing mind-numbingly boring placements. So he has great cheekbones, milk-chocolate-coloured eyes and funky this-way-and-that sandy hair. So what. OK, so he's not too tall, not too beefy but fit. Big deal. And he has good teeth and a gorgeous smile. Well la-di-bloody-da.

So, he's charming and handsome and he's Henry Holden's son.

I am not going to have a flirtation, let alone a fling, with a colleague.

So says your right palm, Fen. What can you read on your left?

Egg-mayonnaise sandwiches never tasted so good. For Fen McCabe, Christmas has come early.

Pastrami on ciabatta is a taste sensation today. Matthew Holden has just appointed the role of rebound to the archivist. No one else need apply.

FIVE

'*A* good day at the office, darling?' Abi jested when Fen took a seat at Snips, the hairdressers, between her and Gemma.

'Save any art for the nation?' Gemma asked her.

Even with her hair sopping wet and the stylist's clips parting it into strange configurations whilst he snipped, Fen looked quite elated.

'I met a man called Matt,' she said with a blush that neither Abi nor Gemma had seen for many many months.

'Please not a frigging statue,' Abi groaned, wanting to lean forward to clasp her head in her hands but finding her hair tugged back by her irritated stylist.

'No no,' Fen breezed, 'but he is Henry Holden's son.'

'So he's as good as a bloody statue,' Gemma concurred, 'God, you're mercenary!'

'Probably just your average office flirtation,' said Fen.

'Yeah right,' Abi snorted, from experience, 'you just try and stop it there!'

Matt hardly gave Fen a moment's thought when he returned home. His ex-girlfriend was still there. Looking very comfortable. She'd cooked him supper. Some for Jake too, but Jake didn't show. Matt didn't have the heart to send her home. Or was it that he didn't have the nerve? He let her sleep in his bed. Again. He felt somewhat defeated by it all. Exhausted. She entwined her limbs around his and gave his ear lobes sweet little kisses, his chest too; she tried her best to arouse his flaccid cock.

'I have a headache,' Matt said, turning away from her but staying awake for hours.

SIX

*J*ames Caulfield was woken by his lurcher, Barry, and, in turn, woke the labrador, Beryl, over whom he tripped on his way to the bathroom. He had a leisurely pee and then yawned at length, hanging on to the basin and staring vaguely at the mirror until the fog of reverie lifted and his reflection gawped back.

'Christ,' he groaned, stretching his chin to analyse bristle length, 'reckon I can go another day?' His dogs did not answer, merely observed him before glancing away in the approximate direction of the kitchen and their breakfast.

'What's today?' James asked, this time not expecting an answer from his canine companions. 'Thursday, I do believe. That means Mrs Brakespeare and as she's rather short-sighted, the razor can wait until tomorrow.' He stroked his chin thoughtfully, sprayed a long blast of deodorant under each armpit and went downstairs in his T-shirt and boxer shorts to feed the dogs. He stood over them, hands on hips, as he always did, while they slurped down their food before staring at him imploringly as if they could eat the same again. 'Come on, out you go.' He opened the arched oak door and the dogs bounded out into the morning.

Standing barefoot on the stone steps of his home, he watched the dogs race each other over the lawn. 'In-digestion!' he called after them in warning, stopping them momentarily in their tracks, before they resumed their intricate chase in and out of the cedars. James looked over to the great house, the gables of which he could see through the shrubs and trees. 'Morning all,' he said quietly, 'apologies, as ever, should my dogs shit in your shrubs.' He shut the front door and went to change. It was ten in the morning and he was running late.

James Caulfield is forty-nine years old. He lives at the Keeper's Dwelling of Delvaux Hall, near Bakewell, Derbyshire. The Hall itself is no longer lived in by Lord Delvaux, or anyone of remotely aristocratic lineage, however tenuous. Fifteen years ago the Hall was converted into ten luxury apartments, the stables, the keeper's dwelling and the forester's lodge into self-contained residences. James is a landscape gardener for whom an address as seemly as Keeper's Dwelling, Delvaux Hall, Near Bakewell, Derbyshire, is essential to his trade. His clientele would be strictly limited if his van and cards gave some cul-de-sac in Chesterfield as his abode. James bought the building as a forsaken shell fourteen years ago, taking on most of the interior renovations himself. Consequently, though his mortgage is relatively small, the upkeep of the place requires a monthly input of funds that his landscape gardening only just about provides for. It certainly does not stretch to fixing the temperamental heating system, or the extensive roof repairs.

While most men his age dress in suits for the office or casuals for tele-working, James's work attire consists of old khakis, a black cotton polo-neck (the polo part becoming unstitched at the neck), a quilted checked lumberjack shirt, thick socks and hiking boots, an old battered wax jacket slung over his shoulder but worn only in utterly antisocial weather. The whole ensemble, clothing as it does a strong six-foot frame, makes James look much more Ralph Lauren than he does Percy Thrower and that's why most of his clients are female. His Italian mother bequeathed him a head of tenacious, dark curls that he keeps cut close to his scalp. Though his hairline has receded a little, it has not drawn back further since he was twenty-six, nor have the silver flecks which pepper the sides increased. Because he scrutinized it daily until he was thirty, and it didn't creep back even a millimetre, James rarely looks at it now – he is more concerned with his torso. When he looks in the mirror, he is always unnerved to see that it is not the body of a man in his mid-twenties that he still fully expects to see. But there again, when he goes for his thrice-weekly run, he is always unsettled that three miles feel much more of an effort than seven ever used to. He fears that age is playing havoc with his memory and powers of logic. Saying that, he is blessed by good looks; working out of doors affords his skin a year-round healthy bloom and his olive complexion accentuates the glint of his nut-brown eyes. His teeth are good. His humour is excellent. His hands are anomalously fine and clean for his job. His self-sufficiency, however, is wholly exasperating.

James is a prime topic of analysis amongst the women he works for. Word of mouth passed him from client to client, and much conversation is devoted to hypothesizing on why such an eligible man is unattached. In their pursuit of the tiniest clue (they've given up on full-blown answers), they rarely allow James to garden uninterrupted. He is paid by the hour and if they choose to force him to spend lengthy periods at the kitchen table drinking tea, or juice, or sometimes, according to the season, Pimm's or spiced cider, then that's their prerogative. Most would love to object to the presence of his dogs, especially the lurcher with the lascivious glare and probing snout, especially the labrador who invariably digs up much of James's work before he leaves; but none voice their concern. Whatever makes James happy. What is it that would make him happy? But is he *unhappy*? He can't be happy all alone, surely. Do you know? No, do you? Any ideas? Any clues?

He's an enigma. In Derbyshire, he is day-dream material, fodder for fantasy. He is Mellors. And Angel. He is Gossip. He's the highlight of many a Matlock Mrs's week. He knows it and he chuckles to himself amongst the hydrangeas. He plays up to it. He likes the attention. The company. And the control.

Once James had arrived at Mrs Brakespeare's near Hassop, had been given a cup of tea, a bun and a run-down on her week, there was just time for him to do an hour's work before lunch-time; a hearty affair of ham and eggs, orange barley water and the recounted ways, wiles and woes of Mrs Brakespeare's daughters and granddaughters.

'And you, James, what are we to do with you?' Mrs Brakespeare declared quite brazenly, folding her arms in a motherly way, for emphasis and persuasion, while she observed him.

'What do you mean, Mrs B?' James asked, quietly enough to disguise his teasing tone.

'Please, after all this time, and all my assurances, *please* call me Ruth.'

James nodded, though both knew he never would. All his clients begged him to be familiar but the closest he came was to abbreviate their surnames to the first letter. Mrs Woodgate, in Hathersage, one of his newest clients, longs for the day when she will finally be Mrs W.

'James, James,' Mrs B chided amicably, 'we don't like to think of you all on your own in Keeper's Dwelling – it's a grand place, perfect for a family. Well?'

'Mrs B,' James replied, clearing his throat and helping himself to an apple which he bit into and chewed for a tantalizing period before answering, 'as far as I can see, the only way a family will live at Keeper's is if I sell it on to one.'

'But you can't be happy, truly so, just you on your own?'

'Oh, but I am,' munched James. 'Best to be with nowt, than with the wrong'un,' he said in an accent that was a whole county north and not at all the Cheltenham-born,

Cambridge-educated, Derbyshire-living gardener.

'But you're not getting any younger,' Mrs B all but pleaded, 'you don't want to become too set in your ways. I mean, you really should shave regularly, too.'

'Mrs B,' James said in a voice that blended warning and flattery, 'Lunch, as ever, was delicious.' He kissed his fingers and threw them theatrically to the air, fluttering Ruth Brakespeare's heart quite intentionally as he did so. Still she knew no more about him than she had six months ago. There'd be little to recount to Babs Chorlton, whom she'd promised to phone at tea-time.

'James,' Mrs B called from the back door. James looked up from the roses and cupped his hand to his ear. 'James,' said Mrs B, 'promise me one thing — keep the door ajar, never let it close completely.'

James, who had understood her very well, nevertheless sauntered over to the garden shed, opened the door a little and gave Mrs B the thumbs up. Exasperated, she blinked skywards and then went in to phone Babs because it just couldn't wait.

James had no more jobs that day and, after an arduous trawl through Safeways, and a demoralizing visit to the petrol pump (he was constantly bemused by the fuel gauge in his Land Rover always hovering at empty), he told the dogs he had spent over half the cash he had earned that day, that it was therefore Safeways' own brand rather than Winalot Supreme for the next few days. After a run which hurt his legs, his lungs and his pride, he sat down to a bowl of Heinz tomato soup followed by a bowl of cereal: Cornflakes, Alpen and Coco Pops, all mixed together and saturated with full cream milk. The combination was delicious and satisfying — and eaten, as often it was, in gleeful defiance of Dawn.

Dawn, with whom James had spent most of his mid-twenties in a gracious apartment in Bath when he was working as a highly paid surveyor, had insisted on providing three courses at seven thirty sharp. With her predilection for well-cooked meat, overcooked veg and stodgy puddings, along with her need to have everything washed and dried just as soon as it was finished with, she made the evening repast about as enjoyable as the taking of cod liver oil as a child. James rebounded into a relationship with an American model so faddish about food that often supper was little more than herbal tea gulped down with air, egg whites blended in the Magimix or, as a rare luxury, liquidized frozen bananas. It was then, in his early thirties, that James decided all potential bed-mates must be dined on the very first date; their choice from the menu and the amount left on their plates determining the level of involvement he was willing to invest.

Ultimately, it cost him a fortune in restaurant bills and redundancy between the sheets. Aged thirty-five, James turned to dogs, Derbyshire and delphiniums for respite. He liked dogs. Dogs ate anything at any time and licked the bowls clean themselves. And Derbyshire was down to earth, with folk whose humour was as dry as their stone walls. And delphiniums? Ah! Delphiniums. The season would arrive soon enough.

And are the Derbyshire dames gems to rival those of the Blue John Caverns? Or are they Bakewell Tarts? Come on, James, don't tell us you've been celibate for fourteen years.

Lord above, no! But you know what they say about discretion . . .

Do we?

Exercise it and you're rewarded – lay after lay.

No one has scratched a little deeper?

No. If I'd been an idiot, I'd have married my childhood sweetheart at twenty-one. Anyway, my father had two wives, several mistresses and innumerable dalliances. I look on him as an example – albeit, one not to follow. Women are complicated. And they are expensive too. And noisy.

And you're forty-nine now.

Yup. Stuck in my ways with my heart shared equally between two dogs and a draughty house. Not much more room in there. Anyway, I'm not that inviting a proposition. I had a couple of women last year, one in Glossop, one in Crookes, for whom I was the height of glamour on account of my age (I was at least twice theirs) and accent. Folk round here would love to see me set up in the Dwelling with a wife and the proverbial 2.4 – but they'll be keeping their ripe daughters well away.

Why?

Because I think they feel if I'm unmarried and with sperm awaiting at forty-nine, there must be some reason for it, something wrong.

OK, what about their older daughters?

It's a truth universally acknowledged that an unmarried man, at forty-nine, is far more attractive a proposition than an unmarried woman of that age.

But are you happy like this?

I'm used to it. Familiarity breeds content.

With a huge mug of tea and a clutch of digestive biscuits, James goes to the room he calls the study to divide his attention between three days of unopened mail and today's *Guardian*. Bill. Bill. Bill. Bill Clinton. James does some hasty mental arithmetic and reckons that the amounts owing will swallow nicely both the amount earned last month and to be earned this.

Swallow nicely – hey, Mr Clinton?

Barry and Beryl look at him with expressions bordering on pity. James studiously ignores them and the pile of red bills, and tries to ignore the fact that he is verging on broke. He turns the page of the newspaper and reads that an anonymous bidder at Calthrop's paid £3 million for a Matisse.

'Shame we don't have a Matisse or two knocking about,' James says, regarding a pair of oil sketches above the fireplace. 'My bank manager hates me.' He looked at the numbers under the Matisse painting. He thought about his bank manager. He looked at the pile of red bills. He thought about the Fetherstones. 'Compared to a Matisse, we'd probably need to subtract most of the noughts if we put the Fetherstones up for auction.' He ventures over and unhooks one of the paintings from the wall. It is about the size of a coffee-table book.

How awful that something as prosaic as a leaking roof and irate bank manager would make me think of selling my Fetherstones. There again, pruning rhodos does not a rich man make.

'Anyway, my lot are probably not even worth half of a pencil smudge by Monsieur Matisse.' He looks at the back of the board he has just taken down. '*Adam*, 1895. *Eve*,' he murmurs, taking down the other, '1894. Biblically impossible – but artists are gods of a type – creating and destroying and having tomes of nonsense written about them.' He looks at the wall and cringes at the two light rectangles edged by dusty outlines. He places the two paintings side by side. He feels ashamed that he's trying to read price tags on them. He feels irritated that, at forty-nine years of age, his finances are in disarray and his bank manager is rude to him. He looks at the oil sketches, butting up against each other. Without the width of the extravagant stone mantelpiece separating them, he suddenly appreciates how they were conceived as much more than a pair. He feels ashamed for having kept them apart.

'Dirty bugger!' he chortles under his breath with deference to the artist. He sees how, if he was to cut the figures from the board, they would entwine together in copulatory ecstasy. 'Hang on,' James says, leaving the room and disappearing out into the garden followed by his dogs. He returns without them, but with a small sculpture of two figures. 'I forgot about you two, pumping away privately under the boughs of the weeping willow. I'll bet you anything – yes! You see!' He brandished the statue as if it was an Oscar, glancing only cursorily at the woodlice clinging haplessly to its base. 'Put the two figures in the paintings together, cast the lot in bronze and this is what you get.' He read the base. *Eden*, 1892.

'That can't be right. Surely he'd have done the sketches first? More to the point, if this is not a culmination piece, is it worth less?'

What am I doing? Am I really thinking of selling them? Just because I'm broke?

He scrutinized the dates on the boards and the bronze and knew he read them correctly. 'I might ring Calthrop's tomorrow. Just out of interest. Or for insurance purposes.'

Clipped tones in the Nineteenth Century department at Calthrop's assured James that they'd be frightfully interested in any works by Fetherstone and, whilst they could estimate nowhere near the number of noughts of the Matisse league, they said they were confident of a sum far more princely than James had ever imagined.

'I say, you wouldn't like to bring them down to Bond Street, would you? Let us have a good old snoop? Valuations are free.'

'I may,' said James cautiously.

'And you say the sculpture is just over a foot high?'

'That's right.'

'That's a bugger.'

'Sorry?'

'We live in hope of the marble *Abandon* being brought in unannounced one day. Now that *would* earn you a bob or two and a place in the history books.'

'Really. Well, sorry to disappoint. But perhaps I will bring the others – I don't know if I want to sell them, though my bank manager would. Do I need to make an appointment? Ask for *who*?'

'A triple-barrelled surname,' James exclaimed to his dogs, before filling a bowl with cornflakes and two crushed Weetabix. *Eden*, now free of woodlice and soil, stood at the foot of the stove; *Adam* and *Eve* were propped against the knife block and the washing-powder box. It was nearly

44

eleven in the morning. Mrs G's at noon, just for a prune, then Mrs M all afternoon, hopefully till tea-time and a good feed. So, no rush then. James perused the *Guardian*. He started the crossword, but without a pen it soon became a little trying. Then the name Julius Fetherstone leapt out at him from the small print of the galleries listings.

'"*Julius Fetherstone: Art and Erotica*". *F. McCabe. Tate Britain. Thursday Lunch-time Lecture. Millbank, SW1*,' he murmured. 'Flavour of the month, Fethers old boy?' He put down his spoon and looked hard at the paintings. 'Doesn't fashion dictate an inflated value?' He rummaged around in a kitchen drawer, found a rail timetable that was surprisingly not out of date, and consulted it for a train for the day after next that would bring him into London in good time.

'Looks like we have a date.'

SEVEN

Wherever you are, it is your own friends who make your world.

William James

I'll just nod, Jake decides over a mouthful of Chicken Madras. *I'll just nod and not comment.*

Matt was remarking on the physical similarities between a girl on a TV advert for dandruff shampoo and Fen McCabe.

I won't comment, Jake thought, *I won't say, 'Yes, but you said that one of the girls we chatted to in the pub last night looked like her'. I'll just nod.*

'Fen's face doesn't have that hardness, though.'

I won't ask you how Fen can look like that girl on the adverts and the girl in the pub and Gwyneth Paltrow and your very first girlfriend.

'Not that willowy, though. Just normal height, I suppose.'

I mean, if she looks like all the above, she probably doesn't look remotely like any of them. A crazy mixed-up kid – which is what you're sounding like, Matthew Holden. You can't possibly go for a healthy rebound brand of zipless fuck with someone occupying your thoughts as much as this Vanilla girl.

'Don't fuck the payroll,' Jake says.

'I've no intention of doing so,' says Matt, who feels suddenly just a little vulnerable, as if he's been caught out.

46

'I'm just saying that it's refreshing to have a nice view at work. She seems like a laugh. Like we could be mates.'

'Like you want to mate her,' Jake counters, offering to swap the foil container with his Madras for the remains of Matt's Rogan Josh.

Matt shrugs. 'Nah,' he says, feigning indifference by appearing incredibly interested in *Newsnight*.

'Anyway,' says Jake, 'if she looks like a hybrid of that model crossed with Gwynnie and the girl in the pub, if she's intelligent and a laugh and all that – well, she's probably happily ensconced with some lucky bloke whom she blows to heaven and back every other night.'

'Probably,' Matt agrees, after a moment's thought. It made sense that Fen would already be taken. 'Bugger *Newsnight*,' Matt says, 'let's go for last orders.'

* * *

'How's Matthew Hard-on?' Abi asks Fen whilst wrestling to uncork a second bottle of Sauvignon.

'I had lunch with Otter today,' Fen replies, taking the bottle and deftly wielding the corkscrew. 'He's recently broken up with a long term girlfriend.'

'I thought Otter was gay?' Abi says.

'Huh?' says Fen, 'Oh. No. I mean Matt.'

'Ah!' says Abi, messing Fen's dark blonde long-crop.

'Aha,' says Gemma, twiddling her dark curls herself.

'I mustn't get involved,' Fen says.

'Nope,' cautions Abi, 'he'll be on the rebound.'

'And the impression you ought to be making at your new job is of archivist extraordinaire,' says Gemma.

'Not slapper,' says Abi.

'You're right,' says Fen. 'Anyway, I don't really know him at all, do I? I just find him attractive because he seems like a nice bloke and he's really sexy looking.'

'When really he might be a total prat,' muses Gemma, having had one too many of those.

'Or a complete sod,' Abi warns, having had one too many of those.

'Exactly,' Fen says decisively. But she goes to bed planning on what to wear the next day. Perhaps she'll be loitering with intent, accidentally on purpose, outside Publications near enough to lunch-time.

Bugger! I can't. I'm lecturing at the Tate at lunch-time. Just as well. Just as well.

EIGHT

Defy the influential master!

Cézanne

'**D**on't moisten too much,' Auguste Rodin told Julius Fetherstone, a little surprised at his student's uncharacteristic ineptitude, 'use your finger to check.' The great master had been slightly perturbed that today, his English protégé seemed fractious, distracted. He had therefore given Julius the simple task of moistening the clay maquettes so they did not dry out and crack. But he observed that the young artist sponged and sloshed the slip as if he was bathing a horse. Rodin suggested Julius stop. That he sketch.

'Don't want to sketch,' Julius said defensively.

'Take over from Pierre and continue the carving of *The Kiss*,' Rodin instructed. Such an exacting task was also an honour – to allow the young Englishman time with the master's current work. The marble was in another studio. By itself. Away from Rodin. An ante-room away from the other students. Away from the six models, of both sexes, moving naked around the studio so that whenever a sculptor turned and wherever his gaze fell he was confronted by the human form and the play of light upon it.

'"Love led us to a single death",' Rodin quoted as he walked his young student around *The Kiss*.

49

'Paolo and Francesca,' Julius elaborated, wanting to impress his master that he had read Dante's *Inferno* and knew the story. 'Paolo's brother goes to war entrusting the welfare of his wife to him. Paolo and Francesca fall in love and have an affair. Hell is their reward.' Rodin nodded sagely. 'Tell me that it is only in the arts that love could lead to eternal damnation,' Julius pleaded privately under his breath. Rodin, who at once now understood the provenance of his student's malady, decided it wise not to comment. He left the room, encouraging Julius to imagine he was stroking the skin of the figures to define their form, rather than carving into marble to reveal it.

Which is precisely what Julius did – and did very well – for an hour.

Then he left the ante-room and returned to the main studio as if in a trance, not seeming to notice that his master was regarding him quizzically and soon with irritation. In fact, Julius was not aware of any other person being in that studio. He scooped up an armful of terracotta clay, cradling it like a baby as he walked to the end of the room. There he sat down on the ground and laid the clay between his legs. He was sweating profusely. Panting. Little under an hour later, Julius suddenly growled, shouted, wailed, as if something was being wrenched from him. His body was twisted into spasm before collapsing and becoming as flimsy as rags. Rodin, quietly, ventured over. His young student looked up at him, tears silently streaming down his clay-smeared face. The great sculptor looked at what the young Englishman had created, had created in a frenzy, that tortured him so.

Two figures. About a foot high. Their bodies simultaneously flowing into each other like liquid but also bucked solid at the moment of sexual ecstasy. The redness of the clay accentuating the sense of flesh, blood and arousal.

'Paolo and Francesca?' Rodin asked carefully, not wishing to intrude on the intensity of personal experience that had so obviously consumed his student.

50

'Yes,' Julius replied. His voice was hoarse, not from the lie but from the exertion of wresting the form away from his soul and out into clay. Rodin told him to go, to rest for two days, not to visit the studio but to indulge himself with time, to work and create alone, slave only to what this inner inspiration was dictating.

'I will keep your clay moist,' Rodin assured him. And he would. For to see brilliance in one's students is affirming for the teacher. A legacy. A testament. A lineage in the making. The future in safe hands. 'I am the bridge between the past and the present,' Rodin muttered at a naked young woman who smiled politely and wondered if she should tell the sculptor that pellets of terracotta clay clung to his great beard like berries to holly.

Oh, how I hunger for her. Never more. Never more. I am full. And yet I starve.

Julius bought a baguette and a hunk of ham. With his teeth, he ripped the bread as he walked to his apartment but his mouth was dry and the bread stuck in his throat.

She has sucked me dry. And yet creative juices overflow and threaten to consume me.

His master had told him not to work and yet Julius broke into a jog. Home, home, he had to be there now! As soon as he entered his apartment, he dropped his provisions on the floor, fell to his knees and, with white chalk, drew Cosima across the floorboards. Where she had been. This time yesterday. Stretched out. Enfolding him. Him in her. Where did he end and where did she begin? That was the point. There was no beginning; there could be no end. And yet it had ended between them. He had to abandon himself to this fact. He would do so willingly. To be enslaved by the memory of Cosima was a captivity he could only welcome, however torturous it might be. Pain is good. Salvation from despair. Growth and creation.

There was a knock at the door.

Cosima!

No. Of course not.

Oh shit!

Thursday.

Rent day.

It would be Madame Virenque who knocked.

This week, as last, Julius was penniless. Jacques Antoine would pay for the portrait bust of his fiancée only on delivery. A small advance had been given for materials. And spent. Oh God, still she knocks.

Julius opened the door. Madame Virenque raised an eyebrow. She saw the chalk drawing on the floorboards and her other eyebrow was raised.

'You have money?'

'*Non, pardon, Madame.*'

One eyebrow down, the other now cocked lasciviously.

Close your eyes, Julius. Imagine Cosima. Forget that your landlady's breasts are pendulous, spongy; the skin akin to used crêpe paper. Remember instead the pertness of Cosima's, the translucence of her skin, the blush of her nipples. Do not allow the more pungent smell of this woman to override your memory of Cosima's sweet muskiness. If where you are dipping your cock now is slack, undefined, hold the base of your shaft and conjure the heat, the tightness of Cosima's sex. Come quickly. If you come, she will go.

Cosima, Cosima. Oh God.

Madame Virenque was disappointed. Her eyebrows told him so. But still, she could not now argue for the rent. An orgasm for her was not a condition of the barter.

The orgasm for Julius emptied his mind as much as it emptied his testicles. The pall had lifted and he was thinking clearly.

'I need money,' he said to himself after she had gone, knowing too that he must eat, so he sat down to his ham and bread. 'I will never fuck for lodgings again.' He wanted to move. He needed money to do so. There was a substantial amount for the taking, merci beaucoup, Monsieur Antoine. 'I must commence the portrait bust of his fiancée.'

That evening, Julius started his portrait of Cosima. Only it wasn't Cosima – not that Jacques or their friends would know. Julius idealized her natural beauty, enhancing her features to create an exquisite face atop an elegant neck and a stunning *décolletage*. Of course, the result would so flatter Jacques Antoine that he would pay the sculptor gladly. And yet Julius could keep Cosima to himself.

'A true sculptor works from the inside out,' Julius said out loud when his wire armature was complete and his fingers throbbed, 'even when you carve away at rock – when you work from the outside in, rather than when you model with clay and build up mass – it must be the essence of the subject which dictates the surface details.' He turned the banding wheel slowly, staring hard through the wire mesh as it rotated before him. It was like a network of atoms, the most rudimentary step towards breathing life into sculpture. 'And yet most people who look at sculpture see only the exterior. Just the periphery. The superficiality of the surface.'

By creating a portrait that was idealized, Julius knew he would be flattering Jacques Antoine's vanity.

Julius took to his bed in the early hours, unwashed even though his hands were bloodied from torn fingernails and cuts from the wire. 'My piece will have pride of place in their drawing room. And Jacques will present it to all those who enter. "See how beautiful is the woman who is my wife!" he will boast. 'Did you ever see beauty more complete? How skilled is this young Fetherstone! Of course I will introduce you – I am sure he will sculpt your wife too."'

Julius slept deeply, dreaming of his work in progress: the portrait bust, also his clay maquette. Wherever he was in dream-time, that writhing twist of terracotta was in sight. When he woke, he knew somehow how significant it was. How the work itself would dictate his future as much as his passion for Cosima.

*

As soon as it was light, Julius began to build muscle and tendon and bone and gristle aboard the armature with nuggets of clay. He worked all hours for two weeks; borrowing money from a rich student of Rodin's to pay rent to Madame Virenque. The bust progressed. It was a virtuoso piece; emotion poured from the tilt of the face or the sweep of the forehead and even now the sculptor knew just how light would catch and suffuse the work once it was cast in bronze. When he carved the eyes and parted the lips and swirled the hair idealistically, then he knew he had hidden Cosima deep within the piece. He had her to himself. She would reappear, he knew she would, whenever he sculpted an anonymous female form again. And no one would know it but him. And ah! how he would know.

He felt a certain smugness knowing how he could con Jacques and his circle into believing that this idealized beauty in bronze was the spitting image of the woman herself. But they would be incapable of recognizing her in *Abandon*, or *Eden*, or *Hunger*, and all the related works that were already in embryo, propagating as rampantly as cells, in the mind of the sculptor.

They would not recognize her. But Julius would see her, possess her again, from this day forth whenever he carved a breast, modelled a pair of lips, shaped a waist, defined a buttock, the run of a stomach, the intimacy of an ear lobe. It would be her. Unmistakably. No one else would know, though. For they would be too caught up in surface details. They did not know her inside out.

This distortion, though slight, was enough to condition all those who saw the sculpture to reappraise the way they regarded and recalled Cosima. Her own face swiftly became that of the sculpted version to all who knew her. Thus, when Julius created his masterpiece, *Abandon*, no one recognized the female figure as Cosima though he had commanded all his power and dexterity as a sculptor to best describe the woman who had both liberated and destroyed him.

54

For the rest of his life, alongside pot-boiling portrait busts and garden sculpture, Julius Fetherstone devoted maquette after maquette and volumes of sketch-pads to the theme of Cosima and *Abandon*. He cast four versions in bronze. There is one in New York, at the Museum of Modern Art, another in Paris at the Musée d'Orsay. A late version was bought by Getty and is on loan to the Art Institute of Chicago. The remaining bronze is at the Neue Pinakotek in Munich.

Julius Fetherstone's masterpiece, his magnum opus, the marble version of *Abandon*, exists now only in photographs. It has disappeared. Presumed stolen. It was at the artist's studio around the time of his death in 1954 because it can be seen in the background of photographs chronicling the artist's last weeks, bedridden in his studio surrounded by his work. There is scant documentation about *Abandon*, only Julius declaring to the great art historian Herbert Read that 'within the rock, all my desires as a man and a sculptor were contained and released'.

Of what value are grainy, monochrome, two-dimensional records of something that was conceived and created to be experienced in the round?

A tease. Torture. A tragedy.

NINE

Love is essentially copulation, the rest is only detail,
doubtless charming, but detail nevertheless.

Auguste Rodin

'*B*limey mate,' said the
cloakroom attendant at the Tate gallery when James handed
him the rucksack containing the Fetherstones, 'what you got
in there? Bleeding crown jewels?'

'You never know,' said James who then wished he hadn't
because the attendant promptly opened his bag for a suspicious look inside.

The attendant smirked and raised his eyebrows at Adam
and Eve enclasped in ecstasy. 'Is that art, then?' he asked
James.

'God no,' said James, 'pornography.'

Matt and Otter both knew why Fen had refused sandwiches
with them. They knew exactly what her prior arrangement
was. And, though they knew that she obviously wanted to
keep her lunch-time lecture secret, they couldn't resist
going.

'We'll keep out of sight,' Otter reasoned.

'We'll be silently supporting her,' Matt justified.

'We'll be fleshing out the audience,' Otter continued.

'We'll sit at the back and sneak out before the lights come
up,' Matt concluded.

Only Fen's lecture was of course conducted not in an auditorium but in the sculpture hall, so Matt and Otter found pillars to hide behind.

'My God!' Otter exclaimed. Matt, though, was speechless.

There was Fen, sitting on the lap of a large stone man whilst a stone woman pressed her back against his, her head thrown back, one arm extended down with her hand firm over her pubis, the other arm stretching above, her fingers enmeshed in the male's hair. Fen sat very still, having positioned herself so that the male form seemed to be nuzzling her neck, his right hand masked from view by her body but apparently cupping his cock. Or wielding it. Or touching Fen's bottom. Or delving right in. The sight was quite something. Quite the saucy threesome. Matt's jaw dropped. Otter giggled involuntarily. James felt his trip to London was already proving well worthwhile though he had yet to visit Calthrop's. Judith St John arrived late. She coughed when Fen was about to speak. Fen swiftly told herself that perhaps Judith simply had the beginnings of a cold. Judith St John had no interest in Julius Fetherstone, whom she considered a second-rate Rodin. But she was interested to hear just what this Fen McCabe had to say. Bloody double distinction from the Courtauld Institute. She herself might only have one distinction but she'd graduated five years prior to Fen McCabe. Hardly second-rate. Standards had been much higher then. And the true distinction was that she was deputy director of Trust Art. And look at Matt Holden, all mesmerized. Oh for God's sake.

'Julius Fetherstone,' Fen started, assessing that Judith's cough had subsided and that the audience of around twenty was all above the age of consent, before stretching her arm above her, stroking the male's cheek before placing her hand over that of the female, 'was obsessed with sex.'

Fen slid from the lap of the sculpture and, with her hand on the male's hand which, it transpired, was indeed lolling over his cock, she ran her fingertips up his arm while she continued. 'Fetherstone seemed to delight in the paradox of capturing in stone, or bronze, and in a frozen moment, all the heat, the moisture, the movement and, most of all, the internal sensation of the sex act.' She brushed the cheek of the man with the back of her hand and then rested her head gently on his shoulder, draping her arm down over his chest. The women in the audience wanted to be where Fen was, wanting to touch and clasp and grapple with the awesome sculpture. Many of the men in the audience, however, just wanted to touch Fen. Apart from Otter who was transfixed by the male sculpture. And by a rather athletic-looking tourist a few yards away.

'This work is called *Hunger*,' Fen said, standing back from it though it meant her all but pressing herself against two young women listening. She gazed at the stone and then faced her audience. She made eye contact with all of them, with Otter and Matt and James and Judith. But she did not glance away, or give a blink of discomfort or recognition. Fen McCabe, art historian, was rather different from Fen McCabe, archivist. Or was this merely the spell of Fetherstone's works? 'It's called *Hunger*,' she repeated, standing much closer to her audience than to the sculpture, 'but the couple themselves seem quite sated, don't you think?' The audience bar James was staring at the sculpture. 'Don't you think?' It was a question. James wanted to answer but could not establish eye contact and didn't really want to raise his hand. Anyway, the lecturer was staring directly, almost at point-blank range, at the two young women near to her. 'Don't you think?'

'Definitely,' one whispered. The other could only nod. They were both flushed. Not from humiliation or embarrassment. But from the effect the mass of copulatory stone had on them.

'Fetherstone worked on the theme of sexual abandon from 1889. His great treatise – titled *Abandon* – now exists in four supreme bronzes. Though the whereabouts of the marble

Abandon – staggering even in the few photos we have of it – remains a mystery. Just look at them,' Fen implored, turning back to the sculpture, 'just look at them.' She gave her audience a tantalizing few seconds of silence. 'Now, this portrait bust of Jacques Lemond,' she said, moving to a plinth nearby, 'is not just conventional in conception, it was staid and boring even for the time in which it was executed.' Fen McCabe had cast the spell and then broken it. The audience had to follow her dutifully to another work, a rather uninspiring, if well executed, head and shoulders. But Fen was manipulating her audience. Her talk ended ten minutes later, having utilized a cross-reference with Maillol and a look at the two oil sketches by Fetherstone (which James was most pleased to deduce were inferior to his in execution and subject matter). She'd answered the obligatory questions (having anticipated, by the look of her audience, what they were to be) and then she'd left the gallery. Briskly. Perhaps to have a sandwich or something. Buy an *Evening Standard*. *Cosmo*, maybe. She knew well what would be going on in the sculpture hall. Most of the audience would remain. She'd observed their reaction to her lecture, to *Hunger*, to sculpture, on several occasions. They'd potter about half glancing at other works. Some would linger at Rodin's *The Kiss*. But all would gravitate back to *Hunger*, however long it took. To circumnavigate. For a deeper look. To feed their hunger.

Judith had left noisily midway through the Q&A. Matt left the gallery unseen, leaving Otter to chat up the athletic young tourist. Matt's semi hard-on disconcerted him.

It's not just the look of her. Not the sculptures, for Christ's sake. I think it's that she's so damned passionate. I don't know!

James took a taxi to New Bond Street. There was a stirring in his trousers too. But he rationalized that he was turned on by the thought of the money his own Fetherstones might generate. Or by art, of course. Not by F. McCabe. No no no.

He peered into his rucksack. Adam and Eve were still at it. Again. Leave them to it. Recall the content of the lecture so he was well armed to rebuff any bluff from the auctioneers. What did she say? That F. McCabe? She called him Julius. What does F stand for? Fiona? Frederika? Frederika probably. Freddie to her friends. Something like that. What had she spoken of? James couldn't remember. He chastised his age as the culprit. But how come he could remember everything about her? Down to her having just the one dimple when she smiled which increased to two when she laughed.

Whilst James sat on a rather hard but aesthetically fine mahogany bench outside the Nineteenth Century European department, he wondered if the higher up you were at Calthrop's was directly proportionate to the number of hyphens in your surname. And whether the number of hyphens to the surname might equate with the number of noughts such an expert might achieve on the sale of works. And how long they were entitled to keep a visitor waiting. Ten minutes and counting. He concentrated hard on two seascapes and thought how he'd really much rather have the Fetherstone oil sketches on his wall than those. Why was he selling them then? Money? Yes. But not because he was greedy. Because he needed to.

'Mr Caulfield? Margot Fitzpatrick-Montague-Laine – good afternoon,' an immaculate woman with a warm smile and affably outstretched hand, who looked too ordinary to have hyphens in her name and too young to hold a job of such stature, greeted James and ushered him through to her office, her eyes wide and expectant at the sight of his rucksack. 'I think it most honest that my colleagues in Nineteenth Century British passed you to me,' she said. 'I mean, Fetherstone was British by birth – but he is so *quint*essentially European.' She looked at James earnestly. 'Wouldn't you agree?'

'Quint*essentially*,' James responded, stressing a different part of the word to imply it was a conclusion he had himself

60

made already, whilst racking his brains to recall anything F. McCabe had said along those lines in her lecture. He couldn't remember if she had. She'd talked about moisture. And sex. And carnal delirium. And this Nineteenth Century European woman was very attractive and she was talking money and was thus all the more attractive because of it. And because she could enunciate words like 'quintessentially' in a most sonorous way.

'So,' she was saying with an eyebrow raised almost coquettishly, 'what do you have for me?'

'Adam and Eve having a fuck,' said James without thinking, because he was thinking how much he'd like to have a fuck. With F. McCabe. Or Margot F-M-L. Whoever. It had been a while. He wondered whether to apologize. Or to bite his lip. Or make light of it. Or just ignore it. But seeing her eyes light up, he decided that to show her Adam and Eve having a fuck was a good start.

'1892,' he said, by way of introduction to the sculpture. He gave her a few moments to feast her gaze upon it and then brought out the sketch of Eve. '1894,' he said, watching Ms F-M-L hone in on the painting. Then he brought out Adam. '1895,' he said, titillated by seeing how excited Miss Margot was. He didn't really care whether this was over their monetary or aesthetic value, or a mixture of both. She looked hungry. And it turned him on. 'What am I bid?' he jested. She stared at him.

'We offer the paintings as a pair,' she suggested in a most conspiratorial voice, as if hatching an illicit plan, leaning close to him with an almost clichéd amount of cleavage on view. 'It would be a travesty to split them. We put the reserve at around thirty thousand.' James worked hard not to gulp because he felt she was scrutinizing him to see if he would. Or to see whether he'd noticed her bust. He had. He didn't gulp. He nodded sagely. 'The bronze,' she said, musing, 'forty thousand is realistic.' James was sure to tip his head to one side and look out of the window as if considering whether this was the most financially viable route for him to take. 'I propose we offer them in the July sale. It's a biggie. Lots of Americans. Fetherstone is growing in popularity over the pond.'

'Would you care to have lunch with me?' James asked.

'I'm hungry,' Ms M. F-M-L said, licking her lips.

She chose two starters. Asparagus. Predictably. And oysters. Ditto. James tried to tuck into a Caesar salad but anticipated it would all be gone in two mouthfuls. Actually, it was five. He was still hungry. Watching Margot do what she was doing to the asparagus, he didn't know what he longed for more – her or one of Mrs Brakespeare's substantial platters of ham and eggs.

'Will you let me have them?' she asked, leaning across the table and exhibiting her cleavage again to great effect.

'No,' said James.

'Or, let me just keep them in the department for a while?' she compromised, her pupils as dark as the espresso in front of her.

'No,' said James.

'Oh go on,' she purred, 'just come back to my office – I'm sure I can persuade you somehow.'

'Roger!' she calls across the vestibule to a man who comes over. 'This is James Caulfield. He's brought in three delightful Fetherstones. They're in my office. Do come and have a look.' This offer she extends to two other men they encounter on the way back to her office. James watches her bottom, clad in a tight skirt, swaying seductively as she takes the stairs. He has to thrust his hand deep into his trouser pocket in a bid to conceal his erection. She opens the door to her office and a shaft of light streams in, soaking Adam and Eve who are still having sex. Right there, on her desk.

'Let me see now,' she says, 'how am I going to persuade you to part with them?' Closing the door with her back, all of a sudden she pulls James towards her and gorges herself on his mouth. She doesn't sip him down as she did the oysters. She doesn't tongue him tantalizingly like she did the asparagus. She doesn't linger over him and take her time. She gobbles him, sucks him, chews and gulps at him. Her hands grab and squeeze and pull at him. Her body is bucking and writhing against his. His face is wet from her mouth. His lips are being bitten both accidentally and on purpose. His hair is being pulled, his shirt tugged, his belt yanked. He isn't kissing her back – her mouth is in the way. And it's all so sudden, he hasn't had the chance to think about it, to object, to stop himself, to participate.

Oh my God! She's going to give me a blow-job! Oh my God! There's someone knocking at the door.

It is Roger from downstairs wanting to see the Fetherstones. Anyone there? James's thudding heart is in his mouth. And Margot has her mouth full. Roger has gone away, thank God.

Oh God, what is she doing?

James raises his eyes to the heavens but they hit the ceiling where fat cherubs are cavorting with whimsical unicorns and baby centaurs. He closes his eyes.

It's been a while. Not since that girl in Hathersage.

Margot has stopped sucking. Her knees crack as she stands up to face him. James doesn't know what to say or where to look. He's desperate not to take leave of his senses but his brain has now taken residence in his balls. Coming is such a priority that it overwhelms any thoughts of intruders or condoms or impropriety or ramifications or repercussions. She hoicks up her skirt and guides him inside her. A few quick thrusts is all it takes.

The relief.

God. Now what? Where to look? What to say?

'Definitely July,' Margot is saying, rearranging her clothing, 'the Americans will be here on a shopping spree.'

'They'll be sold to a private collector?' James asks, zipping himself up, turning away from her and giving Adam and Eve an apologetic look.

'Undoubtedly,' she confirms, walking over to her desk.

'And they'll leave the country?' James asks, staring at his

63

Fetherstones as if they're children about to be committed to boarding-school overseas.

'I would say so,' she says, regarding him levelly.

'Don't you think that would be a shame?'

'With the money they could generate?' she retorts, astutely. 'It's not my job to make sure that works of art go to the right home, wherever that may be, just that they achieve the highest amount possible.'

'Say it's a bank vault in Los Angeles?'

'Then it's a bank vault in Los Angeles that forked out around £70,000 to make space for them.'

James obviously doesn't like the sound of this.

'Look,' she says, too sweetly so that it verges on patronizing, as if she's lost interest with him, as if his soft side or conscience was not the reason for her having fucked him, 'if you're worried about where they'll go, why not offer them to a national institution via the NACF or Trust Art? We can still be your advisors. You will forfeit the whole premise of an auction, of prices rising alongside salesroom hysteria.'

'Phone the Tate?' James asks.

'Wherever,' she says, 'then the gallery will try to raise funds via a grant from, as I said, the NACF or Trust Art. You know who you should contact? Fen McCabe. She works at Trust Art now. She's a Fetherstone fanatic. We offered her a job which she declined because she said she'd protest every time one was sold to a home of which she might not approve.'

'Fen,' James mused.

'McCabe, short for Fenella, bit of a mouthful,' said Margot Fitzpatrick-Montague-Laine, 'we were in the same year at the Courtauld. She was the class swot. Mind you, it gained her the sole double distinction that year.'

James didn't feel like telling her that he knew exactly who Fen was, that he had just been enthralled by her lecture, by her passion. But he was surprised just how pleased he was to learn her first name. How fortuitous it was that he could contact her. And he was surprised that, suddenly, he felt very hungry again.

'Think about it,' Margot said whilst ignoring James, and Adam and Eve, to flip through the documents on her desk, 'call me.'

TEN

*O*tter observed Matt trying to settle. He watched him stroke his chin, scrunch his already short scrunched ochre-coloured hair, rummage through sheaves of paper, tap a number on the phone with a pencil but not make the call, take the pencil to his mouth and drum his teeth lightly. With his spectacles now replacing the pencil and hanging off his lips, Matt had his eyes fixed at absolutely nothing going on outside the window. His mind, Otter mused, was not fixed on the job in hand.

He should be thinking about editing that article on Kandinsky and Schönberg? But I rather think he's thinking about sculpture. But there again, I should be writing the side bars for the Antony Gormley article. And I'm thinking about Jorgen who is twenty-five, Scandinavian and just happened to be listening to the same sculpture lecture at the Tate as I was.

'How's the Kandinsky piece shaping up?' Otter asked Matt, to distract himself from the distraction of the shapely Jorgen. Almost begrudgingly, Matt turned his head, dragging his eyes around, looking slightly baffled. 'And Schoenberg,' Otter prompted helpfully. Matt gave him a slow, thoughtful nod backed up by a noncommittal noise from his throat that told Otter that Matt had given the article little attention.

Matt stretched and yawned in a way that was far too considered to be natural. 'We should ask Fen to write a piece on Fetherstone,' he said in a tone he was employing to be nonchalant but which was far from it. It was four o'clock and Otter felt ready and entitled to a jolly little gossip about Fen, Jorgen, whomever, but Matt was already walking from the room.

'To talk articles with Fen,' Otter said to his computer screen. 'Go on, lad, ask her out for a drink.'

Matt chastises himself as a soft sod for hovering, even for but a second, outside the door of the Archive. That he can hear her rustling makes him want to ease the door open and observe her unseen. See her on tiptoes wrestling with boxes; see her sitting on the floor, making piles; perhaps standing with her back to one of the shelves, engrossed in some catalogue, or comfortable in her chair, mesmerized by a fan of black-and-white photographs. He doesn't knock.

She's sitting on three of the toughened boxes. With her toes turned in. Matt can see down her top.

'How timely,' Fen says, who's had a most productive afternoon and has given little thought to anything but the contents of 1952. 'Have you ever seen these?' She offers him a clutch of old photographs. He looks at them and, from his vantage point, he glances down Fen's top again.

'It's my father,' he says, locking on to her eyes and realizing for the first time that they are blue. 'Who's the old chap with the beard?'

'Matisse!' Fen all but whispers in deference and excitement.

Matt scrutinizes the photos, sneaks another look at Fen's breasts. 'I really enjoyed your lecture,' he tells her.

She's blushing! The girl who practically masturbated herself on a stone man – and woman – is blushing.

'Thanks,' Fen mumbles, feeling the need to study a Post-it on a box that says 'Misc'.

Go on, Matt – ask her for a drink after work. Make it casual – a Trust thing; no ulterior motive, a trust thing. Have a little flirt!

'Maybe you could write a piece on Fetherstone for *Art Matters*?' Matt asks.

'Sure,' Fen replies briskly, tucking hair neatly behind her ears, back ramrod straight. Archivist. Art historian. Colleague. Art is what matters.

Fen pouted and rested her head on Abi's shoulder. Abi stroked Fen's hair, stroked her shoulders, and thought that now was not the time to ask Fen what on earth she was doing wearing *her* Paul Smith top. Gemma came back from the bar with vodka and Red Bull for each of them.

'Fen's sulking,' Abi said to her, 'don't quite know why – here lovey, have a little sippy to help lubricate your vocal chords.'

Fen had more than Abi's suggested sippy, she practically downed her drink in one. Gemma and Abi regarded her expectantly. 'First, I go and bloody blush,' she said.

'Well,' Abi started, wondering why the facts should amount to a pout of such proportions. She wasn't quite sure how to continue so she took a long slug at her drink and filched a fag from Gemma.

'Then,' Fen pouts, 'then I go and get all disappointed that all he wanted was an article from Fen Fen the Fetherstone Fan.'

Gemma and Abi smoke their cigarettes contemplatively.

'I was primed, ready and willing to say, "Why, I'd love to have a drink with you",' Fen said, 'instead the only sane answer was, "But of course, how many words and when's the deadline?".'

'Yes, but . . .' Gemma started. *If that had been me*, she thought, *I'd have suggested discussing word limit over a drink. But it was Fen. And she's as predictable as I am.*

Fen, having finished her drink and having no need for a cigarette (she'd smoked without inhaling as a teenager and inhaled when she was at university, just the once, before throwing up quite spectacularly), was suddenly lucid. 'No!' she exclaimed, 'the point is that I quite *wanted* him to make a pass.'

'Cool!' Abi said. 'You fancy him.'

'About time too,' said Gemma.

'Could be dangerous,' Fen muttered.

'Or the start of something very beautiful,' Abi jested.

'A good old flirt is quite good fun,' Gemma shrugged.

They all nodded. Fen, though, still looked a little perplexed.

'Another drink?' she offered, though no answer was needed.

Abi and Gemma spied her at the bar, having a surreptitious look from her left hand to her right. And though this affectation often irritated them, tonight they praised it as they saw that her eyebrows were no longer knitted together in a furrow of discontent. No doubt she'd be ordering doubles all round. A shot for the right hand, a shot for the left.

It's not just Otter who wants to play a part in bringing Fen and Matt together. And it's all very well Gemma and Abi encouraging Fen to the hilt. And Jake banging on about the merits of a zipless fuck, the necessity of The Rebound. More fortuitous, though, Fate is set to lend a helping hand too. Just like in the movies. Eyes meeting across a crowded bar and all that.

'Crown and Goose?' Jake suggested to the five-a-side team as dusk descended on Regent's Park. 'Who's coming?'

'Sure,' Matt said, slightly disgruntled that he was in jogging bottoms and an old rugby shirt while Jake had brought along a change of trousers and a clean top. 'Are you just vain or merely more organized?' he asked.

'I'm always fastidiously prepared for all eventualities,'

Jake countered, slightly irritated that their team-mates were sloping off to wives and partners and a civilized glass of Chardonnay, 'plus I had lunch with a firm near us so I nipped back home.' Matt regarded him nervously. Jake smiled and slapped his back. 'Fear not,' he assured Matt, 'there was no bunny boiling on the stove, no messages on the answerphone and the flat was just as we left it.'

'Three days of silence,' Matt said. 'Perhaps she's genuinely cool about things. Or do you think she's planning something?'

'Your wedding?' Jake glibly suggested. 'Or your death,' he tempered, on observing Matt's horror.

'Come on,' Matt said, walking into the Crown and Goose, 'lager?'

'Actually,' says Fen, looking imploringly at the barmaid and darkly at Jake, 'I was next.'

'Two pints of Carlsberg,' Jake ordered, momentarily and conveniently deaf; looking squarely at Fen before turning on the charm for the barmaid. Giving Jake an accidentally-on-purpose jab with her elbow and a look of utter distaste, Fen raised her eyebrows at the barmaid in a 'Men! Pah!' kind of way, hoping to appeal to her feminist proclivities or sense of conduct at the very least. The barmaid, however, was silently praising God that the softball season had started early and, though it gave her no satisfaction to blank Fen, it gave her much pleasure to serve Jake, even more so because she had pipped Sonia, who'd worked there longer, to the post. Fen started humming Aretha Franklin's 'Sisters Are Doing It For Themselves' but the irony was lost on the barmaid who was engrossed in Jake's tip and smile; both disproportionate to the service she had provided.

'Come on come on!' Abi implored Fen when she returned with what were definitely doubles, 'more Matt!'

'Yes,' said Gemma, 'details.'

70

Fen, all of a sudden slightly sloshed, was happy to oblige. 'I was chuffed that he came to the lecture. I think he was genuinely interested, his father championing Julius and all.'

'Oh God, not that bloody bloody sculptor,' Abi cried, swiping her brow as if a mammoth headache had descended.

'Come on,' Gemma nudged, 'vital statistics.'

'I told you,' Fen said, 'he's tall. Ish. And good-looking. Ish. And blond.'

'Ish?' asked Gemma.

'Well – dark blond. Ish?'

'Natural?' asked Abi.

'I would hope so,' said Fen primly.

'God, for an art historian, your powers of description are *terrible*,' Abi teased.

'Just because he's flesh and blood and not stone or metal doesn't excuse you from technicolor detail,' Gemma added.

'I've only been there four days!' Fen remonstrated. 'I just quite fancy him. Not specifically for his looks. Or his personality. He just seems . . .' she stopped and her jaw dropped.

'Just?' Abi prompted.

'Seems?' Gemma pressed.

'Over there,' Fen said.

Thank God the bar was noisy enough for the ensuing squeaks of delight and giggles of excitement from Fen's group to go unheard. Thank God the bar was crowded enough to dissipate the heat from three sets of eyes burning into Matt.

'Oh God,' Fen cried, 'what do I do? Smile? Wave? Ignore? Die? Loo? Home?' Gemma took Fen's left hand and gave it a quick but tight squeeze. 'Has he seen me?' Fen asked. 'Has he?'

'Delicious,' Gemma said, not quite knowing if she should be raising a glass to Matt or his friend.

'You certainly haven't done him justice,' said Abi, 'you didn't say about the facial hair.'

'The other one, the other one!' Fen said, wishing she could just stare at one spot and keep her eyes from continually flitting over to the boys.

'I rather like the look of the-other-one-the-other-one,' Gemma said, 'I've never had a man with a goatee. I quite like them. I rather think they could tickle my fancy – if strategically placed.'

'I've had one,' Abi declared, 'very strategically positioned. In fact, it tickled my fancy so much, I had a fit of the giggles and fanny-farted in his face.'

'Shush!' Fen pleaded. 'Stop! Where are you going?'

'Over there,' Gemma said.

'To make our acquaintance,' Abi said, 'to see if he passes muster and whether he warrants our seal of approval and, therefore, whether we grant you our go-ahead.'

'Oh God, he's seen me. I'm going to the loo,' said Fen, who didn't need to go and didn't know why she wanted to disappear. She went, though, and stood by the sinks for a while trying to compose herself, compose what to say. She was simultaneously excited yet felt a certain timidity too. She was bemused.

Abi and Gemma were also bemused.

'Shy? Fen?'

'Why?'

'That girl has spent far too long persuading herself that art nourishes her every need,' said Gemma.

'And she's spent far too long listening to us bang on about the Inevitable Bastard Element Of All Males,' said Abi, 'though it's a risk she'll just have to take. I mean, *we* do, don't we?'

'We *do*,' Gemma confirmed, 'and it's often Fen who picks us up when we're in pieces.'

'But we invariably go for the wrong ones,' Abi rationalized.

'And Fen doesn't go for anyone at all,' Gemma continued, 'so, though Matt might not be a Wrong One, she probably doesn't want to find out the hard way. Hence taking the easy route direct to the loo. Or home. Or back to the bronze of a nineteenth-century sculptor's studio.'

'Oh blimey,' Abi sighed, 'she might so be missing out!'

'That's the risk she'd probably rather take,' Gemma qualified.

'She won't let us give her a helping hand,' Abi mused, 'so let's just shove her right in there.'

Gemma regarded Abi, knowing the idea would be fine if it was she whom Abi was setting up, but just slightly concerned that they were meddling too deeply, too fast, for someone like Fen.

'Feeling brazen?' Abi asked slyly, eyeing up Jake just as much as he was eyeing her.

'When am I not?' Gemma sighed as if it was some great affliction, eyeing up Jake just as much as he was eyeing her.

Oh God, no!

Fen?

Cows!

What's the problem?

They're over there – with Matt and that bloke. I'm not prepared.

You can't map out life like you plan a lecture, you know. See – Matt's spotted you. He's raising his glass. He's grinning. They all are. Just a bunch of people chatting. Go and join them. Go on.

Sometimes, a good cliché is hard to beat. Sometimes, it's priceless, especially if it is obvious that the person delivering it is doing so quite intentionally. Even more so, if they are doing so because it is quite obvious that they need it as a prop, a shield, without which they wouldn't quite know what to say. Therefore, Matt's opening line of 'Fancy seeing you here' – though it was met with Jake raising his eyebrows and Abi and Gemma swallowing down a snigger – made Fen grin.

'Do you come here often then?' she countered.

Refusing to be out-clichéd, Matt retorted, 'What's a nice girl like you doing in a place like this?'

Gemma couldn't resist, 'What makes you think that Fen is a *nice* girl?' and Fen, who was floundering for a cliché to bat back, didn't mind this in the least.

Jake murmured to Abi, 'Can't really say that nice girls are my bag. I like them naughty.'

'I'm downright dirty, mate,' Abi responded, staring at him straight before turning her back on him to give Matt the Spanish Inquisition.

'What does Abi do?' Jake asked Gemma.

'She edits a teenage girls' magazine,' Gemma told him. 'And you?'

'Advertising,' Jake said, 'I'm afraid. You?'

'I,' said Gemma, pausing to make sure her lips were parted to great effect and that her eyes had darkened, 'do most things. But I draw the line at animals.'

Matt and Fen talked mainly about work. But they nattered nineteen to the dozen and were excessively interested in what the other had to say. Even though some would argue that a noisy pub in Camden Town wasn't quite the venue for a lecture on Fetherstone's deconstructionist foray 1927–29. Nor was it a convivial setting for Matt's stories of homesickness at boarding-school from the ages of nine to eleven. But the anonymity of the setting, the background noise, beer and vodka, the unexpectedness of it all, made it seem safe. Fun too.

'See you in the morning, then,' said Matt, because last orders had been and gone and the bar staff had stopped begging the punters to leave and were now demanding they do so.

'Mine's a cappuccino,' said Fen cheekily, 'and a *pain au chocolat.*'

She winked, did Fen McCabe. She even winked. She didn't even think to marvel at the disappearance of all that previous timidity. But Gemma and Abi did. And they knew it could not be attributed to vodka alone. The girls walked home, Fen swelling with pride and joy as her friends assured her that Matt didn't just pass muster but scored very highly on their excessively exacting set of standards.

'Stringless sex?' Jake tosses casually as he and Matt make their way down Parkway hoping to hail a cab before they reach Camden Town tube station and have to suffer the Northern Line to Angel. 'Zipless fuck?' Jake bandies yet detects a momentary discomfort in Matt. 'Fanbelt Macbeth?'

Matt shrugs. 'Taxi!'

'Well, if you don't, mind if I do?' Jake hazards, not because he has any designs on Fen, but merely to elicit a response of more satisfying proportions from Matt.

'Yes, I bloody do!'

Aha! Jake thinks. 'You couldn't have stringless sex with her anyway,' he declares.

'Why not?' Matt says defensively.

'Because she has you nicely knotted up already,' Jake defines.

'Sod off,' says Matt, unnerved by Jake's perception.

'It's true!' Jake says. 'So my advice is not to venture to Vanilla McCabe until you've had a good poke elsewhere.' Matt hopes that his expression doesn't register "why ever not?" but obviously it has. 'You *do* need time out,' Jake defines. 'You can't go from one straight into another. It'll be out of the frying pan into the fire.' Jake assessed it was time to lighten up. 'If she's out of my bounds,' Jake says, with a change of tone, 'what about her flatmates then? The raven-headed sultry Gemma; the feisty blonde sprite, Abi?'

'Be my guest,' says Matt, relieved to deflect the attention away from himself and Fen. 'Which one?'

'Either,' Jake shrugs, as is his way.
Matt raises his eyebrows.
'Both,' Jake shrugs, as is his way.

ELEVEN

*F*en wasn't quite sure what the score was with personal phone calls. Her job didn't require much time on the telephone; just the occasional call, made or received, to a gallery or museum. But on this, the last day of her first week at Trust Art, Fen wanted desperately to make a call. Should she ask? Even if the response was laughter? Or a frown of disapproval? Would Bobbie's switchboard sound the alarm, start flashing in another colour? Would Rodney scurry in and cry, 'Good Grief! Fenella McCabe – we're a *charity*. You are eating into funds that could be spent saving modern art for the nation!' Was it a good excuse to pop along to Publications and ask Matt to specify the rules and regulations concerning communication equipment at Trust Art? Just an excuse, any, to pop along to Publications?

I'll be quick. I only need to say a sentence. It's too good to keep to myself.

Fen phoned Gemma at work, at the TV production company, though she had to hang on for an agonizing few minutes whilst Gemma was located.

'Guess what!' Fen whispered.

'What?' Gemma whispered back but had to repeat herself due to much background noise in the editing room.

'Guess who came into work to find a cappuccino waiting on her desk, piping hot?'

'Blimey, Fen,' said Gemma, 'I'd regard that as symbolic as a diamond ring, if I were you.'

Fen told Gemma to piss off and phoned Abi in search of less sarcasm.

'But did he remember the *pain au chocolat*?' was Abi's response.

Fen told Abi to piss off and phoned her older sister Pip immediately, hoping for less cynicism and a distraction from her sudden concern over the lack of *pain au chocolat*.

'Don't read too much into it,' said Pip thoughtfully.

Fen wanted to tell her sister to piss off, but knew Pip meant well and spoke from love as much as from experience. So she phoned her younger sister Cat, now craving a response that was neither sarcastic, cynical nor common-sensical.

To Fen's delight, her sister cooed appreciatively (though privately Cat felt Fen was reading far too much into it) and said things like 'He sounds gorgeous' with the inflection in all the right places. Feeling bolstered, Fen had no need to further abuse the Trust's trust in her use of their phone; she drank and savoured her cappuccino and then felt well equipped to commence her duties for the day. She didn't feel like a *pain au chocolat* anyway. She'd had toast with her butter, for breakfast, as always she did, before leaving for work.

TO: m.holden@trustart.co.uk
FROM: f.mccabe@trustart.co.uk
RE: caffeine

dear m, thanks for the essential caffeine injection – i'm whizzing through the files at twice the normal speed. for future reference, one sugar too, please. F McC

It took almost seven minutes, and three full edits, before Fen sent that one.

TO: f.mccabe@trustart.co.uk
FROM: m.holden@trustart.co.uk
RE: caffeine allocation

dear f, and I thought you were sweet enough. M

Matt didn't send that one.

TO: f.mccabe@trustart.co.uk
FROM: m.holden@trustart.co.uk
RE: caffeine allocation

dear f, not only will I remember sugar, I'll also make sure it's not decaff. Must be the frothy topping that's enabled you to feel so productive this morning. M

'Oh God,' Fen groaned quietly, hiding her head behind a sheaf of letters from 1965 between Lord Bessborough and Henry Holden discussing the gift of a Barbara Hepworth *Pierced Form*, 'it was decaff, it was *decaff*.'

TO: m.holden@trustart.co.uk
FROM: f.mccabe@trustart.co.uk
RE: RE: caffeine allocation

dear m, froth had fizzled away by the time I prized off the lid. and the pain au chocolat had mysteriously self-combusted because, though I searched in drawers and in a box marked 1965, there was not a crumb of evidence of its existence. f McC (hungry)

Fen fired that one off without so much as checking it.

TO: f.mccabe@trustart.co.uk
FROM: m.holden@trustart.co.uk
RE: RE: RE: caffeine allocation

head hanging low with shame and remorse. No froth? No sugar? No caffeine? No p au c? Would a sandwich lunch make it up to you? If you haven't already expired before you've made it to 1966? M

Fen actually printed that one off, folded it, slipped it into the back pocket of her jeans and reread it at ridiculously regular intervals during the morning. She also checked her e-mail with alarming regularity but her in-box remained empty.

Mind you, I haven't responded to his last.

Playing hard to get, Fen McCabe?

No, just playing. It's fun.

Of course she had a sandwich lunch with him. Sitting in the gardens of the flats opposite the Trust. Otter came too. But neither Fen nor Matt minded. Fen felt a certain pride that their chemistry should be witnessed and later commented on; Matt just didn't mind that Otter was there. Otter, who adored Matt and, in just one working week, felt very tenderly towards Fen, nevertheless couldn't resist a gossip and a little action. That a drama in miniature could be played out before his eyes, under his direction, fed the lascivious and puckish side of his nature. A necessary antidote to his daily grind of correcting punctuation and typos. It was therefore with careful timing and timbre of delivery, that he told Bobbie he would let her into a little secret. But he did so only when he knew Judith St John would be in earshot.

'Love loiters along the corridors of Trust Art,' he said in a hushed but knowing voice.

'Ooh blimey!' Bobbie exclaimed. 'Who is it, Otter? I thought you was the only nancy boy here!'

'I am!' Otter declared proudly, laying a thin hand on Bobbie's shoulder, which was padded extravagantly in the receptionist's enduring homage to Joan Collins.

'You swinging the other way then?' Bobbie asked him almost accusatorily. She looked him up and down, hoping whomever he chose, of whichever sexual persuasion, would be someone kind who'd feed the poor duck with meat and at least two veg on a nightly basis.

'Dearest Bobsleigh,' said Otter, ''tisn't me at all. But lust lurks, mark my words!'

'Who?' Bobbie whispered, eyes so wide that the false eyelashes on her upper lids all but meshed with her eyebrows. 'Where?'

'In. The. Archive,' Otter defined, noticing that Judith's head was unmistakably tilted though her hands rifled through the pile of post in her pigeon-hole. 'Our Matthew has his eye on young Fenella. You mark my words.'

'Ahh!' Bobbie said, tutting with appreciation and high hopes for the young 'uns.

'There'll be all sorts of shenanigans behind the Archive shelving,' Otter prophesied, noting with satisfaction that Judith, post in hand, was nevertheless standing stock-still. 'Debauchery amongst the boxes,' Otter offered as his parting shot, winking at Bobbie and walking past Judith as if she wasn't there.

Not if I have anything to do with it, thought Judith, smiling somewhat disdainfully at Bobbie, whose only crime on this day was a Dynasty-style suit in a lurid cerise.

Judith had no need to go upstairs, but she swanned past Publications and waltzed into the Archive. 'We don't, as a rule, use the Trust phones for personal calls,' she told Fen, 'not even if it's supposedly pre- or post official work hours. We're a charity.'

'I am so sorry,' said Fen, wanting at once to be swallowed by the box on her lap and taken to the safety of 1966 (before she had been even a twinkle in her father's eye).

'You weren't to know,' said Judith, covering her triumph with a spite-sweet smile, 'but you do now.'

If he doesn't want me, he's not having her. Not that I know if he wants me or not. Haven't tried that one. Yet.

Judith swanned out of the Archive and into Publications, inviting Matt to the opening of the Rothko exhibition at Tate Modern the following Tuesday evening.

'Welcome to the end of your first working week,' said Matt, who'd found the pretext of a missing hole punch as the

81

excuse to visit the Archive for the second time since lunch. 'We're going to the pub for a—'

Fen's phone silenced him and he soaked up her wide-eyed excitement at its ringing.

'Archive?' she said, almost with incredulity, on answering it.

'Fen McCabe?'

'Yes?'

I don't recognize the voice yet he's Fen-ing and not Fenella-ing me.

'James Caulfield,' the voice drawled. 'I was told to call you by Margot Fitzpatrick-Montague-Laine – I think that's the right order and the right quota of hyphens – at Calthrop's. You know, or knew her.'

God! Margot! thought Fen, who really hadn't thought about Margot Fitzpatrick-Montague-Laine since leaving the Courtauld.

God! Margot, thought James, who had thought of her on occasions when he couldn't sleep.

'It concerns three Fetherstones in my collection,' he said, clearing his throat and rearranging his semi-hard cock in his trousers.

'Margot,' Fen mused. 'Three Fetherstones! *Three*?'

At this point, Matt backed out of the room, making a knocking-back-of-a-pint-glass gesture. Fen, though, was too engrossed in the notion of three Fetherstones in a private collection to respond, or even notice really.

'I need to sell them,' Mr Caulfield was continuing.

'Sell them?' Fen reacted.

'Yes,' the man continued, a forlorn edge to his voice which Fen would never have detected to be just slightly manufactured. 'But, if at all possible, I want them to go to a public museum or gallery. So that the nation can enjoy them as much as I have.'

I want to marry you and have your babies. Whoever you are. You have Fetherstones. And you have a conscience, thought Fen. 'I see,' was what she decided to say, though.

'What are they?' She tried not to whisper although she felt as though she was about to peep into a box of unknown treasure.

'Adam and Eve,' James Caulfield imparted, 'two oil sketches and a bronze.'

'Oh my God!' Fen exclaimed unchecked, unable to see James grin at the other end of the phone.

'I live in Derbyshire,' he said.

'So do I!' Fen rushed. She could hear James's question mark. 'I mean, I was brought up there. I've only lived in London for five years,' she continued by way of an apology, which for some reason made James smile all the more. 'I come home frequently,' she furthered, as if establishing a link with Derbyshire as well as a common love for Julius Fetherstone would seal the deal and head to an offer of marriage from this man, to say nothing of an offer from the Tate – Liverpool or London – for his Fetherstones.

'Would you like to come and see them?' James proposed. 'Or should I bring them down to London?'

Fen rushes out of the Archive, beams at Matt (who takes full credit for the smile, not being the type to eavesdrop on phone calls, personal or otherwise) and heads downstairs to Rodney's office.

'There are three Fetherstones in Derbyshire!' Fen announces, having knocked and been told to enter. 'A chap wants me to look at them. He wants Trust Art to handle their sale. He wants them to go to a public collection. He's invited me to go next Tuesday.'

Judith St John is also in Rodney's office.

It is Friday. It is home time. Fen feels her week's work is complete. And she feels that her news of three Fetherstones in Derbyshire, the vendor's desire that she should assess them, that Trust Art should handle the transaction, more than vindicates the three or four minutes of personal phone calls that morning.

Rodney claps his hands together, gives Fen the thumbs up with both thumbs and exclaims, 'Crikey! Super! Go north, young lady!'

Judith seethes behind her slanted smile.

TWELVE

'**M**att?' Judith St John had bided her time the next Tuesday morning before going to Publications. She'd loitered in Acquisitions, had a banter with Fund-raising (much to their surprise – the fact that she was visiting, let alone bantering) and even paid more than a fleeting visit to Accounts (much to their trepidation – she only ever came to them when annoyed). With a smile fixed on the accountants, her ear was fixated by any sounds coming from the Archivo. She heard Fen leave, heard her hum, detected that her footsteps were headed down the corridor. Aha! Towards Publications. Judith left Accounts when they were in mid-sentence. With precision timing, she entered Publications to see Fen already perched jauntily on the edge of Otter's desk, Matt standing relaxed with his back resting against the wall, Otter rotating slowly in his chair looking like a puppet from *Thunderbirds*. Judith approved of the way Fen slithered off the desk and looked embarrassed. She liked the way that Matt stayed exactly as he was and regarded her measuredly. She was amused to see how the situation amused Otter too.

'The private view is at seven,' Judith told Matt. 'I've booked Vinopolis for dinner after – if that suits?'

'Sure,' Matt shrugged.

85

'Is that the Rothko exhibition?' Otter asked.

'Yes,' said Judith.

'I absolutely love Rothko,' Fen commented, grinning at Matt.

'I'm afraid I have only a single plus one,' Judith said very quickly, should Matt affably invite Fen along. She was aware that Fen regarded her. Good.

'I'm off home to Derbyshire anyway,' Fen said, realizing there was an attempt to rile her, not quite knowing why that should be.

'Home? Derbyshire?' Matt responded as if Fen had said Dubai.

'Yes,' Fen clarified, 'to see that man with the Fetherstones.'

* * *

I never had Thomas the Tank Engine books, Fen mused whilst browsing in the newsagent in St Pancras, *but I remember Ivor the Engine. I remember watching it on television, with Pip and Cat, at a time when Cat was too young to figure out why Pip and I dissolved into giggles every time we impersonated Ivor's steam sound.*

Shitty Poof. Shitty Poof. Shitty Poof.

Oh God! I'm twenty-eight years old, standing in the fabulously Gothic monstrosity that is St Pancras station and I'm thinking about a cartoon steam train that went shitty poof shitty poof shitty poof. I'm an art historian, for God's sake! I should be comparing the interior of St Pancras with the Gare St-Lazare or Gard du Nord in Paris where Monet was as enraptured by the ephemera of steam as he was by clouds and the fleeting aspects of nature. I should be acknowledging Pugin who said, 'Stations are the cathedrals of our time.' Instead, I'm berating myself – no, Django more like – for depriving me of never knowing the Fat Controller. Or Percy. And I'm more interested in that pigeon limping because it has a stump, than in admiring flying buttresses and trefoils in the clerestory. I don't want to nourish my brain, I want junk food! And a glossy mag. And a throwaway paperback. And I'm excited, unnecessarily so, that the only size of Maltesers is a bumper family pack. Doesn't matter that the price is extortionate, nor that the quantity is obscene for one girl to consume.

Until Luton, Fen fidgeted. She dipped in and out of her magazine with the regularity that she dipped in and out of her bag of Maltesers. She stared out of the window and gazed, as surreptitiously as she could (which was not as surreptitiously as she thought), at her fellow passengers; giving them pasts, presents and futures, names and proclivities which, for the most part, would flatter them all. Her cheese and ham baguette remained half eaten, not because it was tasteless (in fact, it wasn't merely tasteless, but tasted very peculiar indeed) but because there were Maltesers and things to observe and the trolley service from which she ordered a liquid masquerading as coffee. She gazed out of the train window and thought about Matt.

How would it be to kiss him? I think he's a 'take her in my arms and sink my lips against hers' kind of mover.

And you'd like that.

Fen?

If I admit to it – oh dear.

Stop looking from hand to hand! What on earth can you see there? And why on earth is the notion of kissing Matt a dilemma?

Oh, the mating game. Can I really be bothered with it all? The Rules. Men being from Mars? Me, apparently, a Venusian. And all that bollocks.

Jesus, Fen, you've only kissed the bloke in your imagination.

I know I know I know.

Stop looking at your bloody hands. You'll have us thinking that you have an obsessive-compulsive disorder rather than a mannerism that can be amusing and, on occasion, irritating. Most importantly, stop investing everything with such unnecessary significance.

OK. I know. But you don't understand. I haven't felt this fabulous zip of attraction for a bloke for ages. I wonder.

Wonder what?

If the frisson *is a two-way thing.*

What is your gut instinct on it all?

Fen?

Stop grinning inanely out of the window. Stop resting your cheek coyly on your shoulder.

I think so. Oh, I don't know! I think he'd like to take me in his arms and sink his lips deep against mine! I don't know. He might just take me out for a few drinks and then suggest we shag. I don't bloody know!

After Luton, Fen sat very still for a while because she felt a little queasy on account of her stomach becoming a food processor mixing the various incompatible and hastily ingested foodstuffs, coupled with all that flitting of her eyes outside, inside and on print.

But then, despite the wafts of burgers and bad coffee, it was the anticipated scent of Derbyshire which dominated and took her well away from her London life. Back to home, to childhood, to where memories lingered, were vivid and seemed somehow to almost drive her London life into second place, into secondary importance within her scheme of things.

And the train is pulling into Derby and Matt goes from her mind and her aspirations, to be replaced with Julius Fetherstone. Fen McCabe loves being an art historian. Confident. Stimulated. Informed. Assured. It is something she feels she does very well. They're sending her north, by train, after all. No one else could be better for the job. That's what Trust Art thinks. And Calthrop's. And James Caulfield.

'Django!'

How fabulous he looked! A batik smock hastily tucked here and there into a fabulous pair of jeans which were constructed from patches of denim in intricate tessellations. Snakeskin boots (fake) and a neckerchief made from what was salvageable from an old Pucci shirt (original) which Fen remembered vividly from her formative years.

And he's shaved, and his sideburns are fluffy and his hair is the colour of milk, slicked back with God knows what into a pony-tail held in place by God knows what. Ah, a pink towelling scrunchy that Pip must have left on her last visit. Or that she gave him. Or that he asked for. And see, he is holding that Chinese parasol in case of showers.

A *Telegraph* tucked under his arm and, Fen knew, a *Racing Post* tucked within that.

'Don't know how that came to be here!' Django would say – she'd put money on it. 'Oh well, let's open a page at random and see if anything tickles our fancy.' And he'd place about seven bets. And would just about break even. His theory would work next time, he'd assure her. 'If there is a next time,' he'd then say hurriedly and lightly.

'Django!' Fen allowed herself to be enveloped in a hug of prodigious proportions.

'Dearest girl,' Django boomed, 'you come by train. Shitty poof shitty poof.'

The Rag and Thistle was a lively pub and, having been in the Merifield family for four generations, retained many of the qualities that brewery-owned pubs never achieve. One felt, on entering, that this was indeed a *house* for the public – a family's home open to locals and visitors alike, where personal trinkets and memorabilia replaced standard-issue props like horse brasses and Toby jugs.

There were no Toby jugs but there were old pewter tankards, each one of which contributed to Merifield legend in some capacity, believable or otherwise. There *were* horse brasses – but they'd been worn by Badger and Sarge and there were photos of the two Clydesdale horses with Old Man Merifield at the county show in 1929 to prove it. There were no signs saying 'You Don't Have To Be Mad To Work

Here But It Helps If You Are', but there was the present publican David Merifield's graduation certificate from Nottingham University. And in place of mass-produced sepia photos of Rustic Street Scene Anywhere, were a stretch of family snaps of the Merifield dynasty at their various weddings, christenings and hand-shakings with celebrities of a major or minor persuasion.

There was a lovely photograph of Lulu Merifield, aged fourteen, curtseying to Princess Margaret. And a rather blurred one of Polly Merifield in a crowd with Elton John signing someone else's autograph book five people away. (The point being that both Elton and Polly are looking directly at camera, as if the photographer had said, 'Smile for the Rag and Thistle.') The cast of *Peak Practice* had signed beer-mats which David Merifield had framed in a jaunty pattern around a cast photo. And there was an autographed serviette from a woman who told the Merifields she'd been a backing singer in a band that they'd never heard of and that no one since could shed light on, the signature being somewhat illegible. It was still the topic of conversation on occasions when music was being discussed. 'Maybe she was a Bananarama?' Mrs Merifield might muse. 'Panor-bloody-rama, more like,' David Merifield would retort. 'I saw someone similar on *Top of the Pops* – she was singing and grooving behind Ronan Keating,' Melanie, the barmaid, might offer, 'but only similar – not the same.' Whoever *she* had been, whoever she was, whatever she was doing now, She With No Name had plinked her small change generously into the oversized whisky bottle whose contents benefited the local hospice at least once a year.

There were no laminated menus with novelty meals at the Rag and Thistle. Just simple home cooking – pies and ploughmans, chicken and chips, lasagne and a lasagne without meat, chile con carne and a chile without carne. And Bakewell tart. Oh! the Bakewell tart. The Bakewell tart was a permanent fixture on the menu. It was still baked according to an old Merifield secret recipe (a proliferation of ground almonds, plus home-made strawberry jam. Always strawberry. Only ever home-made). Moreover, to deprive anyone of a slice, at any time they might fancy one, was such a terrible notion that the Bakewell tart at the Rag and Thistle was available all the time. Even after the bell for last orders had been rung. So that's why Django took Fen there, to the Rag and Thistle, though it was certainly past lunch-time and really nowhere near tea-time. And that's why, feeling peckish, James Caulfield had popped into the pub on his way back from Mrs Braithwaite's but en route to Tammy Sydnope's.

Melanie the barmaid, nineteen years old and so coquettish and buxom that even the careers advisor at school could come up with no job that would suit her better, had wrapped a slice of Bakewell tart in a serviette for James whilst fluttering her eyelashes. 'And here,' she said, when he was about to leave, 'these are for your dogs.' She gave him a packet of pork scratchings, with much eye contact and hastily moistened lips.

'Thanks,' James said, unable to keep his eyes from her impressive cleavage, 'their favourite.'

'From their favourite barmaid,' Melanie had winked.

'Thanks,' James said again, suddenly wondering what she'd be like in bed, 'see you soon.'

'Hope so,' she said, running her fingertips up and down the phallic truncheon of the keg lever, thinking he'd probably be very good in bed. Not athletic, not energetic, but with decades of tricks and licks in his repertoire.

Feeding himself the tart with one hand and tossing the gnarled knuckles of pork scratchings to Barry and Beryl on the back seat with the other, meant James steered his heavy old Land Rover out of the car park with his elbows. And Django had to swerve his 2CV to avoid him. And stalled. And Fen had to chide her uncle for not fixing his seat-belt. And Django said bugger Bakewell tart, I need a pint. And Fen said that's fine, Django, I'll drive back. And James just looked in the rear-view mirror, caught sight of Barry (Beryl having fallen off the seat with the violence of the manoeuvre) and said oops. Pork scratchings were all over the floor. But the Bakewell tart was working wonders in his stomach and, though late for Tammy Sydnope, he was nicely refuelled to tend her garden with expertise and energy.

Later that evening, after one of Django's inimitable suppers (today utilizing chick peas, coley fillets and green tagliatelle), Fen and her uncle settled down into battered, mismatched but equally comfortable old armchairs for a nightcap.

'Brandy,' Django declared, customarily, 'is medicinal, you know.'

Fen took a sip of her Hennessy and hummed in agreement.

'It's good for your blood, it's good for your brain,' Django continued, as if quoting a fact gleaned from the *Lancet*, or the back of the bottle, as much as from personal experience. Fen raised her glass in support. 'It doesn't do much for the heart, though,' Django said wryly. He observed Fen. 'I hear you have a suitor, Fenella.'

'Django!' Fen remonstrated, swirling her brandy around the balloon rather violently, pursing her lips and frowning rather harder than the situation warranted.

'I'm only reporting on a fact imparted to me by your sisters,' Django shrugged. 'I just want to know that your heart is in safe hands.'

'I'm holding on to my heart,' Fen said rather dramatically. Django was unable to elicit much more from her. But the details imparted by Cat and Pip sufficed. A chap her own age. Educated. Good job. Son of someone to do with that wretched sculptor.

Fen wakes at three in the morning. She has indigestion. Fish and chick peas and pasta. But she doesn't regret her supper. Django concocted and cooked it with love. And she doesn't regret the Bakewell tart. It was always a pleasure to pass time in the Rag and Thistle. And as soon as a mouthful of the tart hit the tastebuds, the sensation was exquisite. Like a physical *déjà vu*. Comforting. No, the culprits must be the Maltesers and baguette on the train. She would refrain on her homeward journey tomorrow. What time had she to be at Mr Caulfield's? Eleven a.m. Sleep. *Come on, slumber, subsume me!*

No. It isn't going to happen.

Fen rises from her bed and looks out of the window. Silver shards of moonlight lick the lawn, tickle the trees and reveal nuggets of platinum in the old stone walls.

God, how I love it here. I forget how it suits me. This is home. I don't think I'll ever be a townie. Why would I want to live in a place where night is noisy and diluted by an orange glow? Night should be dark and silent.

Fen tiptoes down through the house and out to the garden to sit awhile under her favourite tree. Until she feels sleepy and cold and longing for her childhood bedroom.

THIRTEEN

Beauty lies in the hands of the beer holder.

Anon

At three in the morning, Matt is sitting by himself in his flat, wondering where Jake is and what the hell tonight was all about.

Due east, in Bermondsey, Judith doesn't feel tired at all. She's cracked open a bottle of Chablis and is sipping away, triumphantly.

Oh Lord. What on earth happened whilst our attention was focused on Fen and food and Farleymoor?

Sublime nothingness. That was the phrase that the Rothko exhibition inspired in Matt. Where mass is weightless and space is heavy and colour has motion. Advance and recede. Silence and noise. Tangible then ephemeral. Sublime nothingness that was something incredibly specific. The canvases reminded Matt of the moment of reverie. Or of the moments post orgasm. Or perhaps this was what death was like.

'I've always thought Rothko just a little overrated,' Judith said.

This struck Matt as far more insulting to Rothko, and patronizing, than an unequivocal negation of his work. And so Matt suggested that they leave. He didn't want his time and space with the resonant canvases intruded upon. He'd come again. Definitely. On his own. Probably.

'I'll just go and say goodbye to Nick Serota and the others – oh! Jay Jopling,' Judith name-dropped. Matt, however, was far more tickled to observe David Bowie and a couple of supermodels whose names he did not know, from a distance, than to schmooze the great and godly of the British art world. But he didn't say goodbye to anyone, because he hadn't said hullo to anyone, because he thought the purpose of a private view was just that – privileged time with works of art.

'Sublime nothingness,' he said, indulging in another few minutes in front of a vast canvas, while Judith worked the room, 'genius.'

Judith just about let Matt choose the dish he wanted at Vinopolis, but she chose the wines and the conversation topics. Excusing himself after the hors d'œuvres, he sat, perplexed, in the toilet.

She's negative about everything. Rothko. The structure of the exhibition. The service at Vinopolis. The quality of the food. It's giving me a headache. So what if she found a speck of dust on her wineglass? I couldn't see it. Anyway, Jilly Goulden often praises top notes of dust or dirt or pencil shavings when she assesses wine. I'm bored. I'd much rather be having a pint with Jake. Or just watching TV, for that matter.

When he returned, Matt did not notice that Judith's silk shirt had been unbuttoned twice, nor that her lipstick had been replenished. What he did notice was that the wine-glasses had now been filled with a full-bodied red with liquorice undertones and whispers of blueberry. And Matt promptly decided that the way to make the evening work for him was to drink and be merry to counter Judith's drinking and being harsh.

'I'm not so sure how I feel about the New Girl carrying the Trust's torch Up North,' said Judith, running the tip of her middle finger along the rim of the wineglass.

'New girl?' Matt said, wondering if Judith had therefore

finished her discourse on the shortcomings of the National Arts Collection Fund.

'Fenella,' Judith said, taking her finger to her lips, 'McCabe.' She flicked her tongue over her fingertip. 'Gone to Derbyshire.' Matt wondered whether he ought to have more wine to assist his understanding of Judith's drift, or whether he'd had too much wine to be capable of fathoming her point.

'I think you, Matt, *you* should have gone,' Judith purred, with persuasive eye contact.

To Derbyshire? With Fen? Why didn't I think of that? 'To Derbyshire?' Matt asked.

'Yes,' Judith said.

'With Fen?'

Judith's face jerked at such a notion. 'You,' she stressed, '*you* should be the one to represent the Trust.'

Matt looked puzzled.

'I mean, Fen's the New Girl,' Judith reasoned, 'she's *only* an archivist, not an *ambassador*.'

'I'm an *editor*,' Matt shrugged, not liking Judith's point, 'and I don't know diddly about Fetherstone.'

Judith let it lie. She had wanted to draw out of Matt any intentions towards Fen. She had wanted to infuse him with her mistrust of the New Girl. She had wanted to point out Fen's shortcomings, to allude to the fact that it was Matt and *she* who were intellectually and professionally on a par – and above Fen. So Judith turned to chit-chat instead. Which Matt found most peculiar, having never spoken to Judith about anything other than Trust matters. So he drank more wine and she flattered him with questions about where he lived, with whom, where he shopped and where he spent his leisure time. Matt answered them as if he was on a quick-fire round of a TV quiz. Once or twice, he wondered where it was all leading. What the prize at the end would be.

* * *

There wasn't a prize. But there was the most almighty surprise. Up against the vaulted brickwork outside Vinopolis.

* * *

Lord! What is the woman doing?

She's pushed you against the wall.

She's kissing me!

She's working her tongue inside your mouth like she hasn't eaten for days.

Oh God. No, stop. No, don't.

She's pressed against you, grabbing at your groin. And you're stirring, Matt. You're hard. And she's hailed a cab and it's taking you to Bermondsey and you can't remonstrate or even comment because she has welded her mouth to yours. Not that I think you would either remonstrate or comment. If the straining bulge in your trousers is any indication, I'd say you are rather enjoying yourself.

See, now you're kissing her back.

And you have your hand inside her shirt, over her bra, under her bra, her nipple pressed against the centre of your palm.

Matt has ceased to think. He isn't wondering what on earth is happening, nor what the ramifications might be. He has no inclination to touch upon whether all of this is a jolly good or rather bad idea. He is in a Rothko painting, where time is not about yesterday and tomorrow but about the present instant being all that matters, a continual and simultaneous past and future.

It isn't a bad place to be, not least because his cock is being fingered teasingly by Judith as the cab discreetly winds its way east to her apartment. Her tits feel fantastic in his hand. Her mouth excites him. Every time the cab goes over a bump and changes direction, her teeth catch his lips. He likes it.

This must be Bermondsey. Though in the dark and under

a haze of alcohol and a blur of lust, Bermondsey looks pretty nondescript. Judith pays the fare whilst Matt turns his back to do up his flies. Judith isn't aware that her left breast is clearly on view, should the cab driver choose to gawp. Even had she been aware, she wouldn't have cared. She is on a mission. And the final location, where it will be brought, literally, to its climax, is but yards away. The cab driver has noticed the exposed breast. But he is a family man. He tried not to look in the rear-view mirror this past quarter of an hour. Only for the purpose of traffic awareness. He knew what they were up to in the back, the two punters, slightly sozzled. He found it all rather unsavoury. He might well switch from nights to days.

Two hours later. Three a.m. Matt, sitting alone in his apartment, wonders where Jake is and what the *hell* that was all about.

She's so not my type, Judith. I can't go to work tomorrow! There again, I can't not go to work tomorrow. That entire article on the Euston Road School has to be re-subbed. Otter's having a day off, so I'll have to do it.

What was Judith's flat like?

What? Oh. Ultra hip. White walls and very wide floorboards. Bathroom a homage to Philippe Starcke, kitchen a replica in miniature of an industrial kitchen, lots of stainless steel and gruesome-looking utensils I bet are never used. Terry Frost on the sitting-room wall. Dark brown leather sofa. White TV and DVD. Spotless. Bed very low, no headboard, no pillows. Therese Oulton on the wall. Frameless. Sheets the colour and texture of sack.

What was the sex like?

What? Oh, we didn't do it in her bed. On account of the sack-like sheets, I presume. We did it most other places. I came, taking her from behind, while she hung on to a wall-mounted steel rack above the cooker.

But what was the sex *like*?

What? Oh, it was fine. It was sex. Quite good sex.

I mean, was it rampant? Did it last long? Did she go down on you?

I'm a bloke, for Christ's sake. It's not in my nature to workshop through every hump and grind. Yes, she went down on me. No, I didn't go down on her – she didn't seem to want me to. We started in missionary on her sofa, then sideways on the white rug. No, hang on. Before that she went on top for a little while and came that way. I presume. I mean, she sounded like she was coming. Then I said could I come. And she said wait. Led me into the kitchen and took a condom out of the cutlery drawer – which only now strikes me as rather odd.

Did you stay long?

She asked if I wanted to stay the night. She didn't seem that bothered that I declined. She called me a cab and we had a civilized glass of wine whilst I waited.

Do you want to see her again? Sleep with her again?

Jesus – the Spanish Inquisition. She's quite a hard, independent woman. So, no, I don't think it is the start of something beautiful. Where the hell is Jake? I feel like my hangover's coming on now. I'm going to take two Nurofen. Nuro.

Matt?

Fen.

Fen what?

Nuro-fen. If that was the zipless fuck, what are my intentions now towards Fen?

FOURTEEN

While Fen slept in her old bed, Matt sipped a glass of water to make the Nurofen go down and his stomach contents stay down. While Matt sipped water, Jake zipped up his jeans. And Abi watched him, remaining in bed where she lit a cigarette though she knew it was as dangerous as it was decadent. All the while, Gemma, who had gone to bed early with what may well develop into flu, slept soundly; unaware that a man had been in her house, let alone her housemate's bed.

'Seen my socks?' Jake whispered. Abi motioned to the chair by the window, and then to her chest of drawers to the left. Jake found one sock under the former, the other on top of the latter. Fully dressed, he came over to Abi in her bed, and started to kiss her breasts most attentively.

'You'd better go,' Abi laughed quietly, though she'd have been happy for him to stay. 'I'm giving a presentation tomorrow morning and I only want to feel shagged in one sense of the word.' She eyed the flies of his jeans appreciatively. He kissed her, wishing she'd had a drag of fag after, rather than before.

'I'll let myself out, shall I?'

'No bloody way,' said Abi, 'I'll follow you down to chain

the door. Don't want to find you lurking in the broom cupboard tomorrow morning.'

'Why don't you come and lurk in my broom cupboard tomorrow evening?' Jake suggested lasciviously as he stood on the doorstep.

'Can't do tomorrow,' Abi said, matter of fact, 'but I could do the next night.'

While Jake strolls out in search of a black cab, Matt decides his flatmate is a dirty stop-out and goes to bed. Matt and Abi switch off their lights at much the same time. Judith continues to sip wine in bed. None of these three can drop off to sleep. There's too much recent sex bombarding their minds and continuing to make their bodies fizz, throb and ache.

Gemma, though, sleeps soundly – but will wake up with a stinking cold tomorrow. Fen sleeps soundly too. For these two, sex is far from their minds. For the time being at least.

Ten miles from Fen, at Keeper's Dwelling, Barry the lurcher and Beryl the labrador huff and twitch in their baskets. Upstairs, James is out for the count, snoring; but so lightly that he's really just breathing heavily. Margot Fitzpatrick-Montague-Laine comes into his dream, comes into his house. She brings Fen McCabe with her. Fen is wearing wellingtons. She looks dowdy. She has a terrible laugh. And she's scared of the dogs. She has horrible hands. Chewed fingernails and red, blotchy, scaly skin. She keeps laughing at nothing. 'I want to hit her over the head with *Eden*,' Margot whispers to James. 'And then I want you to fuck me like Adam is fucking Eve,' Margot says, eyeing the sculpture greedily.

James wakes from the dream with a hard-on. But he ignores it. The dream, though bizarre, was vivid. He is disconcerted that he is now a little nonplussed by his future visitor. And yet, hadn't he cleaned the house, quite thoroughly, quite excited, during the evening? And bought fancy biscuits and pikelets to be toasted?

'The Fetherstones,' he reminds himself out loud. 'I want her to want them. I need the money.'

Sleep continued to elude him. John Grisham was no help. Nor was a Thames & Hudson book on sculpture. Nor was the thought of a wank, let alone a few trial tugs. He switched on the light and listened hard to the silence.

James had brought the oil sketches and the small bronze into his bedroom. Almost as if this was to be their last night in his ownership. He looked across to them, to Adam and Eve in two dimensions and three. Suddenly, he didn't want to lose them.

Perhaps I'll cancel Fen McCabe. She in the wellies with the ugly hands. Maybe I don't need the money quite as urgently after all. I'll phone the bank first thing. And dependent on their advice, I'll cancel McCabe.

FIFTEEN

The two divinest things this world has got,
A lovely woman in a rural spot!

James Hunt

'Gracious, Fenella,' Django murmured.

'Blimey, Django,' Fen responded.

They'd driven towards Matlock, through the small town of Farley Bath and Django's 2CV had made a brave assault on the 1:4 hill that met them just as soon as they'd crossed the humpback bridge. The steep road ahead was just as twisting as the river they'd been following. An army of oaks and cedars stood to attention as Fen and Django trundled upwards. The density of foliage threw light around the road in shards and pebbles and made the shade seem eerie. Under this canopy, the old stone walls were not grey as those on the moors; here they were mottled with moss and fringed with cascades of ivy. Django and Fen had remarked that they'd been unaware there was a house up this road. They'd thought the whole area was Forestry Commission, that it was a road that merely transported travellers from A to B. They'd never seen the lion and unicorn lurking either side of the entrance of a hidden driveway on the right. When Fen had read through Mr Caulfield's directions, and come upon the lion and unicorn, Django had taken the sheet of paper from her convinced she was making it up. But there they were, the lion and unicorn, licked with lichen, ears chipped or missing, time corroding a clear delineation of their features. Still, though, they were impressive; the lion had one paw draped nonchalantly over a shield, the unicorn reared up with forelegs slicing the air though his horn was only half its original length. They presented a grand herald, but still Fen and Django weren't quite prepared for the grandeur of Delvaux Hall at the end of the majestic drive.

'Gracious, Fenella,' Django murmured.

'Blimey, Django,' Fen responded.

'Don't think I've met this Delvaux chap,' Django mused, whilst a pillared double doorway soared in front of his eyes.

'I think he's probably long dead, Django,' said Fen, thinking the proportions of the windows set into smooth, creamy-peach stone, quite beautiful. 'Anyway,' she said, 'I'm not to go to the main hall, but the keeper's dwelling.'

Fen and Django sat in the Citroën and regarded the smaller driveways left and right of the main house.

'Right!' Django declared. 'Right!' he proclaimed. 'I'm nearly always *right*,' he chortled. And he chugged the car off to the right. Only to arrive first at the Forester's Lodge and then at the Huntsman's Cottage. 'Well, right might have been wrong but we've had a bloody good nosey,' Django said, retracing their tracks, the 2CV coping valiantly with the dinks and ruts in the tarmac forming the lane left of Delvaux Hall.

'Now, you're quite sure you don't want me to accompany you to the front door?' Django offered, having drawn up outside impressive iron gates.

'Quite sure,' Fen assured him.

'And you're quite sure he does indeed possess works of art by Fetherstone,' Django continued, gravely serious, 'and you're sure that he isn't a homicidal axe-wielding madman?'

'Quite sure,' Fen laughed, 'on both counts.'

'Call me if you need a lift to Chesterfield,' Django said, taking the tip of her nose in the crook of his fingers, like he used to when she was young.

'What!' Fen teased. 'You'd forego dominoes afternoon at the Rag and Thistle to drive me to my train?'

'If,' Django paused, lifting his index finger, 'if I really had to. Though I hasten to add that I'd hold it against you and would dock, accordingly, a great proportion of that which I intend to leave you in my will.'

'I'm sure Mr Caulfield won't mind running me in to town,' an unsure Fen breezed. 'He probably drives a white Rolls-Royce with a gold-coloured radiator grille.'

'Not if he has Fetherstones,' Django reasoned. 'They would suggest he has taste. A white-and-gold Roller would preclude that altogether.'

Fen was delighted. She never realized that Django actually appreciated the work of Julius Fetherstone. In the past, he'd remarked that *Abandon* looked like two people being mangled by a tumble dryer. In the past, he'd referred to Fetherstone as 'a dirty old codger'. He'd looked at a maquette for *Hunger* and declared it 'downright rude, just porn legitimized by being in bronze and a century old'.

But that's all a show, Fen thought with great satisfaction, though she did wonder why she hadn't twigged before now, that before now she had truly taken it personally.

'Bye, Django,' she said fondly, wrapping her arms around his neck and giving him a heartfelt squeeze. 'I'll come home again soon. Hopefully, with my two sisters.'

'Hmm,' Django mused, slipping the steering-wheel through his hands, 'and maybe a new lover in tow!'

'Django!' Fen objected, tugging against his slack seat-belt, wishing she could make sure he'd fix it.

'Have fun, young 'un,' he said with a wink.

She watched the 2CV list and lurch its way away. And then she observed the iron gates.

'Julius!' she said under her breath, suddenly feeling absurdly happy. Derbyshire. Delvaux. Django. '*J'arrive*, Mr Fetherstone. I'm here.'

But no one else was.

* * *

Oh dear, James. Did the bank manager tell you there was no need to sell your Fetherstones? Were you not able to make contact with Fen McCabe directly? Up there, on Farleymoor and deep down here, in the grounds of Delvaux Hall, her mobile phone has no signal. Have you gone off to work, then? Mrs Brakespeare's, isn't it? And on to Tammy Sydnope who now wants you twice a week?

The gates, despite their apparent age and in spite of their daunting dimensions, swung open easily and noiselessly. Fen walked towards the front door of the dwelling – which she decided immediately was far too humble a name for the building before her. Dwellings, surely, were constructed from wattle and daub, with a split stable door as an entrance, and sleepy small windows sunken into uneven walls. Would a keeper dwell behind such fine stonework and a beautiful, arched oak door? To say nothing of mullioned windows. And a clock and weather-vane. Fen supposed it depended on what the keeper actually kept. And this one has three works of art by Julius Fetherstone.

The doorbell did not seem to work but a rap on the knocker (it was an iron version of the lion and unicorn) was satisfyingly loud and assertive. Only no one came to answer. She knocked again.

The walls must be thick, Fen thought, *the interior walls too. And maybe Mr Caulfield is old and infirm and takes a while to totter to the door, to displace a dachshund from his lap, to find his glasses.*

Fen, your imagination is far too fertile. I don't think there's anyone home.

Well, I'm going to knock again – in a little rat-tat-tat rhythm.

Oh.

Well, now I think I'll peer through the windows. Kitchen. See! Dogs' bowls. Two of them. Mind you, each about the size of a dachshund. Looks fairly tidy. And over through this

window, on the other side of the front door, a sitting-room.
The back of an old leather armchair. I'll just knock on the
windows, in case he's nodded off.

Oh.
    I'll knock on the door again. I don't want to lurk around
behind the house.

No one answered. Fen stood still, with her back to the front
door, wondering what to do. She felt a little embarrassed, as
if she'd been led along, as if she should have verified details,
phoned last night to check, this morning too perhaps.
    Even if he is, as Django fears, an axe-wielding homicidal
maniac, I'll be just fine because at least he is nowhere
around to butcher me.
    Fen! Your imagination.
    She stood against the door and then decided to cross the
patio, descend stone steps, cross a gravel promenade and go
through into the garden beyond. Because, you never know,
the Fetherstones could well be out of doors. As it was nearly
the second week of April, the rhododendrons were just
beginning to spew their fabulous colour out into the world.
Fen was utterly taken by a particularly violet specimen, at
least fifteen feet high and wide. With her back to the garden,
she gave the shrub her undivided attention, partly because it
warranted it, partly because it gave her time to wonder what
to do next.

Whump! Something has shoved her in the back, face first
into the rhodos. Heavy breathing. Manic panting. Fen gasps
and tastes raindrops from the leaves. She spins around.
Immediately, something hard and insistent pokes at her
crotch. She gasps and looks down. It is an enormous, hairy,
wet lurcher. Thump! Something knocks her off her feet and
she staggers sideways. Righting herself, she is confronted by
a wet, slathering labrador which, standing on its hind legs
with its front paws on her shoulders, is practically eye to eye

with her. Its tongue is lapping at her cheek. She keeps her mouth closed at just the right moment. Fen is not normally scared of dogs. But these two are huge and, momentarily, she is unsure of the sincerity of their welcome. In an instant, she clocks that tails are wagging. And there's all that licking going on. And a moment later, with the shock subsiding, the cogs of memory start to turn.

It's that lurcher – the one whose coat resembles Django's Astrakhan gilet. I've seen this dog before. Recently. Yes! The Rag and Thistle when I was up here last with Cat and Pip.

'Beryl!' Someone is yelling and the labrador barks once, turns on a sixpence and bolts away.

'Barry!' Someone hollers and the lurcher reluctantly drags its face away from Fen's crotch. It too tries to turn on a sixpence but its lanky legs threaten to interweave with disastrous consequences. Shoving its flank against Fen's thigh for support, the lurcher untangles its legs and lopes off with its tongue lolling out of the side of its mouth to make way for a deep, hound-like woof.

Fen stands stock-still, with her hand clasped to her heart in a most Jane Austen-like fashion. Raindrops from the rhododendron seep down the back of her collar and course midway down her spine. She shivers.

It's the raindrops.

You just had the shock of your life, Fen.

Just the raindrops.

Who's this, striding up the lawn with the two dogs running apologetic circles around him?

Lord Delvaux?

Or maybe the keeper of the dwelling.

The man seems to be making a leisurely, if not downright slow, passage towards her. Before her, the lawn sweeps down and away, fairly steeply, bordered on all sides by shrubs and trees and bushes, all well tended, all bursting with foliage or spring flowers. Beyond the perimeter of the

108

garden, the land sweeps upward, clad in the uniform pine and ordered ranks of Forestry Commission land. The horizon, which, due to the steepness of the incline, is high up rather than far away, is punctuated aesthetically by a folly. All glistens; the skies are clearing, there's fair weather ahead, after four solid hours of rain this morning.

Here is the keeper, or the squire, or maybe just the gardener, strolling towards her in a battered old Barbour, jeans and hiking boots. Might this be James Caulfield? Fen doubts it. Could Mr Caulfield really be anything other than a nice pottery old man with a dachshund on his lap, a gammy hip and three Fetherstones he's owned for donkey's years?

'I'm so sorry,' the man calls to Fen while he continues to approach. The dogs look up at the target of his apology and decide to bound towards it, to offer theirs. 'Dogs!' the man hollers and, though they do not return to him, their reaction to Fen is much less demonstrative than before. They don't venture above her knees this time, though her shins and ankles are given a good sniffing. 'Fenella?' The man approaches. He holds out his hand, which is dirty with earth. He wipes it on his Barbour, which has damp patches where a rewaxing is needed and trickles of wet trying to cling to where there is wax. Fen clocks his face; he is handsome – weather tanned with good bones, something a little Mediterranean, perhaps because of the dark hair, the olive eyes. His gaze is quite penetrating and she glances away and down the lawn. He extends his hand again. Still muddy but surprisingly long and shapely. 'James Caulfield.'

'Fen McCabe,' says Fen, politely pretending she hasn't seen the state of the hand she's shaking. 'I thought you'd be old.'

James looks surprised and flattered. 'I'm not as young as I used to be,' he says by way of an explanation.

'None of us are,' Fen theorizes, wondering how on earth the conversation can progress. They stand awkwardly for a few moments. 'Gorgeous garden,' Fen offers, 'it must take some upkeep.'

'The grounds of Delvaux Hall as a whole were loosely

modelled on those at Chatsworth,' James informs, perusing the view.

'How interesting,' says Fen, knowing that her enthusiasm sounds embarrassingly disproportionate.

He doesn't look anything like an axe-wielding lunatic. He looks, actually, rather fine.

'Well, Fen McCabe,' says James, 'shall I introduce you to them? Barry! Beryl!'

'I've seen them before,' Fen says as James leads on to the house.

He stops and regards her, baffled. 'How?' he asks, a little defensively. 'They've never been out of my sight.'

'But I saw them a couple of weeks ago,' Fen corrects.

'Where?' James enquires, frowning, going through the garden gates which swing back at Fen.

'At the Rag and Thistle,' Fen shrugs, uncomfortable that it's such an issue.

'The Rag and bloody Thistle?' James exclaims, opening the front door which was unlocked. 'What *are* you talking about?'

'The lurcher buried its nose in my crotch then,' Fen explains, standing in a rather dark and chilly, flagstone-floored hallway. James flicks on a light and regards Fen. He has a peculiar urge to remove small shreds of shrubbery from her hair. But he decides it wouldn't be seemly. And his hands are dirty. And why does he want to touch her anyway? Just because she's seen his dogs before?

'I thought you meant *Adam* and *Eve*,' James explains, keeping his hands to himself (it's only now he's inside his home that he is aware of how dirty they are). 'The dogs are called Barry and Beryl.'

'That's nice,' Fen says absent-mindedly, not that interested which is which; really craving a nice cup of tea.

James made a very nice cup of tea. And, to Fen's amusement, he served hers in a fine china teacup and saucer, though he poured his into a mug. She thought of Lady Chatterley and Mellors and felt rather refined and just a little flattered.

110

'Biscuit?' he offered, sitting down.

'No thanks,' she said politely because she felt he shouldn't have to get up again.

'They're Belgian,' he tempted, 'slathered in milk chocolate.'

'Go on then,' Fen accepted. James leant back on his chair at a precarious angle, stretched further to open a low cupboard and retrieved a box of biscuits. They looked luxurious. Only Fen didn't take one just then. Her hands remained in her lap. This was so that she could have a surreptitious glance from left to right. For James, though, it was a warning bell that maybe his dream had been prophetic in some weird way. His hands might have been rather dirty when they first met, but he hadn't had a chance to assess *her* hands at all. Scaly? Bitten nails?

'Delicious!' James said, his mouth full, munching contentedly on a second biscuit before the first had reached his gullet. 'Go on!'

Fen reached for the biscuits. 'I had kippers for breakfast,' she told James, as if it was a guilty secret, 'with hash browns and baked beans. Only Django had run out of conventional baked beans so he heated up a tin of kidney beans and added tomato ketchup and a dash of Henderson's Relish.'

Momentarily, James couldn't care what Fen had eaten for breakfast. He was simply pleased to see that her hands were pretty, that her nails were neat and that her skin was pink and even. 'Henderson's Relish?' he said. 'I thought we'd kept that secret from you southerners.'

'I am not,' Fen remonstrated, 'a southerner. I've spent more of my life in Derbyshire than I have anywhere else.'

'I forgot,' James said, glad that she'd reminded him. 'I'm the fraud,' he confided, 'I spent my first thirty-five years down south. I've only been here fourteen.'

God, he's almost fifty!

'Is your mother a Derbyshire lass then?' James asked, interrupting any thoughts Fen was beginning to have on people not looking their age and age being all in the mind and she'd never met anyone who was twenty years older than her yet to whom she was undeniably attracted. Whoa, Fen!

'No. Sutton Coldfield originally,' Fen said, 'but she ran off with a cowboy from Denver when I was small and my dad brought my sisters and me from Battersea to Derbyshire to live with him and his brother Django.'

'I see,' said James, who thought Fen must have a very active imagination, 'and they still live over at Farleymoor?'

'Well, actually my dad died when I was little,' Fen shrugged, 'so it's just Django – who is the best mother and father a girl could have.'

James didn't know what to say to that. He thought perhaps that such childhood trauma had made her bulimic if her inroad into his biscuits were anything to go by. She was already on her third and they were very rich. And of course she'd had kippers and hash browns and some hideous-sounding bean concoction for breakfast. Must be bulimic. Shame. He'd read about how so many young women were unhinged nowadays. Oh God! did that make him sound old. Her hands were lovely though. And her laugh wasn't that horrendous cackle of his dream but a demure little chuckle. And she was far from dowdy – 'nicely put together' being the phrase occurring to James. And she wasn't scared of his dogs and they seemed to really like her.

'Could I see Julius now,' Fen asked, 'please?'

'Of course,' James smiled, wondering how old she was.

Twenty-five? Ish? I had a twenty-three-year old a couple of years ago.

James!

'Can I use your loo?' Fen asked.

Oh dear, she is bulimic.

James! For God's sake don't hover outside the loo. It's intrusive. And it's worrying.

Ah – she's only peeing.

'You're probably the envy of your friends,' James said to

Fen, who was surprised to find him loitering quite so near the toilet.

'Actually,' Fen said, 'their business trips often take them to Europe rather than Derbyshire. New York, even. And their pay is much better than mine. But many of them deal in dull figures. Whereas the figures I deal with are bronze or marble and absolutely gorgeous.'

'I meant,' James said, 'that you can eat and eat but stay slim.'

Fen regarded him as if he were a little peculiar. What an odd thing to say. The comment had suddenly set him apart from her generation. 'In my day—' he might say. 'I remember when—'

Fen was just a little disappointed. And then relieved.

For God's sake, I'm here to represent Trust Art. Let's see the Fetherstones.

They went back into the hallway, which seemed quite warm now that Fen could take in a worn kilim, the grandfather clock, a console table heaped with magazines and papers and gloves and dogs' leads, carpeted stairs up, a door to the back leading God knows where. James led her into the sitting-room she'd spied from the outside, where she'd imagined James as a wizened old man sitting waiting for her but deaf to her call.

And the three Fetherstones were directly in front of her. James had propped the two oil sketches, so that their sides touched, to the left of the fireplace. The bronze was to the right. Fen was speechless, her head turning from the oils to the bronze, back and forth, as if she was watching a tennis match.

'Blimey, Mr Caulfield,' she said, not taking her eyes from the works though she turned her cheek slightly.

'Nice,' said James, 'aren't they?' He watched her absorbing every detail. 'Go up close, Miss McCabe – have a sniff and a feel.'

Fen went to the fireplace and sat down between the oils

and the bronze. She removed her shoes and curled her legs around her. Which should she touch first? Her right hand reached for the bronze and her left hand found the boards. Holding on to Adam's head in bronze, she carefully pulled the oil sketches to her and placed them, one at a time, in her lap. The paint, though used thinly, had such exuberance of application.

'It's amazing,' she said quietly, tilting her head back a fraction to indicate that she was talking to James and not herself, 'he took such delight in the physical handling of media – whether painting or sculpting – sometimes you feel that the subject matter was almost a coincidence, a fluke. Like he was so enthralled with the actual material, then wow! look! what a bonus – I just painted or modelled Eve!'

James had never noticed. But now he did. 'Exactly,' he conferred as if it were a long-held theorem of his own.

'Yes!' Fen exclaimed, turning right round to beam at James, 'Yes!' She turned back to Adam, to Eve, to the two of them together. She ran her hands – fingertips, knuckles, palms, the backs – over all the surfaces that her eyes were dancing over too. She held the oils very very close to her face, loving it that she was allowed to let her nose touch the surfaces, her cheek too. Oh Adam! Julius! She explored the bronze figures, fingering every curve, delving into every space, sensing every twist and dip, delighting in the movement and the stillness, the solidity and the weightlessness, much like foreplay. Clutching the oil sketch of Adam against her, she turned her torso to James.

'Mr Caulfield, are you very very broke?' she asked, one arm holding Adam tight against her, the other encircling the bronze, the sketch of Eve in her lap. 'It's a travesty,' she proclaimed, 'to choose *these* to sell to raise funds.'

'They're really the only items I own of any value,' James told her bluntly. 'The grandfather clock wouldn't pay for the reroofing. And anyway, it has a purpose, a function.'

'So does art!' Fen retorted, 'Jesus, if they were mine, I'd rather sell my soul as well as my body.'

What on earth was James meant to say to that? He thought her histrionics rather amusing, but he wouldn't let it show, let alone say so.

'Are you sure there's nothing else of value here?' Fen enquired, glancing around the room as if James might have overlooked some large solid silver tureen or nondescript but authentic eighteenth-century landscape that Americans are always delighted to pay inflated prices for. She saw, however, that though the furniture was nice and the bookcase was heaving and there was a crystal decanter of whisky, there was indeed a deficit of silverware or landscape paintings. 'Couldn't you, I don't know, *move*?'

But if you'd found a place like Keeper's Dwelling, in an area outstandingly beautiful, would *you* move, Fen?

James, actually, felt a little awkward now. No, not just awkward, *uncouth* even. Like he was being deplorably mercenary, or committing a crime against the most basic standards of aesthetics and worth.

'*How* badly does the roof leak?' Fen persisted.

'I'll show you,' said James, offering his hand to assist Fen to her feet, her left thigh having gone to sleep. She held on to his arm, giggling with the sensation as the blood revived her limb. She limped behind him and he took her upstairs. Three large stained patches were pointed out to her, two on the bedroom ceiling, one in the hallway. 'It's only a patch job,' James explained. 'By this winter, if it isn't fixed, I'll be watching stars from my bed.'

Fen conceded that reroofing was essential, at the same time taking a surreptitious look around the bedroom with great interest and absorbing the tiniest of details. A nicely made double bed. *Bet he has a cleaner.* Sash windows, heavy cream curtains billowing to the floor. *Must be a girlfriend's touch.* Carpet slightly worn but well hoovered. A very distant smell of dog. *A bone of contention no doubt for the cleaner and girlfriend.* Tinted engravings, probably 1920s, most likely of Derbyshire, framed. Four botanical prints, also framed. Camelia. Magnolia. Dog Rose. Field Poppy.

But it was the photos atop the chest of drawers which she found most alluring.

'Who's this?' Fen asked.

'The only girlfriend I split up with amicably,' James replied.

'When was that?' Fen asked.

'When we were twenty-two,' James replied, realizing that such an age was well over half his life away and yet for Fen, probably so recent it didn't yet qualify as a memory.

'What was her name?' Fen persisted.

'Anna,' said James.

'Where is she now?' Fen asked.

'Australia, married, four children, a sheep farm,' James replied.

'Do you live alone?' Fen asked, turning towards him and regarding him directly.

James frowned momentarily. 'Why do you ask?'

Fen turned away. She wasn't sure why she had asked. Nor why she was genuinely interested in this man. 'I thought maybe if you had a very rich lover, she would fix your roof,' suggested Fen limply.

'I don't have a lover, rich or otherwise,' James told her, wondering why he had – and why he didn't.

'Who's this?' Fen asked, looking at a photograph of a dark-haired woman with perfect lips and undeniable sadness to her eyes.

'My mother,' said James.

'Was she from Derbyshire?' Fen asked.

'Italy, originally,' James said.

'And who's this?' Fen asked, scrutinizing a photo so old, so small, so faded, that it may not have been a photo at all.

'My great, great-grandmother,' said James. 'Come on back downstairs.'

Fen looked at the photo a little longer. The lady looked familiar.

*

'So,' said James, back in the sitting-room, in the armchair, while Fen sat on the floor with art on her lap and in her hands, 'who will give Adam and Eve the best home?'

'The best home or the best price?' Fen asked. 'I'd give them the best home – but I could only pay you about £70 a month for the next millennium!'

'The best home,' said James. 'Margot Fitzmontague-Le Patrick-Whatever valued the oils at thirty, the bronze at forty.'

'Thousand,' Fen said sadly.

'Of course,' James said kindly.

'But why sell all three?' Fen persisted. 'The roof can't cost that much.'

James looked at the Fetherstones and Fen thoughtfully. 'It would be a travesty to separate them. Look at them! They belong together. They must stay together.'

Fen looked at the pieces. It was true.

'We have to find an establishment that wants them and can plead a good case for Trust Art to assist purchase with a grant,' Fen said, racking her brains.

'And you could do that for me?' said James.

'I'll do it for Julius,' Fen said with a grin.

'Would you like some lunch?' James asked.

'My goodness,' Fen exclaimed, 'it's almost one o'clock. I think I ought to catch a train home.'

'Why?' James asked. 'Do you need to go in to work?'

'They're not expecting me,' Fen pondered, 'but being the New Girl, I could do with any Brownie points to be had.'

'It's the Sheffield train,' James reasoned, 'they're pretty frequent.'

'Just a sandwich then,' said Fen. 'I had a British Rail sandwich on my way up yesterday. It was very very nasty.'

'Simply cheese and pickle here,' said James, hoping that there was still some pickle, 'if that's OK.'

'Sounds lovely,' said Fen.

'Glass of wine?' James offered.

Fen faltered. 'I oughtn't to – I'm working.'

'Chill out!' James teased. Fen laughed. James looked confused. Fen didn't want to tell him that the phrase sounded funny coming from his lips.

The wine was lovely. But even without it, she would have felt at ease. Strangely, though James didn't bother with small talk, Fen still found him engaging. Plus, she liked the creases around his eyes, they spoke of a person who had smiled for many years – decades, she realized. He seemed wholly different – alluringly in between a contemporary and a grown-up. Conversation flowed naturally, not necessitating polite questions and answers though they did ask each other many things, but only because they were genuinely interested in the replies.

James was stimulated by Fen. A bright girl, and of course, very pleasing on the eye. In recent years, James has consistently gone for the latter at the expense of the former; a compromise that has become dull. It was only when James said that they ought to go, that it was nearing three o'clock, that it was no problem to drive her to Chesterfield, that Fen thought to ask him how he had come by the Fetherstones.

'They were passed down through the family,' he told her whilst regarding his watch. 'Come on, Miss McCabe, we've a train to catch. You don't object to Barry and Beryl joining us?'

I don't want to get to Chesterfield just yet.

'Here we are,' says James, 'it's been a pleasure meeting you. Keep in touch.'

'Thanks so much,' says Fen, 'for lunch and the lift – and calling on me to consult.'

'You should thank Margot,' says James.

Fen suddenly remembers student times at the Courtauld. And those parties. 'Did she make a pass at you?' Fen asks, wondering why her heartbeat is quickening as she anticipates the reply.

'Lord, no!' James lies and laughs. 'I'm just about old enough to be her father.'

Fen smiles.

He's right. Of course he is. What was I . . .?

She shakes his hand and assures him she'll call soon.

James watches her go. What a lovely day. Different. Refreshing. Rather like Fen herself. Oh well, time left to do a couple of hours for Tammy Sydnope.

SIXTEEN

I expect that woman will be the last thing civilized by man
George Meredith

*F*en is standing stock-still in front of the news-stand at St Pancras from which she bought magazines and Maltesers yesterday.

How bizarre. How very unnerving. How really quite worrying. How did I do that? How could I do that?

How did you do what?

Spend practically the whole train journey gazing out of the window wondering what it would be like to go to bed with James Caulfield?

I can't believe she did that, Otter, hovering by the stairwell, thought to himself. He couldn't possibly go straight back to Publications. He slipped out of the building, crossed the car park and, via a gate, took refuge in a tiny peaceful courtyard that only bonafide Tate gallery employees were meant to know about.

'I cannot believe she did that,' Otter said aloud but discreetly under his breath because two dusty-looking art historians were sitting nearby. He shook his head forlornly. 'How bloody dare she?'

It was not so much the fact that Judith had had sex with Matt that Otter objected to. It was the fact that she had shared this information with *him*.

120

'Damn her! How dare she take advantage of me!' Otter was truly experiencing something close to physical pain. He sat on the stone bench; his sticks-and-stalks body so twisted with the pressure of it all that it resembled a mangled coathanger.

'I adore Matt. And I think Fen is quite gorgeous. But bloody Judith had to go and tell me. Me! Of all the people! She goes and tells me.'

Highly perturbed, Otter stood slowly and, stooping, shuffled back to the Trust Art offices.

'I do not like the woman at all,' he said quietly, re-entering the building. He stopped at the foot of the stairwell. 'Damn her! She has provided me with the most fantastic gossip. And it is a huge, burdensome affliction – believe me – that I am so partial to gossip.'

Otter returned to Publications and literally bit his tongue all afternoon whilst trying to focus undivided attention on an appallingly punctuated article on Sir Matthew Smith. It looked, to Matt, as if Otter had chronic mouth ulcers.

Actually, Matt had found it surprisingly easy to go into Trust Art, settle down and work well. He hadn't avoided leaving Publications for fear of bumping into Judith. He'd been down to Reception a couple of times, had had a brief meeting with Rodney and had gone along his corridor to Accounts, to the photocopying room, to the loo. He simply hadn't bumped into Judith. And yet she was around. He'd heard her; her confident voice from which she'd carefully banished any trace of identifying accent. Her officious walk. Her laugh; ballsy and ever so slightly insincere.

It was tea-time. Fen hadn't shown up for work. Fondly, Matt supposed she was still gazing at the Fetherstones in that private collection in Derbyshire. He turned to Otter. But Otter was picking through the article, hunched over his keyboard, bony shoulders and aquiline features compounding the impression of a raggedy vulture. Otter wasn't talking. Sore Mouth. Or Sir Matthew. Or both.

A text message beeped into Matt's phone. It was from Jake.
'HAD SEX LAST NITE.'
Matt laughed and replied.
'ME 2.'
'1ST PINTS ON ME,' Jake responded, much to Matt's approval.

'You hussy!' Gemma gawped admiringly at Abi. 'I can't believe you did that!'

'Did what?' Fen, coming through the front door, asked.

'Yay! McCabe returns!' Abi sang.

'Stop changing the subject, strumpet,' Gemma said with an emphatic crossing of her arms, her raven curls swishing about her face like angry serpents.

'What subject?' Fen enquired. 'What's she done now?' She plonked her bag on the settee and joined Gemma's side, crossing her own arms over her far less substantial bust and, therefore, to a lesser effect.

Abi giggled coquettishly. 'Fen?' she said gingerly, tweaking tufts of her blonde crop.

'Yes, Miss Baker?' Fen replied, arms still folded in a teacher-like fashion.

'You know Mr Matthew?' Abi said with theatrical shyness and an uncharacteristically coy lowering of the eyes.

Fen looked puzzled. Their landlord was called Mr Michaels. 'Who?'

'For God's sake,' said Gemma, more exasperated with Abi than Fen, 'Matthew. Matt. Lover-boy In The Offing.'

'Oh,' said Fen, 'him.'

'Well,' said Abi, all sparkly, 'you know *him*?'

'Er, yes,' said Fen, having no clue where the conversation was going.

'Well,' Abi continued, looking utterly triumphant, 'you know his *flatmate*, horny Jake?'

'Yes,' Fen said, with a slight frown, 'he of the goatee and flirtatious manner.'

'Hmm,' Abi hummed appreciatively.

122

'He *is* good-looking,' Fen agreed artlessly.

'For God's sake,' Gemma exclaimed, 'the girl and boy played doctors and nurses all last night.'

'What?' Fen looked amazed.

'And no, I do not mean that they were in Casualty at the Royal Free,' Gemma added.

Abi raised one eyebrow most lasciviously. 'He was *good*,' she slurred in an impressive southern drawl.

'Blimey!' Fen marvelled, the penny dropping visibly as her eyes widened and her jaw gaped. 'Did *you*? Do *it*? With *Jake*?'

'Yup!' Abi confirmed nonchalantly.

'Matt's flatmate?' Fen double-checked.

'Yup!' Abi shrugged.

'Good God!' Fen exclaimed. 'Where? When? How?' She paused. 'Quick! White wine!'

There was no white wine, and as Gemma and Fen's thirst for details could not be quenched by a time-consuming trip to the off licence, the housemates made do instead with the bottle of port kept for emergencies. They toasted Abi, while Abi toasted Jake's dexterity of digit and tongue and 'stonking great hard-on'. Fen, who had craved a luxuriate in a bubble bath to mull over James and think of Matt, was now pleased for the distraction away from such introversion.

And the fact that I'm saved, by the enormity of Abi's conquest, from divulging my dilemma and having them laid bare for dissection.

'I can't *believe* you did that!' Gemma, impressed, said as more of the previous night's antics were revealed.

'I can't believe *he* did *that*!' Fen exclaimed, wrinkling her nose at a particularly lurid detail concerning Jake's tongue.

'You get a taste for it,' Abi shrugged with a sly grin. Fen pretended she was going to throw up.

'So,' Gemma concluded, draining the dregs of the bottle between the three glasses, 'we just need young Fenella to set the wheels turning with Mr Matthew, then you lot can be quite the cosy foursome.'

'Wait up,' Abi said, sounding a little concerned and looking rather horrified, 'it was one night of unbridled passion. It's not leading on to anything twosomey, let alone foursomey.'

'God,' Fen said, quite indignant, 'you imply that's far more distasteful than half those things you let that he-man do to you last night!'

'I'm going to have a bath,' Abi yawned, 'anyone want my water? It'll be Clarins bath tonic.'

'It'll be contaminated,' Fen goaded, 'I'd catch something! I'll wait, dear. You go and have a good scrub.'

Abi, though, licked the tip of her index finger and scored an imaginary tick in the air.

Matt and Jake were sitting on plush red velvet in a booth encrusted with Aztec designs in reclaimed mosaic. In Soho. Strange noises, which could have been tribal, or workmen, or terribly avant-garde music, or not music at all, filtered through the private members' bar from speakers hidden behind wafts of chiffon. They were sipping a rather peculiar vodka and hadn't ventured into the complimentary nibbles because it was difficult to tell if they were animal, vegetable or mineral. Despite the cutting-edge trendiness of the surroundings and post-modern vodka, the other people looked decidedly normal. Matt wondered whether this was a source of disappointment for the club's owners.

'I thought vodka was meant to be odourless and tasteless,' Matt remarked, 'which is why it is so easy to drink.'

'This has a scent and a taste to it,' Jake agreed, sniffing and sipping.

'Not that I'm complaining,' said Matt, sniffing and sipping.

'No,' Jake hurried, 'nor I. Another? Shall we move on to lager?'

The meticulously attired and coiffured bar staff studiously ignored increasingly obvious attempts from Matt and Jake to catch their attention so Matt went to the bar. He returned with vodka.

'The lager is Latvian,' he explained to Jake, 'I didn't think we should risk it.'

They chinked glasses and Jake lit a cigarette, drawing on it in a leisurely fashion and blowing the smoke through his nose, eyes half closed and fixed contemplatively on a bit of broken glass that was the centrepiece of the mosaic on the far wall.

'I shagged your intended's flatmate,' Jake said, tapping ash into the ashtray and suddenly hoping it was an ashtray and not art or some receptacle for the pips or stalks or inners or outers of the unidentifiable nibbles.

'Who?' Matt said, not thinking of Fen and wondering if Jake referred to his ex, Julia.

'Abi,' Jake drawled.

'*Who?*' Matt responded, because he thought his ex's flatmate was called Josie.

'The bleach-blonde pixie who lives with your Vanilla MeCrave,' Jake explained, slightly baffled and wondering whether the vodka was having a more potent effect on Matt or himself.

'Fen!' Matt exclaimed, half to Jake and half to himself.

Why should he have been thinking of Fen? Judith was the last person he went to bed with. His ex before that. Fen – never.

'She was rather good,' Jake nodded, as if with great discernment.

Matt smirked in that charmingly puerile way that remains the prerogative of all men, whatever their age. 'How? When? More vod!'

'Great bod!' Jake smirked back.

'Will you see her again?' Matt asked.

Jake swished the ice-cubes around his glass and tipped his head from side to side. 'Probably,' he said, 'I'd quite like to check out Gemma too.' Matt shook his head in mock exasperation. 'A glass of white wine,' Jake shrugged, 'a glass of red – sometimes you feel like blonde, sometimes brunette. Milk chocolate, plain chocolate. The one, or sometimes the other. Something sparkly and light, or something dusky and more sultry.'

'I *cannot*,' Matt enunciated, 'believe you are contemplating it.'

'Anyway, what's your story?' Jake moved on, at ease with his personal proclivities when it came to sex. 'Your sweetheart was not home last night. I peeked in her bedroom though. Very spic and span. And with chains and manacles strategically placed above the bed.'

'Sod off,' Matt laughed.

'Anyway, what about you – last night,' Jake encouraged.

'Judith. At work. Deputy director.'

'Matthew!' Jake exclaimed, 'Not *Judith*! Not *at* work?'

'Yes – Judith,' Matt confirmed, 'no – Bermondsey.'

'*Bermondsey*?' Jake exclaimed as if the place were commensurate with some very depraved act. And then he totally took Matt off his guard. 'Nice mess, mate,' Jake proclaimed, with slight disapproval. 'You fancy the English Rose who hides away in the Archive and yet you go and shag the Mad Woman who wants to oust the director and take over the art world. I know all about Judith – and from the way you've spoken about her, I presumed you didn't much like her.'

Matt considered this. Then he shrugged. 'I don't really. We simply had sex.'

Jake considered this. Then he shrugged. 'Believe me, it's rarely simple.'

Matt considered this. Then he shrugged. 'She made a pass at me. I was drunk. Simple.'

'What are you going to do?' Jake asked, 'about Good Girl in the Archive? And Wicked Witch in the Big Office?'

'I'll pursue the former and be mature about the latter,' said Matt. 'I guess I've done the rebound thing now. I'm cleansed and purged and have a clean slate to see what might happen with Fen.'

'Let's hope Judas will be "mature" about it,' Jake said, a little glumly because thrusting career women intimidated

126

him slightly (probably because he had been cuckolded by one once). 'Ideally, a zipless fuck should happen with a woman you won't see again, not one you work with on a daily basis.'

'Zips aside, it was definitely no-strings sex,' Matt said, 'after all, she made all the moves.'

'Sure,' said Jake, who actually wasn't sure at all.

There are always strings, Jake thought as he ventured into the black marble cavern he presumed was the Gents. *There'll even be strings with Abi – if I'm lucky, she'll just want to tie me up with them or, better still, allow me to strap her to the bed with them.*

James sat up late watching television. He wondered, fleetingly, if Fen had arrived home safely. And what she was doing. Asleep? Awake? Eating? Boyfriend? Barry had diarrhoea. Beryl was trying to fuss over him.

SEVENTEEN

*F*en adored both her sisters. Being the middle girl, it was as if she constantly looked from this way to that, from left to right, much as she did the palms of her hands. On the one hand, if she looked up, a year older than her, she'd find Philippa. Pip – unusual and outgoing from an early age. Fen had always been in awe of Pip's ability to entertain, to hold court in such an amenable way. Pip was an accomplished acrobat and an adorable clown, a master of both spontaneous flikflaks and polished slapstick. Fen marvelled at Pip's strongest personality trait – to be bright and carefree but never self-centred. By comparison, Fen felt herself to be dull, unable to do even a cartwheel or to recount the shortest of jokes. Pip, though, wished she could have that serenity that was so effortless for Fen. For Pip to be quiet, controlled, thoughtful, necessitated yogic breathing and a slow countdown for at least five minutes.

On the other hand, if Fen looked down, a year her junior, she'd find Catriona. Cat. Fen admired Cat's single-mindedness and her passion for all things athletic. When in Derbyshire, while Fen day-dreamed in the heather or under the shelter of a drystone wall, she'd marvel at Cat charging around the moors on her mountain bike; whether staying on in the most precarious of situations or falling off dramatically. Similarly, whilst Fen might stroll along the lane, eyes low so she could spy plants and flowers, Cat would belt past, perhaps two miles into a five-mile hill run, her eyes fixed ahead, always forward, always making strides. It was Cat's blueprint for life, Fen decided. And now that her younger sister had chucked out the despicable boyfriend, and though she was suffering so, she was still managing to stride ahead, planning to leave Britain to report on the Tour de France and further her career as a sports journalist.

Philippa, Fenella, Catriona. From the earliest age, they had rarely been referred to by their full names. Unless they were being scolded. Or were lost in the woods. Or had emitted a sonorous belch at an inopportune moment (Django assured them that there *were* times when it was acceptable to do so). Or had sworn with one of the forbidden expletives (*bugger* and *bollocks* and *bloody* were allowed). Or had rejected Django's cuisine. Or had scored an anomalously high grade in any science subject at school.

The day that Fen returned from Derbyshire was the day that Cat finally split from her long-term but poor excuse for a boyfriend. Currently, Cat is desperately low. She fears she will never feel anything but the leaden sickness weighing heavy in her stomach; the feeling of panic lurking at the base of her throat; the notion filling her mind that she might never love or be loved again; the searing pain of her heart cracking – surely moments away from breaking altogether. And yet, lucky Cat McCabe. Her eldest sister Pip keeps her distracted and entertained during the day and her older sister Fen is with her each evening, staying the night; listening, soothing, advising. It is these three qualities, held in abundance by Fen, which Cat and Pip have always depended on; drawn upon; coveted.

Matt, however, didn't know of Fen's younger sister's crisis. All he knew was that, since her return from Derbyshire, Fen had seemed somewhat remote. She'd been keeping to

129

herself, mostly taking her lunch at her desk, or cross-legged on the floor whilst sorting through 1964. He was a little disappointed. She'd hardly been in to Publications. She'd come out for lunch only the once. She was in early and left early; mostly he didn't realize she had gone until he tried her extension or actually visited the Archive. Bobbie asked him if Fen was on a diet, ''cos she ain't been down for her Jammy Dodgers, I save 'em for her and look how many's stackin' up'. Otter wondered whether Fen had somehow found out about Judith and Matt, and he spent another afternoon gurning and grimacing and throwing himself into his work to prevent himself from divulging this theory to Matt, or merely asking, 'Why the fuck did you have sex with the Tyrant?'

'Are you OK?' Matt had ventured in what he hoped was a sensitive and not prying tone of voice.

'Fine, fine,' Fen said briskly and with a quick smile, 'I want to wrap up 1959 and then have a preliminary peep at 1963 before I go.'

Fen hasn't heard from James. She'd dropped him a line to thank him and to assure him she would be in touch as soon as there was any information. But as yet there hasn't been. So, though she has been tempted to call to say nothing in particular, she hasn't. And there's been no point for him to have contacted her. So he hasn't.

Matt arrived at work early. Jake hadn't been around for most of the week so Matt had indulged in early nights and a relative de-tox from alcohol. (The bottles of Budvar in the fridge didn't really count, he decided. 'If they're an accompaniment to *Crimewatch* or *The Bill* or the *News*,' he reasoned, taking a bottle before watching one of the above, 'then it's merely the same as a humble cup of coffee.') This morning, Matt ordered a caffeinated cappuccino, one sugar please, and a *pain au chocolat*. Just a double espresso for himself. *This'll work*, he assured himself as he walked down

John Islip Street, *it may not be the most direct route to a woman's heart, but certainly it is a step in the right direction and should elicit some response. I've arrived, well armed, good and early. I don't think a chat over breakfast would be decadent or even unreasonable.*

But Fen wasn't in the Archive. She wasn't in the building. And, by ten o'clock, Matt hadn't a clue where she was.

Fen was worried about Cat. Her sister had been the pro-tagonist in finishing the already decaying relationship and, though initially Cat had felt brave, she had quickly sunk and was now pretty inconsolable. Her voice was different, tinged with pure sadness and underlined by a frightening flatness. 'This desolation, Fen,' she had croaked, waking Fen at four in the morning, 'how will I get over it? Oh God, *how*? When? I won't! I won't! I will *always* feel this way.' Fen had cradled her to sleep, kissing the top of her head, whispering, 'I promise you, I *promise* you – you will *so* be OK.' Just before Cat had drifted into a numb sleep she had told Fen, quite emphatically, 'I don't believe you.' And Fen, then, could not sleep. An hour later, Cat awoke crying. She sat up in bed and switched the light on. 'I want him back!' she sobbed, her eyes racing from right to left. 'I can't! I can't! I'd rather be unhappy with him than face an unknown future without him.' Fen knew that if she reasoned with Cat just then, if she pointed out the man's vices, let alone his inadequacies (and he had many of each), if she emphasized how miserable Cat had been in that relationship, she would only hurt her sister more. So she cuddled Cat and felt extremely perplexed.

Not just perplexed. Impotent. There is nothing I can say or do. I just hope I can soothe her.

Being there for Cat, physically, meant just that. Today, Fen would not countenance leaving her until Pip was there for her too. Pip arrived, as scheduled, on the dot of ten. And Fen, handing over the care of Cat, imparted all that was needed with just one look. Like nurses checking each other's charts as one shift ends and the next begins.

'I'd have been happy to have taken the whole day off work,' Fen said to herself as she walked to Camden Town tube station, 'happier, actually, than turning up late. Hopefully I'll just slip in unseen and unannounced.' She wasn't to know that Matt had arrived early, and had gone to the Archive armed with cappuccino and cake for her. She wasn't to know that Judith had announced to Rodney Beaumont that Fen wasn't just leaving early in the evenings, it now appeared she was arriving late in the mornings too. She wasn't to know that, by the time she arrived, Matt had removed the stone-cold cappuccino and eaten the *pain au chocolat* himself.

So, Fen arrived at Trust Art and walked lightly, ever so slightly on tiptoes, up the stairs to her corridor. Fortuitously, Matt was just coming out of the toilet.

'Fen!'

'Hi,' Fen said in a friendly but hasty manner. She kept walking, which required Matt to about-turn so that he could at least keep the conversation going. 'I'm a bit late today.'

'Everything OK?' Matt enquired with a tone of voice he hoped was friendly and not nosy.

'Yes, yes,' said Fen, reaching the door of the Archive, 'but I should really crack on.'

'Sure,' said Matt, a little baffled. 'How about a sandwich later?'

'Um,' Fen was reluctant, 'I'll see how the morning's work goes.'

'You have to eat,' Matt said.

'I know, I know,' Fen replied. She looked agitated. 'I'll see.' She entered the Archive and let the door close behind her.

What the bloody hell is wrong with her? Matt wondered as he walked back to Publications, wondering why he was slightly irritated.

With Cat occupying so much of Fen's time and thoughts, it was a relief not to talk about it. *If I let them know here that there are family problems*, Fen had reasoned, because she

132

had at one point thought of mentioning it to Rodney, *then every time they see me they'll ask how things are. And sometimes it's good, it's nice, just to have respite.*

Fen refused Matt and Otter's invitation to join them for sandwiches, but they managed to persuade her that they would be her take-away boys. She wasn't that hungry, but she knew it was because she hadn't yet eaten. So she was sensible and ordered brie and tomato on baguette, mayonnaise no butter, a cappuccino, and an orange juice. It was Otter's idea to add the slice of icing-sugar-coated chocolate finger cake. Fen was touched. She presumed that, because Matt had delivered it, it had been his gesture. When Matt knocked and entered with a cup of coffee a little later, he found her talking quietly into the phone. She just slightly turned her back on him. It seemed furtive.

'I know,' he heard her say, 'I know you do. I just don't know what to do either.'

Then he heard her tell whomever it was she was speaking to that it was breaking her heart too. So he left. He still felt irritated; now he felt disappointed too. He knew eavesdropping was daft and destructive, that picking up fag-ends was unsavoury and pointless. But still, he felt disconcerted all afternoon. And when Judith came into Publications and suggested he accompany her to a private view at the Whitechapel gallery the following Tuesday, he accepted. Slightly absent-mindedly. Forgetting, just then, that he'd even been to a private view with Judith. Temporarily not remembering what had happened afterwards. And then his ex-girlfriend called, in tears, proclaiming love and death. Suddenly, Matt had a huge headache and actually said, somewhat histrionically, to Otter, 'Why can't I be gay! Bugger women!'

'Because,' Otter quipped, 'it would mean bugger *men*! *Literally*, dearest. And men, in my vast and lurid experience, are ultimately far more demanding than women.'

Matt laughed. He rang his ex-girlfriend back and attempted to soothe her by showing concern for her feelings and sympathy for her plight. It served, though, to delude her that he cared because he'd changed his mind. She rang her best friend to inform her that Matt had just rung! 'He was so sweet! Caring! I'm *sure* he feels it too. Shall I call again? Text message him? E-mail?' Matt received a text message some minutes later, about broken hearts now, wonderful times then, and beauty in the future. Nine kisses. Far more than their combined total in the last months of the relationship. Matt's headache returned, nagging the front of his skull and coursing down to his shoulders.

'Do you think Fen fancies me?' he asked Otter, rolling his head slowly, eyes closed.

'Who wouldn't,' Otter said sweetly, reaching over and giving Matt's shoulder a one-handed massage.

'I fancy *her*. And I have definitely, *definitely* felt a reciprocal vibe,' Matt said, eyes open, happy for Otter to continue tweaking his neck. 'I rather think that was more then than now, though.' Matt looked a little glum. 'I think she's gone off me.'

'Oh shut up, boy. Go to her. Now. And kiss her,' Otter said distractedly. Matt, though, took him at his word and left Publications directly. Otter expected Matt had gone to the loo. He had no idea, until Matt's triumphant return ten minutes later, that he had gone to the Archive and done exactly as Otter had told him.

I never liked him. There was always something – some niggle. He's too charming. Too keen to ingratiate himself.

Fen is staring blankly at a clutch of correspondence from 1967 between the Trust and a wealthy collector called Sutcliffe Marton. It is probably riveting, concerning as it does a Roger Hilton and a Victor Pasmore. But Fen's mind is on Cat. And her ex.

He was a con man, really. Mature and affable on the surface, abusive and screwed-up beneath.

'Wanker!' she hisses. 'I'll kill him.' There's a knock at her door. 'Yes?' she all but barks, slamming the papers down on the desk and rising, hands on hips, eyes dark, as if it is Wanker himself knocking.

It isn't. It's Matt. Though Fen is relieved, she's really not in the mood. She wants to be left in peace to indulge in murderous thoughts. Luckily, Matt attributes Fen's mien to 1967 being in a mess – if the scatter and hurl of papers and documents all around her is anything to go by.

'Hi, Matt,' she says in a tone of voice that is cursory and flat and suggests that her greeting is conditioned etiquette.

'Hi,' says Matt terribly seriously whilst taking three steps towards her, slipping his right arm through the loop made by her hand being on her hip. His hand rests lightly at the small of her back. Or is it the top of her bottom? His other hand cups the back of her head.

God, her hair is soft. She has a biro mark on her cheek.

This is Matt's last thought before he kisses her. He locks gazes with her, not caring that she looks slightly puzzled. Then he presses closed lips against hers. Just presses. No puckering. No tongues. Just a gentle but steady push. He sees that she doesn't look so puzzled now, her pupils have dilated, her frown has softened. He lightens the pressure from his lips and feels hers move instinctively forward to find him. She breathes through her nose. She smells chocolatey. Slightly dusty. Quite nice perfume. She makes a small involuntary sound, as if her breath has accidentally caught her vocal cords. It turns Matt on as much as if she'd been gasping in orgasm. He closes his eyes and slips his tongue lightly along the crack of her lips until they submit and he explores her mouth avidly. He holds her tightly. Her hands are no longer on her hips; one is up behind his back grasping his shoulder-blade, the other is grabbing on to the belt loop of his jeans. And she is kissing him back, indeed she is. Energetically. Emphatically.

He takes his tongue away and hers flits along his lips imploringly. He kisses her many times on the lips, quickly. Then he stands back a little and smiles broadly. Neither of them has a clue what to say, really. Kissing, though a long

135

time coming and longed for some time, was not really part of the day's agenda. Matt takes a step back, raises his hand and lets it fall.

He is aware that Fen has looked instinctively at his groin and has blushed. He glances down. Tent pole. Eiffel Tower. You bet! He doesn't blush. He feels rather proud. He also feels unbelievably horny.

'God I want to fuck you,' he murmurs.

And he goes! He's gone! And Fen stands there, utterly seduced, buzzing between her legs, breasts heaving Brontë style. 'Let's go to bed,' one of her boyfriends had said to her. 'I want to make love to you,' another had serenaded. 'Do you feel ready to take this relationship to a fully sexual level?' another had asked.

God I want to fuck you.

God I want to fuck you.

God I want to fuck you.

Matt's words. They linger in her mind just as the sensation of his kiss is lingering in her mouth. It is the sexiest thing anyone has said. And what turns her on most is the dark-horse element. The intensity of his desire was so unexpected. The phrase employed so un-Matt. Lovely, handsome Matthew Holden, whom Fen has grown used to being charming, polite, well mannered.

She sits down, not knowing what to think. His words are in her head, in her heart, in her sex; repeated and repeated in a deliciously rhythmic way. She glances from hand to hand. *I can't believe I'm about to do this.* She slips her left hand between her legs, closes her thighs around it, closes her eyes, and imagines Matt.

Fen comes. Gorgeous. Like a prelude to what's imminent in reality. She opens her eyes and sees Fetherstone's *Adam*, just the Polaroid she took when in Derbyshire. She doesn't think of James. She retrieves the clutch of papers which had been annoying her so, and now finds their contents utterly scintillating.

* * *

TO: f.mccabe@trustart.co.uk
FROM: m.holden@trustart.co.uk
RE: oscillation

Dear Miss McCabe
That was really very interesting. I'd like to delve deeper
and take it further.
Sincerely
M.Holden

TO: m.holden@trustart.co.uk
FROM: f.mccabe@trustart.co.uk
RE: re: oscillation

Dear Mr Holden
Yes, fascinating. I agree – let's.
Kind regards
F McCabe (Ms)

TO: f.mccabe@trustart.co.uk
FROM: m.holden@trustart.co.uk
RE: re: re: oscillation

Dear Ms
Tonight?
Best wishes
M Holden

TO: m.holden@trustart.co.uk
FROM: f.mccabe@trustart.co.uk
RE:

Dear Mr Holden
Tonight no good.
Apologies.
Ms McC

Nothing came back from the office three doors down. It
perplexed Fen; more worryingly, it prevented much
progress with the job she was being paid to do. She thought

she'd wait half an hour. But what if Matt left early? Ten minutes seemed like an elegant time lapse.

TO: m.holden@trustart.co.uk
FROM: f.mccabe@trustart.co.uk
RE:
Matt
Can't do tonight – but could do tomorrow.
Here's my mobile phone number.
Fen

She had added an upper-case X after her name, which she then changed to lower case, and then removed altogether just before sending.

It's been so long for me. I don't actually know what the etiquette is, unlike Abi and Gemma who know all the Rules and the merits of Playing Hard To Get. So, I'll leave off the 'x'.

But why can't you do tonight, Fen? While the iron is hot? And love is in the air? And while he has a tent pole in his trousers? And you're sticking to your knickers? And you're both feeling just a little triumphant, aroused and ebullient?

I can't do tonight – Cat duty. But I just might be able to do tomorrow night because Pip generally tries not to work on Saturday nights on account of the proliferation of unsavoury requests from stag nights. She doesn't mind doing acrobatics in a leotard. But she does object to drunken prats calling for her tits. Someone gave her a ping-pong ball once, and a twenty-pound note. Pip didn't understand. So she improvised and managed to balance the ball on her nose for a few seconds before performing a trick to make the money disappear. She was quite proud. The bloke was livid.

So, you can do Saturday night?

I can. If Pip is free. If he calls. Oh please do! It's bizarre – I've really never felt single, on account of Julius and his works, but being kissed by Matt has . . . well . . . I hope he calls.

EIGHTEEN

Fen's extension just rang and rang.

James presumed that on Fridays the staff sloped off as early as they could.

He rang again.

They've probably gone to the pub.

He tried the main switchboard.

'I just seen her,' Bobbie squawked, 'she's off home for the weekend. Can I take a message?'

'No,' said James, 'I'll call on Monday.'

'Ta-ra,' said Bobbie.

James took the dogs for a walk. Though they'd been bounding around Mrs Litchfield's all afternoon, they were eternally eager to please, thus wagged their tails and lolloped along getting good and muddy in the process.

'I don't really know,' said James to Beryl who'd brought him a wet and gnarled stick to throw, 'what I'd've said had she answered.' Beryl dived off in the opposite direction to that in which James had hurled the stick. 'I didn't really have anything to say,' he said to his dog who'd come back to him with an imploring look. Barry emerged from the thicket with the stick and Beryl chased him. 'I just felt like phoning her.' It was a nice evening. 'I'd like to see Fen again. And soon.'

Maybe James would go to the Rag and Thistle. Flirt with Melanie. Friday nights were always lively there. 'I'll call Trust Art on Monday, on some pretext or other.'

Or maybe he'd just bath the dogs. Look at the state of them!

'Barry! Leave! Beryl! Come!'

NINETEEN

Alas! The love of women! It is known to be a lovely and a fearful thing.

Byron

Abi felt forsaken. Gemma felt overburdened. Fen felt guilty.

Abi felt a little forsaken. It wasn't enough to divulge with anatomical precision the intimacies of her carnal adventures with Jake to Gemma alone. Abi wanted to observe Fen's eyes pop with amazement, perhaps envy, at her debauchery. She really did like Cat, and sympathized with her plight, but she resented her for monopolizing Fen. Fen was such a good listener. Abi felt bereft. Gemma had good ears, but as her sexual past was just as depraved as Abi's present, her reaction wasn't as satisfying as Fen's would be. Gemma could also be a little judgemental. Fen would just be overawed.

Gemma felt a little overburdened. Where was Fen to gossip with over Abi's sexploits? Gemma was finding Abi a little repetitive and dull; too many outrageous positions and far too many multiple orgasms. Gemma was also finding Jake increasingly attractive and tempting.

Fen felt a little guilty. Though she went directly from work to Cat's flat, and though she stayed up with her sister until the early hours, watching TV and listening to Cat, though she slept in the same bed as her sister and woke any time she woke, Fen was not giving Cat her undivided attention. And she felt bad about this. She was there for her suffering sister more in body than in spirit. Moreover, in her mind, she was in fact giving her entire body, inside and out, to Matt. Fen did feel guilty, but then Cat seemed so caught up within the vortex of her angst that Fen wondered how much constructive use she was at any rate. Nothing she could say seemed to soothe her sister, or make much sense to her, nor really have any effect at all. If Fen could be there in body – a shoulder to cry on, arms to envelope, a body to snuggle against – did it matter all that much that her mind was running rampant, ripping off Matt's clothes and imagining the feel of his lips on her body?

For once, Fen wasn't confusing fact with fiction, reality with fantasy, life with art. It was, at long last and for the first time, unequivocally Matt in her day-dreams. At no point did he metamorphose into the male component in *Abandon*. Or melt into *Adam*. Or assume any characteristic of any other of Julius's male muses. More to the point, as she hadn't looked from hand to hand at all, Matt did not become James either. In fact, Fen hadn't thought about James. She hadn't envisaged anyone other than Matt touching her like that. Or penetrating her. Her envisaging was so vivid it made her gasp. Cat presumed her sister was reacting to her recently imparted details on just how ghastly the last holiday had been with her ex.

'No!' Cat implored, suddenly panicking that she was being too negative. 'I mean, we were *both* going through shit. I was behaving badly myself – stroppy, sulky, unaffectionate. I probably set him off. That's what I mean! That's what I'm saying.' Fen passed her the tissues. Fen knew how destructive and pointless Cat's train of thought was. But still she couldn't stop herself from wondering what Matt's body was like.

I think a smooth chest, with just a masculine smattering of hair coursing down from stomach to groin. I doubt whether he's downright hairy. Or completely smooth. And I wouldn't mind either, anyway.

142

'Shall I phone him?' Cat asked Fen, who was herself wondering whether she should phone Matt.

'Don't!' Fen pleaded to them both. 'Sleep on it.'

Phone me, Matthew Holden. Sleep with me.

Matt couldn't phone Fen just then. And he certainly couldn't sleep with her. His ex-girlfriend was sobbing into his shoulder, her hand alternately grasping his arm feebly, or rubbing the crotch of his jeans weakly. Both in a futile bid to appeal to, to rouse, his caring side or his sexual side; *either* side which he had once devoted to her. But it was like calling and calling a telephone number that has been changed. Ringing and ringing. No answer. Nobody's home. Nobody's there – they've gone, left. When? Where? How do I get back in touch?

'I know we can make it work,' Julia wept, 'we've been through so much. How can you just walk away?'

Matt did truly feel for her, love her still. But though he willingly held her, his mind and therefore his heart were not in it.

'Is there someone else?' she asked, her eyes wild. 'Is there someone else?'

'No,' Matt told her.

Not yet.

He felt lousy. His relationship with this woman was categorically over. There would be nothing wrong, furtive, untoward, about taking things further with Fen. And yet, he felt guilty. Phoning Fen tomorrow had now changed from being an event loaded with pleasurable anticipation, to one that suddenly just seemed wrong and now probably wouldn't happen at all.

'I'm going to call you a cab,' he told Julia, who was clinging on to him as if she was clinging on to a glimmer of hope, to a strand remaining of their threadbare relationship.

'Don't throw me out,' she sobbed, 'please let me stay.'

Matt suddenly wanted to yell at her. But he bit his tongue.

He'd yelled at her before. Like she'd screamed at him. It had been pointless.

'I'm going to call you a cab,' he repeated quietly.

He tries zapping through TV channels with a bottle of Bud to hand after she's gone. But nothing catches his attention. Or tickles his fancy. So he goes to bed and tries to have a wank but nothing tickles his fancy and his cock won't rise to the occasion. He tries, fleetingly, to think of Fen, to recall the Archive that afternoon. But he can't bring her face into his mind. He can't even lie in bed looking forward to phoning her the next day because he isn't going to phone her.

Bloody bloody women. I think I need a break from them altogether.

TWENTY

*F*en walked to work with some trepidation. Matt hadn't called her over the weekend and she'd been furious with herself for glancing at her phone with alarming regularity throughout the two days. She had even dialled her voice mail, despite common sense and the most basic knowledge of telephone technology assuring her that if a message had been left, her phone would have beeped accordingly and flashed up a little picture of a telephone receiver. On Sunday morning, she went back to her house, taking Cat with her. 'For fresh air and a change of scene,' Fen told her sister.

More, though, for me to check the home answerphone and see if Abi might offer any information, indirectly or otherwise, on account of Jake being the cad's flatmate.

Neither Abi nor Gemma was at home. And there were no messages for Fen on the answering machine, no Post-its proclaiming 'Jake says call Matt' stuck to the fridge, no scrawled number hastily penned on the corner of the newspaper by the phone. Nor on the back of the paper bag from the bakery lying scrunched by the toaster. Nor on Gemma's bed, or Abi's dressing-table.

Fen's emotional reaction and her behaviour unnerved her. For so long, she hadn't been remotely bothered by love and all its panoply; she had found romantic day-dreaming, or simple masturbation, more than satisfactory. She had deemed the traumas many women suffer on account of men to be self-inflicted and for the most part unnecessary. Now, however, here was she not just experiencing all the pangs and neuroses she'd hitherto read about and ridiculed, she was also exhibiting textbook behaviour of the Forsaken Woman.

Oddly, though Fen had spent most of Saturday feeling unattractive and a fool (*Why hasn't he called?*) and by Sunday she was silently cursing the bastard *(Who the hell is he anyway?)*, now Monday sees her feeling rather timid and dreading seeing him (*Why didn't he call? Why did he kiss me like that? Does he or doesn't he find me attractive? If he does, why didn't he call? And if he doesn't, why kiss me?*).

Standing pensively in the queue for a cappuccino, Fen was struck by a notion so feasible that she felt utterly jubilant and practically skipped to Trust Art.

How could I be such a cow! Poor Matt probably won't be at work today at all! Why on earth didn't I think of this before, why the hell didn't I credit him more? He probably has the flu! That's it! Even if it's just a cold – we all know how such ailments knock a man down and render him incapable of little more than groaning and being bedridden!

Fen, dearest, it's almost May. And mild.

Food poisoning, then. Shut up.

Fen was pleasantly surprised to hear Otter and Matt chatting as she passed by Publications, though she was slightly miffed that there was no e-mail, let alone cappuccino, awaiting her in the Archive. By lunch-time, with no visit and no telephone call, she was starting to feel glum again. This was alleviated by Fen reminding herself fiercely that these very feelings were precisely why she'd forsaken men for such a relatively long time.

All this 'will he won't he', all that 'does he doesn't he' – it's a waste of my time and a drain on my emotions.

146

She threw herself into her work, skipping lunch altogether and not feeling hungry in the slightest. Bobbie's Jammy Dodgers more than sufficed. Most exciting was that, by tea-time, Tate Britain had returned her call, requesting more information and expressing interest in the Derbyshire Fetherstones. She thought of James but then thought she oughtn't to be spending time thinking of him at all. Not yet. Not until there was sure business to discuss. But then she wondered if he'd appreciate a courtesy call.

'Mr Caulfield?'

There was a pause. 'Yes?'

'It's Fen,' said Fen.

There was silence.

'McCabe,' Fen said, a little embarrassed.

'Hullo, Fen McCabe,' James said.

Fen felt a little awkward. 'Just thought you'd like to know that Tate Britain has expressed an interest in your Fetherstones. I mean, it's no done deal but they'd like to know more so I thought you'd like to know.' She was gabbling.

'That sounds promising,' James said, 'but I'm just on my way out. Can we talk some other time?'

'Yes, of course,' Fen rushed, 'I mean Tate Britain would definitely be my first—'

James butted in. 'I really have to go – let's talk soon.' And he hung up. He hadn't told Fen that he was taking Beryl to the vet to have a boil on her paw lanced.

Fen continued to hold the receiver to her ear. She wished she hadn't phoned. She was suddenly tired. She needed a Jammy Dodger.

'It's the Wild Woman of Bleeding Borneo!' Bobbie declared on seeing Fen. 'What have you been up to?'

'Just 1974.' Fen attempted to quash Bobbie's wink wink, nudge nudging. Judith, who was loitering by the pigeon-holes, wasn't convinced.

I'm going to have a lovely luxuriate in Neal's Yard bath oil when I'm home, Fen decided, leaving Reception, *wash my hair in all things Aveda. And then, methinks, drink copious amounts of vodka.*

She enters the Archive. Matt is there. He is seemingly engrossed in a hastily scribbled note from David Hockney to his father.

'Hey, Fen,' he says, with no hint of a cold and good colour to his cheeks putting paid to her theory of flu or food poisoning. She swiftly settles on a weekend-long migraine. Which actually isn't far from the truth.

'Matt,' she says, hoping that she's smiling in a non-affected way though she's been taken off her guard.

Am I meant to be aloof? Alluring? Angry? Amorous? And that's only the As. How about Baffled? Bolshy? Brazen?

'I'm sorry about not calling you,' Matt says and he does look apologetic, his blue eyes searching her face for forgiveness, his hair going this way and that, suggesting his regret has caused him to ruffle and scratch it. He's wearing a crisp, mint-green shirt open at the neck, rolled up at the sleeves and tucked nonchalantly into black jeans. Fen feels a little dusty by comparison. Her white shirt is grey around the cuffs and only half tucked into her jeans, which she's worn all weekend.

'Don't worry,' Fen says, brushing away any awkwardness he might be feeling.

'Did you have a good weekend?' he asks politely.

'Fabulous,' Fen lies, 'but too short.'

'I –' Matt starts, twitching his lips and tilting his head whilst looking at her.

Longingly. He's definitely looking at me longingly. And he looks tired. So I'll forgive him. Because, at the end of the day – literally – he is here, after all, looking for me, in my Archive.

'Are you free tonight?' he asks.

Fen purses her lips apologetically and shakes her head. 'Sorry,' she says, knowing this is the response that Abi and Gemma would have her make. 'Tomorrow,' she ventures, 'I have no plans tomorrow.'

148

*The girls will probably cringe and chastise me. I'm
probably meant to wait at least forty-eight hours.*

'Great,' Matt smiles, 'wonderful.'

Fen sees that he looks awkward. It makes her feel calm,
confident even. She goes to Matt and puts her hand gently on
his neck. Ever so slightly on tiptoes, she kisses him lightly,
mainly on his cheek but just catching the corner of his lips.
Before she can move away, Matt grabs her against him and
slips his tongue immediately into her mouth. She is so
turned on by this forcefulness that she bucks her body
against his instinctively. She laps at him readily. His hand is
grasping her buttock; the other is against her back. He can
feel no bra strap. He is desperate to see her breasts. Feeling
them through her shirt will have to do for the time being.
Until tomorrow. He makes an appreciative noise in his
throat whilst he kisses her, which she echoes when her
breast is being fondled. She's grasping his buttocks too. She
can even feel his straining cock against her despite its being
behind two layers of denim.

And this is precisely how Judith St John finds them. Her
two employees. Archivist and editor. Heavy petting in the
Archive. She is outraged.

'For God's sake!' she barks.

Fen and Matt leap apart and are speechless. Everyone is
acutely aware of wet mouths and the impressive bulge in
Matt's trousers and Fen's flush and Judith's indignation.
Judith doesn't just hold her ground and command their
darting eyes to her steely glare, she steps right into the
Archive. In silence, she holds the door open and raises an
eyebrow which suggests Matt should leave. Immediately. Fen
feels backed into a corner though neither woman has moved.
What excuse can she give? Mind you, what crime has she
committed? What should she say? She shouldn't look guilty.
She should be grinning. She feels incapable of doing the latter
and fears she is doing the former involuntarily. She waits an
eternity for Judith's response. Judith comes close to her and
picks up the Hockney letter, studying it with great interest.

'Fenella,' she says at long last, as if to a gifted but tiresome child, 'I just thought I'd pop in because I know you like to leave on the dot. I was wondering if we could have lunch tomorrow? I'd love to hear an update on the Archive.' She says it with barbed affability and apparently no memory of what she has just witnessed.

'Yes!' Fen enthuses, more from gratitude and relief than from the invitation itself. 'I'd love to.'

'Super,' Judith smiles spikily, 'I'll book the Tate restaurant for one p.m. Come and fetch me from my office at ten to.'

'OK!' Fen gabbles. 'That would be wonderful. I'll really look forward to it. I won't have my morning croissant and I'll try to abstain from Bobbie's biscuit barrel. I've never eaten in the Tate restaurant, just the canteen which is really quite good. And I've loads to tell you. Not just about the Archive but there seems to be some movement on those Derbyshire Fetherstones too!'

Judith, however, smile fixed in place while her mind whirrs behind, is already on her way out.

She passes Otter. Otter looks simultaneously horrified and elated. Matt has just recounted the ambush. In an instant, from a glance at Otter twisting his fingers and desperately avoiding eye contact, Judith knows that he knows.

'I'm taking Fenella for lunch,' she says, connivingly, 'I feel there are a few things she ought to know.'

'Oh God,' Otter wails quietly, though Matt is in a meeting downstairs with Rodney and Fen has left, 'perhaps it is my duty to enlighten poor Fen before Judith does. Otherwise, it could be the end of something that won't have had the chance to unfurl.'

What a bizarre end to a very long day, Fen contemplates, walking down John Islip Street to Pimlico tube.

It isn't over yet, Fen.

Fen had a lousy journey home and, too exhausted to walk up the escalator at Camden Town tube station, she is fantasizing about vodka, lime and soda, Neal's Yard aroma-therapy bath, Aveda hair products and Clarins body lotion, too. She makes a quick detour to the fruit and vegetable market in Inverness Street to buy limes, unwilling for her fantasy to be compromised in any way. When she arrives home, it doesn't seem that anyone is in so she troops, shoeless, up to her room and lies on her bed awhile, waiting patiently for the water to be absolutely piping hot. She dozes off, happy that sleep should prevent impatience with the temperamental immersion heater. She wakes, undresses and wraps a towel around her. She goes down a floor to the bathroom. A floor beneath that, the front door opens.

'Hiya,' calls Abi.

'Hey, babe,' calls Fen, hand on the bathroom door handle, 'just going to have a bath. There's lime for vodka – do you fancy rustling us up a couple?'

Fen enters the bathroom and comes across a rustling couple. It is Gemma. And Jake. Jake has snatched his hand from Gemma's unbuttoned jeans, revealing a glimpse of Gemma's snatch in the process. Not that there's much to see, Gemma having gone for a Brazilian bikini wax over the weekend.

'I'll have one too,' Gemma calls down to Abi, kissing a flabbergasted Fen on the cheek as she leaves the bathroom. 'Jake's just arrived – shall I ask him if he fancies one?' Jake follows Gemma, kissing Fen's cheek too. 'Well?' Gemma whispers saucily to Jake, well in Fen's earshot though she'd rather not hear. 'Do you fancy one then?'

'Sure,' Jake murmurs back, 'with a twist.'

Fen runs her bath full blast, rejecting Neal's Yard for the last glob of her Penhaligon's lily of the valley bath essence for added luxury. She emits a near-orgasmic sigh as she eases herself down into the fragrant foamy water.

Abi comes in with her vodka. Fen thinks how bright and funky she looks, like a pop pixie. She must have bleached her hair over the weekend. Her skin is clear and her eyes sparkle. 'Don't be too long, Fen,' she says, 'Jake's taking us all out for sushi.'

'I don't like sushi,' Fen says truthfully, the weight of the day making her visibly sink a little deeper into the bath. 'Too raw,' she says, 'too fishy.'

TWENTY-ONE

A lover without indiscretion is no lover at all.
                                                Thomas Hardy

Eating   ☐
Drinking   ☐
Both   ☐
W1   ☐
N1   ☐
NW1   ☐
Base 1   ☐
Base 2   ☐
Base 3   ☐
Bullseye   ☐
Breakfast: *Continental*   ☐
               Full English   ☐
               Cappuccino & Croissant at your desk   ☐
               In your dreams, Holden   ☐

Please tick appropriate box(es) and return to Publications (sealed envelope advisable) by lunch-time.

Fen munched the *pain au chocolat* and sipped the cappuccino Matt had provided, whilst she read and reread and giggled at his note. He was a flirt – but a creative one at that. She didn't know which boxes she should tick. She knew which ones, privately, she'd like to tick, but she didn't know if she ought. She felt a little awkward. Matt's inventiveness touched her, his presumptuousness turned her on; the fact that he was obviously looking forward to the evening charmed her. But still she felt a little trepidation. Was all of this just too full on? She had so little recent experience to go by. Was Matt too forward for someone who, after all, had only recently split from a long-term girlfriend?

Two hours later, though, she put 1977 to one side to reread Matt's list once again. She chewed her pen thoughtfully, then made her marks.

Eating	☐
Drinking	☐
Both	☑
W1	☑
N1	☐
NW1	☐
Base 1	☐
Base 2	☐
Base 3	☐
Bullseye	☐

Base 1 ☐ ⎫
Base 2 ☐ ⎪ *ANYTHING BASE . . .*
Base 3 ☐ ⎬
Bullseye ☐ ⎭

Breakfast:

Continental ☐ ⎫ DEPENDS HOW
Full English ☐ ⎪ SATED THE
Cappuccino & Croissant at your desk ☐ ⎬ NIGHT BEFORE
In your dreams, Holden ☐ ⎭ LEAVES ME . . .

Please tick appropriate box(es) and return to Publications (sealed envelope advisable) by lunch-time.

She couldn't find an envelope, so she slipped the sheet of paper into an acid-free folder and stuck a Post-it note to it, on which she'd written 'Information from the Archive. FAO Matthew Holden Esq'. She hovered outside Publications and, believing the room to be empty, entered. Otter was there. No Matt. Good. She knew Otter was both party to the attraction between her and Matt and that he actively encouraged it.

'Hey, Otter,' she said, 'just leaving this for Matt.' She

placed the file on his desk. 'We have a hot date tonight!' she confided in a whisper.

'Oh, dearest Fenella,' Otter groaned, holding his head theatrically in his hands while sheets of paper fluttered and sighed all around him.

'Otter!' Fen soothed, going to him and laying a hand gently on his twig-twist shoulders, presuming it was some finer point of punctuation or the choice between adjectives which vexed him. 'Are you OK?'

'But you're having lunch with Judith?' he wailed, dragging his palms down his cheeks so that he resembled an emaciated bloodhound.

'Yes,' Fen confirmed artlessly, 'but I can eat like a horse at lunch-time and still manage a hearty dinner.'

'Darling girl.' Otter looked and sounded as though he was going to weep. Fen felt a little alarmed. Only, Matt came in and she suddenly felt it was more important to exit hastily and leave him alone with the Archive folder, than it was to discover what grieved Otter so. Matt regarded the head-bowed Otter and thought him to be a trifle odd, which he regularly thought anyway, thus finding nothing ominous in his assistant's deportment today.

'Cheer up,' Matt said lightly, 'it might never happen.'

Otter sighed. 'Oh but it will, sweet knave, it will.'

Matt saw the Archive file instantly but busied himself with a couple of phone calls before looking inside. He was delighted with Fen's response and went to the Archive to return the folder and sneak a snog. Meanwhile, Judith St John entered Publications, and spoke briefly at Otter whilst sauntering over to Matt's desk and glancing at his form for Fen. She noted Fen's ticks. Immediately, Judith sensed lead in her stomach and tasted bile at the back of her throat. But she had more than one trump card up her sleeve. She left Publications making no comment to Otter who was gnawing his right thumbnail, having already chewed the fingernails of that hand.

Otter didn't want to have lunch with Matt. He couldn't

stomach a thing, full stop – not food, nor talk of Fen or Judith. He practically ran down to Victoria station to hide, to get away. He spent a very full lunch-hour browsing around the concourse shops; the tannoy comfortingly loud so that he didn't have to listen to the dilemma in his head.

Fen had spent her frugal freelance days on a lunch-time diet of toast and Marmite (with tinned *alphabetti-spaghetti* if she'd had an article published); her lunch times at Trust Art had been perfectly served by sandwiches from the nearby café. Therefore, to have lunch at the Tate Gallery Restaurant was a real event. Accordingly, she had dressed very carefully that morning, more for lunch than for the evening with Matt which was to follow. She had no desire, let alone the wardrobe, to match Judith's penchant for Armani (always collarless, jacket long, skirt short or trousers slim in navy, black or charcoal, T-shirt in crisp cream mercerized cotton), but she had teamed her most expensive skirt (a lilac-grey, crepey, bias-cut just-below-the-knee Ghost special) with a slate-grey Agnés B cardigan. And a selection of Gemma's Bobbi Brown eye make-up too. Matt of course thought she'd dressed for him. And the notion, along with the indisputably braless fact of Fen's tits beneath the cardigan, had made him kiss her very intensely when returning the folder.

Fen chose from the menu carefully, nothing with any juice or sauce that might splash or stain. Smoked salmon to start. Grilled corn-fed chicken with celeriac mash to follow. *Crème brûlée* to round things off nicely. Judith chose salad to start and a salad with goat's cheese (which she pushed to one side) to follow. And fresh fruit salad for dessert.

Come on! Come on! What was said? What was the conversation like? Did it flow? What was discussed?
Actually, she was really sweet to me!
Did she call you Fenella or Fen?
Fen. Throughout.
Do you suspect it was a veneer?

No! I'd much rather credit her with having an unfortunate manner in company. She was very attentive – asked me lots of probing questions about the Archive.

And?

Was I enjoying myself, had I made friends amongst the staff? You know, usual stuff.

No! More details.

Well, she was even light-hearted about catching Matt and me! She said, 'Fen, I doubt whether the Archive is the most salubrious of setting for clinches with Matthew.' I laughed and she raised her eyebrow and told me to be careful.

To be careful?

Yes. Actually, I wasn't quite sure of the meaning behind that one either. Was she talking about safe sex? Or the metal corners of the shelving being hazardous? Or stains on the papers? Or people not as tolerant as her walking in on us? Anyway, the conversation became quite girly – I told her we were having a hot date tonight. In W1, food and drink – I didn't say about the bases and breakfast.

What was her response?

Actually, she was fiddling with a message on her mobile phone and fiddling with the spun sugar on her fruit salad and trying to summon the bill. I don't think she was that interested.

Not that interested?

No. I think Judith St John is wedded to work and promoting her image as a thrusting young force in the art world. I think respect is what she lusts after, and success is what turns her on. She was interested in the Tate's response to the Derbyshire Fetherstones. There's an acquisitions meeting in three weeks' time. I'll call James Caulfield and see if he can arrange to have the works sent down.

'For fuck's sake,' James sighs, wriggling out of his boots. He is dressed and ready to go to his afternoon assignments, having come home for lunch and to give Barry his antibiotics. He was just about to hold the door open for the dogs when the house phone rings. Whether James is merely stuck in his ways or whether he has standards, he resolutely adheres to a policy of no boots beyond the hallway mat. The phone is ringing.

'Call my fucking mobile, why don't you?'

The boots have to come off. He jars his left ankle in the process and winces. He practically skates across the flagstones to answer the phone.

'Yes!' he barks.

Fen is taken aback by the aggression.

'Who is this?' he demands.

'Mr Caulfield?'

In an instant, James knows it's Fen. The pain in his ankle subsides; the fact that Beryl is chewing his right boot is irrelevant. Barry is engrossed in giving his balls a meticulous licking. James sees that, subconsciously, he is holding his own testicles. It's the sound of Fen's voice. It's a balm. It has smoothed away the furrows of irritability from his brow, it has soothed his ricked ankle.

'Mr Caulfield?'

The fairer sex indeed. Remember, I spend most my life listening to dogs snoring or barking, or to middle-aged busybodies divulging their opinions, and to me droning on to myself.

'Hullo?' Fen says again. 'It's Fen McCabe. From London. From Trust Art. The Fetherstones.'

'Hullo, Fen,' James says in an instantly soothed tone of voice, 'this is James.'

Fen is smiling subconsciously. She can smell Derbyshire. She can feel the spring breeze on her cheeks. She is relatively full from lunch at the Tate but she could easily manage a slice of Mrs Merifield's Bakewell tart from the Rag and Thistle. The Archive is all brown boxes and grey shelving and paint that needs a face-lift. Keeper's Dwelling smells of wood fires and has dogs that are effusive in their affection. And Fetherstones. Three of them. 'How are you, Fen?' James asks. Barry has finished cleaning his testicles and is now humping his rump in a peculiar dragging fashion across the large doormat. 'Bugger – can I worm him on antibiotics?'

'What?' Fen reacts.

'Sorry, Fen,' James laughs, 'Barry is on antibiotics. And I think he's probably got worms.'

'Is he doing that funny bottom shuffle across the floor?' Fen asks.

'Spot on.'

'Worms,' Fen proclaims, 'yeuch.'

'Anyway,' James says affably, 'enough about my dog's anal afflictions, what can I do you for?'

'Yes,' Fen says, becoming the official voice of Trust Art, 'could we have your Fetherstones in London, please? The Tate want to see them and then there's our acquisitions meeting later this month.'

'Sure,' James says, 'sure. Shall I bring them? Send them? Will you send for them?' He paused. 'Come for them?'

'I'll send for them,' says Fen, though she does pause momentarily to think twice.

It was nice speaking to James. It was almost four o'clock. The evening with Matt seemed imminent. She'd arranged that Pip should be on Cat duty, but under no circumstances to tell her that Fen had a date.

It had been nice, speaking to James. He has the most wonderful Fetherstones in his collection. Fen would send for them and see them again. It was something to truly look forward to. For the time being, though, the coming evening was what Fen was looking forward to.

Judith St John entered Publications. She glanced at Otter whose eyes were wide with fear for some reason. She looked at Matt who was tapping a pencil between his top and lower teeth whilst looking out of the window.

'Matthew,' Judith breezed. He looked up. It was very obvious to her that he had been lost in thought, not thinking about the running order of the current issue of *Art Matters*.

'Hi,' he said.

'I suggest we leave here at five thirty-ish.' She said it so nonchalantly, but with such confidence that, though Matt temporarily had no idea to what she alluded, he felt it was more than his job's worth to enquire what, where, why. Luckily, Judith continued. 'The Whitechapel is a bugger to get to from Pimlico. The private view starts at six thirty. I'll order a cab. I thought we'd have a light supper afterwards. I've booked that new fusion restaurant in Hoxton.'

There was no room to comment, let alone protest. Matt kept the pencil in his mouth. His facial expression was neutral. Only the flexed muscles on his cheek gave away that he was biting down on the pencil, hard. Judith, feeling triumphant, smiled in a girly-sweet way utterly at odds with her character. 'It could be an interesting evening,' she said, most beguilingly.

Both Otter and Matt sat with their heads in their hands. Matt has a sense of duty. He has manners. The arrangement with Judith was made before that with Fen. He was hugely disappointed. But he had to do what is right. His father had drummed it into him. Honesty. Politeness. Decorum.

'Bugger,' he sighed, 'what a fuck-up.'

It was five o'clock.

He went to the Archive.

It is five thirty. Matt and Judith have gone.

'Fuck,' says Otter, 'what a fucking fuck-up.' He goes to the Archive. He finds Fen, a brownish smudge on her white vest, typing data into the computer. She has a line of biro ink on her left hand. Whether she is chewing something, or whether she is merely masticating with concentration, Otter cannot tell. But he thinks how gentle she looks, fragile even. Oh dear.

'Fen, dearest,' Otter says, laying a hand carefully on her head.

'Hey,' Fen says. Then she pulls a forlorn face. 'He blew me out. He's spending the evening with Judith.'

160

'I know,' says Otter, not wanting to know more, and therefore not noting that Fen's expression has a theatrical edge.

'Bastard,' Fen says, but Otter, so caught up in what he thinks has happened, does not hear the lightness to her tone of voice, that she uses the term almost affectionately.

Fen is indeed hugely disappointed. In fact, she felt quite annoyed when Matt left the Archive; a little rejected too. She tried to understand. It was work, after all. A prior engagement, that's all.

Otter, however, does not understand what Fen has understood. All he knows is that she has had lunch with Judith, and that Judith had told him that she'd be enlightening Fen on a couple of matters. Otter can only begin to imagine what was said. And what he imagines is enough to compel him to reassure Fen in any way he can.

'She's a manipulative bitch,' he proclaims, now stroking Fen's hair quite frenetically. Fen frowns and ducks her head from Otter's touch; she swivels in her chair to face him and he perches on the edge of her desk like a raggedly crow in a bird sanctuary. 'I promise you, dearest, she'll have made it sound much more than it was – certainly much more than it ever meant to Matt.' Fen is frowning still. 'You have to remember,' he says very carefully, 'that he is recently released from a troublesome break-up of a long-term relationship.' Fen has no idea where this conversation has come from, where it is going, or why Otter is engrossed in it. She doesn't even know who the 'she' is.

'It was only sex,' Otter stresses, 'Matt fucked Judith because he was on the rebound.'

Fen scrunches her eyes tight shut.

Oh fuck. Judith.

She keeps her eyes closed. Otter has presented her with a mapped-out canvas. She has only to fill in the colour. Painting by numbers. Joining the dots. A picture to be revealed.

I don't want to know!

I want to know everything!

161

Matt?
Judith?
Sex?
When?

Otter feels that the best thing to do, the most tactful and constructive way to handle all of this, is to play down completely the coupling of Matt and Judith. He will simply stress the physical and do away with any emotional significance Judith might have – must have – emphasized over lunch. 'And he was drunk,' Otter proclaims, as if this fact further undermines any relevance whatsoever to the fornication between Matt and Judith. 'I mean,' he continues, hoping to calm Fen's darting eyes, 'I know it was a couple of a weeks ago – the Rothko private view – but honestly, *honestly*, it was just a one-off, drunken exchange of bodily fluids. Purely physical. It hadn't happened before – and I promise you, dearest sweetest darlingest Fen, it won't happen again. Certainly not tonight.'

Shut up, Otter.

'It was just sex.'

Stop it.

'Alcohol fuelled.'

Enough.

'Seriously, love – for Matt it was little more than an assisted wank.'

Otter, leave it!

'Don't let Judith have suggested to you otherwise. She's a fucked-up cow. She feels threatened by your success and your beauty and Matt's obvious attraction to you.'

Yeah, right.

'But just because she's trying to replicate that evening again tonight – well, I assure you, Matt'll have none of it.'

Yeah, right.

'I mean, his ex-girlfriend has been trying to claw her way back on the scene – our poor Matthew, he had a lousy weekend trying to wrest her off him. He only wants you, dearest Fen.'

162

Now an ex-bloody-girlfriend is thrown into the equation!

'I give you this privileged information because I will not have you judge this fine boy on the bullshit that Judith fed you over lunch. Nor on the trials of his past. Trust him. You can.'

Privilege? Trust? It's all bullshit. Judith didn't tell me a thing, you bumbling, interfering idiot.

'It was a one-off, drunken, pointless shag. But hey, haven't we all been there?'

No. I haven't, Otter. And I'd rather not consort with those who have.

Otter could not persuade Fen to come out with him for a restorative drink. She said she had cat duty at her sister's, or something. Matt likes cats, Otter thought to himself as, exhausted but with a weight off his mind, he made his way to the tube and home to his meticulous one-bedroom flat in Notting Hill.

Fen sits at her desk feeling shell-shocked. And betrayed. By all of them. Would she rather not have known? She can't think straight. She doesn't think she likes Matt very much. She doesn't like Judith at all. She thinks Otter is an insensitive, gossip-obsessed fool. She stares blankly at the wall. Her focus changes and fixes on a postcard of *Abandon*.

Yes. Absolutely. Abandon. Abandon it all.

Even from the black-and-white two-dimensional repro-duction of this great work, the play of light on mass, the shapes of the spaces in between the forms, the dance between limbs, the intensity of the emotion emanating from within these two lust-locked people, takes her breath away.

It's crazy. A lump of bronze. And yet they breathe.

'What a genius.'

Fen stares and stares at the work of art that has obsessed her for over a decade. A tear oozes from the corner of her eye as painfully as the lump that has lodged itself at the base of her throat.

These people do not exist. The physical forms that are here are merely testimony to this sculptor's knowledge of human anatomy. This is not real. They are as fictitious as characters in a novel, or in a film. I feel I've been conned!

'Con artist,' she spits. She rips the postcard from the wall and tears it in two. She has severed He from She. Not that they were one, anyway. Not that they were anyone at all.

Cat, who had wept on and off all evening, was fast asleep by ten o'clock. Fen flicked channels on the television. Her mobile phoned beeped that there was a message. She hoped it wasn't Matt. It wasn't. Fleetingly, she was disappointed but swiftly chided herself. It was Abi.

'How wz yr date? R U inflagrante?'

Fen snorted. She sent Abi a text message back.

'Pants.'

Abi didn't understand.

'???'

Fen was too tired to phone through the information. She sent Abi a final text.

'Tell U 2morro.'

She switched her phone off and put it in her bag. There were two pieces of folded paper. One was a copy of Matt's list. This she folded into the smallest possible form and expertly launched over to the waste-paper basket. The other piece of paper was a print-out of James's phone number and address. Fen folded this twice and then tapped it contemplatively against her nose. What had he said?

'Shall I bring them? Send them? Will you send for them? Come for them?'

She had told him she'd send for them.

She has changed her mind.

'James?'

'Fen McCabe? Good God, you're not still at work are you?'

'I think I'll come for them.'

TWENTY-TWO

Give a man a free hand and he'll run it all over you.
Mae West

*T*he next morning, if Fen had any second thoughts about her impromptu visit to Derbyshire, then what she found in her house when she returned from Cat's flat, decided her at once that she should be gone from London which, in her eyes, was rapidly disintegrating into a city of iniquity. She wanted to change her clothes, to wash away any vestige of yesterday. Dress not for Judith, nor for Matt. Matt, she thought with a smirk to her face but a churn to her stomach, was probably hunting for his clothes amongst the debris that had no doubt been flung around Judith's flat in erotic abandon.

Or maybe he went home alone at half past nine. Whichever, what do I care?

It was cloudless. Though the sun wasn't yet in appearance, a soft spring day was prophesied. As Fen strolled through Camden towards her house, she felt nicely restored. She'd slept well and now the weather put her in a balanced mood.

I have a fair few postcards of Abandon. I must take one or two in to work.

'God, you've a great arse, babe.'

Jake's lust-soaked voice filtered down the stairs and into

the kitchen where Fen was trying to enjoy a simple, refreshing glass of grapefruit juice. Jake's description was accurate, Fen thought, objectively classing Abi's bottom herself as 'pert and inviting'.

Fen found herself straining her ears to hear Abi's response. There was something simultaneously repellent and yet utterly compelling about eavesdropping on another couple's sex. She felt both awkward but quite titillated. As though she shouldn't listen, as though she really should go, but as though some voyeuristic side to her was revealing itself and goading her to stay. Stay, inch closer, listen more, have a peep! A desirous groan from Jake made Fen clasp her hand to her mouth to hold back schoolgirl giggles. Jake was now really moaning and gasping and the bed was creaking.

With all the noise, it seemed the opportune moment for Fen to make her way quietly up to her room. The house was tall and thin with the kitchen and living-room, open plan, spanning the ground floor. The bathroom and Abi's room were on the first floor and Gemma's and Fen's rooms, separated by a twist in the hallway and three small steps to a landing, were on the top floor. Abi's door was wide open, Jake's clothes were strewn around it. The bed was unmade but empty. They were obviously up a level.

Please God don't let me find her strapped to the banisters or Jake humped over the stairs on the landing. Or the two of them in some yogic configuration on my Lloyd Loom chair!

Actually, they are in Gemma's room, Fen.

What the hell are they doing in there? That's outrageous, she'll be truly pissed off.

No, she won't.

Of course she will be! I would be!

But it *is* Gemma.

Fen knew she should have just tiptoed past and looked steadily ahead. But there was a magnetic force dragging her eyes to the left. And what she saw rooted her to the spot. She

166

was alternately turned on and revulsed, titillated and appalled.

It was indeed Gemma who Jake was screwing. Fen was stunned to the spot, like a rabbit transfixed by the headlights of a car, drawn to danger. She observed through the slightly ajar door, Jake humping and thrusting and gyrating against Gemma's admittedly great arse.

'I'm coming, I'm coming!'

In a tiptoe dance, with an acute awareness of just how creaky the floorboards were, just how noisy her heartbeat was, just how bad all of this was – them, her – Fen sprung along the landing like a pursued antelope and darted into her room.

She sat on her bed, dumbstruck. Appalled for Abi. Livid with Gemma. Disgusted by Jake.

What the hell am I meant to do with that knowledge?

Her right palm said tell Abi, her left palm said don't. Her left palm said confront Gemma, her right forbade it. She wrung her hands for a moment or two and then, lightly clasped, she let them fall into her lap.

My potential new boyfriend shares his flat with this immoral, philandering sod.

She held her head in her hands.

What else do they share?

She squeezed the bridge of her nose.

My potential new boyfriend is already screwing the assistant director at my place of work.

Fen looked out of the window.

I don't think I like these people. Thank God I am going to go to Derbyshire. I belong there.

Fen didn't feel like Maltesers or dodgy sandwiches from St Pancras station. And every glossy magazine seemed to brim with articles she really didn't want to read. 'Dirty Sex For You and Your Man', 'I'm Sleeping With My Best Mate's Fella', 'Can A Womanizer Really Change His Ways?'. So she bought the *Guardian*, the *Independent*, the *Spectator* and

167

the *New Yorker*. She hadn't phoned work. She hadn't replied to Abi's alarming text message of 'CALL ME CALL ME CALL ME'. Fen couldn't have anything come between her and boarding that nine-twenty-five train. In two hours and one minute, she'd alight at Chesterfield and be safely ensconced in her own familiar territory.

She phoned Abi only when the train had pulled out of Luton and had picked up speed.

'Abi?'

'Fen!'

Fen sank back against her seat with relief. Abi's tone was light and energetic and not the voice of a girl whose best friend was screwing her boyfriend.

'Well?' Abi enquired. 'Tell me! Last night? Why was it "pants"? Did he rip yours off with his teeth? Does he wear hideous beige Y-fronts?'

'He blew me out,' Fen said, really not wanting to go into it.

'Where on earth are you?' Abi asked.

'On a train. Going to Derbyshire. To see a man about some sculptures.'

'The same bloke as last time?'

'Yes,' said Fen, 'this time, I'm bringing his works back with me.'

'Gosh, you must have been saving up your pocket money!' Abi laughed.

'Yeah right,' Fen laughed back. 'How are you, Abs? Are you OK? Are things good?'

'Darling,' Abi said, 'when you have the kind of sex I had last night, even the most shit day at work – as today threatens to be – is not just tolerable but almost pleasurable!'

'Jake, then?' Fen said.

Abi's response was to make the kind of appreciative noises that she normally made on eating a decadently large slice of chocolate cake.

'Good,' said Fen, 'good. Gemma?'

'She's fine too,' Abi assured her. 'A girly night is long overdue for us three.'

168

'Yes,' said Fen, wondering if a girly night for the three of them would ever be possible again.

'Why did Matt blow you out?' Abi asked.

'He had to go to a private view,' Fen explained, 'with Judith St John.'

'Ooh,' said Abi, who always listened to everything Fen told her, 'which lady?'

'You know,' Fen said ingenuously, 'the power-dressing, power-crazed assistant director.'

'Yes, yes,' Abi explained, 'I said, Witch Lady.'

'Yes,' snorted Fen, 'whom he's shagging, if Otter's revelations are anything to go by.'

'Good God,' Abi exclaimed, 'thank God you haven't gone further than snogging, then. Do you want me to see if Jake knows anything?'

'Don't worry,' Fen said, 'don't bother.'

'The bastard!' Abi said. 'The cad! The deceptive sod!'

'Don't!' Fen pleaded, horribly aware that the abuse fitted Jake perfectly, probably better, in fact, than Matt – whom she knew, deep down, hadn't actually done anything wrong.

'I'd better go,' Abi said to Fen's relief. 'See you tomorrow – don't drop the sculptures!'

'Bye, my lovely,' said Fen with much feeling.

The train was nearing Leicester. It was a good time to phone work.

'Hello. Trust Art – how may I help?' answered Bobbie, exaggerating her 'h's.

'Bobbie? It's me, Fen.'

''Allo darling, you all right? You 'aven't got the lurgy?' said Bobbie, dispensing with all 'h's in her spontaneous concern for Fen's welfare.

'No, no,' said Fen, all bright and breezy, 'I'm on a train to Derbyshire – can you tell Rodney that I've gone to collect the three Fetherstones?'

'Fen. Derby. Shire. Rod. Three. Feathers,' Bobbie murmured, scribbling a note. 'All done, ducks. When you back?'

Fen looked out of the window.

''Allo?' Bobbie called loudly, thinking Fen's signal must have gone faint. 'When you back? Today? Tomorrow?'

Fen held her phone against her chin and watched the home counties disappear. She cancelled her call.

She redialled Bobbie a few minutes later.

'I lost you,' Fen lied, 'my signal went. Can you hear me?'

'Lovely loud and clear, gorgeous,' Bobbie confirmed.

'Tomorrow,' said Fen, 'I'll be back at work tomorrow.'

But I might not be back in London tonight.

What are you doing, Fen?

I don't really know.

Why haven't you called Django?

I don't really know.

Are you not intending to stay in Derbyshire? At home?

I don't know.

Or if you decide to, are you not sure where and with whom?

I don't know.

TWENTY-THREE

I *wonder why the uncle over at Farleymoor isn't collecting her? I could do without this. I'm having to cancel Mrs Jackman. And less then twenty-four hours' notice – from Fenella to me, and from me to Mrs J.*

Feeling irritated more than resentful, James tried to focus his attention on Mrs Brakespeare's *Acer Palmatum 'Atropurpureum'*.

I suppose, though, that the Fetherstones are going to generate far more income than four hours at £15 an hour with Mrs Jackman. Plus of course lunch with Fenella is preferable to lunch at Mrs J's. I can't stand gammon steaks. And it is always, always, gammon steaks.

'Remember when I took along my own sandwiches?' James laughed, talking to Beryl who was busy digging a rather large hole at the front of Mrs Brakespeare's herbaceous border. Beryl looked up momentarily, but she didn't remember so she returned to her digging. 'She gave them to you and Barry and I had to have bloody gammon steaks most of which I sneaked to you and Barry too.' James wondered where Barry was.

'Shit!'

Mrs Brakespeare's back door was open. Barry certainly was not in the garden. Mrs Brakespeare was not in the house, having told James she was popping out. James jogged over the lawn, rushed out of his boots and walked into the house.

'Barry!' he called in a harsh whisper. Silence. He ventured in further. The sitting-room door, thank God, was shut and the cream sofas remained pristine. 'Barry! Where the hell are you?'

James groaned on hearing the lurcher lollop down the stairs. 'Barry!' he yelled, his dog dropping Mr Brakespeare's slipper immediately. 'You're going to Battersea!' The lurcher, however, sauntered past his master as if to say 'yeah, right'. James looked down at the well-chewed slipper. Barry was now looking very eager to enter the dining-room, the door being ajar. 'Battersea!' his owner warned and the dog thought better of it and skulked outside. James sighed. Maybe he should just feign absolute ignorance but secretly bury the slipper in Beryl's keenly dug hole? He returned to the garden. 'Jesus Christ – where is bloody Beryl?' James marched around the garden, deciding out loud to trade his dogs in for cats. Beryl, it transpired, was fast asleep in the large hole she'd so meticulously excavated.

James waited for Mrs B to return, even though it meant he was running late to pick up Fen. When Mrs B finally returned (at much the same time as Fen's train was pulling in to Chesterfield), James apologized profusely for Barry's altercation with the slipper. And Barry, for his part, did his best to hang his head and look as though he was willing to take a beating.

'James love,' Mrs B cooed, distressed to see him agitated, 'don't you worry about it.' She looked down at Barry kindly, but kept her hands away from his raggedy, soil-enriched coat. 'Mr Brakespeare needed a new pair anyway,' she told the dog. 'We'll keep the tatty old pair for your next visit, shall we?' James thanked her profusely and Barry panted with relief. They bade her goodbye.

'Are you off to Rita's now?' Mrs B enquired.

'I've had to cancel Mrs J,' James said.

'Oh?' Mrs B responded, alarmed and curious. 'Why? Everything OK?'

'All is well, Mrs B,' James assured her. He grinned to himself but regarded his client with a level gaze. 'I have a young girl coming up from London to see me. In fact, I must go and collect her now.'

Young? Mrs B wondered after James had gone, *how young? A floozy? A niece? London – what's she coming to see? And how long might she stay? Well! Who shall I phone first?* Going upstairs, she looked out of the landing window to her garden and regarded Beryl's large hole with some exasperation. Just past the bathroom, her husband's other slipper lay. It had put up a good fight but the rubber sole had been mercilessly torn away from the upper. In her bedroom she gasped. The duvet bore the unmistakable imprint of a very large and muddy lurcher.

'Oh doary,' she said, 'better not let Mr B see this. And better not tell James. He'd be horrified, poor love.'

James had been pleasantly amused by Fen's abrupt and unexpected phone call last night. Now there was something compelling about catching sight of her, unseen. James watched her for a moment or two. She seemed to be lost in thought, sitting a little forlornly on the station bench. He was twenty-five minutes late.

And now here she was, over there. Lovely in the flesh. Yet James suddenly felt curiously reluctant to approach her. Last night, after her phone call, he'd stared hard at the painting of Eve and had attempted to conjure an image of Fen naked, doing to him what Eve was doing to Adam in the sculpture. It had been a titillating fantasy. But he had quashed it abruptly, warned himself that he was old enough to be her . . . And had gone to bed with a John Grisham thriller instead.

James glanced at his watch. Then looked again to Fen, the breeze lifting her hair and laying it down again.

You daft sod, she's come to you because it's probably

Trust policy for personnel to accompany works of art. Plus, a cheap-day return is probably more economical than hiring a courier firm to collect and deliver.

Nevertheless, James gave Barry the honour of greeting her. Fen looked momentarily startled and then soon enough delighted. She looked up and caught sight of James. He waved. She smiled. She left the bench and walked over to him.

'Hullo,' she said, holding out her hand.

'Sorry I'm late, chuck,' he replied, ignoring her hand and kissing her lightly on the cheek. Her cheek was soft and cool against his lips. The contrast in temperature appealed to them both.

'Where's Beryl?' Fen asked.

'She's in the car. Both of them are in disgrace, really,' said James, leading the way to his war-torn Land Rover.

He doesn't have hands like a gardener. I remember from last time.

Fen glanced from James's hand, resting lightly on the handbrake, out of the window to a bustling Chesterfield shopping morning. *His hands are more like Matt's than Alan Titchmarsh's. But there again, I've seen photos of Julius's hands – and that drawing he did of them – and his fingers were fine and long. James has very nice hands. That's a new boutique. Blimey, it's selling Paul Smith! Beryl has bad breath. I'm hungry. What's the time?*

James was just a little disconcerted by Fen's mien. She seemed contemplative. She also looked wan and tired and he found himself quite interested in why this should be so. What had she been up to?

Partying, most likely. Too many late nights. Not eating properly. Her skin looks lacklustre, her eyes have no sparkle, her hair is a little limp. Perhaps she smokes too much.

'Do you smoke?' James asked.

'No,' said Fen. 'My housemates do – sometimes I'll light a

ciggy for them because it amuses them and reminds me why I don't.'

'You look rather tired,' James commented, wondering if it sounded like a reprimand.

Fen, nodding, said she was fine.

'You look a little,' James paused and then thought what the hell, 'pensive.'

'I'm fine,' said Fen but without nodding.

'A bowl of soup when we get in,' James said, all jolly, 'how about that?'

Fen turned to him. Sunlight shot through the windscreen, illuminating her face. It spun the most incredible colours through her eyes – shards of charcoal, turquoise and khaki – and turned her skin from pale and flat to sheened porcelain. He had to look away.

'Soup'll be lovely,' she said, with gratitude.

I want to lock the dogs in the utility room. I want to feed Fen. I want to have sex with her. I want to put her in a bath and ease a soapy flannel over her back and down her arms. I want to make her a cup of hot chocolate. I want her to fall asleep in my bed. And sleep. For hours. And I want her to suck my cock. I want to keep her. I want to lock her up.

James's thoughts turned him on and horrified him.

Don't you bloody dare. You leave her alone. Concentrate on the road. God, Beryl's breath is bad. Must be gingivitis again. Must buy those special chews.

Fen felt a flood of calm when James pulled in to Keeper's Dwelling and switched off the engine. She wanted to curl up with a cup of cocoa and go to sleep. Perhaps have a nice deep bath first. James was bound to have a roll-top cast-iron bath.

'Come on in,' he said, key in the lock. 'Barry, Beryl – have a pee, please.' Fen watched the dogs; the lurcher tottered over to the gatepost and cocked his leg against it while the labrador padded over to the side of the gravel drive and squatted down, avoiding eye contact.

'Aren't they good,' Fen said, the peace and fresh air, the solitude of the place, reviving her. She felt much brighter.

'They're good-for-nothings,' James grumbled.

'You're horrible,' Fen said, and poked him because it felt right, 'you don't mean it.'

James wished she hadn't poked him. It sent his incorrigible thoughts into a stampede.

The hallway smelt lovely. Fen hadn't realized that it had a distinct aroma but standing there again proved that obviously it had. The same as last time. Earth on boots. Wood fire. Old mahogany. Wax on flagstones.

I love all of this. As a lifestyle. It's so me, isn't it?

'Sit in there,' James all but commanded in a tone of voice fairly similar to that which he used for the dogs. He held the door to the snug open and gestured to the particular armchair he wanted Fen to occupy. 'I'm going to fix some soup.'

'Can I help?' Fen offered.

'No,' James said, 'no.'

He didn't want her with him. He wanted her to sit still. And stay out of sight.

When I tell my dogs to sit, I do so to keep them out of trouble. I'm telling Fen to sit to keep myself out of trouble.

James disappeared into the kitchen. Fen was quite happy to sink into the comfortable leather tub chair. The room was still. No fire. No dogs (Barry and Beryl had been confined to the utility room). And no Fetherstones. Where were they? Where? Should she go and ask James? No, she should stay put. He'd said so. Not a lot to do, really, other than to sit still and relax then. Let the mind wander. And wonder.

Fen wondered how on earth she could go on the rebound against Matt when they hadn't even been in a relationship for him to have cheated on her.

He slept with Judith before he even kissed me. I oughtn't to judge him on that. Though I might now think less of his taste.

And yet her desire for James was not caused by a desire to

176

spite Matt, or to bolster her suddenly flagging self-confidence. She simply desired James. All the more so today because of the contrast between him and Matt, between all that she loved about Derbyshire and all that she suddenly loathed about London. Sleepily, she glanced from hand to hand.

I find James incredibly attractive. Not just physically, although he is classically handsome. I like him – he's slightly aloof, set in his ways, self-contained. I'm actually turned on by his age. I suppose it is the notion of his experience and I don't know, his weatheredness.

Fen yawned. Where were the Fetherstones?

On the other hand, what I find compelling and, at the moment, preferable, is his differentness to Matt. And men my age. James – I don't know – he's a grown-up! Makes Matt seem just too laddish. That's not fair. I know Matt is attentive, kind, gorgeous to look at, young, successful and outgoing. But he lives with Jake. Jake is screwing both my friends. I rather think I ought to steer clear of someone ensconced in that milieu. Was Matt intending to have Judith and me at the same time?

She yawned again and wondered if James was a safer bet.

You have to have things in common. James and I have Derbyshire. And Fetherstones.

Yes, but Fen, no matter how impecunious you were, you would never sell Fetherstones if you owned them. Anyway, Matt and you have London and age and art in general, in common.

Jesus. Why am I even feeling obliged to choose between the two? Why am I cross-referencing their pros and cons? I've been doing just fine, these past couple of years, not being bothered by the presence or otherwise of the opposite sex in my life. Why on earth do I now feel I have to decide between these two vastly different and probably equally unsuitable men?

She yawned expansively.

Neither.

She let her eyes close.

Nope.

She thought of Adam and of Eve. She told herself that this was the reason for her visit today.

Nope. Neither Matt or James. Not worth it – not worth the hassle, not worth the gain.

She fell asleep feeling that, above all, she'd been unfaithful to Julius Fetherstone.

TWENTY-FOUR

The only way to get rid of temptation is to yield to it.
Oscar Wilde

James had no ingredients for soup. He didn't even have a tin of Safeways home-brand, let alone Baxters or Heinz with which to improvise or serve as a base. He did have some Cup-a-soup but the fleeting thought of using it appalled him so much that he pushed the box to the back of the cupboard. He didn't want to go and ask Fen what she'd like instead. He decided that he'd make chicken sandwiches. And he'd put lashings of mayonnaise on hers, because she looked like she needed feeding up.

I bet she lives in a shared house where supper is invariably baked potatoes or Marks & Spencer ready meals.

You can talk, James, you who frequently dines on Heinz tomato soup, infrequently on Cup-a-soup, invariably followed by a bowl of cornflakes, then a packet of ham which you eat, slice by slice, while watching the television and ignoring the heartstring-tugging gaze of your dogs. Jaffa Cakes before bed time which, if your dogs are lucky and their soulful looks are imploring enough and if the packet is more than half full, you share.

James cut the bread into doorstep wedges. The chicken, leftovers from a Sunday roast, was still succulent and he licked his fingers frequently. He mixed a little mustard in with the mayonnaise for piquancy and made a potato salad with left-over boiled new potatoes. It all looked hearty and appetizing.

'Fenella,' he called, 'lunch.'

But there was no response. He wanted her to come into the kitchen, so he could have the distance and the propriety and the safety of the table between them. A working lunch.

'Fen?'

Still no reply.

Oh God, I hope she hasn't gone snooping.

James ventured into the snug. Fen's arm was lolling over the side of the chair which he had told her to sit in. It had its back to him. He walked around and came across Fen fast asleep. It made him smile. She looked ten years younger, her eyelids softly closed, her lips parted, breathing lightly and rhythmically. Her white cotton shirt was open at the neck. He saw a pulse twitching calmly at the base of her throat. Her white cotton shirt revealed more now that she was slumped and relaxed. James came nearer and peered carefully, to delight in the soft undulation of her right breast. Her skin looked good enough to lick.

Chicken sandwiches. Chicken sandwiches. Wake her.

He inched closer, captivated more by what the shirt concealed than what it revealed. She didn't so much have a cleavage as a slight dip between her breasts. But that looked good enough to lick too.

Wake her. Sandwiches.

He held his breath the closer he came to her. He didn't want to wake her. His lips were inches away from her skin. He glanced at her face. Fen McCabe gazed back at him. Wide awake. And just as hungry. A suspended moment, a pregnant pause, lips wet and willing. James, though, straightened up.

'I didn't know whether to wake you, sleeping beauty,' he said hoarsely, one hand on his stomach, the other in his back pocket, 'but lunch is ready.' He turned.

'Prince Charming woke Sleeping Beauty with a kiss,' Fen said, the pulse in her neck racing.

James pretended not to hear.

But you woke up. You woke up.

They ate in cordial silence. James was pleased to observe how Fen wolfed down the sandwiches and helped herself to seconds of the potato salad. Conversation was frugal and polite over coffee.

'Where are the dogs?' Fen asked.

'In the utility room,' James replied. 'How's your uncle?'

'Fine,' Fen said, 'Django is fine.'

'Will you see him today?'

'No,' Fen said, looking ever so slightly shifty, 'it isn't that kind of visit.'

'What time is your train?'

Fen's eyes flitted from side to side though she tried to fix her gaze on a piece of potato on the table. 'I don't know,' she said, 'I don't mind.'

'See how things go?' James suggested. Fen nodded.

'I suppose you'll be wanting to see them,' James laughed. Fen's eyes sparkled.

They were in his bedroom. The oil sketches were propped on the chest of drawers behind all the old framed photographs; the sculpture was by the side of the doorway leading to the ensuite bathroom.

'Hullo,' Fen said to them, to James's amusement. She turned to him. Slightly flushed. 'Can I use your bathroom?'

'Sure,' he said, motioning to it with a nod of his head, 'go right ahead.' He could hear her taking a pee. An unmistakably feminine trickle. His cock stirred in his trousers.

For God's sake.

Inside the bathroom, Fen was disappointed. The fantasy of taking a bath in a roll-top cast-iron classic was sadly dampened by reality presenting her with a modern plastic suite in a discouraging shade of peach.

'Can you manage them OK?' James asked, remembering that the sculpture, despite its humble proportions, was heavy.

'Sure,' said Fen, gazing at the intertwined figures. 'I don't want to go home just yet.' She looked a little unhappy.

'The trains are regular,' James offered.

She looked at her feet and caught sight of a John Grisham novel lying on the floor by the bed. She was quite taken aback. She'd imagined Garcia Marquez being James's night-time reading. Grisham was on a par with the peach bathroom suite.

'Fen?' James was saying. 'Train time?'

'What?' Fen said. 'Oh.'

'Or,' asked James, 'would you rather I kidnap you for an extortionate ransom? Then I could keep the Fetherstones.'

'My family aren't very flush,' Fen responded, 'and most of my friends have excessively burdensome overdrafts.'

'Not such a good idea, then,' James replied, wondering why on earth he'd said such a thing anyway. What would Trust Art think? What would Mrs Brakespeare think? What would Fen think?

'You could kidnap me for free,' Fen suggested, shy in voice but coy in her sideways glance and tilt of her head. 'Adam and Eve look very at home here,' she said, 'right here, in the bedroom. They shouldn't be in a gallery. They should be in a bedroom, or outside in a garden of Eden of their own.'

'My roof, remember,' said James, wanting to deflect attention away from the intimacy of the bedroom setting.

'James,' Fen said.

'My sodding roof.'

'Kiss me.'

'No.'

'Yes.'

'No.'

'Kiss me, James.'

'No, Fen.'

'Yes.'

She goes over to the window and looks out over the garden. What on earth did she just say? Oh God. Out loud. James

182

gazes at the back of her head. What did she just say? And he'd said no? Of course he wants to kiss her. But it is absolutely out of the question. She's young enough to be, to be – to be absolutely out of bounds.

Bollocks, James, you've had women far younger than Fen.

It's not right.

Why not?

Suddenly, Fen feels him behind her. He is encircling her in his arms. They do not speak. He takes his left hand and runs his fingertips lightly over her forearm until their fingers lock. They move their bodies around a little. They instinctively find each other's mouths and they lock lips. Fen feels herself dissolve, like bubbles in a bath. She could crumple to the floor because she knows that James's arms are holding her. For James, kissing Fen is like having one's mouth filled with honey. Or petals. Sweet-pea petals, he decides, as her tongue darts lightly over his. James smells heavenly. After a morning's gardening, there's a slight musky sweatiness shot through with pheromones; there's the scent of cold roast chicken, and a very faint linger of a light aftershave. He is tall. He appears to be strong. She can sense his hard-on. She wants it badly.

Fen feels enveloped. Completely enclosed by masculinity. She is overwhelmingly turned on, brought to the edge of orgasm by James's kiss alone.

'I have to go,' she says, pulling away from his lips.

'No,' James murmurs, 'couldn't we—?'

'Yes,' Fen melts, closing her eyes and offering James her lips. He cups her face in his hands, takes his lips to her eyelids, to the tip of her nose, to the corner of her mouth where he flicks his tongue tip tantalizingly.

'No,' says James, 'you're right. You have to go, Fen. You must.'

They stand facing each other, eyes scorching into one another. She wants to be kissed by him again. She wants to stay.

'Take the bronze today,' James says quietly, 'because of course the oil sketches aren't here, are they?'

Fen and he regard the oil sketches.

'No,' said Fen, 'they're not here. They're at the framers. And I'm cross because I've told you to leave them unframed.'

'But though we have been able to stop the process,' James says, 'the earliest I can have them here is next week.'

'Yes,' says Fen, 'next Monday. I can come and collect them then.'

TWENTY-FIVE

'She's switched her phone off,' Matt said, having tried Fen for the fourth time that day. He scratched his head. Otter shrugged. He hadn't told Matt what he'd told Fen. He didn't want it to become an issue between Matt and her. Otter had told Fen because he sincerely thought he would be setting straight what Judith had undoubtedly twisted. He simply wanted to furnish Fen with the facts so that salacious inaccuracies would not hinder her impending union with Matt. Otter cared about both of them. He didn't care for Judith at all. Of course, Matt didn't know that Otter knew about the recent coupling with the assistant director; certainly not that the assistant director had told Otter herself. So, Matt was merely concerned for Fen's welfare on a day when she wasn't at work and her phone was off. He'd been hoping to take her out that night, to make up for yesterday. 'Flu, perhaps?' Matt suggested out loud. 'I wonder if Bobbie has her home number?'

While Matt went downstairs to Reception, Judith paid a visit to Publications.

'Where is he?' she asked Otter, who twisted his legs around each other and placed his bony rump firmly on top of his skinny hands in a bid to prevent himself from going over to Judith and hitting her.

'Loo?' Otter suggested.

'I tell you something,' Judith said, regarding Otter levelly with very dark eyes, 'he's bloody odd. Warped, you could say. Twisted. Sexually – I don't know – unstable.'

Otter couldn't help looking sheepish and shy – because he had absolutely no idea what on earth he could say in response or in Matt's defence.

Matt returned. Otter held his breath, wondering if this was perfect timing or the worst timing imaginable.

'Hi,' Judith breathed, 'I was just telling Otter about last night.'

Matt observed her but remained silent. Then he grinned and laughed out loud, curtly. Judith raised an eyebrow and sashayed from the room.

'And what exactly did she tell you about last night?' Matt demanded of Otter.

'That you're sexually warped, twisted and unstable,' Otter replied with extreme nonchalance, as if simply recounting Matt's age, height and weight. Matt laughed and shook his head. It disconcerted Otter greatly. What was he meant to tell Fen now? Because surely, she'd ask. She'd expect to know, at any rate, and Otter had of course given himself the role of her confidante. There was a sharp pain in his stomach and a pervasive acidy taste in his mouth. He thought he very probably had developed an ulcer, on account of so much stress and responsibility.

'I hear you're in Derbyshire – you skiver!' Matt leaves a message on Fen's phone. 'Just thought I'd ring, though. I was hoping to wine and dine you tonight. Give me a call if British Rail has deposited you home at a reasonable hour. Um. Or I'll see you at work tomorrow. Yes. Bye.'

Matt rings her phone again, almost immediately. Otter pretends not to hear though he is listening hard, peeling his ears to catch Matt's lowered voice.

'Fen, it's me again, Matt. Er. I just wanted to – well, basically I'm sorry again for last night. It was pants, anyway.'

186

He wonders whether that was too corny. But there's little he can do about it. He hopes she'll call. He feels badly about last night. And hopeful for tonight.

But Fen didn't call. The train whisked her back down south. She listened to his messages when there was a signal on her phone. They made her smile. But she didn't want to speak to Matt. She wasn't punishing him. She wasn't playing games with him. In fact she didn't feel cross with him at all. She wanted to linger over memories of James, instead. Uninterrupted. Because it would be nearly a week until she saw him again. She hugged his rucksack close to her, though the bronze was heavy, digging into her ribs and poking her stomach. The bag smelt of James's hallway. She closed her eyes and tried to conjure the smell of the man himself. She felt no regret that they hadn't had sex. Just a yearning.

Jake and Matt met at their local after work. They loved the place. A rarity in London – a pub that has not lost its identity, a pub at ease with itself, a pub whose landlord and clientele had no interest, no desire for even a change of carpet, let alone cosmetic surgery to turn it into a wine bar or gastro-pub or a meetery-eatery with leather sofas and candles. You couldn't order a Sea Breeze because the landlord didn't trust pink drinks. If you wanted vodka, the mixers available were all in little bottles, because the landlord did not trust those one-gun-gives-all gadgets. Tonic. Coke. Ginger. Bitter lemon. No diet versions available. There were glacé cherries for the ladies, lemon slices and lime cordial. Crisps were available in ready salted, cheese and onion and salt and vinegar. There were peanuts too, in bags which were a bugger to open. Sandwiches, and sandwiches only, on white pre-sliced bread, were served at lunch-time, and at lunch-time only. No salad garnish. No cutlery. Kitchen roll in lieu of paper napkins. ('Unnecessary,' the landlord had explained to Jake and Matt one Saturday lunch-time, 'poncey paper napkins would just put up the price of the sarnies.' Kitchen roll was fine for Jake and Matt – more than they had in their flat.)

Though Jake and Matt were lager drinkers, there was something so classic about the bitter at their local – its colour, its luke warmth, its slightly repellent odour of eggy fart, that they rarely ordered anything else. There was a jar of pickled eggs behind the bar, but the contents hadn't diminished in all the time that Jake and Matt had frequented the establishment. A giant whisky bottle sat on the bar, half filled with coins to benefit charity, but the contents hadn't increased much in all the time that Jake and Matt had been frequenting the place. The clientele, integral to the atmosphere, hadn't changed at all.

Ages spanned decades. Personal circumstances probably ranged from flat broke to absolutely loaded. It was irrelevant. All were equal there. They gravitated to this particular pub, because absolutely nowhere else could serve them better. Faces were therefore always familiar, yet the atmosphere was never cliquey. Everyone knew the bar staff's names and the bar staff knew the names of all the clients. But the clients merely exchanged nods with one another. Affable but respectful. Specific seats had invisible 'reserved' signs on for particular people. It was a quiet pub; it smelt – not unpleasantly – of beer towels that needed a wash, windows that should be opened more often, stale Hamlet cigars. It was totally unpretentious and honest, as a good pint itself should be. People went there to sup in peace or in company; not to get drunk, but to wile away an evening. Though it was called the Coach and Horses, its clientele only ever thought of it and referred to it as The Pub. As if there was no choice, no contest; the one and only. Which is precisely why Matt and Jake had gone there. Sitting at a corner table. Two pints of bitter. Salt and vinegar. Cheese and onion. Jamie Oliver would be hard pressed to come up with a better repast for two young men on a weekday night.

'Did you? Did you shag her again?'

From whose lips came this? Because it could have been

Matt enquiring after Gemma, or Jake wondering about Judith.

'Did you?'

'No,' Matt said, 'I didn't. But she spent the whole evening coming on to me.'

'But you didn't,' Jake said.

'Didn't want to, mate,' Matt told him.

Jake understood this to mean that Matt hadn't wanted to mate, as in fornicate. Matt laughed. 'No,' he confirmed, 'I don't. Not with Judith. I'm ready for Fen, now, I think.'

Jake whistled in admiration. He didn't think Matt had gone soft. He actually rather admired his outlook. Partly, because it was so diametrically opposed to his own.

'Abi and Gemma suit me perfectly,' he said, with a tinge of woe, 'blonde and brunette. Night and day.'

'Salt and vinegar,' Matt said, offering the open packet of crisps to Jake.

'Cheese and onion,' Jake responded likewise.

'You'll get caught, you will,' Matt warned.

'But until I do,' Jake said, 'I'll continue as normal.'

Normal? Matt thought, *I don't think so.*

'I don't know how you do it,' Matt said.

'High levels of testosterone,' Jake shrugged, 'interacting with a very, very dirty mind.'

I meant, I don't know how you do it – how you maintain such a clear conscience.

'Abi? Gemma?' Fen called down from her room on hearing the front door open. She had half hoped to avoid both. After all, it had only been that morning – though the trip to Derbyshire made it seem weeks ago – that she had come across Jake and Gemma.

'It's me,' Abi called back.

Shit, thought Fen. Though, had it been Gemma arriving home, Fen's response would have been exactly the same.

'Where are you?' Abi called up.

'In my room,' Fen shouted.

' 'Kay,' Abi shouted back. 'Glass of wine?'

' 'Kay,' Fen called down.

'How was Derbyshire?' Abi asked, settling alongside Fen on her bed and sipping wine as if her whole day had been geared to such luxury and relaxation.

'Oh,' Fen said lightly, 'you know.'

'Will that bloke part with his art?'

'Have a look in that bag,' Fen said.

Abi left the bed and went to pick up James's bag. 'Good Lord above!' she remonstrated, as her skinny arm snagged against the weight of unseen and unexpected bronze. She looked inside and took the sculpture out. 'Good God!' she murmured. She turned to Fen. 'Did you nick it?' She was joking, of course, and turned back to the sculpture. 'Jesus,' she marvelled, 'this is pretty damn horny.' She brought the sculpture over and placed it on Fen's bedside table. She took to the bed again and Fen passed her the glass of wine. They gazed at the sculpture. 'You win, Fenella McCabe,' Abi conceded, 'you win. It's bloody gorgeous and erotic and I'm going to have to phone Jake and tell him that he's to take me to bed or lose me for ever!'

Fen laughed. Now *that*'s what she should have said to James. 'Where on earth did you get that line from?'

'Meg Ryan,' Abi admitted, somewhat reluctantly.

'*When Harry Met Sally*?' Fen asked.

'*Top Gun*,' Abi elaborated. 'She had a bit part as the zany wife of Dr Green from *ER*.'

'Goose,' Fen corrected, 'Anthony Edwards played Goose.'

The girls chattered away, about movie stars and quoted classic lines; glancing every now and then at *Eden*.

Gemma arrived home at almost ten o'clock. Fen told herself not to be suspicious.

But Abi has tried to call Jake. He's not answering land-line or mobile.

Just because he's not with Abi doesn't necessarily mean that every other moment will be spent with Gemma.

'Wow!' Gemma said, catching sight of the Fetherstone as

soon as she came into Fen's room, 'did you steal it?'

'Piss off!' Fen laughed.

'God,' Gemma murmured, looking closely at the bronze, turning it, touching it, touched by it, turned on, 'that's pretty horny.'

'Isn't it just,' Abi agreed. 'It's got me all dressed up with nowhere to go – as it were.'

'Not seeing Jake tonight?' Gemma asked Abi, while Fen tried surreptitiously to analyse her housemate's body language and tone of voice. She could detect nothing untoward.

'Any idea what time he left this morning?' Abi asked her.

'We left together – he took a taxi and dropped me off en route,' Gemma said.

'I'm tired,' Fen suddenly announced not because she was, but because she didn't want either girl in her room talking about the man they were both having sex with.

'Poor petal,' Gemma teased.

'She's lugged the Bronze Bonk all the way back from Derbyshire,' Abi said in Fen's defence.

'I'm going back on Monday,' Fen said, 'to pick up two oil sketches.'

'What's he like?' Gemma asked, her eyes drawn again to the sculpture.

'I've told you a million times,' Fen said, not minding that she was to say it again, 'he's greatly underrated and yet his *oeuvre* – in subject matter and execution – is absolutely seminal in the development of figurative sculpture of the late nineteenth and early twentieth century.'

Gemma and Abi regarded Fen a little blankly. And then with exaggerated pity.

'I think Gemma meant the bloke in Derbyshire,' Abi said, as if to a simpleton.

'Oh,' Fen said. Don't blush. Don't blush. 'He's nice enough.'

'Rich?' asked Abi.

'No.'

'Eligible anyway?' Gemma pushed.

'No, no,' Fen breezed, 'he's old. I'm tired.'

'She blushed,' Abi remarked to Gemma in a whisper when they'd left Fen's room.

'I know,' Gemma connived.

'She says he's old,' Abi remarked, 'but that could mean anything over thirty – if age is to be assessed in comparison to us.'

'I want her to have Matt,' Gemma said, 'then it'll be ever so cosy.' She looked at Abi. They giggled.

'Shall I call Jake again?' Abi asked.

'Yes,' Gemma agreed, 'good idea.'

Jake's phone rings in the pub. He sees it's Abi's – or Gemma's – home number.

'Hullo?' he answers, not quite sure which girl it'll be and not minding.

'Hey,' says Abi. The line is bad.

'Dodgy signal,' Jake says, rising, 'I'll call you back in a mo'.'

He leaves the pub to return the call, and then returns to his pint not long after. He drains his glass. 'I've been summoned,' he says to Matt, eyes glinting.

'By whom?' Matt enquires, with mock disapproval, wondering what could have the urgency to take Jake away so willingly from last orders.

'Abi,' Jake says, licking his lips. 'She said something bizarre about Fen bringing home some porn.'

'Porn?' Matt says, startled. 'Fen?'

'Porno art was Abi's precise term,' Jake says. 'Come with me, Matt. Sounds like they've been quaffing the Chardonnay whilst we've been enjoying our civilized pints.'

'Come with you?' Matt asks.

'Yeah,' Jake shrugs, 'why not. Surprise Miss McCabe.'

Matt drinks the last third of his pint. Art? Porn? Fen?

Jesus. Abi. Gemma. Jake.

'Come,' Jake says, rising.

'Sure,' Matt says, following him out.

There's a knock on Fen's door. She's reading a paperback, she's cleaned her teeth. She's sitting on her bed in a vest-and-boxer-shorts night set.

'Yes?' she calls, wondering when Abi or Gemma has ever bothered to knock.

Oh God, don't let it be Jake trying to seduce me!

'Fen?'

Oh God! It's Matt! Oh Jeez!

Matt pops his head around the door while Fen is rooted to the spot, be-vested and blaspheming.

'Hullo,' he says.

Oh my God, she's practically naked.

Fen is too stunned to close her gaping mouth.

'Jake was coming – I thought I'd just pop in. You know, just for a minute or two.'

Fen nods blankly. Matt is still mostly in the hallway, just his head in her room, and his hand steadying the door.

'Bloody hell, Fen – did you nick it?' Matt exclaims on catching sight of the Fetherstone on her bedside table.

'Of course I didn't nick it!' Fen laughs. '*How* amazing is it?' She caresses Adam's head between her thumb and forefinger.

'May I come in?' Matt asks.

His manners touch Fen. 'Of course,' she smiles.

Matt concentrates very hard on the Fetherstone because he knows that unless he keeps his eyes trained on the forms of Adam and Eve, they will gravitate over to Fen in her vest. He doesn't want to notice that her toenails are neatly varnished the colour of aubergine, he doesn't want to acknowledge that her bare legs are just as toned and smooth as he'd imagined they'd be. He starts to discourse on Julius Fetherstone and cross-references this particular sculpture with Rodin's *Adam* and *Eve*.

'Of course, the figures of Adam and Eve were never

entwined,' he said, 'they were to stand to either side of the Gates of Hell.'

Fen nods. She knows all that. 'How was the Whitechapel yesterday?' she asks because kissing James has put a perspective on Matt.

'It was OK,' Matt answers honestly, 'nicely curated – but I didn't like any of the exhibits. There wasn't one piece I'd have had in my home.'

'And Judith?' Fen probes.

Did they? Shall I? Shall I ask him if they did?

Matt looks fleetingly a little alarmed. 'Judith really liked the show,' he says diplomatically. Fen nods. 'She's odd.' Fen raises an eyebrow and cocks her head encouraging Matt to elaborate. He doesn't.

'I think she has the hots for you,' Fen says, with an edge of mischief to her voice.

Matt groans. 'You may as well know—' Fen puts her fingertips to his lips. She does know. Quite enough. She doesn't want to hear any more.

Matt takes her fingertips from his lips and kisses them. He holds her hand. 'Fen McCabe,' he drawls huskily, 'do you know how horny you look, in that white, semi-see-through vest?'

Fen giggles. 'They're my jim-jams, silly!'

'Could we take it off, please?' he asks. Matt's manners delight her, as do his slightly glazed eyes. Fen knows from James's example that such a gaze at such a moment is caused by blood flow and energy being focused down to the groin. She glances at Matt's lap.

Unmistakable.

But still it surprises her. And arouses her. She doesn't quite know what to do. She plucks self-consciously at the straps of her vest and stares awkwardly at her knees.

'Can I?' Matt whispers, running his fingers over hers over the straps of her vest. 'Let me,' he suggests, easing a strap over her shoulder. Fen lets him gently lift her vest over her head.

Can he see my heart thuddering?

'Je-sus,' he whispers, 'you are absolutely *gorgeous.*' His hand reaches out and then stops, hovering, inches away, as if he is politely waiting for the go-ahead. Gently, he cups his palm over her skin. He gulps. She gasps. His breathing is quick. The feel of his hand on her skin, the sensation of her perky nipple at the centre of his palm, is lovely. Matt kisses her throat, at the exact location James had wanted to when Fen had woken up. Matt raises his face to Fen's. The deeper he kisses her, the more insistent his fondling becomes. He eases her down, flat on to her bed, and his face hovers over hers, half his body pressing over her. His hand travels along her ribs, over her stomach, his fingertip dips in and out of her navel. Lightly, he traces the curve of her waist and trickles his fingers back up to her breasts. He is tonguing her with some abandon, every now and then nipping her bottom lip with his teeth. Her hands are enmeshed in his hair. Her eyes are closed. Her mind is empty of anything other than savouring this moment.

Matt stops kissing her. He takes his face away so they can look at each other. 'More?' he asks. Fen doesn't know whether her heart is beating so fast on account of apprehension or arousal. 'I'll be gentle,' Matt says. To answer, Fen lets her eyelids close gently while she touches his chin and pulls his face close so that their lips meet again.

'OK,' she whispers.

Matt slips his hand down the elasticated waistband of her shorts and skims over her pubic hair. He cups her entire sex in his hand. Fen moves, to catch against his finger. He stops kissing her but the feeling of his breath on her face is just as lovely. Without preamble, he suddenly and deftly has a finger between the lips of her sex. The feel of his hot smooth finger against her clitoris, and at the wet opening of her sex, turns them both on immensely. He alternates between dabbing her clitoris and slipping his finger deep inside her. She is on the verge of coming. As his finger is working magic on her, she kisses him, forcing her tongue deep into his mouth. She is close to climax. Now she is moving enthusiastically. She is almost there. Not quite. Excruciatingly close. Wait! Almost. Almost. Nearly there!

Matt pulls away from her mouth and his finger is suddenly still. Fen stares at him.

'God I want to fuck you,' he whispers, staring back, his face close.

Fen comes. Ultimately, Matt's words brought her to orgasm.

When her sex has finished its spasms of pleasure, he takes his finger away and feeds it into her mouth. The release of sexual tension, pent up from her feelings for Matt, her feelings for James, leaves Fen languid and exhausted. Glazed, she gazes at Matt's handsome face. Glancing to her left, she sees *Eden*. James's face comes into her mind's eye. She closes her eyes.

'Sleep,' Matt demands, 'you look spent. I'll see you at work tomorrow.'

He kisses her forehead sweetly. Though her feet are at the pillow end of her bed, she allows him to place the duvet over her. Her eyes remain closed. Her lips are relaxed into a satisfied half-smile.

Matt made his way through the house. All the bedroom doors were closed. He had no idea which was Abi's room, which was Gemma's room, and which room, exactly, his rakish flatmate was in. Matt caught the tube home to Angel. If he licked his lips, he could taste and smell Fen.

It's not just sex. Not now. It's more. Now I want the whole her.

'It's not just sex,' James told Barry, 'I've had plenty of good sex in my time. It's *her*.' Barry's eyes twitched to show his master he was considering his words very carefully. Beryl sauntered over, sat by the armchair and sighed. 'I want her back here now.' James got up and went to the kitchen. Aimlessly, he looked in the pantry and the fridge. He wasn't hungry. He made milky coffee but he wasn't thirsty. He stood with his back to the stove. Barry and Beryl were hovering in the doorway, looking concerned. 'I can't be falling for someone her age – not at my age.' It was midnight. James presumed she and her housemates would still be up. Drinking wine, no doubt; gossiping and theorizing, probably. He picked up the phone and dialled Fen's home number.

'Don't they have an answering machine?'

He let the phone ring on.

'Isn't anyone in?'

The phone rang until it rang off.

'Where is she, I wonder?'

He tapped the receiver against his chin contemplatively. He was disappointed. It was suddenly very obvious that he was alone in a leaking house in Derbyshire with two dogs.

'I'll call her tomorrow,' he said quietly, taking the dogs outside for a last pee. 'I'll suggest she comes to me sooner than we've arranged.' The dogs seemed reluctant to come in. It wasn't even a particularly nice night, with heavy cloud-cover blanketing stars from view. 'God, to have her in my bed tonight.'

TWENTY-SIX

Whoa. Time Out. Calm down, cool it a little. It seems that everybody in this book — whether male or female, flesh and blood or bronze and marble, has sex on the brain. They are either having it, wanting it or simply spending far too much time in pursuit of it. They think about it while journeying into work by tube, or whilst driving Land Rovers down Derbyshire lanes, or when sipping absinthe with fellow artists at Les Deux Magots on the Boulevard St Germain.

Fen's sister Cat, and Matt's ex-girlfriend Julia, go to bed lonely and alone, trying hard to pretend that the last time they had sex with their exes was wonderful. In truth, both girls' sex lives diminished rapidly in the last months of their relationships. Lovemaking had been a contradiction in terms; because the love was no longer there and all that had been made was an effort to provide or achieve some level of physical gratification. Both women are struck with horror at the thought of their ex-boyfriends being with other women and yet both women had ceased to fancy their partners in those last horrible months. It hasn't yet occurred to them that one day, perhaps sooner rather than later, they will actively want to sleep with another man, that another man will desire them and take them to bed. Both women are even mourning the children they will never have by their exes, though babies had never been on their agenda.

Jake is physically exhausted. Sleeping with two different but equally insatiable and sexually adventurous women leaves him with little time for musing; whatever spare time he does have he uses to rest up and prepare for the next session with whomever. He has no preference. Sex is incredible with Abi and Gemma. It would be impossible to choose.

Judith St John can't sleep. She's too wound up by work, and works even harder at relaxing. When she arrives home, she flicks on classical music, opens a bottle of good wine and cooks for one, healthily and colourfully, in her designer kitchen. She's seen people on American TV series and films behave like that in their apartments after work. It works for them. They are successful at home as well as at work. They are also successful at being single or having casual relationships. It is not Matthew Holden whom she wants and desires; but control and superiority. What she had enjoyed about sex with Matt was not the physical sensation, but the sense of conquest. It wasn't about Matt. It was about Fen. If it hadn't been so obvious that Matt had designs on Fen, Judith would never have made a move on him. She was appalled that she should feel remotely unnerved by the mousy archivist. But she was, not so much because of Fen's intelligence, her suitability for the job, her prettiness; but because almost on sight Matt had had eyes for her and yet he had never looked twice at Judith. Matt had been an easy lay, that first time, plied with alcohol and compliments, her hand thrust uncompromisingly down his trousers, her tongue stuffed into his mouth.

But it didn't work yesterday. I had the bait laid but he didn't even sniff or nibble. What can I do? What can be done? It's not the sex I crave, nor his person – it's the success of my little project. It's as if Fen is proposing a takeover bid. I want it to fail. I cannot have anything at all operating behind my back and beyond my control.

Matthew doesn't regret having sex with Judith. It makes him cringe when he thinks back on it – but only at himself. He is pretty ashamed that, at nearly thirty years of age, a combination of alcohol (for which he had a strong, well-trained constitution) and a grope (which he was well experienced at giving and taking) could have been persuasive enough for him to have taken leave of his senses. But back then, he hadn't yet kissed Fen. And once he had, everything changed. The ex-girlfriend at last became very much part of his past. Judith became something daft that happened after too much booze. Last night, at the private view and then hip Hoxton, Matt was neither flattered or amused. He just felt awkward. Judith was on the verge of making a fool of herself with all her unbuttoning and pouting and bedroom eyes and fondling of pepper-pots. Tonight, he could smell Fen and taste her and see her gorgeous breasts clearly in his mind's eye. He wants a relationship with this girl. And he wants to consummate it soon.

James doesn't feel terribly comfortable. He has banished the dogs to the utility room so he can have a long think about the consequences of today. Something about Fen unnerves him. He's had affairs with women younger than her, but there's a freshness about Fen, a naivety, something a little old-fashioned, chaste even, which warns him to keep a respectful distance. Water is now coming through the roof. *Adam* and *Eve*, one propped on the dressing-table, the other on the window-sill, seem to be flirting and goading. You know you want it. You do. You want to do to her what Adam is going to do to me, Eve seems to be saying. She is offering you an apple, take it, take it, Adam abets. Take her. Have her. She wants you.

'Shut up, Adam!'

James takes both paintings and places them, oil sides facing each other, under his bed. Then he hurries downstairs in search of buckets and pans. As he tries to sleep with an atonal chorus of tinkles, plips and splashes all around him, he pulls the pillow over his head and chants that he will *not* mix business and pleasure.

Abi and Gemma go to sleep with smiles on their faces and their bodies throbbing. It's only sex. It's leisure, it's pure pleasure. Why wouldn't they want more? Once their bodies aren't quite so sore.

And Fen. She is asleep, upside down in her bed. She's kissed James in the morning and Matt in the evening, and when she came, though Matt brought her to orgasm, she throbbed for both men. Sleepily, she had wondered whether she's just doing a Jake. And what exactly is it that Jake is doing? Having a taste of this, a soupçon of that so that he can make a choice? Does one need to decide between two? She's not sure. Does she have a moral obligation? She's not sure. She'll have to go further to find out. It concerns her that she could feel so moralistically disapproving of Jake when on paper, she knows she is behaving little differently to him.

And Julius.

As Julius prophesied, and to Rodin's delight though to Madame Virenque's dismay, friends of Jacques Antoine wanted to commission Fetherstone for portrait busts of themselves, their wives, even their dogs and children. Soon enough, the young sculptor was able to afford an apartment overlooking the Musée Cluny. He paid rent every Thursday without fail or discount, to a middle-aged landlord who wouldn't have said no to sex but preferred the money and anyway, didn't have the temerity to ask. Sex dominates Julius's life though he has lived celibate for two years since Cosima. Every day, however, through the ooze of the plaster of Paris with which he constructs, or the clay with which he moulds, or the marble which he carves; through the exploration of anatomy, how ecstasy causes bodies to writhe, his life is dominated by sex. Sex doesn't sell, though. He has learnt, when a potential patron visits his studio with the commission for a bust of his wife or children or himself, not to show him the 'other works'. He tried that, two or three times. The visitors to his studio were at once sucked into the

201

scenes of lust and yet spat out, too. The works were so uncompromising in design, so blatant in subject matter, so confrontational, they were quite terrifying. How could a mind so perverse, so obsessed, claim also to be a master of the conventional sculpted portrait? *Non, Monsieur Fetherstone, non.* Wives and children would not be safe in his company.

TWENTY-SEVEN

*F*en woke in a fabulously good mood. After all, when she opened her eyes, there was a Fetherstone by her bedside. Gazing at *Eden*, she felt simultaneously calm yet ecstatic. Swiftly, she made it all make perfect sense to her.

I like to look this way and that, to consult right hand then left. It's what I'm like – if anything, I'm rather cautious. I like to feel that there are two sides to every coin – and the coin that makes me the person I am has lovely Matthew on one side and gorgeous James on the other. The men are as distinct as heads and tails, as individual as my right hand is from my left. I suppose you could say that there are two sides to every story.

Ah, but you don't credit Jake with this.

Jake is different.

Why? He's involved with two beautiful women. He's hurting no one. For him, Abi and Gemma are your Matt and James.

No. There is a slim but subtle difference. There's the question of deception. Jake is only in it for sexual gratification, for a spot of bedpost-notching. In fact, Abi is too – she only ever talks about the physical side.

And Gemma?

Gemma's just wanton.

God, Fen, you sound sanctimonious.

The difference between their triangle and mine is the issue of deception. Poor Abi. Furthermore, theirs isn't so much a triangle as a knot, a mess. And it's downright torrid that they all know each other. It's horribly incestuous. At least Matt and James don't. Just me. I'm the key. And I hold it with respect and care.

But in which hand do you hold it, Fen?

Abi stares hard at the front door long after Fen has shut it behind her. Gemma giggles irreverently once she deduces Fen to have walked a sufficient distance from the house.

'Honestly,' Gemma says, shaking her head in disbelief and pity, 'Maria Von Trapp watch out.'

'We kissed! We kissed!' Abi mimicks Fen.

'Actually, it's quite sweet,' Gemma concedes, 'and it wasn't just a kiss – what was her terminology?'

'She said that Matt "had a good rummage" – those were her words,' Abi muses.

'Actually,' Gemma says seriously, 'it *is* quite sweet, in this day and age. A little bit of old-fashioned decorum.'

'Don't sound so wistful!' Abi reprimands. 'Just because we're such trollops – it doesn't make Fen's morality higher than ours. Just different.'

'Are you seeing Jake tonight?' Gemma asks.

'Not if I'm still walking like John Wayne!' Abi declares and, to make her point, she swaggers to the front door, wincing theatrically, and leaves for work. Gemma follows a few minutes later, once she's sent a ludicrously lewd text message to Jake's mobile phone.

Matt was shaving and emitting a tuneless, absent-minded hum. Rivulets of foamy water trickled down his forearm, clung to the edge of his elbow and then oozed off to drip on to the floor of the bathroom or his bare feet. Today was the first day of his adult life that he had actually enjoyed shaving. When he had been a child, he loved his father to daub his face with shaving cream from the badger brush, which he then had much pleasure removing with an old kitchen spoon, tracing tracks through the cream like a toboggan careering down a hill. Since adolescence, however, Matt had found shaving the most terrible bind, had even surreptitiously read articles in his ex-girlfriend's glossy magazines about laser hair removal. Once or twice, he'd toyed with the idea of not shaving, of going for the beard, but gave up after four or five days; hating the feeling of grubbiness from the stubble and the way his whiskers caught on his pillow or pullover. Usually, he shaved in a rush, because he was hopeless at getting out of bed when the alarm went. Usually, he nicked himself here and there, and missed little patches which then irritated him supremely during the day. He'd tried aftershave once, which stung so much that his eyes watered and he'd been late for lectures on account of obsessive splashing of cold water against his cheeks. Although a goatee suited Jake, Matt felt it was the worst of all worlds – all the pitfalls of facial hair design coupled with all the inconvenience of shaving.

Today, though, Matt hummed and shaved, wielding the razor in swift strokes decapitating bristles but leaving his skin unscorched. Today, he was 'full of the joys'. It was a phrase his nanny had used in his childhood, one she had never qualified – thus it was perfect to express the joys of season, time, or general mood. Full of the joys of spring. Full of the joys of tea-time. Full of the joys of being a six-year-old with a new red bicycle for his birthday. Full of the joys of success at school, at university; of being in love. Today, Matthew Holden, two days away from his thirtieth birthday, is full of the joys of simply being out there. Of being young and living in a vibrant city; of having a stimulating job in addition to the stability of family inheritance; of being blessed with a lively social life; of being blessed with good looks and a fine figure; of being on the verge of falling in love with a sweet yet sexy girl.

205

With his face now smooth and pink, Matt patted it dry –
a pointless procedure preceding, as it always did, a long
hot shower. With the mirror steamed up, Matt wiped a dry
corner of his towel over it. Unlike Jake, Matt had looks but
little vanity. He was using the mirror not to marvel but to
prove a case in point. Ah, yes. There was his reflection,
clear and bright; external proof of his internal sense of
vitality. Great shave, smooth as a baby's bottom. Time to
get dressed, to greet the day, hooray! to see Fen. If Matt
had been remotely religious he'd have praised the Lord
for his good fortune; if he had lived in biblical times, he'd
have offered a sacrifice in thanksgiving. Some pieces of
gold perhaps, not sheep. No. He liked sheep. He'd grown
up in Gloucestershire surrounded by fields peppered with
them.

He dressed quickly, yesterday's trousers and a badly
ironed polo shirt, but still looked fresh and becoming on
account of his excellent demeanour. Jake, in comparison,
looked wan and tired.

'Sow your oats last night?' he mumbled in response to
Matt's verve, handing him a cup of coffee. Matt,
momentarily, looked confused. Sex had not been on his
mind this morning; the thought of it, the imminence of it
happening with Fen, was simply one element contributing
to his fantastic mood.

'No,' Matt grinned, 'not yet. You look *terrible.*'

'I'm shagged,' Jake groaned, 'literally. I really don't think I
can keep it up.'

'Ha!' Matt joshed. 'And I thought you were famous for
your powers of sexual endurance.'

'Ha bloody ha,' Jake answered, but with humility and not
rancour. 'By the way your mum called. You were humming
and la-la-ing so loud that you didn't hear the phone ring. She
says call her, that she hasn't spoken to you in ages, bla bla.'
Jake rubbed his eyes and then kept them closed, his
muscular frame slumped on the sofa. 'Bla bla.'

Matt checked his watch and phoned his mother. Their

relationship was a good one, good enough for no guilt to be foisted or felt if phone calls weren't returned promptly or visits home were not more frequent.

'Mummy,' Matt said, because he had never abbreviated it to Mum.

'Darling!' Susan Holden, in Gloucestershire, exclaimed, a little alarmed. 'Are you all right?'

'Fine,' Matt assured her, 'why?'

'Well, I only phoned half an hour ago,' she said with friendly sarcasm.

'I was having my shower and I'm actually on time for work so if we have a quick chat I'll still arrive my normal quarter of hour late!'

'Now, darling,' Susan said, 'your birthday. Of course there'll be the dosh from Daddy's will, but is there anything specific I can give you?'

'Honestly, Mummy, I'm fine – whatever,' said Matt, who had forgotten about his birthday and didn't want for anything anyway.

It had always delighted Susan that an only child, brought up by a rich and aged father and a rich, younger mother, could be so unmaterialistic. 'Well, how about a suit from Armani? Or a scooter?'

Matt declined, having no need for the one or the other.

'A VD machine?'

'DVD player?' Matt laughed. 'Jake has one.'

'Darling, I do so want to give you something special,' Susan paused, 'my baby boy is turning thirty!'

'I'd quite like that book about the Beatles,' Matt said honestly.

'Bugger the Beatles on your birthday!' Susan remonstrated. 'Well, for the time being, shall I just put a tab behind the bar at the Groucho or the Cobden again?'

'I'm not a member of either,' Matt reminded her.

'But I am,' she declared, 'you can leave it to me, Matthew.'

Matt was touched. 'Thanks,' he said. Just before the call ended, he spoke up. 'Mummy?'

Susan hoped he wasn't going to request the Met Bar or somewhere else she had no strings to pull.

'I met someone.'

Because historically, Matthew had never really imparted much detailed information about his private life, his mother came to the wrong conclusion, presuming the someone to be someone she knew. 'Who, darling? The Smythes are in town this week – did you bump into them?'

'I mean,' said Matt, 'a girl. I've *met* someone. Wanted you to know.'

Susan was touched and rendered silent momentarily. 'Well,' she said at length, 'that's super.'

'Yes. Hmm,' said Matt, now clamming up which was far more normal a response to his mother's ears. 'She's lovely,' he mumbled.

'Super,' his mother repeated, eager to know everything but too tactful to probe. 'Well, I'd better go. Nanny and I are going to do ruthless things to the vegetable patch. You should see it. Your poor father would turn in his grave. It's a veritable riot. A disgrace. Bye bye, darling.'

In Gloucestershire, she replaced the handset and observed it a while. Her only child, her beloved boy, turning thirty. Met someone lovely.

'Nanny?' she called.

'How was my boy?' Nanny, suddenly appearing, asked.

'Top form,' Susan said, 'and he's Met Someone.'

Nanny placed the Mr Muscle on the occasional table with care, and sat down beside Susan on the Chesterfield. They stared at the fire-guard. 'Ooh,' said Nanny, 'someone nice?'

'Lovely – apparently,' Susan said, 'he wouldn't bother recounting dalliances.'

'Good for Matthew,' said Nanny, tapping Susan's knee. 'Come on now, there's the spinach to be done before elevenses.'

Fen was walking down John Islip Street ahead of Matt. He

wanted to call out to her, wolf-whistle even, run up to her; instead, he indulged himself watching her unseen.

She wiggles. Unintentionally. But an unmistakable and utterly alluring sway to her bottom. Oops! Easy girl – watch your step.

'Fen!'

Fen turned around and blushed. They walked the last few yards together, slowing their pace, not quite knowing what to say. They knew their awkwardness was natural, acceptable, after last night's impromptu intimacy. Chit-chat seemed a good idea, despite being surprisingly hard work. It was therefore a relief to arrive at Trust Art. They said good morning to Bobbie and rifled through their respective pigeon-holes. A delighted and intuitive Bobbie filed her nails with gusto, happy to presume that Fen and Matt had arrived at work together because they had left home together after an evening of passion and a night cuddling cosily together.

Matt hovered at his door and Fen faltered alongside him.

'I'm a gentleman,' he shrugged, escorting her the extra few yards to the door of the Archive.

I'm a soft sod, more like!

'See you later, then,' Fen said, with a shy smile.

Matt walked back to Publications. No sooner had Fen sat down to check e-mails, than he had returned. He perched on the edge of her desk, fiddling with a paper-clip which he kept dropping.

'Fen,' he started, 'last night – well, I had planned to woo you with the whole seduction thing, you know, dinner, wine, candles, Barry White background music. So, I mean, last night – I mean, this morning. I mean, are you OK about it all?'

Fen was touched. 'Very OK,' she said.

Matt tipped her chin up and bent low to kiss her. 'It's not good for my balls,' he whispered, 'to fill them with such expectation. They're aching for you.'

'I'm on Cat duty tonight,' she said apologetically, laying her hand gently in Matt's groin.

'That just makes me want to make a pun on pussy,' Matt said, dejected.

Fen smiled. She tapped his knee. 'We can do dinner whenever,' she said, 'foreplay or post-coitally!'

'Fen McCabe!' Matt marvelled and laughed. 'Actually, it's my birthday on Friday.'

'I'll tie myself in a big red ribbon then,' Fen said coyly.

'I can unwrap you at the end of the evening,' Matt mused. 'My mother is footing the bar bill – bring Abi and Gemma, your sisters too, if you like.'

Fen was happy for the focus to shift from an evening entirely centred on consummation. She would invite Pip and Cat to Matt's birthday drinks. She quite wanted to show Matt off to her sisters. She valued their opinions more highly than her flatmates's.

TWENTY-EIGHT

*J*ames was well aware that *Adam* and *Eve* were under his bed, but he resolutely refused to bring them out; ignoring them rather as if they had misbehaved. He had been chastising himself since last seeing Fen. What could he have been thinking? Utterly ridiculous. Impossible too. He was standing over his dogs whilst they wolfed down an early tea or a very late breakfast.

'I have to nip it in the bud,' he said out loud, pleased with the horticultural allusion.

Her gorgeous rosy nipples were like little buds in the centre of my palm.

'For God's sake!' he scolded himself, though Beryl thought she had done something wrong and hung her head over her bowl until her master apologized and reassured her and urged her to eat. He checked the time. Four o'clock. He rather thought the London workforce stopped at around this time on Fridays to steam into pubs.

Better phone her. Better cancel Monday. Better explain that it suits me better to have the two oil sketches sent to Trust Art via courier.

'Archive?' Fen answered her phone.

'The oil sketches – they're back from the framers.' *James James James James James!* Fen rejoiced to herself.

'Unframed, I hope,' she said, surprising herself at the steadiness of her voice and her readiness to jest.

'Of course,' said James.

'Ought I come to collect them then?' Fen asked.

'Yes,' said James, physically rapping his temple with the telephone.

'In fact,' said Fen, 'it might be practical to come up on Sunday – save myself a tiring day return.'

'Yes,' James agreed.

'I could stay the night with my uncle,' Fen said.

No! thought James. *I mean, yes!*

'But he may not be there, of course,' Fen mused, wondering when was the last time that Django had spent a night away from home. 'In fact,' she said, 'I think he might have said that he thought he probably was definitely not going to be in, in all likelihood.'

James was silent.

I don't want to hear this. I'm not listening. The paintings will be sent down by bloody Parcel Force, if needs be.

'Perhaps I could stay with you?' said Fen softly.

'Yes,' said James, 'of course you can.'

James replaces the handset and stands in the kitchen shaking his head at himself. Barry and Beryl sit in silent companionship either side of him. They don't like to hear him groan. They head-butt him with desperate affection.

'Phone her back,' he commands, 'now!'

But he doesn't.

Fen replaces the handset and feels very pleased that the call came just before her meeting with Rodney and Judith – she will be showing them the Fetherstone bronze before taking it to the Tate for secure keeping prior to next week's acquisitions meeting. Fen leaves work. She is really looking forward to Sunday.

TWENTY-NINE

'*B*ut I haven't anything to wear!'

Pip and Fen observe Cat who is sitting in shabby tracksuit bottoms and a shapeless sweatshirt; toying with the idea of actually eating, or rather sucking, cold baked beans directly from the tin with a teaspoon.

'And I won't know a soul!'

Pip and Fen, arms folded across their breasts, regard their youngest sister benevolently but sternly.

'I'm not ready – please – I'd rather stay in and watch *Eurotrash*. I don't want to go out. I'll be a wallflower. A burden. It's pointless.'

She looks and sounds quite pathetic. If her elder sisters were not aware how hard her pain has been, they'd have thought her unnecessarily melodramatic.

'Do it for me,' says Fen, as if requesting a very large favour. 'If Matt doesn't warrant your seal of approval, then I'll know not to sleep with him.'

'I mean,' Pip colludes, 'say you don't come, and Fen doesn't take a blind bit of notice of my opinion – say she sleeps with him then you meet him and proclaim him the devil incarnate? Well!' She does a handstand and walks upside-down over to Cat. 'Please, Funny Face, please come?'

213

Cat regards her topsy-turvy sister. And thinks about her responsibility in the development of Fen's love life.

'OK OK,' she sighs. 'I'll do it for you,' she nods at Fen, 'and for you,' she nods at Pip, suddenly feeling the urge to tickle her upended sister's midriff, 'but I'm not looking forward to it. I don't want to go. I'd like to leave early.'

Fen and Pip nod at everything she says.

'I suppose I could wear my Whistles dress,' Cat says quietly. Fen pretends she's engrossed in a magazine about bicycles. Pip, who has righted herself, nods with necessary nonchalance. 'I could just wear my jeans,' Cat suggests. Again Pip nods while Fen continues to read about yellow jerseys.

Cat emerges fifteen minutes later. She looks gorgeous. She is in the Whistles dress, her hair meticulous in a mussed-up chignon, her pretty facial features enhanced with a flick of mascara and a swipe of lipstick.

'Come on then,' she says glumly, as if on her way to the gallows.

Throughout the evening, at various intervals, Fen stopped to ponder the fact that tonight was the night when she'd have sex with Matt. Once or twice, she wondered if tonight wasn't really the right time. It was his birthday, he was having an impromptu party. There were loads of people. She felt, sometimes, as if she was something of a hanger-on – wearing her genial smile rather fixed because she knew so few people. Actually, she hadn't been remotely clinging and had, in fact, spent more time chatting to her sisters and flatmates than she had spent with Matt. He'd catch her eye, though, and smile, or they'd just gaze for a suspended moment. Times like those she'd think yes, let's sleep together tonight. However, observing him at other times, knocking back a drink or laughing in an overanimated way with his friends, she'd think no, let it wait. His friends were very warm and chatty, fuelled as they were by the champagne on tap, courtesy of Susan Holden. In the toilet, Fen looked from left hand to right.

It's very odd. I've been taken aback when some of his friends have said, 'Oh so you're Fen McCabe,' but I've been equally offended if they've said, 'What's your name? Do you work with Matt then?' and obviously haven't a clue who I am to him.

Matt had spoken at length both to Cat and Pip, separately and together. The McCabe sisters reported back to Fen that Matt was gorgeous, a honey, a gent, obviously enamoured with her and that she should go for it, lucky lucky girl, what a catch. By midnight, Cat was fairly plastered. She hadn't been drowning her sorrows – far from it – her inebriation was merely a physical reaction to a simple glass or two of champagne on a stomach that had churned with distress over the past month or so and been deprived of regular meals.

'I think Cat should go home,' Pip said surreptitiously to Fen. 'It is her first outing after all – it should end on a high note. It could well devolve into drunken overemotional rambling and tears if she's – or we're – not careful.' Fen agreed. She looked over to Matt, the life and soul amidst a posse of pals.

Perhaps I should go now too. We could go to bed tomorrow. Or whenever. Anyway, Abi and Gemma are in full swing – literally. So I might feel a little uncomfortable without my sisters.

'I'll go and say goodbye,' said Fen. Pip regarded her as if she was totally insane. 'I'd rather leave with you two,' Fen explained.

'It's the boy's birthday,' Pip said, with incredulity, 'why on earth would you leave?' Fen shrugged and looked uneasy. 'He glances over at you with charming regularity,' Pip said. 'Half the time, you don't even notice. You are making his night. You must stay. You're his biggest birthday pressie, you daft cow.'

'I'm not saying I'll leave on account of being a dutiful sister,' Fen told her with honesty, 'I just might feel more comfortable leaving now, that's all.'

'Oh shush,' Pip said, asserting bossiness that was the prerogative of the eldest sibling. She walked over to Matt to wish him a happy birthday, to thank him for inviting them, to say how lovely it had been to meet him. 'Hope we'll meet again soon,' Pip said, shaking his hand. 'You take care of my sister – and she'll take care of you.'

Matt grinned. 'Pip, it's been a pleasure. Is Cat OK? It must have been a tall order for her tonight – I hope she's enjoyed at least part of it.'

'Oh, she has,' Pip assured him, 'but it's time we left.' She kissed him on each cheek. 'If I wasn't so sozzled, I'd juggle with those empty champagne bottles. But I am, so I shan't. Good-night.'

Gemma seemed to be monopolizing Jake and it was winding Fen up. Abi was very merry, flitting among Matt's friends all chatty and effervescent. Fen watched as every now and then Abi would return to Jake and Gemma briefly before skipping off to socialize elsewhere. Because Fen did not know what to say to Gemma and Jake, she steered well clear of them. But she avoided Abi too, because she did not want her to spend too much time away from her boyfriend. Matt was attentive towards Fen, introducing her to people he'd already introduced her to, bringing her into conversations by changing the slant or the subject matter, or just giving her hand a squeeze or her shoulders a rub or bestowing upon her a very lovely smile.

At gone one in the morning, a couple of Matt's friends made a suggestion that Fen didn't feel so sure about.

'Come on Matt, let's go back to yours.'

No! Go back to your own homes. For the past half-hour, I've been wanting him to come up to me, to whisper, 'Come on Fen, let's go back to mine.'

'Sure!' beamed the birthday boy, taking Fen's hand. 'Who's coming?'

Five others, it seemed, excluding Matt and Fen. Not Jake or Abi or Gemma – they were happy to stay put, Jake holding

216

court while the two girls gazed at him starry-eyed and laughed heartily at anything remotely humorous, hanging on his every word and quite often, his arms or trouser legs too.

'You don't mind, do you?' Matt whispered to Fen.

'Of course not,' Fen said. She was happy to leave. It unnerved her that Gemma's interest in Abi's boyfriend should be so brazen.

And now it is almost three in the morning and the last of Matt's pals are waiting for their cab. Fen is tired, so tired that she keeps popping to the bathroom to splash cold water on her face. This means that, with her mascara now gone, she looks exhausted. Her right hand says, 'Just chill out – you want more from Matt than One Night anyway.' Her left hand says, 'Slap your face, splash more cold water, brush your teeth and as soon as those bloody people have gone, give Matt the birthday present you've prepared for him.' Fen makes a compromise; patting her face with more cold water, sucking a fingerful of toothpaste, pinching her cheeks to give her wan expression a bit of colour.

Matt's friends tell her how much they've enjoyed meeting her, how they hope to see more of her, that they're sure they'll be seeing her again soon. All the while, they smile their seal of approval on Matthew. It cheers Fen up.

Matt closes the front door.

'Phew!' he says, though his back is towards her. 'I thought they'd never go!' He turns and smiles. 'Brilliant birthday,' he says. They sit on the sofa and appreciate the silence. Fen tells herself to go home, to stay, to kiss him, to stay put.

'You look gorgeous,' Matt says.

'I've washed off all my make-up,' Fen replies a little gloomily.

'I don't like make-up,' Matt says. Fen worries in case he thinks she uses too much.

'I just use a little mascara, a little eye shadow,' she rushes, 'actually, I pinch it off Gemma.'

'Gemma wears too much, you see,' Matt says, to qualify, 'for my liking, anyway.'

'Not for Jake's,' Fen mumbles.

'Sorry?' says Matt.

'Nothing,' says Fen, knowing it to be dangerous territory.

'It was great meeting your sisters,' Matt says and then stifles a yawn.

'Yes,' says Fen, 'I'm really pleased that Cat came.' She yawns expansively.

'Miss McCabe,' says Matt, 'can I entice you into my bed?'

'Of course you can, birthday boy,' says Fen.

Fen and Matt tried to have really good sex. They really tried hard to enjoy it, and tried hard to pleasure each other, and Matt tried hard to be hard, full stop. Fen tried not to be put off by the alcohol on his breath and she tried not to take his feeble attempt at an erection personally. Matt told himself that Fen must just be tired, that's why she didn't want him to go down on her. Actually, Fen was concerned that after the long night in a cramped, hot bar, coupled with a microfibre G-string and far too much excitement early in the evening, her nether regions might be a little unappetizing. But she was too shy to say so. They did manage to have sex, but the only conclusion they came to was that seduction was daft at four in the morning. No amount of bump-and-grinding was going to change that. Sleep was a much better idea. Matt brought his body against Fen's back, so that he was curled around her and she was sitting in his lap almost; lying like a pair of spoons. Just before a dreamless sleep swept down on her, she remembered the feeling of Matt nuzzling the nape of her neck. Then she remembered nothing else. When she awoke, she remembered bad sex but the stronger memory was how comforting she had found sleeping with Matt. It didn't matter that he was making odd gruffles, or had morning breath. What mattered was that she felt safe and at ease with him.

Funny, that! From work flirtation to prospective boyfriend! I actually rather like the idea of that.

218

THIRTY

*T*he more imminent it became, the more Fen and James absolutely dreaded seeing each other. Both prophesied a horrible, animal inevitability to it all. It would only take a phone call, a quick one at that, from either of them, to cancel the arrangement. They both knew that. Easy.

If I see her, I'll sleep with her. It's not a good idea.

If I see him, I'll sleep with him. Bad idea.

But they will see each other. In a matter of hours. It's inevitable.

Throughout her life, Fen had steadfastly refused to lie. Whereas Pip could concoct fabulously inventive stories, while Cat could just fall irritatingly silent, Fen preferred to be simply evasive. She would omit certain details – always primarily to prevent hurt – but she would never out-and-out lie. Therefore, she told Matt that she was going to Derbyshire to collect the Fetherstone oils, but that's all she told him. She omitted to call her housemates or her sisters – she didn't phone them because they hadn't phoned her. If she told Gemma and Abi, and if Pip or Cat then called the house and were told Fen was in Derbyshire, they'd presume their sister to be with Django. If she called Pip or Cat, they'd want to know why she wasn't staying with Django. Matt simply knew that Fen had family in Derbyshire, so had no need to ask where she was staying, assuming that she was going up on the Sunday so that she could indeed stay with this Django chap. It was so logical that he didn't ask, and therefore Fen didn't need to tell any untruths.

So, Matt took her to St Pancras and settled her on the train with the Sunday papers and some chocolates.

'See you tomorrow,' he came close to her ear to whisper.

'Tomorrow,' Fen smiled. She was already looking forward to it. 'About lunch-time.' She kissed Matt's neck and he left the train, waving briefly before leaving the station. With a contented smile on her face and a warm feeling in her body, Fen settled back into her seat (she had decided to upgrade herself on the Sunday special rate to first class) and organized the papers into her own idiosyncratic order of preference. TV guide first (not that she ever watched much), then the main newspaper, followed by the travel supplement (not that she'd taken a holiday abroad in two years), magazine, newspaper review section, children's comic supplement, finally the appointments. She always read the appointments with great interest, not that she needed a job, or was remotely interested in any on offer, or that she even qualified to apply for any advertised.

I just like to see what's out there – all those interesting-sounding careers with a host of applicants waiting in the wings. In comparison, my world is so small. It isn't really even a notch on the cog of national industry.

Today, though, Fen couldn't really settle with the papers. It wasn't the landscape that distracted her, nor her fellow passengers. It was the free rein she had to think about Matt. Before they had cemented their relationship, she would fantasize about what might be. This was exciting to do, not least because he was the first man of flesh and blood rather than bronze or marble to captivate her in some years. But now there was something much more satisfactory about gazing out of the train window and replaying events that had really happened. Now she wasn't having to write a script and envisage; she was remembering fact. It was as if her recent days had been secretly filmed. Whilst living them, she was far too caught up in the here and now to really appreciate them. But here on the train, she could rewind and then press play, settle back into her comfortable first class seat with the cotton anti-macassar and the complimentary coffee, and indulge herself reliving the immediate true past in glorious technicolor detail.

This she did with ease, and much replaying of certain details, until Leicester. She rewatched herself having sex twice – first on Saturday morning, though it was nearer noon when they awoke. In truth, that had been just as bad an idea as trying to consummate their relationship a few hours before when they were exhausted and somewhat drunk. Although revived and not too badly hungover, morning breath precluded any kissing – which Fen had always rated as one of the most erotic elements of lovemaking, one of the fundamentals of foreplay, probably due in no small part to her love of Rodin's *The Kiss*. It was straightforward, safe sex during which Fen did not come and Matt did not seem to notice though he enquired after her pleasure after the event.

Sitting on the train, Fen thought back to strolling along Upper Street desperate for a post-coital, post-hangover carbohydrate overload. In the event, they forsook a traditional greasy spoon for Pizza Express because the garlic wafting out into the street was just irresistible. Fen shifted in her seat and remembered how they had been overcome by a fit of giggles over God knows what. Dough balls really have little comedy value but that afternoon, Fen and Matt had tears streaming down their faces while their bodies were racked with laughter.

Accepting a refill of not-too-bad coffee, Fen indulged in replaying images of the early-evening lovemaking she and Matt had taken their time over a few hours later. Their bodies smelt fresh and though their breath would have kept the vampires away, they were immune to it because they shared it. They thought each other tasted rather delicious, actually, Fen decided, looking out of the window thinking that a large herd of sheep looked like a flurry of litter.

It was a turn-on watching him as he climaxed. Me on top. He locked on to my eyes as he was building up to it, then they glazed over and ultimately closed altogether with the intensity of his orgasm. His gasps and moans really excited me. As did the feeling of his cock jumping for joy. I was rather chuffed that he was so spent and speechless for some minutes after.

Did you come too?

Almost. Nearly. No. Not that it mattered. He was sweet and asked if it had been all right. He didn't ask outright if I'd climaxed. I told him that it had been lovely, that he had been more than all right. I didn't lie. I don't lie, you see.

The train pulled out of Leicester and gathered momentum. To Fen's horror it was as if Matt had been left standing on the platform she was hurtling away from. And though she tried to crane her neck, she lost him. She lost him. And though she tried to read 'A Life In The Day Of' profiling some athlete she'd never heard of in the back of the *Sunday Times* magazine, James Caulfield appeared in her mind's eye and refused to go away. It was bewildering for her. Matt had quite categorically disappeared. James held her thoughts until Chesterfield. She disembarked the train with butterflies rampaging around her stomach. It no longer seemed a bad idea, morally doomed, to spend a night with this man. It seemed a fantastic opportunity.

Though, if it's so good an idea, why is my mouth so dry?

There's Beryl! Or is it Barry? The Land Rover must be parked outside. There's James. Smiling. Approaching. Here.

'Fen,' he greets, laying his hand on her shoulder, leading the way out.

It was lovely to be back at Keeper's Dwelling. There felt nothing untoward in being in such close proximity to this man. Fen was in no moral maze because she had no thoughts of Matt whatsoever. Now, feelings for James – positive and good – were at the forefront. Which is why, when she went to the loo, she was so horrified by the knickers she had chosen with such care that morning.

What was I thinking? I am wearing tatty old knickers, chewing-gum grey, back to front. I know my trousers don't allow for Visible Panty Line – but why did I improvise? Why didn't I wear one of my G-strings? Why have I tried to emulate the G-string effect with a pair of shabby pants, back to front?

She knew it was for the same reason that she hadn't shaved her armpits or legs – because this morning, full of the joys of her union with Matt, she wanted to dissuade herself from the temptation that is James. She thought shabby underwear and stubbly limbs would deter her. Alone in James's toilet, she tried to return to that mind-set.

Art. Art. Think and talk art. Phone Django.

'Where are *Adam* and *Eve*?' she asked James, who was sitting in the snug with Barry lolling over his feet and Beryl slumped over Barry, both dogs sharing a plate of Jaffa Cakes with their master. James didn't want to tell her they were on top of each other upstairs under his bed. He didn't want to say the words 'upstairs' or 'bed'.

'Don't worry,' he said instead, 'they're in the other room – nicely unframed, of course.'

Fen took the easy chair opposite him and accepted a Jaffa Cake. He watched as she nibbled all around the edge and then levered off the orangey bit to suck and savour. It was both seductive and charming – rather like Fen. On the one hand, James found her mesmerically sexy; on the other, he sensed a freshness and naivety. He imagined he could take her to bed and subject her to the rudest of sex, or he could sit her in his chair and treat her like a porcelain doll.

'James?'

Sit still, Fen.

'Fancy some exercise?'

Just you sit in that chair and stay as you are.
'James, shall we take the dogs out for a walk?'
Marvellous idea.
'Marvellous idea.'

Striding through Forestry Commission land near the Folly, James and Fen let their bodies touch, even bump, accidentally-on-purpose. Every now and then, Fen would fall back a step or two. She liked to see James ahead of her. His hands slung into his pockets, his head cocking this way or that to locate some bird or admire some tree. His profile fine, a smattering of bristles enhancing his rugged, out-doorsy mien. She felt he was leading the way, setting the pace, taking her for a walk. She liked his control, his dominance. He took natural paths at random, the carpet of pine needles making footfalls soft and springy. She loved the way his walk was so confident, so in tune with the environment. The dogs were like balls on a bagatelle, careering this way and that, bounding between trees and over logs and through dank-smelling marshy patches; every now and then depositing chunks of well-chewed branch at Fen or James's feet as a gift.

'Tell me about Django,' James said, because it was a safe subject and one in which he was genuinely interested. 'It's highly likely that we have crossed paths at some point.'

'Django is our mother, our father, our guardian angel, our best friend,' Fen said without gushing, 'and you'd certainly know if you'd crossed paths with him!'

'Your mother?' James probed. 'How did you cope?'

'Easily,' Fen said, 'as far as I can remember. I wasn't even three when she eloped with her cowboy from Denver. My only real memory is Battersea. Of our front room. The room is more vivid in my mind's eye than my parents, though. It had fabulous wallpaper – a little like the opening of *Doctor Who* – lots of receding circles and stuff.'

They walked on quietly.

'In fact,' Fen said, with a chuckle edged with slight

remorse, 'I used to think of those shapes as advancing – only in recent years, I think of them as receding.'

James observed her; she was smiling lightly but there was a fatigue to her eyes. 'Must be your advancing years,' he jested gently, 'you're getting old.'

'I wouldn't want the memory ever to fade altogether,' she said.

'It never will,' said James, as if with authority, 'I assure you.' On they walked. James put his arm across Fen's shoulders. 'On the face of it, you're practically an orphan.'

'Not with Django,' Fen remonstrated.

'No,' James nodded, 'by all accounts. Plus you have sisters, of course. I hated being an only child.'

Barry interrupted them, hurtling at great velocity on account of being pursued by Beryl who was carrying a branch of such menacing proportions in her mouth, that Fen was sent flying.

'Bloody dogs!' James muttered as he righted Fen and brushed her down. 'Mangy mutts.' Fen was laughing, having taken no offence from the dogs' behaviour and having been amused by James's response. Beryl and Barry squirmed around Fen and James, their noses trying to detect the humans' true mood, to work out whether punishment or forgiveness was imminent. Dirty paws scratched imploringly at trouser legs whilst brown eyes gazed adoringly upwards; the combined effort saying, 'Sorry! We love you!'

'There there,' Fen soothed, patting heads matted with forest-floor debris.

'Bloody dogs,' James said, but not unkindly. 'Fancy a drink?'

Fen knew the Cross Oaks public house – but not as well as she knew the Rag and Thistle. She was confident therefore that she would not be recognized. Momentarily, she was disturbed by her desire for anonymity. Soon enough, though, she settled in and enjoyed a half-pint of lager and lime to James's full pint of bitter. She helped herself to the lion's share of the quite sizeable packet of cheese-and-onion crisps he brought to the table.

'How about you, James,' she said, with crumbs at the corner of her mouth, 'are your folks Derbyshire people? Are they alive?'

'Both dead,' James said, 'my father more recently so. Though it was my mother to whom I was closest as she brought me up and I saw little of my father for many years.'

'That's sad,' said Fen, because she could truly empathize, 'you really are a bonafide orphan!'

'All alone in the world,' James chuckled, 'though far from lonely.'

'I love my sisters,' Fen said, ignoring the internal voice asking why she was keeping such fundamental secrets from them, then.

James drained his glass and chinked it against Fen's. 'You're privileged,' he said. 'Come on, we ought to walk back – it's a good mile and a half from here.'

'I'll phone Django,' said Fen, with little conviction, as they collected the dogs who had been tied up outside and were now excessively pleased to see them.

'I can drive you over there later,' said James, unconvincingly.

'Django!'

'Hullo there!'

'I'm sure I saw that niece of yours today.'

'Niece? Who?'

'The middle one – the arty one.'

'Fenella?'

'In the Cross Oaks.'

'I doubt it – she's in London. Lives and works there.'

'Well, I've not seen her for a year or so, mind, but I'll say it were her all right.'

'Can't have been – though she has been up recently. On business.'

'She was with that Caulfield chap – you know, fancy gardens and all?'

'Lives at Delvaux.'

Django took his leave of the bar-proppers at the Rag and Thistle and returned home. Just in case Fen was here. Just in case she was trying to call. Bugger. He must buy an answering machine. Poor girl might have resorted to bedding down on the moors. If she is indeed here. Ah, but she'd ring – of course she would.

But Fen doesn't ring Django. And when he phones Pip to clarify her younger sister's whereabouts, Pip tells him that Fen is far more likely to be in the bed of her new suitor than on a bed of heather.

'Matt lives in Islington,' Pip tells her uncle.

'Does he now,' Django says, wondering if Islington is impressive.

James sleeps the opposite way to Matt. Fen has awoken at four in the morning, thinking she may as well be alone in a bed. James is very much on one specific side of the bed. If she lays a hand on his shoulder, or touches his leg with her foot, he moves over even more. Not in a flinch, just a slight but undeniable shift. It occurs to Fen that James Caulfield is as self-contained in sleep as he is in his life. She lies there, wondering if she is taken aback by this. No. She feels that if he was not happy for her to be in his bed, it would be she who would be shunted far over to one end. He is sleeping peacefully. She recalls his words, whispered in the dark, earlier.

'I *will* sleep with you, Fen McCabe,' he had said, 'but I won't *sleep* with you.'

Because he had said so, whilst his hands had expertly traversed her body, she had been unsure of his intention. Would they have sex and then he'd sleep in the snug? Or would they not have sex but sleep together in his bed?

Despite two bottles of Fitou shared during the evening, despite the dogs being banished to the utility room, despite

Fen and James gravitating from facing chairs to sitting on the floor with their backs to the couch, no direct pass was being made by either of them. Though he laid his hand on her leg and fondled her knee, the conversation contradicted this, focused as it was on Fen's opinion of *fin de siècle* sculpture. Though she ran her fingertips over the back of his hand, tracing his veins, stroking his knuckles, he spoke to her of rosebay willowherb and, tangentially, of having seen Jimi Hendrix play live on the Isle of Wight. Actually, they both found this momentarily a little disconcerting, privately acknowledging that Fen would have been in nappies at the time.

At not even eleven o'clock, Fen yawned first. James yawned very soon after.

'Did you know,' Fen said, knitting fingers with him, 'that the yawn is the most contagious thing in the world? It's the same yawn, being passed around and around, ad nauseam.'

James laughed. 'No, I did not know that,' he said, encircling her wrist and then stroking the inside of her elbow. 'Out of the mouths of babes and sucklings!'

There was silence. Fen was acutely aware of his touch and of the hush and she felt awkward. 'Pregnant pause?' she remarked, not to be witty but to break it. James looked at her, looked a little uneasy. 'I'm tired,' Fen said. 'Bed?' As soon as she heard the words out in the open, she wanted to take them back again.

'We can,' James replied. 'You'll have to share my toothbrush, though.'

And she'd used his toothbrush. And she did notice that his physique bore no vestige of youth, that gravity was doing its thing. And she didn't really mind because to her James was incredibly masculine. She thought how some would say that this man was no longer in his prime. To her, though, he was. Because this is what he looked like right now, and it was right now that Fen had him. In her eyes, there was no room for improvement – because she had no knowledge of his physique when younger to serve as a point of reference or comparison. She wasn't self-conscious about undressing in front of him. And she didn't mind if he did notice her strange improvisation at a G-string. James didn't notice. For him, the beauty of Fen's naked body far exceeded his anticipation.

Then James had said about not sleeping with her, but sleeping with her. Fen had lain in the dark, wondering what he meant. She didn't think, therefore, that she should reach for him though she so wanted to. In the dark, after a while's silence, James touched her. Lightly at first, then assertively. For Fen, it was like him taking her for a walk in bed. Leading the way again. His pace. His territory. It turned Fen on to be passive under his expertise. James was absolutely silent. It was pitch-black in the bedroom. Hands explored and tongues danced and mouths tasted and sucked. James's lips enclosed Fen's mouth, swallowing her moans as she came on his hand. She was then ravenous to return the favour but James resisted her. They didn't have penetrative sex. He didn't come. And, at the time, it didn't seem strange.

Odd, Fen thought much later, as she lay awake with James asleep far on the other side of the bed, *but in truth, that was the best sex I can remember having.*

THIRTY-ONE

Intelligence designs but the heart does the modelling.
Auguste Rodin

Henry Holden had family money – unlike other members of his family, however, he did not put it into ships, but art. His father was appalled – especially when it transpired that the art his son was purchasing was of the modern school. It would have been different if his son had invested in oil paintings of great seafaring vessels. But no, Henry Holden Junior, at the age of seventeen, purchased a nonsensical scrawl by some Russian chap.

'Wassily Kandinsky!' Henry marvelled in a whisper, holding the painting up like a father worshipping a new baby. To Henry's father, it sounded as though his son was blaspheming. However, though strict and not particularly demonstrative with his children, Mr Holden Senior's particular view on parenting and child development was neither to discourage nor encourage.

'Courage!' he had declared to his wife before their first child had been born, 'Courage is the key! It is attainable only through personal choice. Our offspring must make their own mistakes. They must be accountable for their actions, positive or negative.'

And so, though Mr Holden thought little of Henry's taste for the seeds of German Expressionism, and though he thought even less of his son's utter lack of interest in boat building and its history, he allowed his son to spend his funds in whichever way he felt was best.

In Henry Holden's collection, the Kandinsky sketch joined a small Pissarro drawing, a Sisley snow scene and a Lautrec lithograph. But with the Kandinsky, Henry felt he was bringing back to Britain an example of something not yet seen by his countrymen but which was life-enhancing. It made him feel both archaeologist and pioneer – that he had unearthed a treasure and would start a whole movement of appreciation. And that was the keyword – appreciation – he never bought art for its potential as investment, but only ever on purely aesthetic grounds. He loved passionately every work he had purchased. He bought them to hang on *his* walls, to illuminate *his* room and the lives of *his* family and friends. And when Henry founded Trust Art, he decreed that the acquisitions policy should remain faithful to his own. He would not fund galleries which wished to acquire works of art for any other reason than that they greatly enhanced the institutions' walls, or floor space, or display cabinets; would thus enrich the lives of those who worked there or came to visit.

When Henry Holden first met Julius Fetherstone in Paris between the wars, all funds for art, for anything really, were at once directed towards the British sculptor. Julius felt suspicious at first, rather sickened by such a sycophant, and he overcharged his young patron accordingly. Before long, he realized that Henry – or Holden as he had decided to call him – was a genuine fellow with a rather charming and unadulterated zeal for art. He was soon at ease with the notion of the young collector being his long-term patron, rather than merely a client. He knew that Holden bought the works to keep, never to sell; that his near doe-eyed interest had absolutely no homosexual overtones, that when he made his frequent trips to Paris, he had no desire to be entertained by the artist, to creep into his world. He came to

Paris to sit in Julius's studio, to gaze at the sculptor while he worked, or thought, or napped; to part with good money and often accompany his acquisitions home personally. Much to his first wife's exasperation.

'Who is she?' Henry Holden, circumnavigating *Abandon* or *Hunger* or *Desire* or any of the other works featuring Cosima, would marvel. 'Who *is* she?' But Henry asked not out of inquisitiveness, but rather out of wonder. He never expected or craved an answer.

'Do you really want to know?' Julius once asked Henry.

Henry regarded the sculptor with alarm. 'Lord, no!' he gasped. 'If she exists, if I am to know her name, if it transpires she has crooked teeth, or a lazy eye, or a pungent scent about her, the spell she has cast over me would be broken!'

Julius nodded and returned to chiselling. He remembered Cosima having straight pearly teeth, eyes which swallowed you like a whirlpool. And the scent of her – ah! lilac and musk, lilac and musk.

THIRTY-TWO

*B*y mid-June, the acquisitions committee have met and made their decision. Fen, Tate Britain and James Caulfield are delighted that Trust Art has agreed to contribute funds towards the hallowed gallery's purchase of the three Fetherstones. Matt has postponed Otter's article on Winnifred Nicholson to make pride of place for Fen's assessment of the Derbyshire Fetherstones. Otter hammed up how offended he was. Fen had to dampen down how honoured she was. The works themselves are to remain in Derbyshire until the transaction is finalized. The Trust saw it as an honour, while the Tate saw it as practical, that Fen McCabe should accompany the works back up north. She took the bronze back to Mr Caulfield's last weekend. The sketches are being X-rayed and analysed and she is to return them soon. Mr Caulfield actually came down to London a fortnight or so ago – at the invitation of Margot Fitzpatrick-Montague-Laine from Calthrop's, who had sent him a train ticket.

'You could make much more if we handled the sale for you,' she had said seductively, whilst eating her prawns most suggestively and running her fingertips up and down the stem of her champagne flute, licking her lips and fixing her sultry gaze on James.

'I'm perfectly happy with the amount agreed with the Tate,' James had replied graciously. 'I really wouldn't want the works going anywhere else.'

Margot F-M-L didn't want James going anywhere else that afternoon either. She'd manicured and pedicured and primped and preened that morning in anticipation of his visit. To her amazement first and foremost, and secondly to her disappointment, he informed her (whilst she was flicking her tongue fantastically over spoonfuls of zabaglione) that he really had to make this a day visit and needed to catch a train in an hour or so.

James had lied. He had gone directly to a small, insalubrious but nevertheless clean and orderly hotel in Paddington to wait for Fen. Fen, as we know, doesn't lie. Accordingly, that day she had three cups of coffee on an empty stomach, gave herself a headache, told Roger and Bobbie the truth that she had a headache and left work three hours early.

Fen took two ibuprofen on the tube and felt her headache shifting by the time she alighted at Paddington.

'I hope you haven't brought the oil sketches,' James said, when she arrived.

'No,' Fen laughed, 'they'll be back next week – I'm intending to return them the following weekend.'

'Let's go to Whiteley's,' James said, gathering his wallet and picking up the room key. Fen had envisaged Tate Modern. Or the Wallace Collection. 'I fancy a matinee,' said James, 'something trashy.' As always, whether on a walk through the country or in bed, James was leading the way and setting the pace. Usually, it turned Fen on. Today, though, she'd planned on a cream tea at Brown's Hotel. Not nachos in the afternoon whilst watching Bruce Willis rampage around the big screen.

'Where can a guy get a gal a candlelit dinner?' James had asked, to Fen's delight, after the film. Fen didn't want to stray too far afield. They found a gorgeous Moroccan restaurant where they lounged on tapestry cushions on low

234

benches. James held her hand between courses. He kissed her neck when he topped up her glass. She was so hungry for him that she lost her appetite for cous-cous.

'Let's go back to the hotel,' James suggested. 'Now.'

The room seemed more cramped on their return. And overheated. And just as a small hotel room should be, where urgent sex is concerned. Though the establishment was clean and well maintained, there was a seediness to it all. But it turned James and Fen on all the more.

Fen had excused herself during the meal to leave a message on Matt's answering machine. Just for a moment, she hated what she was doing. Sneaking away from James. Making excuses to Matt. She left a message saying that, although she was feeling a little better, she would probably end up staying the night with Cat. *Probably*, she said. Not definitely. Just a possibility. No untruths told.

So Fen has two suitors and she wonders only now and then whether she will at some point have to make a choice, make her mind up. At the moment, there is balance; there is therefore no need to weigh up the situation by gazing from one hand to the other, or one man to the other. Her heart beats steadily, beats as strongly for Matt as for James. Her mind runs with ease, day by day, week after week. It's summer now. Bright and breezy. Fen feels life could not get much better.

Matthew took her home to Gloucestershire for a weekend not long ago. For a girl whose mother ran off with a cowboy from Denver, to be welcomed by two fabulously maternal women – Matt's mother and nanny – was the realization of a day-dream years old. Matt found Fen's story in some ways quaint. 'I mean,' he'd reasoned to Jake, 'you hear of women who run off with the milkman, or the husband's best mate – but only Fen could have a mother who left for a cowboy.' Matt's mother found Fen's story horrific – and was alarmed that the child's upbringing had been entrusted to an artist-cum-jazz-musician-cum-whatever.

'Derbyshire, dear?' Susan Holden had repeated, as if perhaps she had heard incorrectly. 'Wasn't it terribly cold and – wild?' She'd always craved a daughter but her body would allow her only one child and she reasoned it was fitting that it should be a son and heir to the Holden name and fortune. However, had she had a daughter, no cowboy – not even Cary Grant – would have tempted her away from providing the very best, safest, most privileged childhood. 'Poor duck,' she said to nanny, 'but she seems well adjusted. And doesn't Matthew adore her!' Nanny had agreed. 'I believe,' Susan continued, 'Matthew has fallen on his feet. I do so hope they'll make it work.' Nanny looked out of the window at Matt and Fen strolling hand in hand across the lawn. 'They do seem dreamy,' she commented with an approving sigh.

After some furtive corridor creeping, Matt snuck into Fen's bed. She lay in his arms, sleepy but awake, in a room of beautiful proportions, cosy in the soft silence of the Gloucestershire night. And she nestled closer to him. She felt incredibly lucky, happy too. It was only in the silence of the early hours that she could admit to herself that she was falling in love. And though she was apprehensive about this, she was essentially happy and excited.

I want nothing to come between us.

And just a few weeks later, as she lay awake while James slept on the other side of the bed in the hotel in Paddington, Fen knew that she was in love with this man. In the darkness, the accompanying feeling of warmth which seeped along her veins, felt like a very good thing.

THIRTY-THREE

*D*jango sat with his head in his hands. His supper of cod in beer batter had turned cold on the kitchen table. He had no appetite. He had no desire to watch *Coronation Street* despite the previous episode having ended on a cliff-hanger of vertiginous proportions. The phone was ringing but he had no inclination to answer it. In fact, Django had no time to think on anything other than the scene he had witnessed that afternoon. It wasn't that his niece hadn't told him of her visit to Derbyshire. He'd always encouraged his nieces to live their lives with vigorous independence. Derbyshire was her stamping ground too; he did not own it. It was not betrayal that he felt, though he was a little hurt that she could be within a stone's throw and yet had not contacted him or his new answering machine. Django's head was in his hands, a weary weight on his shoulders, not because he perceived Fen to be deceitful. No, Django's discontent derived in whole from his fear that the grown-up Fen exhibited traits more akin with her mother than with her father, his late and beloved brother. That's what troubled him so. The duplicity of it. The insincerity. How could she tell him how lovely her boy-friend Matthew From Islington was when it was plain she was also gallivanting around Derbyshire with Another Man?

Django had seen her, in the Cross Oaks, cosy as you like, nestling into the neck of a man very obviously not Matthew From Islington.

Django took his head from his hands and regarded the battered fish. 'An older chap,' he told it, not quite sure whether he spoke to the head end or tail end, the batter being thick and dark enough to cover up any vestige of either.

He really didn't want to flatter Fenella's mother by wasting too much thinking time on her. But his brother's desolation when deserted still made Django wince; the vivid memory of the three tiny girls, wide-eyed and out of sorts, still made him weep. He blamed his brother's untimely death in part on the trauma of his ex-wife's action. The woman had never acknowledged her daughters' birthdays, or Christmas. The last time she had made contact was a year after she left, when she phoned her ex-husband to say that she and her cowboy were moving from Denver to Albuquerque and that, once settled, she would furnish him with the address. But she never did. So when her ex-husband died, Django was unable to contact her. When Pip was picked to represent her county at gymnastics, there was no way of letting her know. Nor when Fen achieved a double distinction from the Courtauld Institute, nor when Cat broke both ankles and one wrist in a fall from her bicycle. Ultimately, what irked Django so was that, though he had utter confidence in his parenting skills and was convinced that the girls had wanted for nothing, he felt fundamentally that they should have had a mother. He felt that, at the very least, they should have had a mother who hadn't behaved the way theirs had.

And now there's my Fenella. Lying in the arms of one man whilst lying to another. I can't judge the chaps in question, for I have met neither. But I can judge Fen. She should have one or the other. Not both. She should know that. It isn't wholesome. Someone will get hurt. Is she morally inept? Damn her mother. God rest my brother. God bless my girls. God knows what I'm meant to do with this information.

'When will I see you next?' Fen asked James sleepily, with a beguilingly childlike petulance to her voice. She was lying naked in his bed, her head in the crook of his shoulder, her fingers skating patterns over his chest. 'I've returned your art, secured your funds – you no longer have any need of me.'

'Quite true,' James jested, 'you've served your purpose – and served it well.'

'And you've serviced me and serviced me well!' Fen laughed, slipping her hand down his body and finding that a particular part of him was very wide awake indeed. Not even the archaic central-heating system, groaning and protesting and whistling and spluttering, could intrude on the peace felt between Fen and James. The curtains were open but of course there'd be no one to look in. An early owl could be heard in the distance. The window was ajar and a breeze filtered over their bodies. Fen reacted with goose bumps which James stroked rhythmically away. Couldn't they just never get up? Fen wondered. Suspended moments like these were blissful. She'd never experienced them before. They were unique to this man, this place.

I'm sure I couldn't achieve this sense of centredness in London. Or with anyone other than James.

'When will I see you next?' Fen asked again.

'Well, I assume that you'll be visiting your uncle? Soon?' James said. 'And of course, you really ought to check up on me – I might store the paintings incorrectly, might position the sculpture in the pond as a water feature.'

'I don't want to check up on you,' Fen said softly, 'I just want to know that I'll see you. Soon. When?'

They began to kiss. Though he was taller than Matthew, James's physique was softer, rounder here and there. Yet, without comparing the two men, the unique and precious sensation Fen always derived from James's embrace was that she was utterly enveloped and safe. His age, his experience, his self-containment all contributed to this. She nuzzled against him, feeling him soft here, very hard there. Their groins rocked gently, automatically. Their kissing became deeper. Lust started to seep through love and soon enough sexual desire and satisfaction became their prerogative. James's post-coital habit was to withdraw almost immediately, to lie on his back, on his side of the bed, eyes closed, and sleep. Fen didn't mind. She rather liked feeling that the experience of making love with her could render a man speechless and exhausted.

THIRTY-FOUR

Love and scandal are the best sweeteners of tea.
                                    Henry Fielding

*T*he smell of her. Matt's eyes closed with heady pleasure.

'Can't we hook up once you've seen Cat and Pip?' he murmured, his lips touching her ear lobe, his hands grasping her buttocks and pulling her tight close against him. It was stuffy in the Archive but he didn't notice. The door was ajar but he didn't care. His desire for Fen was so strong that he would tolerate an audience, and subsequent dismissal, if only she would let him take her here and now.

'Let me take you from behind,' he said hoarsely. Fen giggled. 'Come on,' he said, deadly serious, leading her hand to the rod-stiff protuberance in his trousers, 'fast and furious. What do you say?' He fondled her breasts, the intensity of desire causing him to stay only just within the limits of being downright rough. Fen gasped. It turned Matt on. 'God, Fen – it might sound clichéd and cheesy but I find you so bloody horny.' Fen felt herself melt and throb, offered her mouth to Matt and drifted away from the Archive into his arms.

There was a knock at the door. Fen and Matt sprang apart.

'For the love of Jesus,' Otter declared with theatrically exaggerated disapproval, covering his eyes with one skinny hand whilst feigning a faint by grasping on to the desk with

241

the other. He cleared his throat and stared hard at the middle distance: 'It's the *Burlington Magazine* on the phone for you, Ed.'

Matt was facing away from him, in a valiant attempt to hide his hard-on. 'Coming,' he said.

'In the conventional sense *only*, I hope,' Otter said with great disdain, opening one eye, 'and watch you don't knock over that entire shelving unit when you turn around, big boy.'

Fen laughed and bit her lip.

'Strumpet!' Otter growled at her before flouncing out of the room.

Matt turned around and Fen raised an eyebrow approvingly at the tent pole holding his trousers out. 'I shouldn't be long this evening,' she said, touching his cheek tenderly. 'Pip said it was a family matter – Cat's off to the Tour de France soon, I presume we're to assess whether this is a good or bad idea.'

'Just head over,' said Matt, 'whenever.'

He didn't dare look at her, let alone kiss her. He had only just physically calmed down sufficiently to leave the Archive for his office and take the call from the *Burlington Magazine*.

Recalling the afternoon made Fen smile intermittently during her journey home. She strolled up Camden High Street with a spring to her step. It was nice and early – she'd nip home, have a bath, pop over to Pip's and then head straight to Islington. Once home, she took her post into the kitchen and flicked the kettle on. She wondered, as she did every month, why her bank statements always arrived on the same day as her credit card statement. The latter demanding that she pay X whilst the former proclaimed that her funds were basically minus X minus a whole lot more. She tucked the envelopes into her back pocket and made what Django would term an NCT. A Nice Cuppa Tea always soothed problems, whether of a financial or emotional nature, even if it was in a chipped Spice Girls mug. She took a KitKat and decided she'd have the NCT in her bath, rather than waste time watching TV. She wanted to see Pip and Cat and then head over to Matt's as soon as she could.

Oh God.

Unmistakable.

Fen hovered at the bottom of the stairs, listening to the creaking bed springs, male grunts and female groans from upstairs.

Which one, though?

Because recently, she'd spent so much time at Matt's flat, she'd not been confronted with the unsavoury reality of her boyfriend's best friend bedding both her housemates.

Unfortunately, in a very literal sense, that's precisely what she'll have to confront now.

Fen sighs as she makes her way up to her room. She can feel that the KitKat is starting to melt against the mug of tea so she slips it into the pocket of her shirt. The moans are increasing in regularity and intensity.

It's Abi. That's a relief. Hopefully it's over between Jake and Gemma.

Up she goes. Only, the door to Abi's room is wide open, as are the curtains, and there's no one in there. Fen crosses the landing and climbs the next flight of stairs. Gemma's door isn't shut.

But I can still hear Abi. I'll just walk calmly by. I'm carrying a hot mug of tea, after all. And, after all, I'm home early. Abi would presume she had the house to herself so I'll just tiptoe quietly and quickly past.

Now, Abi is a great giggler, but the short laugh of delight that rings out just as Fen approaches is at odds with the sprightly trill that is Abi's trademark. Deludedly, for one moment, Fen justifies that Jake must be doing something quite extraordinary to so alter the timbre of her voice. It really doesn't sound like Abi at all. Listen.

243

Don't look don't look don't look.

But as she passes by the threshold of Gemma's room, and hears the squelching and the panting and the creaking and the giggling, Fen's head is turned against her will. And her eyes alight on a feast of flesh writhing around Gemma's bed. It is Abi. Of course it is. And it is Jake. Of course it is. But it is Gemma too. Without a doubt. No need to do a body recount. Gemma, gloriously butt naked, is part of the mêlée. The door is open but only ajar. Fen cannot be seen and though she doesn't want to see, she is rooted to the spot, unable to take her eyes from the action.

Gemma.

Jake.

Abi.

Jake and Abi enjoying Gemma.

Gemma, by all accounts, enjoying it very much indeed.

Jesus Christ.

Fen is as intrigued as she is horrified. Though she adores both her flatmates, she has never felt the slightest inclination to snog either of them. Certainly not to fondle their breasts or have hers fondled by either of them. And most definitely not whilst being penetrated by a man who isn't officially her boyfriend. But that's what's going on in there. Abi's boyfriend is having sex with her best friend whilst Abi's tongue flicks over her. Wait a minute, Abi is now straddling Jake and Gemma is embracing her.

'God I'm close,' Jake says and Fen can see that his cock looks as though it will torpedo right off his body. 'OK, ladies, ready for tea-time?'

For someone fully clothed, holding a very hot mug of tea, with no proclivity for a threesome, let alone a smidgen of sexual attraction for any of the participants, Fen finds Jake's words risibly ridiculous. Not only does his huskily drawled term 'ladies' make her toes curl, but the fact that he has referred to his imminent climax as 'tea-time' has caused her to spill hers. Jake might be hot, but Fen's tea is hotter.

'Fuck!' Jake yells.

'Fuck!' Fen yells. As she drops the mug and tea spills all over the carpet, Jake drops his load – his 'tea', as he has so delicately termed it. Fen is already bolting down a level to the bathroom to hold her hands under the cold tap.

'Fen?' Abi calls down.

'Fen?' Gemma calls down.

'Fen?' Jake calls down.

She doesn't reply. There's no way she's going back upstairs. If the tea stains the carpet, the landlord can take cleaning costs out of her deposit. For now, she wants to be out of the house immediately.

'I just came . . .' she calls up, 'I just came to, to – dump my stuff.'

'So did I,' Jake calls down. Fen hears them all laughing. She feels suddenly offended. Are they laughing at her?

'I have to shoot off now,' she calls.

'That's precisely what I've done,' Jake calls down and Fen can hear them all giggling in a horribly self-congratulatory way.

Fen wants to cry. She isn't sure why. She isn't sure what to say next.

'Bye,' she calls, because it's neutral and safe and has no opening for a *double entendre*. Even if it did, she's closed the door and is marching up the street on the double; out of sight, out of sound.

When Pip opened the door to her flat, Fen thought how the look on her sister's face must mirror her own. An element of shock-horror mixed with a dose of bewilderment, a dash of unease, all laced with unhappiness. How could Pip know, though? Had Abi or Gemma phoned her?

'Urgh!' said Fen, flopping down on to the settee next to Cat, whose facial expression matched both of her sisters'. Pip perched on the coffee table in front of Fen and Cat, her knees practically touching Fen's. 'You'll never guess,' Fen continued, holding her throat as if to quell nausea. 'Honestly,' she went on, 'it's not as if I'm a prude – but . . .'

245

Cat and Pip regarded their sister with level gazes. Fen shook her head forlornly. 'It'll sound like the juiciest of gossip,' she explained, 'but it isn't – it's horrid. I feel very very uncomfortable.' Still Cat and Pip watched her. 'I feel I should move. But first I want to have a bath – it's made me feel dirty, which is ridiculous.'

'No, it isn't,' said Cat.

'It isn't,' Pip agreed.

'What?' said Fen. 'It *is* ridiculous – *I* catch both my flatmates having sex with the same man at the same time and I feel so appalled and revulsed that *I'm* the one who feels she should scrub herself clean!'

Pip and Cat observed Fen in stony silence. At length, Pip spoke. 'How could you, Fen?'

'Oh,' said Fen ingenuously, 'I wasn't peeping – it was unavoidable, the door was open and they were all making such a racket.' Her sisters were giving her very odd looks indeed. 'Do you know what Jake said – oh Jesus – he said, "OK ladies, time for tea," when he was – you know!' Fen giggled and blushed and covered her face with her hands. 'Oh God – I shouldn't laugh but it is so toe-curlingly revolting,' she said, all muffled.

'How could you do it to Matt?' Cat probed, shaking her head and looking quite miserable.

'Matt?' Fen asked. 'I haven't told him yet.'

'Are you going to?' Pip asked.

Fen fell silent.

'Because it isn't fair on him,' said Cat, 'not one bit, not at all. He's so so lovely.'

Fen considered this. 'Jake has probably told him,' she said, 'I mean, I bet it wasn't the first time. I wonder how Matt will respond.' She looked from sister to sister. 'That will be telling, won't it?' she theorized. 'If he reacts as I have, all well and good. But say he thinks it's not that untoward? What then? Do I really want to be with someone with such dodgy morals?'

'Dodgy morals!' Pip cried. 'Dodgy sodding morals!' She

regarded Fen, fire in her eyes and a harshness to her voice that Fen had never heard. 'Pot!' Pip yelled. 'Kettle! Black!' She leapt up and paced around the room.

Fen looked utterly flummoxed. 'I don't follow,' she faltered.

'What we've been trying to ascertain,' Cat said coldly, 'and the reason for us having you here, is how on earth you can do what you're doing to Matt.'

Fen stared at Cat. There was no penny dropping just yet. 'I don't follow,' she repeated.

Pip returned to the coffee table and sat with her face inches from Fen's. 'You have a lovely boyfriend,' she said in a horribly controlled way, 'who is obviously besotted by you – and yet you choose to jeopardize what you have with him so you can fuck around in Derbyshire.'

Fen's jaw dropped. The penny dropped like a lead weight straight to the bottom of her stomach. The crossed lines of the previous minutes unravelled and wrapped around Fen's throat.

'*Derbyshire,*' Cat stressed, 'your own bloody doorstep.'

Fen had not yet closed her mouth.

'How could you?' Pip asked, a look of utter revulsion crossing her face.

Fen changed the aperture of her mouth but no sound came out. She put her hand to her throat. 'I . . .'

'Django saw you,' Cat elaborated, 'in the Cross Oaks, snug as you like with some bloke.'

'I . . .'

'Couldn't you be more discreet?' Cat spat. 'Couldn't you just hole up in your lover's pad – rather than upset Django so? I mean, it's one thing not to even call him – but it's another to flaunt.'

'Django?' Fen whispered.

'Saw you,' Pip confirmed.

'You know what,' said Cat, slapping her hands down on her knees, rising from the settee to pace the room, 'what I don't get is how you can dare to come here, all hurt and shocked and self-righteous about Jake and Abi and Gemma. I mean, they're consenting adults, larking about with sex. But you – *you*. The deception, Fen. The dishonesty.'

Fen looked from hand to hand.

'Stop looking at your bloody hands,' Pip barked, 'and look into your soul. What you are doing is *wrong*. We presume that they don't know about each other?'

Silence. Fen shook her head.

'Have you stopped to imagine,' Pip continued, 'how either would feel if he found out? Have you stopped to consider how much unhappiness you have the potential to wreak?' She took two apples and an orange from her fruit bowl. 'I can juggle, Fen,' she said, doing just that, 'but you can't.' She let the fruit fall. The orange caught the side of the coffee table and then thudded to the floor. One apple rolled underneath the table, the other bounced, bashing the skirting-board before coming to rest, bruised. The orange was alone in the centre of the floor. 'Where do you get it from?' Pip enquired, quietly, bewildered. 'Where do you get it from?'

It was all too much for Fen. She started to cry. Neither sister was inclined to comfort her. Both felt let down and confused and very cross with Fen. She stood up.

'The lies,' Pip sighed, disgusted, 'the lies.'

'I have not lied!' Fen protested. 'I haven't – to anyone.' There was uneasy silence. 'Piss off, both of you!' she cried. 'Piss right off! Who the hell are you two to judge?' And yet Fen knew she should stop, sit down, sob her heart out and then pour her heart out. She knew, most importantly, that she should say no more. She knew she'd regret it. But she continued. 'Who are you to judge me! Cat with your fucked-up love life, and Pip with no love life to speak of. You have no right, no authority!'

With that, she stormed out of Pip's flat.

THIRTY-FIVE

'Tis an awkward thing to play with souls,
And matter enough to save one's own
Robert Browning

'**B**ugger,' said Fen out loud on the top of Primrose Hill. Her indignation at having been told off had subsided. She felt ghastly. Though, as we know, she has a slight obsession with her hands, Fen has never bitten her nails. But sitting on one of the benches on the top of Primrose Hill, she had her fingers in her mouth and was half-heartedly chewing away. It seemed, really, the only thing to do. The McCabe sisters rarely argued. Never had Cat and Pip united against Fen. Never had she spat such spite at her sisters. It simply wasn't her nature. Thus, the top layer of the distress Fen was currently experiencing focused on the insults she had cruelly levied at Cat and Pip. Under that was the wretchedness she felt, now that home truths had been unequivocally pointed out. On all fronts, her behaviour had been bad. To Matt, to James, to Pip, to Fen. Even, unwittingly, to her beloved Django.

'Mess,' she whispered to herself, tears coursing down her cheeks, 'my fault.' She looked over to the aviary in London Zoo. It depressed her. Is that what she had been doing? Kidding herself that she was flying free, flying true, when in reality she was far from her real territory and heading for a bump at any moment? She hadn't been to the zoo in years, she had no intention of visiting it again. On Primrose Hill, lone dog walkers strolled around, friends flopped on the grass chatting, couples walked hand in hand. Fen didn't dare look at her hands. She knew she'd only reprimand herself, whichever palm she consulted. Instead, she just sat there because it was cathartic just to do so, crying quietly, feeling miserable. After a few minutes, though, she knew, too, that it was thoroughly self-indulgent.

How much courage do I have? she wondered. Enough to return to Pip's and apologize? Enough to go to Matt's, hold him close and tell him that I love him? Because I've already told James how I love him.

Do you love James more than you do Matt, then?

No. Ironically, it's because James is so guarded with expressing his emotions that I wanted to tell him how I feel – like it might prompt some kind of reciprocation from him. Matt is much more open and demonstrative. But no. I certainly do not love one more than the other. But this is not the point, this is skirting the issue. How on earth do I manage to leave Primrose Hill?

You should prioritize, Fen. Matt and James are both safely in the dark. It is to your sisters that you should go. It won't be easy, there will be music to face and it may well be dissonant.

Saying sorry is one thing – but they'll judge me, they'll judge me.

Fen dragged her heels. She looked in all the shop windows in Regent's Park Road though she knew their wares well, having spent Saturday browsing there with Matt. More to the point, it was futile because she knew she could not afford any of the things she fancied. She switched her mobile phone on. No messages. She switched it off again. Then on again. She dialled her voice mail. No messages. No surprise there. She bought two apples and an orange, also a bumper-size block of Galaxy chocolate, Cat's favourite, and walked with resigned purpose – if slowly – back to Pip's.

*

The beauty of true sisterhood – whether women are united by blood or friendship – is the ability not to hold grudges. Men, after disagreements or fallings-out with each other, will invariably just bury the hatchet and pick up where they left off. Women, though, will relish the chance to work through the issue. When they have done so, they are further on than they were when they left off. They move forward, on foundations which are firmer than they were prior to the rift. Simply saying, 'Sorry mate,' might be easier; to agree quickly over a pint to let bygones be just that might be very agreeable, but making up shouldn't be easy – if it is, then surely it wouldn't be difficult to fall out again.

'She's back,' Cat said, seeing Fen's legs descending the stairs to Pip's basement flat.

Whilst walking back to Pip's, Fen had polished up three or four variants on an impressive soliloquy. However, by the time she was hovering her finger over Pip's doorbell, all were utterly redundant. The knot in her throat had already lodged itself as she approached Pip's building. When Cat opened the door, Fen felt her eyes smart over. When Pip greeted her with a gentle, 'Hullo, slapper,' the tears fell. The three sisters sat together on Pip's sofa, though it was only a small two-seater. Pip and Cat were silent, Pip's hand on Fen's shoulder, Cat's hand on her knee. They let her sob. And snort back the snot. And be quiet for a moment before starting up again. Eventually she was all cried out.

'Here,' she croaked, thrusting the plastic bag at Pip. Pip smiled at the replacement fruit and laid them gently in the fruit bowl. She and Cat had eaten the surprisingly unbruised apples while Fen had been on Primrose Hill. Cat handed out great big chunks of the chocolate to each sister and they slouched back on the couch and munched.

Pip spoke first, loving chocolate so much that she found it impossible not to gobble it down. 'Fen,' she said, with no anger to her voice, 'what I'd like to know is exactly *how* you can do it? Not just on a moral level – but on a practical one too?'

Fen stared at Pip's wall so intently that Pip and Cat could all but see the cogs and wheels of her mind turning. They gave her time and more Galaxy. Fen arose and took a pew on the coffee table, facing both her sisters. 'I know it sounds odd – especially for someone as hooked on romance as me.' Pip and Cat nodded. 'They're just so different, these two men,' Fen continued, 'yet it's not as if either lacks anything physically or in personality that the other makes up for. That's what's so odd.'

'But don't you feel *guilty*?' Cat enquired.

'It's been effortless to keep them apart – in my soul, mind and heart. Matt lives in London, he is my age, my milieu. James lives in Derbyshire. He's forty-nine.'

'Almost fifty!' Cat exclaimed.

'A sugar-daddy?' Pip asked.

'A gardener,' Fen explained.

'Oh,' said Pip, whilst Cat just looked disappointed.

'I've a clear picture of Percy Thrower,' Cat said, referring to the *Blue Peter* TV gardener of their childhood.

'I'm thinking Alan Titchmarsh,' Pip said, slightly perturbed.

'You're both far off the mark,' Fen assured them. 'Think back to the Rag and Thistle – to that chap you were ogling with the dogs.' Pip and Cat's jaws dropped. Fen nodded confirmation. 'Him.'

The sisters gazed up through the window to street level where disembodied legs made their way either late home from work, or out for a drink or meal or movie. 'Both these blokes enhance my life,' Fen said, 'because I've come to realize that there are two very different sides to *me*. On the one side,' she said, careful not to look at her right palm, 'is the city-dwelling young thing that I am – enjoying London life, having a hip and gorgeous boyfriend like Matt. On the other side, though, are my rural roots, my love of Derbyshire, of the outdoors and all that is different to the city.'

She regarded her sisters.

252

'Two sides of the same coin,' she shrugged, 'town and country. Rich and poor. Young and old. Matt and James.' Pip and Cat wore furrowed brows. 'Put another way,' Fen said, 'it's like really enjoying a programme on television but flicking over to another equally interesting programme during the advert break.'

'Fenella,' said Pip, using her sister's name in full to stress the anxiety in her voice, 'you mustn't toy with men just for your *entertainment.*'

'And Fen,' Cat said, 'who is the main feature and who is the intermission break?'

Fen shook her head slowly. She shrugged. 'I couldn't tell you,' she said, 'honestly. But I assure you that I am *not* using them for my amusement. I am, I think, I suppose, dare I say it, simply in love with two men.'

'And do you know what to do about it?' Pip pushed.

'Carry on?' Fen said, after a very loaded pause.

'OK. But what do you think you *ought* to do about it?' Pip persisted.

Fen shrugged. Pip used her name in full again, in a soft low voice with an unmistakably menacing edge to it.

'Minimize the potential for hurt and thus make my bloody mind up?' Fen suggested.

'Now say that without the question mark at the end,' said Cat. Fen twisted her brow and her hands. Cat and Pip waited. Eventually, in almost a whisper and with a tear glassing over her right eye, Fen did as she was told.

'Who is it to be?' Cat asked.

Fen wiped her eyes and shrugged, shaking her head vigorously as if to try to forget the weight and urgency of her responsibility.

'Who loves you more?' Cat asked. 'Matt or James?'

'I don't know!' Fen declared, because she had put herself right at the centre of both men's worlds and hadn't really stopped to think.

'Mind you,' Cat continued, 'ultimately *you* should choose according to *your* heart.'

'I don't know, Cat,' Pip cautioned, 'I think Fen's head should keep a close check on her heart. Which man is least likely to hurt you?'

'I can look after myself,' Fen declared with a certain petulance.

'Bollocks!' Pip said. 'That's my line and even I know it's bullshit, deep down.'

'What are they like?' asked Cat, not so much because she wanted to steer the conversation back on track as that curiosity had simply got the better of her. 'how do they compare? These two sides of the coin?'

'I don't compare them,' Fen insisted, 'but I can try to describe them.'

Pip and Cat snuggled deep into the sofa, as if story-time on the radio or at nursery school was about to commence. 'Well, you sort of know Matt,' Fen began. 'I so love the way he combines old-fashioned manners with cosmopolitan funky liveliness. He's also incredibly attentive on an emotional level – very caring, romantic. He sends me little e-mails and text messages and sticks Post-its on my computer monitor for no reason other than he cares for me. That makes me feel wonderful. And in bed – well!' Fen broke off to blush. 'At first, it was a little nondescript, but now we don't so much make love as have rude and rampant sex. He's amazing – dirty and desirous. I feel very adventurous and abandoned with him. The things he can do with his lips and tongue – a sort of magic-whispering in any of my orifices!' Fen regarded her sisters, both of whose jaws had dropped. 'He's had a long-term relationship that broke up finally just before I arrived on the scene. He cares about her. I'm glad he does. But I'm gladder that it's now me whom he wants. I'm even cool about his fling with mad Judith at work. I can in no way wonder if I'm his rebound shag. And also, he has a lovely, conventional family. His mum is a real honey. And there's Nanny too.'

'And the country pile,' Pip added, but not wanting to sound cynical, 'and Daddy's inheritance.' Fen poked her tongue out at her sister.

'We like Matt!' Cat proclaimed with a wriggle to grab the Galaxy from the table. 'He's gorgeous on the eye and a really lovely guy. Hey! I'm a poet – not that you'd know it. Sorry!'

'Continue,' Pip encouraged, her mouth full of chocolate.

'James Caulfield,' Fen started, as if it were the title of a lecture about to be delivered. She refused the chocolate. 'Is incredibly and compellingly self-contained. He's classically dark and handsome – looks slightly Mediterranean. True, he's turning fifty – but I really, truly don't think about the age gap. It's not an issue, not for me. He was a surveyor in Bath but he down-shifted to Derbyshire and took up landscape gardening. He's not as sociable, as outgoing as Matt – in fact he can be a little outspoken or else frustratingly quiet.'

'He sounds like a sulky old git too set in his ways,' Pip muttered, because she'd already decided Fen should forsake all others for Matt.

Cat, however, was suddenly rather taken with the idea of James. 'He sounds rather brooding and exotic to me,' she marvelled.

'He is,' Fen assured them, 'he's intelligent and experienced and, I don't know, *smouldering*. What I love about James is essentially a wavelength thing,' Fen mused. 'His family background is similar in its dysfunction. Even his house is a bit rumble-tumble down. So it's comforting – and it's a refreshing change from London pretensions. Plus he has two gorgeous dogs. And of course, we share a love of Fetherstone.' Fen reflected for a moment. 'James and I tried to resist the strong mutual attraction – initially, it was most definitely a physical desire that existed between us, on account of him not being that sociable and me meeting him with my art historian's hat on. Yet, when we went to bed, it was really quite tender. The hunger we initially felt gave way to gentle lovemaking rather than raw sex.'

'Who's the better in bed?' Pip asked.

'Again – incomparable – both great, both different.'

'Who do you fancy more?' Cat pressed.

'Neither one,' Fen said. Both her sisters raised their eyebrows. '*Honestly.*'

'Who gives you the better orgasm?' Cat asked, with a giggle she couldn't help.

'Believe me,' Fen shrugged, 'both leave me begging for a break, rather than wanting more.'

'Do you worry that you're James's totty?' Pip probed. 'That it's every fifty-year-old's fantasy to have a nice nubile bit of skirt?'

'Do you worry that you might be a mere conquest for Matt? He and Jake being lads-about-town?'

Fen wasn't offended. 'They're both special,' she said, 'and I know that they both adore me. It's lovely to hear it from Matthew, and just to sense it from James.'

'Does James not tell you how he feels?' Cat asked. 'Has he not told you that he loves you?'

'He doesn't need to,' Fen said.

Pip opened her mouth and then closed it. She tilted her head and twitched her lips. 'That may be so,' she said, 'but actually a women deserves to be told.'

Fen shrugged. 'It doesn't make me doubt the depth of his affection.' Pip nodded to concede that this may well be so. Deep down, though, she felt that her gorgeous sister was perhaps being somewhat short-changed by this mature gardener.

'At the end of the day, though,' Pip said, 'I still feel you should choose one or the other. The more involved you become with both, the more hurt is in the offing.'

'They say men are like buses,' Fen said, 'that you wait and wait and suddenly two or three come along at the same time.'

'But Fen,' Cat pointed out, 'you can only get on one bus at a time. What's the point of hopping off one just to hop on another? You'll never get anywhere.'

'Different routes?' Fen tried feebly. 'Different places to visit?'

Cat and Pip regarded their sister looking from palm to

256

palm. Fen didn't tell them how analysing each man to the nth degree had actually made her realize just how much she loved both of them.

'Matthew Holden,' Fen said, holding up her right hand. 'James Caulfield,' she said, holding her left. She grasped both together and clutched them to her heart. Then she dropped her head to her hands and sighed. Pip took her right hand. Cat took her left. They all sat still and silent, holding tight.

THIRTY-SIX

*F*en left Pip's, having phoned Matt to ask if he'd mind if she just went home. He sounded touchingly disappointed. Family pow-wows, she explained to him, always left her exhausted. While they spoke, she heard Jake return.

Oh to be a fly on the wall, thought Fen.

Gemma and Abi were sitting very comfortably, sipping wine. They looked neither surprised nor embarrassed to see Fen. In fact, if the clean, extra wineglass was anything to go by, they were actively anticipating her return. Fen wondered why on earth it should be her who smiled sheepishly. Anyway, smiling sheepishly, she accepted a glass of wine and took her seat in the armchair opposite Abi and Gemma snuggled on the sofa together.

'Are you horribly shocked and disgusted?' Abi asked with true concern, her pixie crop looking far more tousled by tension than by passion or pillow.

'Do you judge us and hate us?' Gemma asked, in a tone that suggested that she truly hoped Fen didn't.

Fen sipped and contemplated.

How can I judge? I'm hardly a paragon of moral virtue myself. Anyway, what is it I feel about the torrid triangle?

She sipped and contemplated some more.

And which torrid triangle? My own? Or theirs?

Fen took another sip. 'What can I say?' she said, wondering what to say.

'You can call us a pair of slappers,' Gemma suggested, as if it would make her feel better if Fen did.

'Because, categorically, that's what we are,' Abi said. It was as if both girls actively wanted Fen to be livid, insulted and moralistic, that if she was, they'd then not feel quite so badly.

Fen sipped her wine and replenished all three glasses.

'I mean, we know you're a one-man woman,' said Abi to Fen's undetectable wince, 'and we're one-man women too – it's just that he happens to be the same man.'

'Yes,' Gemma said, 'it's not like we're promiscuous and out shagging anything in trousers.' Her voice carried an edge of relief, as if it had suddenly occurred to her that she was not wanton at all. 'It's not like I'm sleeping with two men at once,' Gemma continued, 'just that the sole man I'm sleeping with happens to be sleeping with two women at once.'

Fen nodded vigorously. She felt hot and bothered. Put the way Gemma had theorized it all, Fen felt that it was *she* who was morally inept.

'We're all happy with this arrangement,' Abi explained, 'jealousy doesn't figure.'

'But your best mate is sleeping with your boyfriend,' said Fen, to make herself feel not so smutty.

'But I've ceased to see him as my boyfriend,' said Abi.

'And he certainly isn't my boyfriend,' Gemma agreed.

Fen frowned. 'But you two . . .' she said, gesticulating with her hands and knotting her fingers together in simulation of writhing bodies.

'It's sex as a recreational and non-emotional, physical activity,' Abi enlightened.

'It's not like we're in love with him,' Gemma agreed. 'I don't know whether the sex would be as exciting if that was the case.'

'But the more emotionally involved you are with someone,' Fen said, 'the more erotic the sex.'

Abi sipped. Gemma sipped. Both regarded Fen with absolute tenderness and respect.

'That's why you're blessed with fulfilling relationships,' Abi reasoned genuinely. Her innocent use of the plural hit Fen in the solar plexus. Fen didn't dare say a word, though. She wasn't going to tell Abi or Gemma about her own infidelities.

They wouldn't understand. They might even feel let down. They'd probably only see the situation in a titillating light.

'God knows what Matt'll make of all of this,' Abi said. 'I only hope he wouldn't dare to judge you by it.'

And how you and Gemma would judge me if you knew what I'm involved in.

'It's odd,' Fen said out loud instead, 'and I mean this with no disrespect – but I've been worried that he'll share Jake's traits.'

'I doubt it,' Gemma assured her. 'Jake often moans that a revelation of his sexploits falls on deaf ears and withering looks from Mr Holden.'

Shit, thought Fen, excusing herself and soon staring menacingly at herself in the bathroom mirror. *Shit. I can't, then, behave like this to Matt. He deserves more. Cat and Pip are right. Someone is going to be very hurt. I've been thinking solely of myself, focusing only on me – that I'd be the one hurting.*

So, you are going to finish with James?

Finish it with James? No!

You intend to call a stop with Matt, then.

I couldn't do that!

But you can't go on like this, can you?

No.

So you have to do something about it.

I know.

What, though?

I don't know! I don't know! I do love them both so.

260

Fen returned downstairs.

'So you don't think we're wicked, wanton wenches?' Abi asked.

'Well,' said Fen, 'I do – actually – but it doesn't change my depth of affection for you. And just don't ever – *ever* – even *consider* inviting me to participate.'

Abi and Gemma laughed. 'Just as long as you promise you won't take it personally that ultimately we simply don't fancy you,' Gemma said slyly.

They finished the wine and watched a terrible game show on Channel 5. Fen gave an expansive, half-fabricated yawn. 'I'm going to have an early night,' she said. 'I'm off home to Derbyshire tomorrow.'

I'm so looking forward to seeing James. But I miss Matt even now.

Fen sits up in bed, the phone in her lap. Matt or James. James or Matt. God, it was difficult enough deciding which man to phone first. She has a headache and a leaden taste in her mouth.

When I'm in James Land, Matt is safely far away. When I'm in Matt World, James is totally out of the picture. But just now, alone in my own space, these two men collide. And that's not right.

THIRTY-SEVEN

'*C*hildren!' Django boomed as his three nieces piled out of Pip's car and bounded into his kitchen where they stood in line, hands behind their backs, rocking their bottoms against the Aga though it was nearing July and no one was cold. 'It's an outrage that you haven't been to see me, en masse, since I don't know when!' He loosened his Pucci neckerchief. 'I can't remember who is who.' He then proceeded to incorrectly name each of his girls. Soon enough, they were all falling about laughing and hugging and wondering why on earth they didn't come home more often. Tea was taken in the garden. Django had run out of jam so cranberry jelly had to do. But it was very nice on malt loaf. He'd forgotten to buy chocolate biscuits but had improvised quite successfully making a paste from cocoa, muscovado sugar and a dab of margarine, trowelled on to rich tea biscuits slightly past their prime. It was a beautiful day and the garden looked magnificent though, as Django said, it basically looked after itself.

'I know your mother ran off with a cowboy from Denver,' Django reasoned with Cat, 'but you chasing through France after a bunch of boys on bikes – well, isn't that taking the family tradition to new extremes?'

The family chatted about Cat's imminent departure.

262

Though they worried that a month away, travelling as a journalist with the Tour de France, might take its toll on the still emotionally fragile Cat, they all agreed that it was potentially a very good thing, the chance for adventure, the opportunity to move on. The conversation soon turned to the other two sisters. Though Cat and Pip teased Fen in front of Django for having a choice between two men to make, no one acknowledged that Django had spied his middle niece with her gardener, nor that he had discussed the fact with her two sisters. This enabled him to deliver something of a pep talk, and it also meant that Fen had to listen openly, rather than switch off or jump to the defensive.

'Fen,' he said, eyes closed under a battered Panama hat, 'you are undeniably gifted with fall-in-loveable qualities. This is both a blessing and an affliction. It is something you have that you must respect and must never take advantage of.'

'But it's the reverse,' Fen remonstrated quietly. 'You misunderstand. I didn't set out to ensnare these two men. I've just gone and bloody fallen in love with both of them.'

'I did the 1960s,' Django proclaimed wearily, as if the experience had been a most tiresome one. 'The only conclusions I drew were that marijuana smokers are boring sods, the Aldermaston march gave me frightful blisters, Joe Cocker did a better job on 'With a Little Help From My Friends' than the Beatles and, fundamentally, monogamy was a very good concept.' His nieces gawped at him. They wanted to know more about everything. 'Believe me – but please, without questioning me too probingly – I've done them all. I was there. I did it, saw it, smoked it.' He sighed and sipped a Pimm's into which he'd put coriander in lieu of mint. 'Hash, acid, mushrooms. Credence Clear Water. Barclay James Harvest. Ten Years After. Free love, paid-for love, secret love, open-air love, love under the influence of drugs, love under the instruction of Mahringi Yogu Prishna,' he listed. 'They were all so –' Django paused. Pip held her headstand. Cat and Fen hung on his every word.

'*forgettable*. Ultimately. Damn tiring too.' He observed Fen. 'You see, Fen, you look *peaky*,' he commented, 'thin, too. Love should make you bloom. But alongside your well-being is the fact that I do not want you turning into a cavorting self-obsessed moral imbecile.' The accusation sounded harsh to all the girls. Fen looked at her uncle steadily. 'You might be in love with both men,' he said, 'but do not lose sight of the fact that each is in love with *you* exclusively.'

Fen looked at her lap.

'They deserve to get what they give,' Django qualified, 'they do not deserve to be toyed with just so that you can indulge your whims.'

Fen plucked blades of grass and nodded. 'I'm not playing with them,' she said, 'they are not toys. I feel deeply for both.'

'I will not have you turn into your mother,' Django said, staring at her hard. 'This has nothing to do with your father's memory, nothing to do with the fact that it was he who was my sibling. It has only to do with a moral judgement I believe I am informed to make.'

Fen felt all eyes upon her. She bit her lip.

'It's make-your-mind-up time, Fenella,' Django cautioned, using her name in full to emphasize the gravity of the situation.

Fen went to bed and really tried to make her mind up. But by the next afternoon, she is sitting in James's kitchen watching him singe the Scotch pancakes. His shirt sleeves are rolled up and revealing his gorgeous forearms. His lips are pursed in concentration of preparing tea. He's in socks. So is Fen. They both leave vaguely damp imprints from their footfalls. They've been for a vigorous walk. It was gorgeous – the weather, the land, the privacy, the togetherness. Now Beryl is spark out across the doorway, Barry is slumped over Fen's feet and James is preparing food for her. She looks from dog to dog to man.

I daren't move. I can't get out anyway. I'm being held captive. Willingly.

'Here,' says James, proffering a plate heaped with heavily buttered drop scones and toasted teacakes, 'eat.'

Fen feels revived. And nourished. By the food, but mostly by her feelings for James. The thought of denying herself its sustenance seems utterly idiotic.

THIRTY-EIGHT

'*B*ugger Matisse,' Fen said under her breath, but not quietly enough for Matt not to have heard as he passed by the Archive after a heated exchange with Accounts, who were suggesting that *Art Matters* be printed on cheaper paper of a lesser quality.

'Beg your pardon?' he said, poking his head around the Archive door. 'Doesn't that constitute blasphemy?' Matt enquired, coming into Fen's room and swivelling on the chair while she remained cross-legged on the floor, papers and illustrations scattered about her like the skirts of some old fashioned petticoat. In fact, she was wearing a tight little T-shirt under a strappy navy-blue sun dress which, when she stood, skimmed an inch or so above her neat knees. As she was sitting cross-legged, though, it hitched itself up to reveal a glimpse of white knickers.

'Love the white knickers,' Matt said with a lascivious wink.

'But they match my top and my trainers,' Fen protested with a cheeky pout, 'that's all.'

Immediately, it struck her just how easy it was to slip back into London, into life and love with Matt, despite the fact that her afternoon with James in Derbyshire was all that had filled her mind that morning. And yet because of her sisters challenging her, the pep talk from Django, the impact of coming across Jake and Abi and Gemma, for the first time, Fen felt a fleeting stab of guilt.

'What has Monsieur Matisse done to piss you off?' Matt probed. Fen was grateful for the change of subject. She could put the guilt and what to do about it to the back of her mind for the time being and put her art historian's hat on instead. Actually, Matt had changed the subject to distract himself from incorrigible thoughts of molesting Fen in her white knickers.

'He died the same year as Julius,' Fen explained, '1954.'

'How very inconsiderate,' Matt said.

Fen nodded vigorously. 'Much as I adore Matisse, I wish he'd died the year before or after Julius. I just feel that Julius didn't receive the recognition he deserved. He wasn't even granted a respectful measure of obituary column inches. *The Times* merely mentioned his passing most cursorily.'

'I'd boycott the paper if I were you,' Matt teased gently.

'Oh, I already have,' Fen answered.

'What's brought all this on?' Matt asked.

'Actually,' said Fen, rummaging around the papers, 'you'll find this quite interesting. I came across a clutch of photos from your father's collection taken in the artist's studio a few months before his death.' She presented Matt with a fan of photographs. Though the studio was lofty and capacious, the space seemed dwarfed by the proliferation of sculpture. Despite there being only seven humans in the studio, the room seemed packed on account of the crowd of characters cast in bronze, hewn from marble or modelled in clay or plaster. Though wizened in stature and sitting in a bath chair piled high with blankets, Julius nevertheless dominated the room in each photograph. It was as if the sculptures and the visitors to the studio were on pilgrimage, paying homage to the great artist in the last months of his life. Henry Holden was in each frame, standing close to Julius. A couple admiring the works kept a respectful distance from the sculptor. Elsewhere, a tall woman, her back to the camera, appeared to be lost in her own world, staring into the middle distance, or at the elbow or ankle of one of the works. A small child was captured in each frame, darting here and there. In one, with a tiny hand on the arm of the old sculptor, the child appeared mesmerized by Julius's beard. In another, the child seemed to be mid-hop – holding on to Henry's trouser leg for balance. In another, the child was clambering over a headless reworking in plaster of *Eve*. In another, the child was skipping out of shot.

'Did Julius have children?' Matt enquired.

'No,' Fen confirmed, 'I reckon he belongs to that tall lady. It is a boy, isn't it? The Peter Pan collared smock and little straw hat are ever so girly – but a girl wouldn't have been dressed in trousers back then?'

Matt scrutinized the photo and shrugged. 'Looks like a little chap to me,' he said, 'but we only see profile or back view. Could well be a tomboy called Marie-Celeste or something.'

Fen looked at the photos. 'I wonder who the mystery lady is?' she said. 'It's almost as if she's avoiding the camera on purpose.'

'Oh Fen,' Matt laughed, 'your imagination is overactive – I mean, look at the other couple, are you telling me they moved intentionally so their features would be blurred?'

Fen looked hard. 'Maybe,' she said.

'This is a sculptor's studio photographed in the 1950s and deposited in an archive,' Matt teased, 'it isn't a still from a security-camera in police records!'

Fen smiled sheepishly. 'It's just that Julius's last months are not well documented. We have a fragmented jigsaw,' she said. 'I'm just trying to piece the possibilities together.'

Matt made to leave. 'Well, if you get bored with the day job, you could always be a researcher on *Crimewatch UK*!' He kissed her nose and slid his hand fleetingly up her thigh.

Alone, Fen looked at the photos again. Really analysed them because she didn't want to consider Matt's honesty, his affection. And she didn't want to hear Pip and Cat and

Django. And she didn't want James appearing in her mind's eye. The photos, the photos. From the brace of the woman's back, she could detect an emotion. What was it? Not shyness. Tension? Not really. Sadness? No. Loneliness? No. What then? Unease. That was it. Made all the more apparent by the ebullience of the child, obviously having a fabulous time.

Look at the little mite utterly enthralled by the mass of Abandon! *All the adults are engrossed elsewhere; Henry and Julius deep in conversation, the tall woman gazing at the knees of* Eve *on one side of the room, the couple – his hand at her waist – sharing thoughts on Julius's late work,* Tristan and Isolde. *The child has been left to his own devices, given free rein to explore what to him must seem a fantasy adventure playground peopled with the most extraordinary characters – including a man old enough, with beard white and long enough, to be God himself!*

'Lucky little bugger,' Fen said aloud, 'I bet he doesn't even remember the day he visited the sculptor's studio.'

HH. Paris. June 1954. That was all that was documented on the back of each of the photos. The HH was from a stamp, enclosed within an oval. The place and date were written in copperplate, in blue ink. Four months later the sculptor would be dead, buried and – to Fen's enduring consternation – really rather forsaken. Abandoned. The studio would already have been rented out to an abstract expressionist called Brochard. Fen shuddered when she thought how Julius would have turned in his grave had he known of the hastily discordant action painting being produced in his studio.

'Where did *Abandon* go?' she wondered out loud. 'Within four months, this huge work had disappeared. Where did it go? Who took it? Who has it?'

By fair means or foul, she prayed the work still existed.

Please let it have been stolen to order.

The thought of it having been destroyed was unbearable.

As Fen travelled home, she comforted herself, downright

amused herself, imagining *Abandon* having pride of place in some opulent casa in a secret location in South America. She conjured a huge open-plan room with white walls and a ridiculously thick cream carpet. Monet's *Impression: Sunrise* on one wall. *Abandon* with ten feet of floor space all around, positioned near to the window-wall. A faceless figure sitting in a chair gazing at the work – some art-loving drugs baron perhaps, or maybe a reclusive spaced-out rock star whom most presumed to be dead and buried in Père-Lachaise.

Wherever it is, and with whomever, as long as Abandon *exists, as long as it's safe and adored, and gazed upon regularly and marvelled at, then Julius can rest.*

Still, though, Fen would love proof. As would the rest of the art world.

THIRTY-NINE

Being entirely honest with oneself is a good exercise.
                                        Sigmund Freud

Although Fen's relationship with Abi and Gemma was restored to its former level of intimacy, she felt very much that it had also moved on. It was different. The affection each had for the other was as strong as ever it had been – but oddly, Fen felt left out. Saying that, however, she had no desire to be included in the antics of their lifestyle. Threesome syndrome, that's what it was – an inevitability that a pairing will always materialize leaving an outsider. It had never transpired amongst the McCabe sisters, whose inter-relationships were utterly equal. Fen didn't even think that the sexual angle of Gemma and Abi's relationship had that much to do with it. It was a wavelength thing. She simply wasn't on theirs – nor did she aspire to be. Furthermore, though she had accepted – without approving or disapproving – the situation with Jake, it did not necessarily follow that she felt any easier about it. Gemma and Abi spoke openly about their open relationship but at such times, Fen politely and subtly switched off.

Consequently, she's been spending more and more time at Matt's flat – where Jake spends less and less time. The quality of the time that Matt and Fen share is beginning to change. As it develops and deepens, ironically it becomes more mundane. But it is the very way in which it fits so

271

snugly into everyday life that makes it all the more enjoyable and fulfilling. Not all evenings now lead to sex, not all conversations are fact-finding missions or focused on flirtation. In fact, Fen and Matt have started to coexist as a couple very nicely, sharing silence, snuggled up watching television, doing their own thing but in close physical proximity to one another – Fen reading whilst Matt snoozes; Fen pottering about his kitchen whilst he checks page proofs; Fen luxuriating in his bath whilst he chats to friends on the phone. They fit in and around each other's space as fluidly and comfortably as Fen's head fits in the nook of Matt's shoulder, or when their bodies gravitate into spoons position during the night. Fen has woken up on occasions to find Matt's hand gently and almost subconsciously cupping her buttock. She had started to wake up to check. She doesn't need to wake up now. She sleeps very well.

'Do you know what I like?' Fen mused one day, stopping midway along the soft-drinks aisle in Marks & Spencer in Islington.

'Doggy position?' Matt tried. Fen laughed. 'Monty Python?' he persisted. She punched him lightly. 'Slightly burnt toast with an inordinate amount of butter?' he said, because he'd noticed that was precisely what she liked.

'What I like,' Fen persisted, 'is coming back from work together and doing this whole homey thing.' Matt, blushing a little, turned his attention to a bottle of ginger-and-lemongrass carbonated drink. Fen continued. 'But also, I like meeting up elsewhere – having primped and preened myself at home. I like it that we have hot dates!'

'Best of both worlds,' Matt quantified.

'I suppose so, yes,' said Fen.

Fen is exhausted yet wide awake. She can't sleep – despite Matt sleeping soundly, cupping her buttock in his hand.

Django is right. Matt is placing his heart in my hands. I have the potential to handle it with all the care this deserves. But I also have the power to drop it and break it. I am, to a degree, responsible for his emotional welfare. And James too. Yes he appears all set in his ways and emotionally self-sufficient. But the vibe that we share is strengthening. He has bemoaned the physical distance between us. He sighs, 'Oh Fen,' when he comes. What did Matt say? The best of both worlds. Oh God.

So you're lying there thinking of James, while Matt sleeps with a handful of your buttock.

I have to start treating these men better. Djungo is right. I'm being selfish and unfair. I must treat Matt, treat James, with the deference they deserve. I must start, finally, to make my mind up.

And thereby lay your own path to walk confidently along. Hand in hand with one other.

I feel stifled. Not by Matt. Not by James. But by my own actions. I can't think straight. I can't breathe.

See her lying there, hot tears coursing silently down her face? She's wondering what she's done. What on earth *has* she done? What *is* she going to do? What the hell is she going to *do*? Her breathing is shallow and short. She is perspiring at the back of her neck. Her head hurts and her heart is very very heavy. Partly because it is filled with the enormous weight of loving two men. Partly because she knows she is overstretching it. She must let one go, for her health, for their sake.

'Babe?'

Instinctively, Matt has woken. He reaches for Fen and finds her damp and distressed.

'You OK?'

He senses that she nods. He turns towards her and places his arm gently, protectively across her shoulders. He kisses her cheek. He tastes salt.

'Bad dream?' he mumbles, sleepily.

'A nightmare,' Fen admits.

'Go back to sleep,' he says, with a little squeeze and another kiss, 'I'm here.'

FORTY

*F*en gave little warning to Matt, or James, of her departure with Pip for a long weekend in France. The Tour de France was in full swing and their aspiring journalist of a younger sister had left England almost three weeks before to join this circus of sorts. Django approved the mission to the extent that he wired money to facilitate their surprise visit to this lycra-clad world, currently heaving its way up and over the Alps.

Fen had in fact planned to visit Derbyshire that weekend but hadn't told Matt of the fact. Matt was thus musing whether to whisk his girlfriend away to Suffolk for the weekend, but had not told her because he loved planning surprises. James, expecting Fen for the weekend, had eschewed Safeways in favour of the lovely delicatessens and butchers in Bakewell, buying lots of fresh food, which he'd hidden carefully from the dogs. He'd also ironed his sheets (for the first time in his life), placing them carefully in the airing cupboard (which he'd forgotten he had), though he had scolded himself thoroughly for being a 'soft bastard', and had scalded his wrists from the steam on Egyptian cotton. He'd also bathed Barry and Beryl with a particularly expensive brand of human shampoo-conditioner – a somewhat overzealous reaction to his dogs having found a secret stagnant pool to which they were paying a daily pilgrimage, its whereabouts a mystery to James.

*   *   *

'How does a room with a view, a four-poster bed, complimentary shortbread and sherry, fluffy towelling robes *and* gourmet dinner in the heart of Constable country sound to you?' Matt asked Fen in the queue at the sandwich shop.

'Pretty idyllic,' Fen grinned. She licked her lips – though her mind was mainly focused on potential sandwich fillings. She had reached the head of the line and was changing her choice for the umpteenth time. 'Emmenthal and tomato on granary,' she ordered. 'No! on baguette, please. And a little mayonnaise. Large cappuccino, one sugar. Slice of that too. Hang on! Does that one have nuts in it? OK then, a slice of that other one, then. Thanks!' Matt ordered salt beef and mustard on rye, a double espresso and a caramel brownie, which Fen insisted on paying for – though Matt jokingly put her arm into a half-nelson while attempting to hand over his cash to much remonstration from Fen. Their larking and laughter gave others in the queue cause to grin or sigh wistfully.

'Shall we take a half-day?' Matt said, as they strolled to the gardens opposite Trust Art.

'A half-day?' Fen replied, confused – and ultimately more interested in making headway into the foot-long baguette. 'What for?'

Matt finished his mouthful. The salt beef was unnervingly stringy. 'The four-poster gourmet weekend in Constable country,' he said.

'Oh!' Fen responded. Then she looked at him and prayed he hadn't gone ahead and done what she suspected and now dreaded.

Not this weekend. Please don't let him have booked it for this weekend.

'When?' she asked a little shyly.

Matt leant forward, his eyes sparkling. 'I'm going to whisk you away for the weekend tomorrow!'

Fen's appetite had suddenly disappeared. Even without France in the equation, her weekend would have been doubly booked. Upsetting one person was one thing, upsetting two was quite another. France was going to cause upset to both James and Matt. Yet France was also saving her the task of choosing between the two. And there was the rub. Suddenly, Fen had no idea which she'd have chosen. Derbyshire or Suffolk? Who did she want to spend time with more? James or Matt? Who did she wish to hurt the least? James or Matt? Who would hurt the most? James or Matt?

She had no idea.

She hadn't really been thinking of anyone but herself.

She was appalled.

'Fen?'

This was just the sort of knot her sisters had prophesied her behaviour could create. However, instead of it having a humbling effect, Fen's feeble reaction was one of irritation. Though this was of course directed mainly at herself, it seemed much easier for the time being at least, to assuage her guilt by redirecting her frustration on to Matt.

It would have been enough to have merely told him that actually, she was off to France at the last minute with Pip to find Cat. But for some reason, she saw fit to preface this by accusing Matt of being presumptuous and hasty. Furthermore, why she had to also employ such an impatient and unkind tone of voice, I do not know. To top it all, her facial expression was unfriendly and hard. Insult to injury.

Matt, stunned by content and delivery, simply stared at her, his face criss-crossed with hurt and bewilderment. For Matt to display such a clear reaction to Fen's total lack of tact and sensitivity served only to compound her guilt. Ironically, the worse she felt the more badly she behaved. It caused her to lose her appetite – but that meant she could not even manage the smallest portion of humble pie. Therefore, she steered well away from apology or remorse by walking away from Matt instead. Briskly. Swearing audibly under her breath.

Matt sat there, stunned. He couldn't swallow – even without the salt beef stuck in his throat. He coughed it back up into the sandwich bag. He threw the bag in the bin and went directly to his office. He spoke to no one for the rest of the afternoon. He didn't even phone the hotel in Suffolk to cancel his reservation though he was aware that he'd lose his deposit because of it. He just couldn't find his voice.

Shit. James.

James, of course, was busy gardening. His phone rang. He could see from the caller display that it was Fen. It made him smile. However, James was handling manure. Mobile phones being fiddly things, the thought of having to gouge out bits of dung from the keypad meant he did not take the call. He'd phone her back. He went about his work again, now with a jaunty whistle.

Tammy Sydnope phoned Ruth Brakespeare immediately.

'He's whistling,' she told her furtively, though James could neither see nor hear her. 'Has he ever, *ever*, whistled whilst at yours?'

Mrs Brakespeare wished she could affirm that he had. But he hadn't. James? Whistle? How very out of character. Whatever can be the matter?

'He's in love,' Tammy deduced, with a very flat edge to her voice. 'He's working very productively, so much so that he can afford to stop every now and then to gaze at nothing in particular. He's in love, I tell you.'

'Or he's won the lottery,' Ruth added with a glimmer of hope for this preferential scenario.

'If he had won the lottery,' Tammy reluctantly philosophized, 'he wouldn't be working for us for £15 per hour.'

'Who is she?' Ruth wondered out loud.

'How about the young 'un he was seen with in the Cross Oaks?' Tammy wondered back.

'Who is she?' Ruth repeated. 'No one seems to know who she is.'

James was working his way around her garden with such conviction and efficiency, even his dogs were reduced to lying very still in the middle of the lawn and regarding their master suspiciously.

'All done, Mrs S,' he said, his eyes glinting, 'I shovelled the shit must faster than I anticipated so I did a little cutting back too.'

'Rushing home?' Tammy Sydnope probed. 'Plans?'

'Not really,' James said, 'not today. Tomorrow, though.'

'Tomorrow?' Tammy repeated with persuasive vagueness whilst gazing at her potentilla in a bid not to appear too nosy.

'I have a guest for the weekend,' said James, swinging his key fob about his index finger.

'Oh yes?' Tammy said, stooping to fiddle with her well-tended pieris. 'Family? Friends?'

James just grinned. His clients amused him, and it amused him to be stubborn about imparting any personal details. It was very flattering, after all, to know that you fluttered the hearts and dominated the conversation of the section of your clients who were female and under seventy years old.

James continued to whistle behind the wheel of his Land Rover. He stopped, however, when Barry and Beryl joined in, yowling and whining and inadvertently filling the air with dog breath. James found it difficult to tell whether they were singing and happy, or downright distressed.

'Hullo, Miss McCabe,' James says, phoning Fen's direct line at Trust Art.

'James,' she says, a little slowly, wishing it was her who had made the call.

'You rang?' he says. 'I was up to my wrists in horse shit.'

'I'm not coming tomorrow,' Fen states briskly, after a moment's silence, 'I can't come at all this weekend.'

278

Images of the ironed sheets in the airing cupboard and the larder full of fine provisions flit across James's mind. 'Any particular reason?' he enquires flatly.

'I'm going to France,' Fen tells him.

'France?'

'With Pip,' she informs him, 'to find Cat.'

'Is everything OK?' James asks.

'Yes,' Fen replies. There's silence. Fen's uncharacteristic aloofness and lack of manners astound James. Cancelling him is one thing – indeed, the reason for doing so would be totally understandable – but the manner Fen has seen fit to employ is quite another.

'Sorry,' she says perfunctorily.

'Fine,' James replies with a coolness equal to hers.

However, it merely makes Fen stroppy that James should sound cross. 'It's last minute,' she says, but not by way of an excuse. 'I have to prioritize,' she adds in a tone to suggest that James is being unreasonable.

'Fine,' James says again, tonelessly.

Fen really doesn't feel remotely flattered that both her men are obviously discomfited by plans which exclude them. Instead, she feels encumbered.

Thank God it's France tomorrow. And the focus can be on Cat.

Fen goes home. Both Abi's and Gemma's beds are unmade. Jake's shoes are in Gemma's room but there's a pair of his jeans strewn on Abi's floor. Fen packs a rucksack and phones Pip to say that doesn't it make sense for her to stay the night at Pip's.

'I'm working this evening,' Pip reminds Fen.

'That's fine,' says Fen, 'I'll just watch TV at yours, if that's OK.'

'Of course it is,' says Pip, wondering why Fen would choose not to spend her last night with Matt, but also knowing instinctively when not to probe.

*

Both Matt and James do a fair amount of carpet pacing and blank-wall contemplation that evening. They both feel uncomfortable. It occurs to both just how much they were looking forward to seeing Fen. And both feel singularly perturbed at her behaviour. Because it is anomalous, is it ominous? They hope not. They are both rather in love with her, you see. Thus, they both feel somewhat rejected. No one sleeps particularly well that night.

FORTY-ONE

No, when the fight begins within himself,
A man's worth something.
                                        Robert Browning

Who is it to be, then? Any ideas? Preferences? Inklings? Does one man deserve her more than the other? Is she truly deserving of either? Can and ought she to carry on as she is? Sense would suggest Matt, who adores her so vocally and looks after her so well. If we were to feed his attributes and those of James into a computer love-compatibility programme, Matt would probably score higher on account of age, logistics, job, personal wealth. But then, the romantic would suggest James. There's an undeniable, almost indefinable, wavelength link that Fen shares, mostly unspoken, with him. Here, age and location, pasts and circumstances are irrelevant. The still point of the turning world. But that's just it. In life, time can't stand still and it's unrealistic to attempt to create a state where it does. There again, time passes all too quickly and lives are too short to make the wrong decisions and have regrets. Should Fen follow her heart or her head? Therein lies the nub – because it is not as if Matt exclusively occupies the one place, or James the other. Fen really is in love with both men – head, heart and body.

Is this a moral dilemma, then? What is morality but a human construct? Just because morals differ, does that mean that one set is superior, more correct, of higher virtue, than another? Who decided that monogamy is the morally superior way? Ah! this is where the issue of consent swings the pendulum. Abi, Gemma and Jake consent to a non-monogamous way of life. Fen, however, has gone ahead and chosen this for herself but without the go-ahead from those with whom she is now deeply involved. There is, therefore, an element of deceit and duplicity and though she won't admit to lies, essentially they are there too; in abundance. Would Matt and James agree to their arrangement if they knew about it? If they knew about it, how would they feel? Appalled? Amenable? Hurt? Happy? Betrayed? Or just bewildered?

Pip, Cat and Django firmly believe the choice and responsibility lie with Fen. But maybe it won't be that simple. Perhaps the best solution, the ultimate conclusion, won't lie with her at all.

*   *   *

So, Fen McCabe has, quite literally, left the country. She has no idea where she and Pip will be staying for the next three nights, just that they are heading by train for Grenoble. Her phone has no network in France. There is little room in her rucksack for much other than a weekend's worth of clothes, the *Procycling* official guide to the Tour de France, the current issue of *Cycle Sport* and packs of Mars Bars for Cat. She has left behind, in a messy pile, all her ditherings. She is focusing instead on the welfare of her sister. Because she cares, does Fen; she truly cares for those she loves. And those she loves, she loves intensely.

FORTY-TWO

Women – their nature is not ours, we are far from grasping it.

Auguste Rodin

*B*arry and Beryl joined their master in a spectacular meal, taken as a carpet-picnic in the snug. They dined on duck-liver pâté, the finest slithers of cold cuts, olives drenched in Provençal herbs and garlic, the most pungent of premium cheeses. To accompany were melt-in-the-mouth breads, an exceptional potato salad and chutneys so delicious that it was completely acceptable to scoop fingerfuls direct from the jars.

'Lovely,' James said out loud though his dogs were asleep at his feet, bellies distended. James was convinced and satisfied that the food would not have tasted better for Fen's presence. It would have tasted no different. In fact, there would have been less to go around, on account of her hearty appetite. She wouldn't have added anything at all, James decided.

Bedtime, though, would have been more fun.

Matt had a really nice meal too. He and his ex-girlfriend. Cosy as you like in their favourite restaurant. Alberto, the manager, welcomed them back to his bosom as if they were his children, presenting her with a stem of white freesia, clasping his heart and cooing, '*Bene bene,*' while regarding the couple

283

with hope and benevolence. Julia was glowing, her cheeks flushed, her eyes bright and expectant. She could hardly eat for gazing at Matt and making every effort to appear chatty and gorgeous. And she did indeed look gorgeous and Matt found her very amusing and entertaining. There was lots of laughter, and gentle sighs, and 'remember when'-ing.

Are you shouting out, 'No, Matt! Don't be tempted! Give Fen a chance!'? Or are you quietly thinking, 'Go for it, Matt, give Fen a taste of her own medicine!'?

What will he do? How well do we know him?

'Come back to mine?' Julia suggests, the candlelight spinning sparks into her eyes. Matt shrugs and nods and says, 'Sure.' They go back to her flat and she pours Amaretto and dims the lights and puts their all-time favourite Neil Young CD on softly for maximum background ambience and subliminal memory manipulation. Cleverly, Julia now steers away from talking about 'us' to focus instead on simply chatting and conversing about work and politics and television and gossip, just like new couples out on a date tend to do. As stimulating intellectually as it's been, she is desperate now to reach over and trace her fingertips down his neck, to slip her hand under his shirt and feel his chest and find his heart beating. She sits on her hands while Matt pours more Amaretto.

'Have you seen the new Sean Connery film?' he asks her. 'It's good – fairly standard brain-rest fare, but entertaining. And that man is so damn cool.'

'No,' Julia says, 'I haven't, but I intend to. Who did you go with? Jake?' She asks as nonchalantly as possible while her heart races in anticipation of his answer.

'A colleague from work,' Matt says, noncommittally.

I went with Fen. I went with Fen. I went with Fen. I bought her a Häagen-Dazs choc ice – she nibbled off all the chocolate outer, got bored with the remainder after a couple of licks and gave it to me to finish. She grabbed my hand at the twist in the plot, then she softened her grasp and knitted fingers with me.

Matt awoke at four in the morning. He wasn't in his own bed. Nor was he in the four-poster in the charming country house hotel in Suffolk. He was in Julia's bed. Her limbs were wrapped around him; her head was nestled against his chest. Her breath smelt of garlic. Her hair smelt very fragrant. Her shoulder was digging into Matt's side. The only thought in Matt's head was what was the best way to extricate himself. It was difficult to tell whether she had wrapped herself around him like a cocoon or a praying mantis. He wasn't comfortable, that was for sure. Physically or otherwise. He debated whether to go for speed or dexterity. He went for a mixture of the two. She woke up of course.

'Where are you going?' she asked, a tinge of panic underscoring her sleepy voice.

'Home,' Matt whispered.

'Don't go,' she pleaded, sitting up in bed and holding her arms out.

'I'll call you,' he said.

'Stay,' she implored, hugging her knees and rocking, 'please?'

'I'll call you,' he said, kissing her forehead lightly and leaving her flat for his.

Matt felt very at peace walking home because he loved London passionately at a time like this, at 4.37 in the morning, when the city was dozing without actually being asleep.

Jake rolled home just after lunch-time the next day.

'What are you doing here?' he greeted Matt.

'I live here,' Matt said, 'I own the place.'

'I thought you were going for a dirty weekend?'

'So did I,' Matt said glumly.

'Where's Fen?' Jake asked, actually looking around the flat because it was so normal to see her there.

'France,' Matt said.

'France?' Jake said. He regarded Matt and decided that they should watch the cricket on the television whilst getting drunk. Matt thought this a splendid idea.

'I spent the night with Julia,' Matt told him between innings.

'For fuck's sake,' Jake exclaimed, with extravagant displeasure.

'Not sexually,' Matt stressed. 'I called her. We went out for a meal. We went back to hers. Had half a bottle of Amaretto. I slept in her bed.'

'Did she try and seduce you?'

Matt had to think hard on that one. 'No, actually – oddly – she didn't.'

'Whoa!' Jake said, waving his hands, 'There's a reason for that! She has a cunning plan, something up her sleeve – you know, take the pressure off to lure you and insure you return?'

'Possibly,' Matt agreed. 'She did beg me to stay.'

Jake turned a glance out of the window into a contemplative gaze at the window-sill. 'Don't do it. Don't take a leaf out of my book,' he said, quite seriously. 'The chapters may be full of fun and frolics but I have a hunch that the ending won't be a particularly pretty one.'

Matt raised his glass to Jake.

'I'll talk it through with Julia tomorrow,' he said. 'I think Fen's back on Monday.'

The next day, Matt did just that – he phoned Julia and took her out to lunch. As gently as he could, holding her hand and maintaining unflinching eye contact, he told her that he really did love her, that he always would, but that their romantic and sexual relationship was over and no amount of hope or elaborate plans could possibly revive it. Julia stared at her plate, dabbing her fingers on the cocoa-powder-and-icing-sugar design that had encircled the chocolate mousse cake. She gazed up at Matt. Ironically, it was the care and kindness in his gaze that convinced her it was indeed over. She knew then that he loved her. But in the past tense.

'Is there someone else?' she felt confident enough to ask.

Matt dabbed at her plate. Shyly, he nodded. 'Yes,' he said, 'there is.'

'Did you go and see the Sean Connery film with her?' Julia asked, but non-accusatorily.

'Yes,' said Matt, 'we went last week.'

'Did she enjoy it too?' Julia asked.

'Yes, she did,' said Matt.

'More than I would have,' Julia stated without malice. 'Not really my sort of movie.'

'No,' Matt affirmed, 'you're probably right.'

'What is her name?' Julia asked.

'Fen,' Matt said, 'Fenella McCabe.'

Julia went very quiet, Matt's heart felt heavy. He had loved Julia very very much. In their early days, he'd seriously entertained theories of marriage and babies and happy ever after. He felt sad now, but without feeling that they had failed in any way. It wouldn't have worked. But he knew that neither of them was at fault or to blame. They had grown over the years – but grown apart instead of together.

'I do love you very much,' Matt told Julia.

'I know you do,' Julia said. Oddly enough, she felt rather calm. She couldn't feel any tears welling, could not detect a knot in her throat, experienced no desperation in her heart, sensed no longing in her soul. 'I know you do.'

They smiled meekly at each other. Matt asked for the bill.

'Do you mind if I go?' Julia asked.

'No – do,' Matt said.

'One last thing,' Julia said, standing then sitting again, 'was there an overlap? Between me and Fen?'

'No,' Matt smiled gently, 'there wasn't.'

Julia had suspicions about indiscretions on Matt's part in the latter months of their relationship. Yet one-off shags or brief physical flings were suddenly easier to stomach and accept than if he'd fallen in love and left her for someone else. For this Fen.

'Bye, then,' Julia said, standing again, tilting her head and giving him a little wave.

Matt stood, cupped her face in his hands and kissed her forehead. 'You take care,' he said and he really meant it.

Matt leaves the restaurant and emerges on to Hampstead High Street where the pavements are awash with the usual proliferation of nattily dressed Sunday shoppers browsing the windows for this week's must haves, despite having to dodge the young families with three-wheeled baby buggies heading for the Heath. Poor Julia. Lovely Julia. She'll be fine. I know she will be. Bye bye, sweet girl. I'm sorry, I'm sorry. I'm sorry that it didn't work out. Matt feels like crying. He heads for a bench on the Heath and sits quietly with his thoughts. Telling Julia that there was indeed someone else was to end the relationship once and for all. No room for hope, no doors left ajar. You can't come in here now. I know – I won't try again. Her acceptance was surprisingly hard on Matt, too. Though he was relieved that the anger and tears and delusions she had foisted on him over the last few months were now resolved, though he truly wanted her to move on, he also knew deep down that it had been just a little comforting, secretly flattering, to have her in love with him from afar. He was having to say goodbye to that. No more e-mails or text messages or voice mails or phone calls from her. Would he miss these? Quite possibly. But you'll have Fen, Matt.

I don't think so.

Pardon?

'I don't think so,' Matt says aloud, rather hoarsely, which causes the couple sharing his bench to move off promptly, pushing their baby, in the three-wheeled buggy with mini mountain-bike tyres, over the grass with ease.

Matt! All she said was that she was going to France rather than Suffolk!

'No,' Matt repeats, 'I don't think so. Not Fen. I don't think it's what I want.'

Matt marched to Highgate, stopping at benches along the way to collect his thoughts and regain his composure. He now realized why he had found Fen's behaviour so unnerving. He felt utterly compromised. It was a feeling he hadn't yet encountered with regard to women. Work, occasionally. Mates, once or twice. Women? Never. Had he always had the upper hand in relationships? Probably. What did that mean? Did it mean that his women had always felt more deeply for him than he for them? Possibly.

I've never had to do much chasing. I've never had to look around or hedge my bets or worry about rejection. If anything, I've had pick of the crop.

Women falling at your feet?

Well, I may have caused many a heart to flutter but, to my knowledge, I haven't made anyone faint.

I mean, there's always been someone – you've never really been single, have you?

No, not in my twenties. I was blessed with a veritable succession, a queue, if you like. Always someone in the offing, no need to spend a night – let alone a week – on my own.

But your relationship with Julia finished before Fen was on the scene.

Yes. But that was my longest relationship. It had staled long before I met Fen. I succumbed to temptation a fair few times. It didn't make me any happier. But I knew, I guess, that it was wrong just to keep it going whilst keeping my eyes open for a viable alternative.

A Viable Alternative dressed in a skirt and making eyes at you?

Yes. But though I was no longer in love with Julia, though things were pretty grim – non-communicative, complacent – I still had a certain respect for her. And for myself. I didn't want to spend years to come having furtive shags behind her back. Been there, done that. It had become boring. Thrill of the chase – and then what? Feeling guilty, feeling flat. Though I was no longer in love with her, I didn't want to hurt her. And I really didn't want the reason for our split to be the presence of someone else. I had to believe unequivocally that the relationship was over purely because it had run its course.

You didn't want to string Julia along, keep her dangling, then cut the rope and have her fall.

Exactly. When I met Fen, I had already left. So when I met Fen, my slate was already wiped clean.

And yet initially you balked at the idea of going straight from one relationship into another.

That'll be a testosterone thing – Jake's notion of The Rebound seemed both healthy and what was expected of me.

So you shagged Judith.

Yes. But in truth, the idea of the sex was far more titillating than the physical reality itself.

'So I got to shoot my load. I came. Whoosh! Big bloody deal.'

Matthew Holden! Hush! You're sitting by Highgate Ponds, there are children in earshot!

And then along came Fen. And shagging Judith could well have jeopardized my chances there. So that's when I thought how contrived it would be to delay the possibility of getting it together with Fen just so I could embark on a conventional rebound and put some space between proper relationships.

You got the girl. And you've been very happy.

Really happy.

So why on earth are you contemplating finishing what has only just started?

Has she gone off me?

'Has she gone off me?'

'Who?' asks a small boy in red shorts and red wellington boots and a T-shirt that was probably white this morning but is now speckled and splodged, Jackson Pollock style, with foodstuffs, vegetation and pondlife.

'Maybe it's actually been too fast too soon? Right person, wrong time?' Matt tries to reason with the child. The boy takes a seat beside Matt on the bench. Suddenly Matt wishes he was young enough, small enough, to wear shorts and wellies and swing his legs because his feet were a long way from touching the ground. Oh, to be trouble free, so full of energy.

'Maybe that's true,' says the little boy very seriously though of course he doesn't understand a word of what Matt is talking about. He's just picking up on Matt's tone and contemplation and is trying to make friends in the way he knows best – mirroring.

'Or do I just feel emasculated by her rejection?' Matt theorizes.

'Yes,' agrees the boy, 'you probably do. I often am emastilated.'

Matt knows not to laugh. 'I don't know,' Matt says, 'has it been a little one-sided? It's not a good idea to start off with an inbalance, is it?'

'It's very bad idea,' the boy comments sagely, 'isn't it?'

'But,' Matt says, 'wooing and pursuing her – was that for my own amusement or because I truly wanted Fen? Did I crave light relief and a laugh – in the shadow of my break-up with Julia?'

'I do that,' the boy says encouragingly, 'I do.'

'If I think about it,' says Matt, not knowing where or how to start really thinking about it.

'I have to think about it too,' says the little boy and he holds his finger to his lips, frowning with the effort of Thinking About It. 'I have thought about it,' he tells Matt, 'and my answer is yes.'

'I should call it a day?'

'It is Sunday. My birthday is never on Sunday. It is on Wednesday November the twenty-first.'

'Is she worth it?' Matt asks, affectionately ruffling the boy's hair. 'I wonder.'

'Is she indeed!' the boy exclaims, raising his hands and letting them fall down on his knees. He sighs, as if he is shouldering Matt's worries plus the weight of the entire world.

'Who's leading who a merry dance?' Matt probes.

'We do country dancing at playschool – shall I show you?'

The little boy clambers down from the bench and holds out his hand. Matt takes it and stands. The boy darts around, clapping and singing tunelessly. 'Do a merry dance!' he shouts gleefully. 'Do it with me!'

Matt laughs. 'Actually, I ought to go home now,' he says. 'Anyway, I have two left feet.'

The boy looks at Matt with alarm and very slowly drops his gaze to Matt's feet. Matt ruffles the top of his dirty blond head and says goodbye.

'Bye,' says the boy, scampering off to do a commendable long jump into a puddle.

FORTY-THREE

Matt wasn't much looking forward to Fen's return. James was, though. Firstly, he was intrigued; genuinely interested to hear of her trip. He was sure she'd have an adventure or two to recount. Secondly, he wanted to gauge her manner. Her brusqueness last week had been so out of character, unattractive too, that hitherto he'd attributed it to PMT or some other hormonal affliction unique to women.

Fen, however, did not return on Monday. Nor did she phone Matt or James to let them know. She stayed in Paris, alone, for a night. She made the decision to do so on the spur of the moment – right beside the Eurostar gates at the top of the escalator in the Gare du Nord.

'I can't come home yet,' she told Pip, 'I'm not ready.'

Pip regarded her sister. 'Don't tell me!' she jested gently. 'You're going off to find Julius Frigging Fetherstone?'

Fen nodded. 'Now that I'm here, it would be daft not to – there are documents in the Bibliothèque Nationale – it would really benefit the Trust Art Archive.' She didn't tell Pip that her desire to find Julius had next to nothing to do with art history – more that she felt confident that Julius would help her decide what to do. She didn't have to – Pip knew her well enough to know that, though rifling through documents sounded plausible, it wasn't the only reason for Fen to stay. As the train headed for home, Pip had a very vivid picture of Fen strolling dreamily along the streets of the Latin quarter talking quietly to a long-dead nineteenth-century sculptor. She'd be OK, she'd be in safe hands. The thought made her grin.

I mean, if I can spend half my life as a clown called Martha – with a separate wardrobe, completely different voice and portfolio of facial expressions – my younger sister can certainly have an imaginary friend in Julius Flipping Fetherstone.

And so Fen McCabe went back down to the Métro and headed for the Left Bank. She found a small *pension* near the Musée Cluny where the owner let her choose between two rooms available. Fen chose the smaller, though it was the same price, because it was like one she'd seen in a hundred black-and-white French films. Curled up on the bed, she left a message on Rodney Beaumont's voice mail, exaggerating both her tone of enthusiasm and the benefit to the Trust Art Archive. She didn't even entertain the idea of making any other calls, not least because the telephone rates were exorbitant. It was tea-time. She'd leave the research until the morning. She was anxious to be out, to see where she might find Julius.

Nowhere. He simply wasn't around. Not even in the tiny street near the Rue de Buci where his studio had been. He wasn't taking coffee at tea-time in any of the cafés, or Pernod early evening in any of the bars; nor did he join Fen for a buckwheat *galette* and an earthenware cup of *cidre* in a cheap, cramped, delicious restaurant populated mainly by art students. He wasn't passing the time on the pedestrian bridge of Pont des Arts, though plenty of other people were. He wasn't sitting on any of the benches in the Luxembourg gardens. By now it was getting dark and Fen didn't want to be sitting by herself in the gardens either. Deflated, she returned to the *pension* and watched the highlights of that day's stage of the Tour de France instead. She thought of Cat, amongst new colleagues and friends in the cramped press rooms, with her new boyfriend in some cramped two-star hotel in the evenings. Cat had worn a veritable sparkle on top of her creased clothes. She had shone. Luminous. Energetic. Her sisters were reacquainted with the Cat of old, whom they had not seen for so many months they had all but forgotten about her. How lovely to see her again. Fen and Pip had left the Alps knowing that they were leaving their sister in safe, loving hands.

Fen looked at her own hands. Were they safe and loving? She didn't want to look too hard. She fell fast asleep with the small table lamp still on.

Fen awoke very early. She swung open the tall, elegant windows and peered over the intricate railings to the street below. The pavements were being washed. *Boulangerie* vans were driving recklessly half on the pavement, half on the roads. There were few people around. The sky was an interesting mix of hopeful pale blue fighting for space against bruise-grey clouds and scorches of orange from the sunrise. She was glad she was in Paris, though how fruitful her day would be she had yet to discover. She climbed back into bed and refused to allow herself to think of Matt or James. That's why she was in Paris – to ask Julius what she should do. There was little point, therefore, in worrying about it before then. She zapped through the television channels and came across the *Magic Roundabout* in French, where the personalities of the characters seemed entirely different to those so infamous in the English version. She sat in the bath – a classic deep square structure where the water covered her shoulders – and practised her French accent, making it more and more extreme with a strong nasal inflection, until she giggled out loud.

'Come on, girl, there's work to be done.'

*

It was good to be back with the Fetherstone Archive. She hadn't been there since researching her Master's dissertation. There were no new documents, nothing really to benefit Trust Art at all, or to justify a day away for Fen and the expense of the hotel. Fen just sat with the pictures and letters spread before her and gave herself a sizeable but silent pat on the back.

You've done well, you've come far. You worked hard and can feel good about reaping rewards.

She felt acutely the passing of time; able to remember herself vividly as a fresh-faced student, always earnest, on a mission to publicize and canonize Fetherstone. Now, six years later, she was a salaried expert on the sculptor whose reputation was growing thanks to her efforts.

Oh look! Here are duplicates of those photos that I found amongst the Holden collection – of Julius in his studio months before death with the couple and Henry and the small boy and enigmatic woman.

The pictures were identical. It was difficult to tell which were the originals – Paris or London. Fen scrutinized the backs. They didn't have Henry's stamp but were inscribed instead in tiny wiry writing in black ink. She couldn't make out the words at all. Collection Someone-or-other. The librarian couldn't tell either; he shrugged and made murmuring noises with suitable facial gesticulations, all in a quintessentially Gallic way. Fen asked if he might photocopy them for her. The librarian obliged – he vaguely remembered her from years ago and was amused anyway that someone should have expressed interest in this folder. He checked his books – the Archive had only been requested twice in the six years since Fen was last here.

Julius, Julius, where the bloody hell are you? I've come all this way, all this way. Please come!

Fen toyed with the idea of visiting either the Picasso museum or the Pompidou. But she felt sceptical whether she'd find Julius in either place.

I could go to the Musée Rodin – but as Brancusi said when a student of Rodin, 'Nothing grows under the shadow of a great tree,' – so I'm unlikely to tune into Julius in that place.

She had over two hours until her train and decided that she wouldn't mooch or mope, or get gallery guilt, she'd indulge herself with some shopping instead. She headed for the Galeries Lafayette where she tried on many things, procrastinated over all of them but left the store having bought nothing. She went to the station, chose a bar-restaurant nearby and marvelled to herself over the quality of such establishments in comparison to those around the London stations. She ordered a sandwich with cheese and piquant *cornichons*, also a *pression, s'il vous plaît*. The combination was perfect, the meal was satisfying.

'I prefer ham.'

Fen didn't need to turn – in fact, if she did she'd run the risk of breaking the spell. 'Do you, Julius.'

'I do, child. And I would refrain from coffee, dearest – you'll feel queasy on the train.'

The waiter came and Fen requested a bottle of Evian.

'I cannot believe that water is bottled and good money paid for it,' Julius said.

'I couldn't find you yesterday,' Fen said. 'I looked hard. It upset me.'

'You should know by now, child, that it is I who comes to you.'

The waiter brought Fen's water, and a pastry too. He'd been watching her. She seemed so absorbed, so deep in thought, that he presumed some unkindness had befallen her. Mind you, had he known that she was chatting away merrily to an artist dead for almost forty years, he would have given her the pastry anyway, out of pity. Insanity in one so young and so pretty – how cruel!

Fen glanced at the old clock above the bar; she synchronized it with her watch and knew that she needed to pay, to go, to catch her train, to return to England.

'I have to go, Julius. I have to go home and sort my life out.'

She felt like crying – but the innate knowledge that, in reality, no one was there to wrap a protective arm around her shoulders, kept the tears at bay.

'Tell me what to do,' she implored, crossing the road.

'One is ultimately responsible for the progress and path of one's own happiness – but one also has a degree of responsibility to safeguard the happiness of others.'

'Can you love two at the same time? Is it possible? Is it right?'

'I only ever loved one woman.'

Fen had reached the escalator. She really had to get a move on.

'Where's *Abandon*?' she asked, now out loud and to the bemusement of an elderly lady who spoke no English. Fen mounted the escalator. 'Tell me, Julius – it's a travesty that the world is denied this monumental, seminal, magnificent work.'

She looked around her. The station was full of people. She knew no one. Certainly there was no sculptor with sage beard and the answer to her question. Of course there wasn't. He died almost half a century ago.

It's time to go home, Fen. You're in danger of missing your train. Hurry.

FORTY-FOUR

Matt wasn't in work the next day. Otter told her that he'd gone for a meeting at the printers about paper quality and charges.

'I love Matt very much,' Fen said instead, looking as though she was about to weep.

'I know you do,' Otter soothed, 'of course you do.'

'I *do*,' Fen stressed, as if Otter had argued otherwise.

'I know you do,' Otter reiterated, unable to fathom why such a positive declaration should be accompanied by eyes stung red with tears held at bay. 'Now, girl, I want news of all those bike boys – in glorious technicolor detail.'

'I have to speak to Matt,' Fen said, her voice wavering, 'today. But his phone is off.'

'He's in meetings with the printers,' Otter told her again, wondering whether his arm around her shoulders would blot tears or create a deluge. He gave her a light punch instead. 'Ed is on a crusade today, dearest, to save Trust Art money – and to save the reputation of *Art Matters* as a quality read on good paper.'

Fen nodded.

'He'll be back tomorrow,' Otter said. 'You can talk slushily to him then. For now, though, you have to furnish me with what you saw out on the Tour. Dimensions, Fen! I demand dimensions. How much is just padding? And how much is truly Boy Bulge?'

Fen sits, forlorn, in the Archive. She has the photocopies of the backs of the photos from Paris but the writing is no clearer. She looks at the shelves. The boxes are now in impeccable order. In fact, she has only four years to organize – and they being more recent, that shouldn't take long at all. Perhaps a month. What then? Will she be out of a job? With whom should she discuss this? Rodney? Judith? What is the etiquette? Should they be approaching her? Should they have done so by now? The fact that they haven't – is it ominous? Should she reconsider the PhD that her tutors at the Courtauld were so keen for her to undertake? Would the British Academy still grant her the award that they had offered but that she had turned down?

Maybe I should just move back to Derbyshire.

'I wish Matt was here today. I hate this! I hate this!'

But why should everything tick along to your timescale, Fen? Why should you always call the shots when it suits you?

I have to speak to James. But I'd like to speak to Matt first.

Well, you can't. Unless speaking to James can wait until you've seen Matt tomorrow.

It can't wait.

'James?'

'The return of the native!' James says, happy to hear from her, slightly perturbed that his heartbeat should have picked up so. It is difficult to deduce her tone from her brief opening. 'How was France?' he asks. 'How was your sister?'

'We found her to be in fine form, high spirits and rather in love,' Fen tells James.

'Good,' he says, pulling Barry's ears gently and twisting them around his fingers, much to the dog's delight. Beryl, craving attention, head-butted his thighs.

'Then I had a day in Paris by myself,' Fen says, 'trying to find Julius.'

'Productive?' James enquires, pleased that Fen today bears no resemblance at all to the snappish girl of last week. He crooks the phone under his chin so he can dispense physical affection to both dogs at once.

'Yes,' Fen says.

She's gone slightly quiet. Barry, leave Beryl's tail.

'Fen?' James says, encircling his hand around Barry's snout.

'Can I come and see you?' Fen asks. 'This weekend?'

'Of course you can,' James says, 'we'll look forward to it.'

'How are Barry and Beryl?'

'Very well,' James says, looking at the two dogs with a mixture of pride and exasperation.

'I love them,' Fen says with great certitude. James thinks this is a little exorbitant.

She must be tired from her weekend.

'We'll see you in a couple of days, then?' he clarifies, his dogs looking at him expectantly.

'Yes,' Fen says softly.

'Bye for now, then,' James says.

'Bye,' says Fen.

She phones him back immediately.

'James?'

'Hullo again!'

'James – I do so love you.'

FORTY-FIVE

How sad and bad and mad it was –
But then, how it was sweet!

Robert Browning

'**I**s Fen back?' Matt asked Otter, looking at his diary as if trying to find an opportunity to slot her into the day.

'Yup,' Otter confirmed, 'she was back yesterday – seemed pretty lovelorn, if you ask me, absence obviously made her heart grow fonder.'

Matt chewed his lip thoughtfully. 'Yesterday was something of a mercy mission,' he justified, 'and I return victorious – I've negotiated the same quality paper, ten per cent price reduction.'

'Without selling your soul or your body?' Otter enquired with much scepticism. Matt raised an eyebrow. 'I'd love to be a fly on the wall when you tell Accounts – ha! they can put that in their pipe and smoke it!' Otter remarked with glee.

'I'm going there directly,' Matt said, with great reserve. He couldn't keep his grin at bay any longer. 'Then I'll go and blow my trumpet a little in Rodney's office.'

'We should celebrate,' Otter said, 'a triumphal luncheon to celebrate *Art Matters*' honour being safeguarded.'

'Abso-bloody-lutely,' Matt agreed. 'I'll book the Tate restaurant. Right, I'm off to lord it over Accounts.'

*

What about Fen, Matt – when will you have time to see her?

Fen had so many butterflies that there was no room for croissant or cappuccino. Not that she'd eaten last night – for the same reason. She'd psyched herself up so much yesterday, needing to see Matt, that she had slept badly on account of all the adrenaline still surging around her. This morning, it had dissipated only slightly into a rampage of butterflies. Seeing Matt was a foregone conclusion. In a matter of hours. Soon enough, in a few minutes. Only, the minutes cruelly stretched back into hours. Fen waited in the Archive. She'd sent an e-mail as soon as she'd arrived; sweetly if rather formally requesting his company at his earliest opportunity. Only he hadn't shown. He hadn't replied. And Publications' door was closed – the blind down to signify a meeting. When it was open again, just before lunch, only Otter was in there.

'Miss McCabe!' he welcomed. 'Have you heard what a hero Holden is?'

Fen shook her head.

Where is he?

'He's in with Rodney at the moment,' Otter said, reading her mind. 'He's probably being given a golden crown, or Freedom of the Corridor – or a pat on the back at the very least.'

I really have to speak to him.

'We're going out to lunch,' Otter was saying, checking his watch which, on account of his skinniness, always twisted around so that the face rested on the inside of his wrist, 'to celebrate the continued use of quality paper at a rate less than that which we were paying!'

'Good old Matt,' Fen murmured, for whom this talk of paper and prices was somewhat irrelevant on both professional and personal levels.

I have to see him. I have to tell him. It really can't wait. For his sake, as much as mine.

'Will you tell him, Otter,' Fen said, 'will you tell him that I'm here? That, when he has a mo', I need to see him?'

'Of course, Funny Face,' Otter assured her, never having seen her looking so serious. It became her though, investing her everyday prettiness with a certain soulful beauty.

Rodney was delighted at Matt's victory. His immediate reaction was to leap from his leather chair and give Matt a double thumbs up. When he'd finished pacing around his office, punching the air with pleasure, he then invited himself along to the lunch at the Tate restaurant.

Why shouldn't he, Matt remarked to himself quite happily, *firstly he's director of Trust Art, secondly he's offered to foot the bill from his own pocket.*

The three men returned from lunch at gone tea-time. To those who did not know the reason for their lengthy boozy lunch, the trio looked slightly the worse for wear. The men themselves, though, felt fantastic.

'Crikey, am I squiffy!' Rodney commented with a boyish giggle as he negotiated the stairs up to his floor.

'I'd say I'm downright pissed,' Otter clarified, to Rodney's great amusement.

'Pissed!' Rodney whispered, as if in awe of a major expletive.

'Drunk as a skunk, me,' Matt said, with much thoughtful nodding.

'Go to your desks and push paper,' Rodney said, 'lovely, lovely quality paper! Actually, shall we go to the pub?'

Otter looked horrified, having always thought that the director of Trust Art ought to display the same sort of discipline and authority as a headmaster.

'Maybe after work,' Matt said diplomatically.

'Jolly jolly fantastic idea,' Rodney enthused, 'fan-*tas*-tic.'

Watching their boss sway and falter off towards his office, Matt remarked to Otter that it was a good job the director's office was a flight of stairs below theirs.

'He'll have a stonking hangover in about half an hour,' Otter concluded.

They entered their corridor as Fen was coming out of the Archive, ostensibly to go to the loo, or down to Bobbie's for a biscuit – anywhere so that she could walk past Publications. She stopped in her tracks. Otter and Matt appeared not to have seen her. She watched them weave and swagger into their office.

'For fuck's sake,' she said under her breath, 'they're pissed!'

She'd be packing up for the day in an hour or so. She had to talk to Matt before then, whatever his capabilities of comprehension. She walked to his office, knocked and entered.

'Fen!' Otter, with very flushed cheeks, exclaimed.

'Fen,' said Matt, his eyes really rather beautifully dark with dilation.

'Hey,' Fen said, with a little semicircular wave, 'do you have a moment? For a chat?'

Matt sighed as he looked down at his desk and the scatter of papers and Post-its that had collected during his absence. He looked at his watch. Looked at his desk again. Looked at Fen. 'Sure,' he said. He stood up, a little unsteady. 'Otter,' he said, raising his hand in a wave of sorts, 'I'll be five minutes. Vet my calls!'

Otter saluted. As soon as Matt had left the room, he let his head droop and drop on to his desk and fell sound asleep.

In the Archive, Fen feels shy about facing Matt. She has to say what she has to say and she wishes he wasn't drunk but she realizes, perhaps for the first time ever, that she simply cannot stage-manage everything as she'd like.

'Fen,' Matt says, at the very moment she turns to him, saying his name. 'Please,' he says, sweeping through the air with his hand to invite her to continue.

'You first,' Fen says, who finally acknowledges it is important to let Matt have not just an opinion but the forum

305

in which to express it. She will listen. She will listen and then she will talk.

Matt rocks very slightly from side to side and back and forth. He nods his head and tries to keep it steady, staring at the top button of Fen's Agnès B cardigan. He lifts his eyes to her face and smiles a little meekly. In an instinctive but uncontrolled gesture, he cups her breast in his hand and kisses her a little clumsily.

'The thing is, Fen,' he slurs though he is obviously trying hard not to, 'I actually really love you.'

She stares at him.

'I do,' he nods vigorously, 'I really do. I love you.'

Still she stares. Tears welling.

'But I don't think it's going to work out.' He shakes his head and looks desperately forlorn.

What? What did he say?

'I don't,' he shrugs unhappily, 'it's not. Nah. I actually want just to be on my own for a while.'

Did he just say—?

'Single,' Matt is saying, 'bachelor,' he continues, 'for a bit.' He tilts his head, regarding her with a mixture of benevolence, love and the simple effort to focus on just one Fen. 'It's too much,' he explains, 'to go from one to another so quickly.' He looks at her and looks at his feet. He has about five of them, he thinks. 'It's unwise.' He shrugs, bringing his head up, though his eyes continue to count his many shoes. 'Unfair on you because it's not right for me.' Finally, he raises his eyes. 'Sorry,' he says, with real remorse, 'I do love you, Fen – but it is the wrong time. It really is.'

And he leaves, does Matt, he leaves the Archive. He goes back to Publications, vaguely notices that Otter is spark out at his desk. He collects his wallet, his mobile phone and, for some reason, a thesaurus, and leaves for home.

306

*   *   *

Fen?

Fen?

Are you crying?

I am crying. Of course I am. Wouldn't you?

But hasn't he just made it easy on you? Saved you a ghastly task?

Fen awakes in the early hours. She flicks on her bedside lamp. No Matt in her bed. No more Matt full stop. She glances around her room. There were things she wanted to say to him, too. Quite a lot, actually. It would be wrong to, she decides, now that she knows the score. She leaves her bed and sits on the floor with her back to the wall, focusing intently on the temperature knob of the radiator on the opposite wall. Though it is summer, her room is always just a little chilly, not that she's had the radiator on. Radiators only work from October to April – Django had told his three nieces so, and they still believed him. Django. Django. She'd be home in a day or so.

   'Oh Matt,' she murmurs, 'I so love you. I am so sad. So sorry.'

   She goes to her window. There is no vestige of dawn at all. She hears sirens. An ambulance, she presumes, on its way to or from the Royal Free Hospital. She crosses her fingers, as Django taught her, to invest the unfortunate with luck and life.

   'Matty,' she says, though she has never called him that. A tear oozes from the corner of her eye. It makes a very slow, hot and stinging passage down, along the side of her nose, to under her nostril where her tongue, stretched to the limit, dabs it up. 'Oh Matt.'

Fen goes back to bed.

'I wanted to tell you,' she sobs into her pillow, 'that I am deeply in love with you. I'd realized that it is you with whom I want – wanted – to walk forward. I'd made my mind up – and it was *you*. It was *you*.'

FORTY-SIX

*B*eing at Trust Art for the remainder of that week was hard for both Fen and Matt. Fen arrived early, left early, bought her lunch on her journey in and ate it in her Archive. She also exerted the powers learnt as a schoolgirl, managing to restrict her trips to the toilet to once mid-morning, once mid-afternoon. Matt had taken a day off on account of his hangover and, on his return, had so many outstanding obligations that he barely left his office, sending Otter to fetch his post or bring him sandwiches.

'It's over with Fen,' he told Otter, but not until the close of the week.

Otter, bewildered and unhappy, could elicit little from Matt. He went to the Archive. No Fen. She'd obviously left early for the weekend.

*   *   *

Fen had phoned Django from St Pancras to announce that she was coming home on the next train out. Django knew his niece well enough to know when to probe and when to just let her be. He had always been able to judge Fen's level of distress by her degree of politeness. He deduced that she was troubled indeed, extremely sad, on account of her being so

309

excessively formal and courteous. Varying degrees of quietness meant the girl ranged from out of sorts to downright angry. Excessive chatter meant she was fretting about something. But politeness had always signified sadness.

'Darling!' he had said. 'How the devil are you?'

'I'm very well, thank you,' Fen had responded, 'how are you?'

Later, he had asked after her job.

'It's going very well, thank you,' Fen had told him.

Django had had a bit of an accident with the Tabasco bottle and rather too much of the fiery condiment had hurled itself into the gazpacho soup he'd made. He'd apologized for it, assuring Fen that he wouldn't be remotely offended if she left it and had cheese on crackers instead.

'It's very nice, thank you,' she told her uncle, sipping demurely from the spoon to prove it, 'a little spicy – but in a piquant way. Honestly.'

He ascertained that her sorrow must run to a great depth indeed when he offered her After Eights that evening. Almost absent-mindedly, she worked her way through the entire box, thanking him for each and every chocolate, whilst listening very courteously to all that he rambled on about that evening. Django knew, unequivocally, of the depth of her distress when she took her leave of him to have a very lengthy but silent bath.

'She always sings in the bath,' Django said to himself, finding two After Eights that Fen had overlooked, camouflaged at either end of the box. He took both chocolates and slipped them into his mouth, hamster style, to the inside of either cheek. It was the way he ate satsumas too. And cherry tomatoes.

'She always sings in the bath, that girl, always.'

Fen?

If things are about to slot very nicely into place, why are you so out of sorts? With Matt now out of the picture, you can at last develop your relationship with James on an equal footing. The contract on your house is up for renewal next month. You could indeed take up the option on your PhD and move back to Derbyshire too. Where else would you find an atmosphere as conducive to study as your beloved home county? It all makes sense. You were equally in love with two men. Now there is only the one man available to you. So why the melancholia? Yes, yes, we all know how dear Julius denied himself love after he lost the one woman for him – but life needn't imitate art, Fen. You have a home with James, and he has a home in your heart.

* * *

'There's something I have to tell Fen,' James says to himself, quietly but sternly, whilst tending to Mrs Brakespeare's roses. 'I've put it off and put it off, but I shall tell her this time. I have to.' He wields his secateurs with expertise. 'I have no idea how she'll react, really.' He pricks himself on a thorn. It's actually such a rare occurrence that it shocks him. 'But I have to tell her.' There's blood. 'She deserves to know.' He sucks his thumb tip. 'She needs to know as soon as possible.'

'Whatever happens – however she is – I must tell her. At all costs. The cost will ultimately be too dear otherwise.'

FORTY-SEVEN

All the best work of any artist must be bathed in mystery.
Auguste Rodin

*B*arry and Beryl bound up to Fen, slathering on her, shoving her, whacking her with their tails.

'Hullo, dogs,' she says, rubbing the tops of their heads and trying to keep her face well away from their slobbering, 'hullo, you two.' Beryl scoots off, haring from Fen to nowhere in particular, returning at full pelt to welcome her again. Fen stands with legs apart and braces herself for Beryl's hurling rebound. Barry then runs circles around Fen, hampering her passage to James, who is standing on his doorstep laughing. She trips just as she's about to reach him and he catches her, planting a kiss affectionately on her forehead.

'Hullo, gorgeous,' he greets her.

Fen throws her arms around his neck and keeps herself pressed against him, her mouth at his neck, the smell of him filling her nose. Remember it. Remember it. Her eyes are scrunched closed. She will not allow herself to cry.

I must not wimp out.

'That's some welcome,' he marvels, trying to keep his arms around her while protecting her from the paws and claws of his dogs who are leaping up at her.

I mustn't put it off. I have to tell her today.

As she sat in the kitchen, watching James make coffee, Fen realized how much she loved being there. With both dogs resting their chins on each of her knees while gazing up at her adoringly, she thought how much she loved them too.

'The money came through for the Fetherstones,' he told her. 'That's why we're having Jamaican Blue Mountain coffee rather than Nescafé.'

'Coffee beans won't fix the leak in the roof,' Fen said, sipping the hot, delicious liquid though she knew that caffeine on top of her current high levels of adrenaline was a very bad idea.

Start! Stop putting it off.

'The Tate has invited me down to the unveiling next month,' James told her, 'but I don't think I'll go.'

Fen was relieved, but nevertheless asked James why he wouldn't attend. He took a seat opposite her. Though his dogs regarded him thoughtfully, they chose to return their chins to Fen's knees.

'It wouldn't seem right,' James explained. 'It's not as if I'm a philanthropic benefactor – I did it for the money.'

Fen nodded.

'You can represent me, if you like,' James said.

I must tell him. I must talk to him. The longer I leave it, the more uncomfortable I'm feeling – and the more unfair it is on him. I'm boiling hot but my blood has turned cold. Darling James – forgive me.

'James –' Fen said, staring at her plate. She continued to stare at her plate. James waited for her to continue. 'May I have more coffee?' she requested lightly.

Stupid girl! I'd kick myself – and hard – if I didn't have these two gorgeous dogs monopolizing my legs.

'Biscuit?' James offered, regarding her quizzically – not that she'd know as she was avoiding eye contact at all costs.

Maybe right now is not the right time – but I have to do it soon, before she goes.

'Thanks,' said Fen, taking a chocolate Bourbon and

scrutinizing the glints of sugar crystals scattered on its surface. *Come on, come on – you need to do this.* 'I – it's –'

'Oh dear,' said James, looking into the biscuit tin and knowing for a fact that the Hobnobs were well past their best-before date, 'gone stale?'

Fen snorted quietly at the irony – but turned it into a blow of her nose so as not to be hurtful. Or, rather, to steer clear of the imminence of broaching the subject she'd come all the way from London to discuss.

James was now well aware of her unease. It unnerved him. After all, today was the day he had to tell her that which he'd been putting off. She was still holding the Bourbon biscuit, she was still staring at her plate. She was twitching her lips and he could see that she was simultaneously trying to talk but stopping herself, too.

Does she know? Has she somehow found out? She was quiet, obviously uncomfortable. *Shall I own up right now? Is that what she wants? Is that why she's here?*

'Fen,' James began, 'I wonder – I need –'

'Wait!' she butted in. 'It's just that I –'

'Shall we go for a walk?' James suggested briskly, taking the uneaten Bourbon biscuit from her fingers and holding her hand. He tried to look into her eyes but they were resolutely downcast. He thought how neat and shapely her eyebrows were.

''Kay,' Fen said.

'Come on,' James said softly, giving her hand a squeeze.

You're a funny girl – I do rather love you, I suppose. But –

The dogs, blissfully unaware of the impending but major event, charged about the garden, head-butting hedges and nose-diving into the shrubbery, barking spontaneously with delight every now and then. James took Fen's hand as they walked. She let it be held. In fact, she didn't want him to let go; *she* didn't want to let go. But she knew she had to. They walked through the garden, where James hovered once or twice, and strolled out into the woods. They talked about the weather, they talked at length about the dogs, Django, Fetherstone; they veered sharply from talking about that which they needed to. They continued to hold hands. Every now and then, Fen took James's to her lips, kissing his fingers lightly (*he smells heavenly, he smells of wood smoke*), having to turn away from him should he spy the tears prickling her eyes. Every now and then, he'd touch her cheek with his thumb, or kiss the top of her head (*she smells of apples, she smells delicious*), or place his hand gently on her bottom.

There's never going to be a right time, he thought, but chose instead to point out tiny violets growing with determination in seemingly the dankest of places

There's never going to be a right time, she thought, but decided she'd rather tell James all about the Alpine stages of the Tour de France, specifically the statistics of L'Alpe D'Huez.

Both knew, however, that timing was essentially in their command. Both knew they were ignoring the fact. They were helpless to do otherwise. Soon enough, of course, they were heading back again. Through the woods. Into James's garden.

For Christ's sake, he reprimanded himself, *I'm practically fifty years old – why on earth do I feel so bloody timid? I know the difference between right and wrong by now.*

Jesus, Fen chastised herself, *get a fucking grip. Do what you know is right.*

Their pace had slowed dramatically. James was now hovering by the great cedar, under whose boughs the wooden hut, like a miniature Swiss chalet, was nestled. James's hands were thrust deep into his pockets. Fen's fingers were pulling at her lips, itching her nose, scratching her forehead. Barry and Beryl, having dutifully peed, were racing each other up the incline of the lawn, over the gravel promenade and up the stone steps. There they sat, waiting for their master to catch up and let them into the house. But James stayed put. And so did Fen. The dogs turned to statues.

'Um,' he said, 'you need to know something.'

'Er,' Fen replied, 'so do you.'

Oddly enough, now the time had come, there was no need for deep breaths. She could hear her voice out in the open.

Thank God, it will all be out in the open.

It was time.

With a hand on each of James's shoulders, she gazed lovingly, sadly, into his face. 'James,' she whispered, because it was all she could manage, 'it's just – I can't.' She shook her head and tears were flung from her eyes like heavy raindrops preceding a downpour. Two sharp, painful swallows kept sobbing at bay for the time being. James was scanning her face, his eyes darting here and there, as if to find clues, as if to guess how her sentence would end, as if he knew what she was about to say, as if to commit to memory every detail of her.

'James,' Fen said, her voice loud but broken, 'I do so love you. But I feel – I really do – that I must call it a day.' He stared at her. She couldn't gauge his reaction and therefore was obliged to elaborate. She turned away from him and gazed up at his charming house, at his two gorgeous dogs sitting expectant at the top of the steps, still stock-still like statuary. She breathed deeply the sweet clean air and tuned her ears to the skylarks. Underfoot, the lawn was springy. All around her, the land was fertile and verdant. It was peaceful. Beautiful. It was Fen's idea of paradise. 'It's over,' she said. Fleetingly, he frowned and a muscle twitched along his jaw. 'It's just,' she elaborated, touching his chin with her fingertips and longing to kiss him there one last time, 'I come here to escape – that's the crux of it. To escape London, my week, my house – all my day-to-days. I come here to retreat. And when I melt into your arms, I'm sort of escaping, retreating, too. When I'm here,' she continued, having paused to gaze at his Adam's apple, 'when I'm with you, it's like make-believe come true.' Her eyes locked on to his. She shook him gently in rhythm with her words. 'But only whilst I'm here.' She held him at arm's length to judge whether he understood. She wasn't sure. 'The love that I have for you, James, is very real,' she told him, 'but the circumstances under which it is generated are not.'

She dropped her gaze. Regarded his feet and hers. Stared at the lawn, the mossy springy grass. She heard James take in breath and release it.

I won't tell him about Matt. It would just be an easy way for me to dump my guilt elsewhere, shift the weight of it away from my shoulders.

She brought her eyes up to his. James smiled at her; a gentle, mature smile infused with regret, sadness, acceptance.

'Fen,' he said, brushing away hair clinging to her tear-slicked cheeks, 'there's something you need to know.'

He brought keys from his pocket and unlocked the door to the wooden den. He pushed the door ajar. 'Go in,' he said, placing his hand on her shoulder almost sternly. He walked off up the lawn to let his dogs into the house.

Fen felt his hand on her shoulder long after he'd taken it away. Then she felt a little flummoxed. She frowned and wanted to swear.

'I've just finished the relationship and he wants me to go and look in his sodding shed?' she said out loud. She turned and watched him walking up the steps. Barry and Beryl had metamorphosed from elegant statues to hurling, leaping mutts.

'Doesn't he have anything to say? Doesn't he feel a thing? Does he not give a toss?'

Fen felt somewhat ungratified.

I suppose I thought we'd talk through our feelings. I feel, perhaps, my words have fallen on deaf ears. Or perhaps his reaction suggests this was never the relationship for him that it was for me. Perhaps the love never had the depth for him that it has had for me. Maybe he's simply not bothered in the slightest.

Actually, Fen, James Caulfield is sitting at his kitchen table with his head in his hands. Oh, he understands all right. He understands perfectly. But he is sad. He is so sad that not even keeping his outdoor boots on indoors, not even the adoring faces of both of his dogs resting their chins on his thighs, comforts him in the slightest.

Leave him be. Grant him his space, his privacy, his prerogative to react in his own idiosyncratic way. Go and look in his shed instead.

The shed has one window, the frame subdividing it into four panes, one of which is cracked diagonally. The interior is not visible because the window is nearly opaque with dust. Fen creaks open the door. It is heavier than she anticipates; than the somewhat ornate design of the exterior would suggest. The shade of the huge cedar tree casts shadows over everything under its boughs. The shed itself is dark inside.

Fen enters. She stands still, waiting for her eyes to adjust to the gloom. Underfoot, she can detect leaves from last autumn – perhaps the autumn before, or even before that. Gradually, shapes emerge from the darkness. To her left, there are sun loungers. A rake is propped immediately to her right. There are some tea chests stacked up just further along. A dog's carrying basket. Jerrycans. A neat pile of dust-sheets. And then not much else. It's quite roomy inside. Quite spacious. A fabulous structure for a Wendy house, Fen thinks distractedly, or for children to play at the Swiss Family Robinson. Only James doesn't have children, she remarks to herself, he just has his dogs. *You can buy battery-driven lighting*, she muses. *A lick of whitewash inside would work wonders. Little gingham curtains at the window. Some brightly painted furniture – however mismatched.*

'Mismatched,' she says softly, 'me and he.' There's something cathartic about the rhyme, about grammar abused for emotional ends.

Her breathing has calmed. Her hostility has abated. Eventually, her eyes growing accustomed to the darkness, she peers deeper into the interior. There is something very large looming at the back of the room. As it takes form, it

318

gives Fen a jolt – it looks like a monster, whatever it is, lumbering under its heavy shroud. She takes a step forward. It's all that's needed. She stops abruptly. Her heart is in her mouth. It is as if she can see through the heavy canvas cover though she has walked only a step further into the darkness. She has started to cry – painful chucks of her voice; tearless. She continues to edge in deeper. Gingerly, she extends her left arm and her fingertips make light, quick contact with the canvas. It is thick, waterproofed; an industrialized tarpaulin of sorts. She's only touched it briefly but the entire form it cloaks is known to her at once.

Though dust and moths and cobwebs and even a bat start careering around the shed, Fen pulls and hauls and heaves the covering away. She is choking. She can't see a thing. Mind you, she doesn't need to keep her eyes open any longer. She puts out a hand to steady herself. She has touched down on stone. It is smooth and cool but not cold. A marble elbow. Dust settles. Fen stops crying. A little light seeps in from the garden. Light radiates out from the marble. Fen stands still. Dust and dirt and her heart are in her mouth. She looks up. Her hand is holding a marble elbow. She looks up. Fetherstone's *Abandon* towers above. She is dwarfed by it. She is absolutely terrified.

FORTY-EIGHT

*F*en stayed in the shed for a long time, though she was utterly unaware of the passing of seconds, minutes or hours. Time was suspended. Initially, she just stood there, mouth agape despite dust and debris catching at the back of her throat. She backed up a few paces and sat on one of the tea chests awhile. Then she crossed the room and heaved down a sun lounger, reclining on it to gaze at the sculpture. Finally, she stood and went over to the marble, circumnavigating it, her hands never leaving its surface; touching, feeling, grabbing, groping. She smelt it and she licked it, she pressed her face, her torso, her back, against it. She stared and stared and stared. She hadn't a clue what to do. She knew, though, that she'd never be the same again. It was one of those life-defining moments.

She remembers *Cold Comfort Farm*, which she'd read years ago as respite from studying for her A levels. She thinks she'll probably become like Stella Gibbons's character of Aunt Ada Doom who was never quite right having seen what she saw in the woodshed.

I will never be the same again.

That took care of the future – but what, exactly, should she do right now? Should she call the police? The Tate? Django? There again, if she told no one, *Abandon* could well be hers.

She could leave London and live here. With James. With Julius. Should she go back to the house and say she hadn't meant what she'd said and that, actually, she'd rather like to live with him until death did them part?

Hang on.

How the hell did it get here?

How the fuck did James come by it?

'Oh my God!' Fen cried, believing she knew the definitive answer. 'Of course! He's a thief! Is he? Is he a *thief*?' Suddenly, she felt sick at the thought of the *Adam* and *Eve*, the bronzes and oil sketches, about to take residence in the Tate gallery. Ill-gotten gains. Illegal, full stop. She'd have to do something. Because, it struck her, she'd had something to do with it. But what? And what could she do? And would she? A tiny, evil little voice was telling her that *Abandon* could well be hers.

No one need know – because no one knows it's here.

But Fen felt trapped. The pressure of making sense of the immediate situation, of trying to figure out what to do, was all too much for her. Instead, for some reason, all she could think of was *The Thomas Crown Affair* – a favourite film of hers in its original and remade state. 'Steve McQueen! I mean, Thomas Crown!' she whispered. 'Pierce Brosnan! – James Caulfield! Suave! Elusive! And he's conned me! He lured me into his bed so he could pass the buck and heap his filthy secret on to me!'

Fen was absolutely enflamed with rage. She was livid – a state she had seldom experienced; certainly never this degree of anger. She stormed out of the shed, stomped up the lawn, stamped over the gravel, marched up the steps two at a time and strode into the house, not taking her boots off.

Fen barged into the kitchen, stood still momentarily with her hands on her hips, and glowered at James. Instinctively, Barry and Beryl slunk off to the utility room and curled up together in just one of their baskets. James arose. Fen went directly to him and, with all the force she could muster, belted him with the flat of her palm smartly across his cheek.

She couldn't even hiss an insult. She simply stood there and shook.

'I —' James attempted. He certainly hadn't anticipated that she'd react like this. Fen thumped him hard on the shoulder. Then she pummelled his chest with her fists, the effort finally opening the sluice-gates to her torrent of tears and rage and frustration and fear.

'You bastard,' she sobbed, backing off him before returning to his body. She had little strength left but feebly, she tried to punch him some more. 'Bastard!' she cried, her sobs heaving her entire body which started to crumple. James supported her, literally holding her up.

'Fen, *listen*,' he implored, 'just sit down and listen.'

'You're a thief!' she exploded, unable to listen. 'You've conned me! You've conned everyone.' She stamped her foot. 'I'll see you go down for this!' she cried histrionically.

'Fen!' James exclaimed, as if to a child. Fen, behaving like a child, hurled the biscuit barrel on to the floor, shoved James hard and ran out of the house, down the steps, across the promenade, down the sweep of the lawn and back into the shed, slamming the door behind her. Then she heard the latch lock behind her. She held her head, scrunched and pulled her hair, and yelled with exasperation.

James left her there. Not as punishment but because he knew it was the only place that she would calm down. If he was honest, he was, quite literally, knocked for six. Knocked, hit, punched, shoved. And he felt bruised, inside and out. He'd anticipated that divulging his secret would elevate him to hero status in the eyes of Fen. In reality, it had served only to disgust and distress his now ex-lover. He picked the smashed biscuits from the floor. Glancing round, he saw his dogs lurking at a safe distance in the utility room. They looked uneasy but they couldn't help themselves from glancing longingly at the crumbs and fragments of Bourbon and Hobnob.

322

'Come on, dogs,' James invited. They came into the kitchen with caution, regarding James, regarding the floor, regarding James again. 'Go on,' he encouraged. They began to lick the floor cleaner than it possibly had ever been. 'Poor Fen,' James said, sitting down watching his dogs. 'I mean, it's not every day one comes across a long-lost work of art in a shed in Derbyshire.' He suspected that, in her rage, she'd locked herself in the shed. He felt it would do her nerves good to stay there awhile. She needed to calm down. She needed time to formulate questions – all of which he could answer.

'My ex-lover is locked in my shed,' James said aloud. He laughed. There was, undeniably, a comedy element to it all. 'Shall we keep her there? Ranting and fuming?' he suggested to his dogs. 'A twenty-first-century Mrs Rochester?' The dogs didn't seem to understand. 'She's locked in my shed, she is,' James said quietly, 'my ex-lover.' The dogs seemed to understand that. They came and sat by his side. James felt sad, an emotion that years of self-sufficiency and contentment had kept at bay. 'We're not right for her,' he told them, with conviction. He fell silent. He thought over her words – about how their love really only existed outside their day-to-day lives. How it took form and flight only in the confines of the house, the grounds, a hotel room in Paddington; when it was just the two of them. And now she was confined to the shed. With *Abandon*. James glanced at his watch. She'd been in there three quarters of an hour.

'I'll go and release her.' The word struck James as highly appropriate.

Sweet Fen. I will release you. I could plead with you to continue with me – just the way we have been. But I have a responsibility to your future – and I think you are right, I am not your future. Nor are you mine.

Fen looked at her watch. She did not know precisely how long she'd been locked in the shed but she reckoned it was almost an hour. She'd been clambering all over *Abandon*.

She'd felt the breasts of the woman, the pectorals of the man; she'd run her hands over his smooth buttocks and fingered the woman's lips which were parted in a gasp of sexual ecstasy. Being with the marble apotheosis of a work so familiar to her was incomparable. Hitherto, the bronze casting she'd been so captivated by as an A level student visiting the Neue Pinakotek in Munich had been her most intimate experience of the work. But she hadn't been allowed to touch, just to look, to marvel, to study every aspect of it. She thought she knew *Abandon* by Julius Fetherstone. But it was only now, today, having had hands-on, direct contact, that she really felt she understood the work. It was about climax, she defined. Not just the thematic depiction of the throes of sexual ecstasy. Somehow, there was tragedy imbued in it – Fen sensed that the work marked the climax of the figures' relationship. That when they pulled apart physically, they left each other too. In terms of technique, of anatomical awareness, it was unarguably the virtuoso highpoint of the artist's career.

'But who *are* you?' she asked the figures, her face on a level with their stomachs. 'Who are *you*?' she asked the man, looking up at him. 'Are you Julius?' She thought he very probably was. 'But then, who are *you*?' she asked the woman, staring intently at her beautiful face. 'I mean, I know you are Eve – and every non-portrait female form Julius ever sculpted – but who – *who* – were you?'

'Fen?'

James.

'Tell me!' Fen pleaded quietly, as if she believed the sculptural figures could do so only whilst the shed door was locked and they were together.

'Fen?'

James. Don't! Don't let me out! Don't unlock the door! Don't break the spell!

James, though, had no intention of letting Fen out until she so requested.

Fen walked behind *Abandon* and looked towards the

324

window of the shed. She couldn't really see much, just blurs of green and, once or twice, a dark patch she realized was James's shadow. With one palm pressed against the woman's shoulder-blades, with the other pressed against the small of the man's back, Fen held her cheek to the heavy space their bodies created. She breathed deeply. She sighed. She left them. Why should they speak to her? Who on earth was she, Fen McCabe, to them? They were utterly self-contained in their desire for one another. As they had been since Julius Fetherstone had released their forms from the great chunk of marble a century ago.

'James?' Fen called a few feet from the door.

'Would you like to come out?' James's voice replied.

'Yes, please,' said Fen.

She comes out, blinking, into the light; into the late July late afternoon. She walks with James over and up the lawn, across the gravel promenade, up the stone steps and into the house. He has his hand on her shoulder, lightly, very supportively. She's comforted that it should be there.

'I expect,' said James, 'that you have a fair few questions for me?'

Fen nodded. James settled into an armchair in the snug. He turned over his hands so his palms were uppermost, signifying that she should start, that he was ready and open.

'Did you,' Fen faltered, '*steal* your Fetherstones?'

James was not offended. 'No, Fen, I did not, they were left to me by my father.'

She believed him. 'But why do *you* have *Abandon*? How did your dad come by that? Why *you*?'

'It was decreed that he should have it,' James said, 'to hold it for me.'

Fen stared at him, her eyes darting around his face to try and glean some tiny particle of sense.

'Come with me,' James said. He led her out of the snug, across the flagstone hallway and up the stairs to his bedroom. There, he opened the drawer of his bedside cabinet and placed a clutch of photos on his bed.

Fen sat down and looked at them. 'How odd!' she said, 'these are like the photos in the Archive at Trust Art and in the Fetherstone files in Paris.' She turned them over. From what she could remember, the handwriting on the back was identical to that on the back of those in Paris. There were five photos, she'd seen them all before. She looked at James expectantly. He handed her three more. Fen took them from him, looked at each quickly and then drew breath sharply. Her hands began to shake.

In the first, the elusive woman was staring directly at the camera, standing posed formally between Julius and Henry. In the second, she was half out of frame, Henry and Julius were in deep conversation, and the small child sat on Henry's knee, his back to the camera. In the third, a close-up, Julius was hazy in his bath chair in the background. The frame cut off half of Henry and half of the woman. It was focused entirely on the child. The child was holding the hand of the woman, the hand of Henry. It was unmistakably a boy. About four years old. Smiling at the camera. Filling the frame. It was, unmistakably, James Caulfield.

Fen stares at James who nods, silently. Fen looks at the photos again. James takes her hand and leads her to the chest of drawers, with the lovely old framed photos.

'This is my mother,' he says, and Fen recognizes her as the lady in the studio. Is that why she looks so familiar? But didn't Fen feel she was familiar, for some unknown reason, when she first set eyes on James's photo? Fen is tired and overawed and can't really remember. 'This is my father,' says James, showing Fen a photo in a silver frame she hasn't seen on the chest of drawers before.

'No, no. Actually, this is Henry *Holden*,' Fen explains to James, as if he might not know, as if he might be mistaken, misled; as if he hasn't realized.

'I am Henry Holden's son,' James says, 'and Theresa's son too.'

Fen is frowning with the effort of trying to absorb too much near-surreal information. James sits her down on the bed, allowing her to keep hold of the two framed photographs. 'Theresa Cattaldi was the granddaughter of Cosima Cattaldi.' These made no sense to Fen. 'Cosima married Jacques Antoine.'

'Oh!' Fen interrupts artlessly. 'Julius did a portrait bust of Cosima *Antoine*!'

'Fen,' James says, 'this is privileged information. Julius had an affair with Cosima. Brief. Passionate. That's all I know. She is the Woman – the anonymous woman. In *Eve*. In *Abandon*. In *Hunger*. In *Desire*. In all the works where the sitter is unknown. We're so used to knowing Cosima's face from the official portrait bust and sketches, we would not recognize her in any other way.'

Fen is dumbstruck.

'Henry Holden had a brief affair with Theresa Cattaldi. He was married to his first wife at the time. Theresa fell pregnant. Henry, therefore, had an illegitimate son.'

'You.'

'Yes.'

'But you're English!' Fen remonstrates, as if it is the one true fact she knows. 'You're not French! Or Italian!'

'Henry brought Mother and me over the year after this photo was taken. I was four and a half years old. *Abandon* was left to me. Julius told Henry I was to have it.'

'But Henry was married,' Fen says, slotting the jigsaw together, 'hence the need for discretion – secrecy.'

James nods. 'We didn't really see him,' he tells her, a little sadness tingeing his voice, 'but he ensured we were comfortable which, in those days, counted for a lot. I adored my mother,' he says taking the photograph of her that Fen is holding, 'I *adored* her. Anyway, when I was a teenager, Henry married a second time and lived happily ever after until his death, I do believe. I did so adore my mother.'

It is difficult for Fen to find her voice or think of what to say or ask next. She lies back on James's bed and closes her eyes and drifts off into a numb sleep.

They awake, wrapped in each other's arms, very late that night. They undress and slip between the sheets. Fen snuggles up to James.

'I love you, James.'

'I know you do. And I believe – truly I do – that what you're suggesting is for the best.'

'Being born of Cosima's blood,' Fen says sleepily, 'you are probably as near as Julius came to having a son.'

'He liked to think so,' James says.

'That's why he bequeathed you *Abandon*,' Fen defines, feeling at ease for the first time in days. It all makes sense. Or at least, much more sense than it had made earlier. It makes enough sense to allow her to go to sleep relatively content.

Over breakfast the next morning, Fen and James talked easily.

'You do realize,' Fen said, 'that if we put *Abandon* up for sale, it's not just a new roof you can buy!'

'I do know that,' James replied, 'but it simply isn't for sale.'

Fen looked at him. 'What are you going to do with it?' she asked. 'I mean, there's something of an indignity about it being in a shed in Derbyshire under a smelly old sheet.'

'I'm not going to do anything with it,' James said, quite abruptly, staring at her squarely, 'but you are.'

Fen is back in the shed. She has a train to catch. She wants time alone with *Abandon*.

'Goodbye, Julius,' she whispers, gently touching the man's forearm. 'Goodbye, Cosima,' she whispers affectionately, lightly stroking the woman's knee. 'I'll find somewhere safe and beautiful for you both, I promise. Goodbye, lovers, goodbye.'

*

James drives Fen to Chesterfield station. Fen hugs the dogs so tightly they yelp. James walks her to the platform. He gives her an envelope.

'It's a letter from Julius to Henry, about *Abandon*, about me,' he tells her.

'We can do this,' she assures him, 'discreetly.'

'In your hands,' he says, 'in your hands. *Abandon* couldn't be safer anywhere else.'

Fen smiles at him. She gazes into his eyes. For a moment, there's the possibility they will sink their mouths against each other. He clasps her against him in an enveloping hug and kisses the top of her head four or five times. 'I could ask you to think again,' he says, 'but I won't. You have so much ahead of you, Fen — so much to do. And, truthfully, I am very content as I am, as I have been for some time. I love you and I will miss you but I am happy to part as we are parting today.'

When I woke this morning and gazed at you sleeping, I realized that, unknowingly, I had been waiting most of my adult life for you. You came with the key to unlock my Fetherstone dilemma, but not the key to my heart. Now you have done so, you can go, I can let you go.

Fen's train is pulling in. Should she tell him? Should she tell him? Now? She touches James's cheek. 'You have a half-brother, James,' she tells him.

But should I tell him?

'He works at Trust Art.'

Should I tell him everything?

'He's called Matthew,' says Fen. She looks at her feet. She thinks of Matt. She smiles.

'He's lovely.'

FORTY-NINE

*F*en didn't tell a soul about *Abandon*. She knew that when the time came to divulge, to share, her private audience with the work – still vivid to her – would have to be relinquished. She kept Julius's letter under her bed, in the shoebox that contained all her childhood treasures. She knew that when it came to handing the letter over – to validate, authenticate and legitimize James's loan – that then she would be grown up. She wouldn't be able to chat to Julius thereafter, nor to refer to him by his Christian name. She wasn't quite ready for that just yet, so she kept the letter under her bed and didn't tell anyone what she'd seen in the shed.

She thought of James often, wistfully. But she thought of Matt even more – despite seeing him every day. They were friendly towards each other. Fen, though, did not make a play for him. She didn't feel entitled. She'd regarded her right palm which said, 'Fight for him! Tell him you demand the relationship is given a fair chance! Ask him if abstaining from the comforts and commitments of a relationship is making him happier!' Her left palm, however, said, 'You blew it, girl. This is your just deserts for wanting everything your own way, for not respecting the potential you had for abusing his honesty, for damaging him, should he ever have found out that you were spectacularly unfaithful to him.'

Otter just wants to bang their heads together hard, to then enable them to kiss each other better. He wants to tell Matt that he's being ridiculously self-righteous, he wants to tell Fen she's being a feeble martyr. He can see that neither of them is happy being apart, and because he knows both of them well, he is absolutely adamant that a romantic attachment between them is fail-safe.

'You're perverted, you are,' he jested with Matt, 'letting Fen go!'

'Pervert!' Matt remonstrated. 'Me? It's you who indulges in poking around bottoms of the same sex – I rather think Pervert is *your* middle name!'

I shouldn't have let Fen go! I shouldn't! But I felt I ought. And now I feel I ought to stick with that. Partly, I suppose, because I'm not quite sure how to get her back. And if I were to, it really would signify that we embark on a full-on bona-fide relationship

'For God's sake, Ed,' Otter said, exasperated with Matt. He clasped his fingers and stretched them back on themselves, the ensuing hollow crackings setting Matt's teeth on edge. 'Now I have your attention,' Otter said. 'I just feel – really believe – that you are making a mistake. Fen is charming and gorgeous and sexy and you interact and interlock together beautifully.'

Matt stood up and stormed out. 'What would you know,' he barked, 'gay boy!'

'Woo him!' Otter pleaded with Fen. 'Pursue him!'

'I wouldn't know how,' Fen told him, 'and anyway, his reasons for ending the relationship make sense. I don't like them, but I *do* understand.'

And then came the day when, without fanfare or palm-consultation, Fen brought Julius's letter into work. She came across Rodney by the pigeon-holes.

'Please could you spare me five minutes?' she requested.

'Good Lord, Fenella!' he remarked. 'Are you telepathic?' He took a custard cream from Bobbie's biscuit tin and left Reception, shaking his head. In her pigeon-hole, Fen found a note, hand-scrawled from Rodney, suggesting a quick chat in his office after lunch. Fen half wondered if perhaps James had called or written. Oh well, she'd soon find out.

By lunch-time, it became immensely important to her to let Matt know before she told anyone else. She went along to Publications.

'Hullo, Matt,' she said, really wishing she could simply not notice that he looked very fine in indigo jeans and a quite tight T-shirt. She glanced at Otter with a faint but perceptible raising of one eyebrow and he took the hint immediately.

'Dying for a slash,' he said, rising and leaving the room with a highly exaggerated bladder-about-to-bust walk.

Fen hovered. 'Um –'

Matt looked up. He refused to be swayed by her smooth bare legs and the fact that she was in the little navy-blue sun dress that had secretly been a favourite of his. 'Hiya,' he said. He swivelled in his chair and Fen walked over to him.

'I wanted to tell you something,' she said.

Tell me that you love me, Fen. Tell me that you refuse to allow me to be so stupid. Tell me that you will not tolerate this relationship being over, just when it was on the verge of really taking off.

'What's up?' he asked instead.

'I've –' Fen regarded him. 'It's just – I wanted to tell you something.'

Matt looked at her expectantly. Fen approached his desk and perched on it. Her knees, all he could focus on were her knees. He sat on his hands for safety and made a rotation swivel on his chair.

'I've found *Abandon*,' Fen said.

Though of course it would have appalled Fen, if truth be told, she really was the only person – possibly anywhere –

332

who thought about Julius Fetherstone on such a regular basis. Matt, though appreciative of the sculptor's work, certainly didn't think about him on a weekly basis, let alone daily or hourly. Consequently, he stared at Fen rather vacantly and, because her revelation did not blow his mind, it did not divert his attention from the pressing distraction of her neat knees.

'In Derbyshire,' Fen continued, as if that was the further information Matt required to comprehend the magnitude of her announcement. 'Julius Frigging Fetherstone's *Abandon*!' she marvelled. 'In a shed in Derbyshire!'

The penny dropped for Matt and he was suitably impressed. 'Blimey!' he said. 'Well done you.' To emphasize his praise, he felt a friendly tap on her knees was appropriate. God, he wanted to linger. God, did Fen want him to linger!

'I have a meeting with Rodney this afternoon,' she told him. 'I can't wait to tell him.'

'Good for you,' Matt said, 'good for you.'

And then he didn't really know what to say next. Nor did Fen. What she wanted to do was fling her arms around his neck and be kissed by him, to have him suggest champagne and celebration. But, sadly, she acknowledged that wasn't going to happen. 'Anyway,' she shrugged, 'you're the first person I've told. Because I wanted you to know first.'

Matt liked the sound of that. 'Let me know how Rodney reacts,' he told her. 'My bet is that he'll jump up and down on his desk and say, "Yippee!" and then charge around his office giving the thumbs up!'

Matt and Fen shared laughter at their director's expense.

Only Rodney didn't behave like an overgrown schoolboy. He didn't jump for joy and shout, 'Yippee!' and dart about brandishing his thumbs. When Fen knocked on his door, Judith's voice told her to enter. Fen came into Rodney's office to find him and Judith sitting there, looking very serious indeed.

'Have a seat,' Rodney said. Fen sat down. Her director looked very unhappy indeed. Oh well, news of the Fetherstone would no doubt lift his spirits and make his day. How could it fail to do otherwise!

Rodney fiddled with paper-clips on his desk and pursed his lips thoughtfully. 'Dear Fenella,' he said, 'dear Fenella.'

Judith took the reins. 'With the Archive so near completion,' she said, wearing a smugness across her face utterly opposed to the clear distress etching Rodney's, 'we thought it only fair to alert you to the fact that the job itself will also be complete.'

Fen looked a little blank. Weren't they meant to be talking about Julius Fetherstone? Judith watched for Fen's reaction. Fen obviously hadn't understood. Judith would have to be more blatant. Rodney wasn't going to be much help, Judith noticed, seeing the director poking paper-clips into an empty juice bottle nervously. 'Fen,' Judith said, with kindness so gracious that it was jarringly false, 'we're going to have to let you go.'

'Go where?' Fen asked, her mind still being firmly in the shed in Derbyshire.

'Well, with the Archive project finished,' Rodney said, snapping to attention and wresting control from Judith so he could add the tact and sensitivity Fen deserved, 'unfortunately, the job is finished too. And there isn't anything else here that we can give you.' Fen stared at him. He looked as if he was going to sob. 'I wanted to give you warning – so you could start scouting around. I wish the Archive had been bigger!' he rued. 'Then you could still work with us.'

I'm being given the sack, the push, the elbow! I've lost my job. I'm unemployed. I won't be working for Trust Art. I'll have to go job hunting. I'll have to buy the Guardian *every Monday and Saturday. I'll have to tell my bank. I'm going to be broke. I'm going to be dismissed.*

The shock of it rendered Fen incapable of saying anything other than a mumbled thank you for having me I've loved working here; all she could do, really, was leave the director's office to seek sanctuary in her Archive.

Matt had been awaiting Fen's appearance in his office, anticipating her effervescence at Rodney's reaction to the reappearance of *Abandon*. But she didn't show. She couldn't still be down there. He phoned her extension. A very very small voice answered at the other end.

'Fen?'

'Matt?'

He went directly to her. As soon as she saw him standing in the doorway, as soon as she clocked the genuine concern on his face, she cast her eyes to her lap and let her tears fall. Quietly, Matt came into the room, shutting the door.

'Was it a fake?' he asked. 'Or stolen?'

'I didn't tell them,' Fen croaked. 'My job is finished. Unrenewable.'

'What?' Matt said, though he heard and understood clearly.

'They're letting me go,' Fen whispered, 'when the Archive is finished in a fortnight or so.'

Matt was stunned and horrified. Not so much because he felt that Trust Art would be the poorer for the loss of a talent like Fen's, but because he suddenly thought how dull his days would be without her floating around. Fen would always be in the Archive — surely? Invariably sitting cross-legged with a clutch of documents in her lap, enthusing over pamphlets of some long-forgotten exhibition, marvelling at photographs of artists and patrons, delighting in hand-written letters by people dead for years. Fen *was* the Archive. The Archive was what Fen did. What would it be without her? An empty room, door mostly closed, contents meticulously and lovingly organized within.

'I can't believe it,' Matt said, squeezing her shoulders though he felt he was in need of comfort himself. 'It's appalling that they'd do that to you.'

Fen sniffed snottily. 'I didn't tell them about *Abandon*,' she said, 'I forgot.'

*

Matt phoned her late that night. She'd gone to bed early, having put Julius's letter back in the shoebox. Her heart lifted to see it was him calling. How she'd love him to be here in person.

'Just phoning to check you're OK,' he said.

'I am,' said Fen. 'I'm just sad – I always knew the Archive was a project to be begun and therefore to be concluded too – but I'm just sad that I'll be leaving.'

'Me too,' said Matt, 'me too. But listen, you must tell Rodney about the Fetherstone. If Trust Art could handle its placement, there'd be no better man for the job than you.'

'Do you think so?' Fen asked.

'Of course,' Matt encouraged. 'Promise me you'll go and tell Rodney tomorrow.'

'OK,' said Fen.

'And you just watch him leap with unbridled joy and give you a huge thumbs up!'

'Thanks, Matt,' said Fen.

'Night, babe,' he said.

Why did I phone? I should've just gone round there.

I'm so glad he phoned. And I don't want to sound ungrateful but I sort of wish he'd just turned up on the doorstep.

Easy, you two, one step at a time.

*   *   *

Rodney did indeed bound around his office on hearing of Fen's discovery. He shook her hand so vigorously it hurt. He slapped her on the back too, hard. And when she left his office, he gave her an ecstatic double thumbs up.

'Marvellous!' he exclaimed to himself. 'Good old Fenella McCabe – she's an asset to the Trust and now it seems we can keep hold of her.'

*

There's just a minor spanner in the works to cause a little last-minute disruption. After all, we can't have a happy-ever-after immediately. It would all be just a little anti-climactic, just a little too cosy and therefore slightly unsatisfying too.

In a quirk of symmetry, the potential disruption at the close of the story comes in the same form as it did at the start of this tale – in the sharp-suited guise of Judith St John. Judith didn't particularly like Julius Fetherstone. Nor was she particularly taken with Matthew Holden. She didn't like Fen McCabe at all – mainly because everybody else did, plus she found Fen's femininity somewhat cloying. The trouble with people like Judith, who find it easier and more pleasurable to dislike rather than like, is that they really don't care if they themselves are disliked. Judith wasn't sly or cruel, she didn't want to ruin Fen's life or consciously cause her unhappiness. However, Fen had something Judith wanted and Judith simply couldn't see why Fen should have it if she herself could have it instead. And if, in the process, Trust Art would benefit, surely that was all the more reason to pursue something that was ultimately for the best.

Fen's salary as archivist had been provided by Lady Helena Minchey – widow of the Sir Michael who, along with Henry Holden, was surely one of the greatest benefactors of the visual arts. Lady Helena ruled her late husband's charitable trust meticulously and constructively. Whereas Sir Michael would have bestowed thousands of pounds on any impoverished artist, Lady Helena maximized funds available by demanding detailed presentations and documents from applicants. This scared away individuals who thought that merely holding out a begging bowl would be enough. She had ensured that Trust Art had taken her to lunch twice, plus produced a ten-page paper to justify the donation from the Minchey Foundation to fund the Archive.

Now she was back in the offices in John Islip Street, being nattered to by Bobbie whilst awaiting Judith and Rodney and lunch at St John's, Smith Square. Bobbie didn't care for airs and graces. If someone was wearing a suit from Marks & Spencer that was the same as her sister's, she'd remark on the fact.

'It's not from Marks & Spencer,' Lady Helena all but hissed.

'It is too,' Bobbie remarked, 'and your hem's down at the back.'

'This is Daks!' Lady Helena declared, appalled that her hem was down at the back.

'Whatever you say, ducks,' said Bobbie, who then thought that Lady Helena would be interested in her sister's husband's gout and thus proceeded to tell her all about it.

Rodney put the case to Lady Helena for a continued salary for Fen McCabe.

'The thing is,' he said, 'she's discovered *Abandon* by Julius Fetherstone.'

Lady Helena looked up from her pavlova sharply. 'Where is it?' she asked.

'In a shed in the country,' Rodney elaborated, because for a Surrey boy, anywhere rural and north of Watford was simply 'country'.

'Good God!' Lady Helena exclaimed. 'Is it all above board? Is it stolen?'

'There's a letter of authenticity from Fetherstone,' Rodney said, 'which specifies to whom he bequeaths the sculpture.'

'Who?' Lady Helena demands. 'Who has it?'

'It's a very, very sensitive issue,' Rodney says honestly and with no manufactured ambiguity. 'The chappy wishes to remain anonymous.'

Lady Helena nods. 'But what do you want from me?' she asks.

'Lolly!' Rodney cries. 'Dosh! The placing of this work will have to be sensitively handled – we can't just give it to the first institution which offers it a home. The publicity surrounding it needs to be carefully handled. There will be scholars and sceptics to entertain, too. The process itself – from the shed to a gallery – could take half a year or so.

Anyway, Fen McCabe discovered the work so I feel we should set her up to see it to completion. She's done magnificently with the Archive!'

'Granted,' Lady Helena agreed, 'OK. I think it's a worthy enough cause. If I do sponsor the role, I would like to be privileged to all this guarded information – just for my own amusement.'

'Of course,' Rodney nodded. 'Oops! Little boys' room, I rather think!' And he disappeared off to the loo.

'You're frightfully quiet,' Lady Helena remarked to Judith.

'I'm just thinking,' Judith said. 'Do you mind if I think out loud?'

'Please,' said Lady Helena.

So Judith delivered the theory she'd formulated and honed all evening the night before. 'However exciting this project, I'm not entirely sure that it warrants a full-time position within the Trust,' she told Lady Helena, 'or even a part-time position. Yes, Fenella found the work – but the job would be about coordination, in the main.'

By the time Rodney had returned from the toilets, settling the bill on the way, Lady Helena was looking very pleased and Judith was looking decidedly flushed.

'Golly, Judith,' Rodney said, 'have you had a little too much wine?'

'God, Rodney,' Judith sighed.

'Judith is a fabulous administrator,' Lady Helena told Rodney. 'She's pointed out that the placing of the Fetherstone is well within her capabilities, well within the specifications of her job and will hardly eat into her ongoing responsibilities. So there is no need for a separate individual. Judith has saved the Minchey Foundation funds that could be so usefully applied elsewhere. I am therefore going to make an extra donation to Trust Art this year. Marvellous.'

Rodney listened carefully. He had to agree, Judith's theory made sense. Damn! He'd have to disappoint Fenella yet again, poor girl.

This hit Fen far harder than the end of her role as archivist. Whereas Matt and Otter wanted to do voodoo on Judith, Fen displayed enormous dignity and generosity.

'But she's right,' she said softly, 'it makes sense, it saves money – which of course means there's more money there to save art for the nation. Judith's just doing her job.'

'But Julius is *yours*,' Otter remonstrated huffily.

'Hear hear,' said Matt.

'You'll have done all the hard work – over years,' Otter stressed, 'for that harridan to reap all the glory.'

'God, has the woman no pride,' Matt muttered.

Fen contemplated her baguette of brie and pickle. She placed it in her lap and took a sip of cappuccino. 'But boys,' she said, 'it isn't about glory and ownership, it's about the greatest work of late-nineteenth-century figurative sculpture.' They looked at her. 'I just want to see it placed in a safe and loving home.' She shrugged.

'But you found it,' Matt protested. 'Surely you'd like to accompany it?'

'Of course I would,' Fen said, 'but I didn't find it, Matt, it found me.'

'What do you mean?' Matt asks as he walks with Fen back to the Trust offices, Otter having made a detour to the news-agent for a copy of the *Evening Standard*, 'about you not finding it? I thought you said it was in a shed in Derbyshire?'

'It is,' said Fen, 'but I was no detective, Matt. The chap who has it came to me. I didn't really have to do a thing.'

Matt stopped in the middle of the pavement and looked at her. 'He came to you?' he verified.

'Yup,' Fen said, 'I handled the transaction with the Tate for his other Fetherstones.'

'*Eden*?' Matt checked.

'Yes,' said Fen, 'so I presume I simply sprung to mind when he decided to reveal *Abandon*.'

340

'Right,' said Matt thoughtfully, 'right.'

Later that afternoon, when Otter had gone down to raid Bobbie's biscuit tin, Matt made a phone call.

'Hi, Mummy. Hey? Oh, I'm fine, I'm fine. Listen, are you around this weekend? Can I come home? I want to talk to you about something.'

FIFTY

Every woman should have one old love she can imagine
going back to . . . and one who reminds her how far she has
come . . .

Anon

*T*he last day of August was
Fen's last day as archivist for Trust Art. Rodney had
organized a send-off on a par with the welcome brigade he'd
prepared for her arrival in the spring. A breakfast in the
boardroom with *brioche* and Bollinger. Rodney had made a
gushing speech and there'd been cheering – and tears too,
from Bobbie and Fen. Otter and Matt were to take her out to
lunch. Before then, she spent the morning checking and
double-checking that the Archive was in order and could
rest until it was needed. She was pleased with her work. It
had been fascinating, however dusty and disorganized it had
been along the way. She decided to leave her Fetherstone
postcards on the pinboard. She had plenty more at home and
liked the idea that whoever visited the room could have
them to gaze upon should they glance up and catch sight of
them.

'I'll always be looking for converts,' Fen said to the
postcards. 'I'd make a great Jehovah's Witness!'

She sat and swivelled in her chair, checked her e-mails
and noted down addresses – electronic and otherwise – of
friendly contacts she'd made at galleries and collections over

the last few months. It all felt like the last day of the school year. Only she wouldn't be returning next term. There was a knock on her door. Otter poked his head around.

'Lunch-time, sweetie?'

'Great,' said Fen.

'Matt can't make it,' Otter said, 'he's having lunch with Rodney and Judith – very last minute.' Otter could see disappointment cross Fen's face. 'Won't I do?' he asked her with a sorry pout.

'Of course you will,' said Fen, giving his waist a squeeze, hoping she hadn't crushed his hip bones in the process.

They walked along the corridor. 'Ooh, I am cruel,' said Otter. 'I'm bullshitting you something rotten – it's me who can't make lunch, not Matt. I met a charming boy at a revolting club over the weekend – and, well, he said he'd love to meet me for lunch.'

Fen was happy for him. And very happy that it meant she had Matt to herself for an hour.

Matt had roast beef and horseradish on rye, Fen had egg, cheese and spinach in a granary bap. They took their lunch to the gardens opposite the Trust building.

'End of an era,' Matt mused.

Fen nodded. Her mouthful was suddenly stuck in her throat because of a knot tying itself there. She put her sandwich to one side and took thoughtful sips of her apple juice. Matt was wittering on about work, weather and the weekend. She was only half hearing him. She was staring very intently at each of her palms in turn. He watched her. He didn't know what she was thinking but he could see that her mind was whirring away. She had very neat hands, but he wasn't sure quite why her palms so frequently invited such utter scrutinizing. He slipped his hand on top of her left, he placed her right hand on top of his and then held that himself. The best sandwich ever.

Fen panics for a moment.

I need to see my palms!

No, you don't.

But I do! I do!

No, you don't.

But I haven't quite finished my ponderings.

Yes, you have. Go on, Fen.

Fen contemplates their interleaved hands for a moment. She can sense Matt is looking at her.

'Just because you were in one long-term relationship that went wrong is no reason whatsoever to prevent you from embarking on another,' Fen blurts. 'Sorry,' she says meekly. Matt is silent. But he's keeping his hands in place. 'I just feel,' Fen says, 'that we were very good together. And I respected the space you wanted. But I don't any more.' Matt raises his eyebrows. 'You see, since we split up, we've actually been able to maintain a friendship,' Fen says, 'and friendship is the most fundamental basis for a relationship.' She nods. Then she nods again because she doesn't really know what to say now.

'But there has to be sexual attraction, too,' Matt says, out of the blue.

'Well,' Fen mutters, 'well.' Then she looks at him directly. 'I fancy you like *crazy*, you daft, annoying sod!'

She wishes he'd smile. She cannot gauge his reaction, or how he's feeling, or whether she should just shut up now and save her dignity. It would be ghastly to be chucked again when already chucked.

'I think,' she says quietly, 'that for us lot – hitting our thirties – it was impossible to sustain relationships started in our twenties. That's the decade during which we grow and develop into who we really are – with all the opportunities and experiences laid at our disposal.'

'Oh, shut up, Fen,' Matt says. She doesn't really hear him, nor does she feel him squeeze her hand.

'And, if I'm honest, I wasn't entirely sure whether or not I actually wanted you,' Fen says with honesty that hurts her, 'and I'm worried that I've blown it.'

'Oh, shut up,' Matt says again, though again unheard.

'But I really think that you shouldn't deny yourself the

potential happiness of a relationship just because you've been there, done that and it didn't work out.'

'I agree,' says Matt.

'And the rebound is utter nonsense,' Fen continues.

'I agree,' says Matt.

'And –' says Fen. She stops. 'What did you say?'

'I'm holding your hands, agreeing with everything you say,' Matt shrugs. 'Will you take me back? Will you take me on?'

'*Me*?' Fen says. '*You*? But I feel I should be asking you the same!'

'Will you?' Matt asks.

'Will you?' Fen asks back.

Hand squeezing is all that's needed. And a deep kiss, in full view of the other workers taking their lunch, in full view of Judith glancing out of her office window, seals it all.

'One thing,' Fen says, as they cross the road to the Trust Art building. 'If we do the whole love and, in time, the living-together thing – promise me we can still have rude sex. That we don't have to go for lights out and missionary position just once a week?'

Matt looks perplexed. He bites his lip and furrows his brow. 'I don't know if that's possible,' he says, running his hand down her back and cupping her buttock in his hand. As she climbs the stairs a step ahead of him, he slips his hand right up her skirt, right between her legs. They stop on the landing and have a really good snog, not caring who might see them. No one does. 'Once a week?' Matt says, with mock horror. 'How exhausting!'

Matt has requested a meeting with Rodney and Judith. Rodney is suddenly irrationally terrified that Matt is going to hand in his notice and inform them he has a job editing a lad's mag. He confides this fear to Judith who looks at him as if he's a halfwit.

'Come in!' Rodney cries, to Matt's knock. 'Have a seat! Coffee? Tea? Something stronger?'

Judith is seriously worried that Rodney is going to come straight out with some huge pay-rise offer. 'What can we do for you, Matthew?' she asks.

'It's like this,' Matt says. He sits down and settles himself very comfortably in the chair. 'I was at home a couple of weeks ago. And the long and the short of it is that my mother would like to direct further funds from my late father's trust to Trust Art.'

Rodney beams. Judith has to stop herself licking her lips. Rodney can't help himself from giving Matt the thumbs up. 'Specifically, the funds are for a salary,' Matt continues, 'for a job position to be titled the Henry Holden Research Fund.'

'How terrific!' Rodney enthuses, though still unsure of the precise demands of such a job.

'My mother wants to encourage other collectors – or their families – to donate or loan documents or works of art for the Holden Researcher to organize, to collate, to disperse.'

Judith and Rodney are absolutely hanging on Matt's every word. 'Such people need to know that there's a place and a specialist who will analyse and archive and, if they wish, rehouse their collections.' Rodney starts clapping.

'Did you realize,' says Matt, looking at his nails and then looking from Judith to Rodney and then back again, 'that Fen McCabe did not come across *Abandon*?'

'She didn't?' Rodney looks horrified, Judith looks very interested.

'No,' Matt confirms, '*Abandon* came to her. Or, specifically, the man who owns it. He approached Fen because he trusts her, because he knows that her absolute love for art would mean that hers are the safest hands in which to entrust his beloved collection.'

Now Judith is starting to look a little horrified while Rodney just looks riveted.

'The Holden Research Fund should sponsor Fen,' Matt says. 'She's a brilliant scholar, a thorough archivist and she's a respected art historian.'

'Hear hear!' Rodney cries, thumping his fist on his desk and grinning at Matt and at Judith.

'So that's a weight off your hands,' Matt says to Judith. 'You can get on with your work without worrying about managing the rehousing of *Abandon*.'

Judith shifts in her seat. Her eyes are dark with distress and humiliation.

'It's right that the project should be given to Fen,' says Matt, 'don't you think?'

'Absolutely,' says Rodney, 'Judith?'

Judith coughs but manages to nod.

'Crikey,' says Rodney to Matt, 'can I thank your mum in person?' Matt smiles. 'Righty ho! Bloody waste of time and money Fenella's leaving do this morning – we'll have to have a welcome-back do now, too!' Matt smiles. 'I say,' says Rodney, 'who'll go up to the Archive to tell her? Shall you or I?'

Matt smiles. 'I think Judith should,' he says.

EPILOGUE

*F*en McCabe is packing her bags. She glances out of the window. If London leaves are dull brown this morning, she knows for sure that those in Derbyshire will be burnished copper, all shades of russet, auburn and gold. She considers what to pack. It won't be cold enough for her Puffa jacket but the nip in the air will necessitate a couple of layers plus a chunky polo-neck. Thick socks and walking boots. Nivea for the face, after an afternoon stomping the moors with the wind and probably some rain and an overall chill. Invigorating! She can hardly wait to arrive. She's taken a day off work. Now that she has a salary, she has proper holiday entitlement too.

Fen leaves her room predictably neat and tidy. Gemma's room, surprisingly, is meticulously spic and span. It appears, from the stripped bed and upended mattress, that some major autumnal spring clean is going on. If that's not a contradiction in terms. Down a level, Fen goes to the bathroom. When she comes out, whistling for some reason, she is halfway down to the ground floor when she hears her name being called. It is Abi's voice, coming from her room.

'Hang on,' Fen calls back. She places her bag by the front door and lightly springs back up the stairs to Abi's room.

'Abs? You OK?' says Fen. 'I was trying not to wake you – I'm off to Derbyshire, remember.'

'Fen?'

'Gem?'

'Come and say goodbye,' Abi is saying.

'Yes,' says Gemma, 'come in and say goodbye.'

Fen pushes open Abi's door. Why anything should surprise her where her flatmates are concerned is baffling, but still she is slightly taken aback to find them both snuggled up in Abi's bed. Fen actually scans the room for Jake, or evidence of him.

'Are you looking for Jake?' Abi asks.

'Because we chucked him!' Gemma giggles, her luxuriant curls all tousled by the demands of sleep. Abi and Gemma sit up, clutching the sheet demurely to their breasts.

'He had become,' Abi drawls, 'superfluous to our needs.'

Fen stands there and takes it all in.

'It's just us two now,' Gemma explains.

'Two's company,' Abi shrugs.

'Three's a crowd,' Fen colludes.

'Are you shocked?' Gemma asks.

Fen thinks about it. No, not shocked. 'No,' she replies, 'seeing your room so clean and tidy – that was far more of a shock.'

'We thought we'd have my old room as another lounge, a sort of non-TV, chill-out kind of den,' Gemma explains enthusiastically. 'Are you OK about that?'

'Sure,' Fen says.

'And are you OK about this?' Abi asks, tenderly and with hope.

Fen regards the two of them. They look relaxed and

happy. They really look rather sweet. 'Sure,' she says, 'more than OK. You're my friends!' They look so relieved. 'And you make a beautiful couple,' Fen purrs in an American accent. They all giggle. A car's horn sounds. 'I must go,' Fen says, 'see you Sunday.'

'Have fun!' they call after her.

'I will,' Fen calls back, the front door open. 'You two have fun, too.'

'We will!' they call back as the front door closes. They snuggle back down under the sheets. It's very early. They don't have to get up for a good hour.

'Sorry!' Fen said, throwing her bag into the back of Matt's car under a barrage of irritating horn parps from the cars behind. She settled in and put her seat-belt on. 'Only Abi and Gemma wanted to inform me that they've chucked Jake for each other.'

'I know,' said Matt. 'Jake had his head in his hands all last night. He says it's the most emasculating thing that's ever befallen him.'

'Oh dear!' Fen responded, mingling concern with just a touch of sarcasm.

'He'll bounce back,' Matt assured her. 'He was talking about going to Amsterdam for the weekend with a couple of his old pals from college rugby.'

'I doubt whether they'll be spending much time in the Rijksmuseum,' Fen mused. She went a little quiet.

Matt glanced at her and put his hand on her knee. 'Jake is talking about moving out by Christmas,' he said.

'Oh?' said Fen.

'You might think about moving in,' Matt said, 'once he's gone, of course. Three being a crowd and all that.'

Fen laughed. And then she smiled to herself. Three *was* a crowd, a triangle with sharp edges. She slid her hand over Matt's forearm. She kept it there. He glanced at her, after negotiating a dustcart and some school children. Fen was smiling at him and her eyes were sparkling.

Matt and Fen arrived in Derbyshire just after elevenses. This was Matt's second visit. In preparation, he had had only the lightest of breakfasts this time and was therefore well able to tackle the lunch Django had spent all morning concocting with great imagination and practically every ingredient in the house.

*

On Saturday morning, Fen and Matt decided to take advantage of the dry day and go for a good long walk, made all the more tempting by the promise of ploughman's lunches at the Rag and Thistle halfway round. Mrs Merifield's pickled onions were incomparable, as were the hunks of unpasteurized cheddar. The pub smelt delicious, cosy and warm and beery. It was crowded.

'You can't leave that!' Matt remonstrated, eyeing the celery sticks and mound of home-made chutney on Fen's plate. 'It's an insult!'

'I'm full,' Fen protested, stretching back and patting her stomach for emphasis. 'What's it worth to you?'

'To *me*?' Matt joked back. 'What's it worth to *you* – you'll be hitchhiking back home tomorrow otherwise.' With that, he tucked into the remnants on her plate. Fen settled back into the chair and soaked up her surroundings: the smell of the place, the laughter and chatter, the familiarity of it all. Her territory. She felt safe. She gazed over at Matt, sipping his beer, unaware of the splodge of chutney on his chin. She felt superbly content. She was so happy to have him here with her. She reached for her bitter shandy. And suddenly, her knee was soaking wet with it. So would yours be, after an energetic head-butt from an amorous labrador and the snout of an adoring lurcher being thrust into your crotch.

Barry?
Beryl?

Fen was being licked and nudged and gruffled at by the two dogs.

Oh my God, she thought, stroking them, pulling their ears, scrunching her fingers into their necks, *oh my God*.

'Dogs!' The voice came from right across the pub.

Oh my God. James!

She couldn't see him. Nor could the dogs so they ignored him and drenched Fen with their affection instead.

'Dogs!'

She couldn't see him, she could only hear him.

'Dogs! Battersea!'

Reluctantly, Barry and Beryl took their leave of Fen and slalomed through legs and bodies to the door.

'Excuse me a mo',' she said to Matt.

'Someone you know?' he asked. Fen nodded and touched his cheek.

She's in the car park. The Land Rover is there. Where are they? Suddenly, the dogs bolt back at her and James's arms prevent her from being thrown to the ground.

'James!' she gasps.

'Hullo, Miss McCabe,' he says. All the excitement has exhausted Beryl, who is sitting and leaning hard against Fen, nudging her every now and then. Barry is having a lengthy pee against someone's particularly shiny Jaguar. 'How have you been?'

'Great,' Fen beams, 'very well. You?'

'Just dandy,' James tells her. 'How's Django?'

'In fine form,' Fen says. She looks at James's boots. 'There's someone I'd like you to meet,' she says.

'Oh yes?' says James.

Fen nods.

'A bloke?' James asks.

Fen regards him and nods.

'The chap you were sitting with? With chutney on his chin?'

Fen smiles and nods.

'Someone special?' he probes.

Again, Fen nods.

352

'Then I'd be happy to meet him,' James assures her.

'He's special to you, too,' Fen whispers, keeping her eyes fixed on James's face to gauge his reaction, 'it's Matthew Holden.'

Just momentarily, a tiny part of James wants to shout, 'Not fair! *I* want you!' But seeing Fen so happy is balm indeed. 'Bloody hell!' James says instead.

'Shall I' Fen asks, 'fetch him?'

'Of course,' says James. Fen walks briskly across the car park. She is gorgeous, James thinks to himself, but nostalgically and without longing or regret. It's so lovely to see her. It really is. 'Good to keep her in the family,' James says out loud, 'hey dogs?'

Matt is about to come looking for Fen, fearing that the huge hounds have dragged her off somewhere. But here she is, returning, looking flushed, looking as if she's wet herself where the spilt shandy has stained her jeans dark. She doesn't take her chair, she comes to sit beside him, presses close next to him.

'Matt,' she says, holding his hand, 'there's someone I'd like you to meet. There's someone who wants to meet you. There's someone it is important and wonderful for you to meet.'

'Not your mother returned from the cowboy in Denver?' Matt gasps, because that's the only person he could think of just then who would warrant such a serious preamble from Fen.

'No, no, no!' Fen says, brushing the air with irritation. 'James Caulfield.'

'Who's James Caulfield?' Matt asks. Fen's eyes are darting around his face. 'Oh!' The penny has dropped. 'The chap with the Fetherstones?'

'Yes,' says Fen, 'and two dogs.'

'I'd love to,' Matt says.

They stand up.

'Matt,' says Fen and she cups his lovely face in her hands

and kisses the smear of chutney off his chin. 'Matt,' she says and she takes his hand and kisses the palm of it, laying it against her cheek. She closes her eyes for a moment. 'Matt,' she says, with an ecstatic smile, 'you have a half-brother.'